SHAYNE WHITAKER

The Fields of Bentonville

I visited Daniel Morgan Camp on 2-16-2023. Please enjoy this book and leave a review on Amazon or Goodread's. Best Wishes Always.

Shayne Whitaker

Sixth & Walnut Books

For Anne and Charlie, perhaps my first fans, among people who didn't already know me at least. Their touching words and efforts to contact me after reading my first book moved me deeply. Their friendship is inspiring. This book is also dedicated to Angel and Pam. They are a wonderful, loving example of how we all should see people.

Could a greater miracle take place than for us to look through each other's eyes for an instant?

— HENRY DAVID THOREAU

Contents

Preface

As is often the case, the genesis for this story came from personal experience and observing the world around me. It's always fascinating to see where inspiration comes from and how experiences and ideas coalesce into a story. Before you embark on the journey within these pages, please allow me to impart how this story came to be.

I passed the Bentonville battlefield several times over the years but never had the time to stop and tour it. The largest battle ever fought in the state of North Carolina took place there, yet many people know little or nothing about it. I finally visited Bentonville in 2013, as the country was roiling in the aftermath of George Zimmerman's acquittal in the death of Trayvon Martin. Like so many people, I watched as protests sometimes turned violent. A great despondency seemed to blanket the entire United States, a sort of collective melancholy. Americans drifted apart. Neighbors became enemies. Friends stopped speaking to each other. People seemed only to see that which divided us, and nothing that brought us together. Some behaved as though slavery and Jim Crow never happened, while others declared nothing had changed since those days. Even as the son of a black man and a white woman occupied the White House, Americans appeared as disconnected as ever. I read the words of people like Dr. King and Lincoln, including speeches and sermons each delivered. While many Americans claimed to respect and honor such men, few exemplified their qualities of compassion and integrity. People were no longer judged based on merit or individual standards, but as part of a larger group. Tribalism took root in American culture and started rotting it. Few people kept their feral emotions in check. Instead of seeking truth and knowledge, people made up their minds based on preconceived notions and only sought to make things fit their view of the world.

Touring Bentonville deeply moved me. Seeing burial markers, trench remnants, and the breadth of the battlefield, as well as imagining myself in that time, brought the events that occurred there vividly to life. But two things I saw there profoundly touched me. First was seeing the vestiges of a bloodstain on the floor of the house used as a field hospital. The second was the slave quarters. As I observed these things, I thought to myself, "Everyone should see this." I then wondered if one might see the world differently if they could experience it as it once was. If you could go back and live in the past briefly, would you still see the world the same today? From those thoughts, this book was born. The story took shape in my mind as I drove home. I couldn't get Bentonville and all I had seen out of my head. I wrote a rough draft screenplay as an outline in a few weeks, something I often do as a first step in writing. The story changed and developed over the years to become what you now hold in your hand.

We have all seen the best and worst in each other. I'm sure some will determine the opening chapter of this book to be controversial. What isn't contentious these days? However, I based the chapter on an event I experienced in the 1980s when living in a tough neighborhood in Nashville, Tennessee. It's an event I wrote about in my first book, *The Homeless Man's Journal*. Shortly after my family moved into a rundown house on Fifth Avenue North, I walked down the street to explore Morgan Park. Several African-American young men approached me as I walked on a dilapidated tennis court's cracked surface littered with shattered glass. The first words one of them spoke to me were, "hey white boy, I heard you said something about my mama." I had met none of them before. They left me as battered and bruised as the ground I laid on. Shortly before writing this book, I stopped for gas where a car full of young men arrived blaring music with some of the most vulgar lyrics you would ever hear. An elderly woman got gas on the other side of the pump from them. When a man politely asked them to turn down the music, they threatened him and several other people with violence. We've all seen the worst in each other.

I hope we have all seen the best in each other as well. Despite those negative experiences, I didn't allow myself to become bitter. Good people showed me the folly in painting with a broad brush. While I remember that day in a park decades ago, I also recall these things: laughing over dinner with Charlie and Anne. Leonard and George leaving work and driving forty-five minutes to meet me at the funeral home after my grandmother passed away. Thanksgivings spent with Angel and Pam. Discussing important things with Private Pullen in a small tent while it poured rain outside at Fort Jackson. The encouragement of Mike, Greg, Purvis, Jerry, and Art during basketball practice at Gardner-Webb. The trust Nikkita and Jamier had in me. Giving clothes to the homeless with Bobby on a crisp Christmas Eve night in Atlanta in 1995, and holding a young child as her father tried on a hat and gloves. Sharing lunch with a homeless man named Robert. Sharing tears and hugs with black and white children at the Baptist Children's Home because I once called an orphanage home, and I knew the agony of their hearts. Cutting up with Ernest and Mo at work. Laughing with Marsella, Mrs. Barbara, Jasmine, Allen, Claudia, and so many others. The pleasant experiences with people far outweigh the bad. A broad brush can't create fine detail, and those elements often make a picture truly exquisite.

I don't intend to "preach" to people or push an agenda with this story. Most will probably get out of it what they bring into it. But if you keep an open mind, you may learn a little about other people, perhaps some history you may not have known, and maybe even something about yourself. I hope the story entertains you as well. We need to understand each other better. We must stop branding each other with labels. It's important to look to the past and learn from it, but we can't stare at it and walk backward. We have to see what lies before us in order to choose the best path forward. Simply, we have to be better. Every one of us.

Acknowledgement

For their unwavering support and encouragement, I am eternally grateful to the many friends who have become family—Tommy and Joy, Mrs. Moore, Alan and Amy, my old Mauney Hall brothers, and my fellow Orphans.

I offer sincere gratitude to Angel and Pam, who set a place for me at the table. To Leonard and George, my TWC crew, Craig, MCD, Marsella, Jodell, Kaye, and my C-Link pals. Nikkita, Jamier, Jasmine, Claudia, Allen, and my DE friends. Massey, KB, my GW teammates, Anne and Charlie, Justin, Jeni, Chris and Amanda, and Mr. Clark. Thanks to the homeless man who trusted me to hold his baby daughter as he tried on clothes Bobby and I were giving away. They all embody the spirit of this book.

As I wrote this book, I couldn't help but find inspiration when I thought about Campbell, Grover, Axel, Carter, and Kendall. I hope they grow up to be brilliant points of light.

I am indebted to the following people for helping to make this book better than I could alone: Julie, whose attention to detail and knowledgeable mind proved invaluable. Thank you Georgann, Elaine, Wendy, Pam, and Kim for taking the time to read pages and offer your thoughts about the story, cover, and language of the book.

Special thanks to Sharon, Syvonne, Linda, Sue, Mr. Cox, Mr. and Mrs. Singleton, Mr. and Mrs. Weeks, Julie and Mike, Linny, Michelle, Mrs. Morris, Dianne, the other Diane, Josh, Jessica, Micah, Julia, Cindy, Mr. Roberson, Cathy, John, Emmily, Wendy, Mr. and Mrs. Reaves, Glenn, Aunt

Jackie, Benny, Lori, Carmen, and Lorraine. Your kind words about *The Homeless Man's Journal* touched my heart and inspired me to keep writing.

1

Choices

Cities mask their pain. Beautiful parks, expensive sports arenas, grand concert halls, and fine museums are sometimes a veneer that conceals the underlying troubles of a city. But the city screams out through the sirens that shatter precious silence. It sends forth its angry bellow through the boom of gunfire. Hungry children and battered women are the source of its tears. It suffers silently in the lonely drug addict and the friendless person, and those that dismiss them.

Every town has a part of itself that it tries to keep secret. Neighborhoods infected with crime, poverty, and blight are not a source of pride for any city. Durham, North Carolina, is no different. While home to excellent universities, venues of culture and entertainment, and beautiful neighborhoods that resemble a slice of Americana, Durham also had a less picturesque area. This part of town had all the prerequisites of a slum.

A variety of vehicles traveled on cracked streets, dodging the occasional pothole. A loud train crossed over the street on a trestle decorated with graffiti. Bars covered the windows of a run-down convenience store. A mangy dog sniffed the ground aimlessly, its tail tucked between its legs. People gathered at a bus stop where a woman and child sat on an overturned shopping cart. A homeless man used another shopping cart to haul his belongings. A woman wearing a short skirt stood on a nearby street corner. A skinny white teenager with glasses walked alone, staring at the ground

1

and slouching his shoulders.

Like the flowers that bloomed after the eruption of Mount St. Helens and the glimpses of life that returned to Chernobyl, hope and possibility also take root in places as desolate and barren as the hood. A constant battle between optimism and despair rage in the neighborhood. But an absent father, the influence of gangs, or the tempting promise of instant gratification can thwart even the most auspicious start. Surrounded by crime and violence, survival becomes the primary aim. The consequences of life in the hood can be great. The struggle for existence often leads to the company of people who do not have your best interest in mind. It led a promising young man named Douglas Timmons to associate with some local troublemakers.

Doug hung out with his band of agitators at the park most afternoons. Jordan Benjamin and Derrick Randall were classmates of Doug's. The trio stood in front of a picnic table as if it was a throne. Sitting upon the pedestal was Isaiah Skinner, a resident bully who was said to have gang ties. Isaiah was easy to spot around the neighborhood. He often wore tank top shirts to display his muscular arms that were covered in tattoos. He kept his hair in distinct cornrows. Many kids thought Isaiah had money, given the expensive-looking watch he wore and the late model sports car he drove. There were whispers he was "hood rich" and drove the car with expensive wheels, but could hardly afford gas and lived with his drug addict mother. Regardless, nobody was brave or dumb enough to question him about it. Isaiah's propensity for violence was well established. The brute was so sure of his neighborhood status that he sat on the picnic table with an open bottle of beer, making no effort to conceal it, despite park rules. Isaiah was keenly aware of the power he held over his young disciples and exploited it. He took a drink from the bottle and let out a sigh, exclaiming his refreshment.

"Take a swig and pass it around," Isaiah ordered as he held the bottle in his outstretched hand.

Jordan took the bottle and immediately drank. He paused for a moment, squinting before passing the bottle to Doug. Doug held the bottle, silently bracing himself before taking a drink. He took a gulp and quickly pulled the bottle away from his lips. Doug almost spat the drink out, but held back and tried to keep a straight face. The grimace and contorted features on his face betrayed his efforts to appear nonchalant about drinking booze. He composed himself and swallowed the foul-tasting drink. Doug's facade broke, and he coughed after swallowing the beer. His associates laughed as Doug tried to collect himself. Doug handed the bottle to Derrick as Isaiah lit a cigarette.

"There you go," Isaiah said as he handed the cigarette to Jordan.

Jordan took a puff, then wiped his lip and passed the cigarette to Doug. Doug took a drag and immediately coughed again.

"Damn, man," Isaiah said as he laughed.

"It went down the wrong way," Doug replied, trying to catch his breath.

"It tore him up," said Derrick, still laughing himself.

"It's a little rough at first," Isaiah said. "We need to get you smoking some weed. That's a lot smoother."

"Hell yeah," Doug replied, again trying to appear cool.

The park was a green oasis in the seemingly colorless and bland neighborhood. Like the desert watering holes, the park served those who were depleted by the scarcity of hope in the neighborhood. People gathered there to escape the mundane routine of life and partake in a variety of activities. A group of guys played a half-court basketball game on a goal with no net. Several girls jumped rope and laughed. The meek and lonely white kid wearing glasses entered the park and walked toward a crumbling tennis court. While the park was a wellspring of hope and escape for many, it did not repel the trouble that accompanied Isaiah.

"Check it out," Isaiah said, pointing to the bespectacled boy a short distance away. "Damn, Harry Potter."

The comment elicited more laughter from the group.

"What's that goofy-looking fool doing in the hood?" Derrick wondered aloud.

"Come on. Let's go find out," Isaiah said as he jumped off the picnic table.

Isaiah's lackeys followed as he hurried toward the nerdy boy meandering around the tennis court. Isaiah tossed the cigarette on the ground and quickened his pace.

The skinny white teen stared at the ground. The surface of the tennis court was cracked and littered with small shards of broken glass. The remaining fragments of the net sat tattered on the ground between two poles. This derelict corner of the park was a blunt reminder that you were still in the hood.

Isaiah tossed the beer bottle to the opposite side of the tennis court as the group entered the fenced-in area. The bottle broke into countless pieces after it landed. They approached the meek kid and formed a semicircle around him. The lone boy sheepishly turned away from Isaiah and the group, acting as if he was just casually taking in the scenery, but his nervousness was palpable. Turning his back to Isaiah and his minions made the hair stand up on the back of the kid's neck. He could sense that trouble was afoot and didn't want to antagonize the group.

"Hey, white boy," Isaiah began, "what are you doing around here?"

The young kid timidly turned toward Isaiah but continued to face the ground.

"I just moved to the neighborhood, and I thought I'd explore a little," the bashful teen said.

"Oh, you're just exploring," Isaiah confirmed. "That's cool, that's cool. But we have a little problem. You see, I heard you said something about my mama."

"I didn't say anything," the boy replied. "I don't even know anybody around here."

"That's not what I heard," Isaiah said. "I heard you said something about my mama. Didn't you hear that, Doug?"

"Yeah, that's what I heard," Doug answered.

The unassuming kid lifted his head, hoping his accusers could see the sincerity in his eyes.

"I didn't say anything about nobody," the kid began. "I don't know you. I just moved..."

Before the boy could finish his sentence, Isaiah blasted him in the face with a powerful punch that sent his glasses flying. Reeling from the blow, the boy spun around wildly, as if someone had thrown him from a moving car. Unable to see clearly, the kid bumped into Doug. The crown of the boy's head hit Doug right in the face, causing Doug to jump back and hold his hand over his mouth. Doug took a moment to absorb and evaluate the stinging pain in his lip. Doug withdrew his hand from his mouth and saw blood on his palm. His split lip was swelling.

"Did you hit my friend?" Isaiah asked angrily.

"No," the boy declared as he held his hands over his face to shield himself against another volley of punches from Isaiah.

Isaiah paused the assault and stood with clenched fists as he stared fiercely at the boy. Isaiah glimpsed Doug as he dabbed some blood from his lip with his white t-shirt.

"Doug, don't let him get away with that crap," Isaiah advised. "Bust his ass, man."

Doug wiped his hand on his shirt and looked almost confused, hesitant. The kid pulled his hands from his face for a moment, revealing a swollen lip and a black eye. It felt wrong to hit the kid again, but peer pressure and street cred are relentless enablers.

"Hit his ass, man," Isaiah demanded.

"I know you ain't gonna let this punk bust you in the face and get away with it, Doug," Jordan interjected.

An angry expression suddenly swept across Doug's face. He flared his nostrils, yelled through gritted teeth, stepped into a punch, and hit the teenager upside his head nearly as hard as Isaiah did. Derrick and Jordan buckled over laughing, each of them holding their hand over their mouth. Isaiah grinned approvingly.

"That's what I'm talking about, Doug," Isaiah said. "Don't let nobody disrespect you."

Isaiah stepped forward and hit the kid again, knocking him to the ground. The kid stayed down but reached for his glasses, which were within arm's reach of where he fell. Derrick booted the glasses away before the boy could grasp them. Isaiah kicked the boy in the stomach, causing him to curl into a fetal position.

"Don't let me see your stupid ass around here again, white boy," Isaiah warned.

The four bullies walked away from the tennis court, leaving the boy holding his stomach and crawling toward his broken eyewear. The hostile crew gathered on the sidewalk beside Isaiah's car.

"You knocked the hell out of that guy, Isaiah," Derrick said admiringly.

"Doug got him pretty good, too," Jordan added.

"Yeah, he did. That was nice. I bet we don't see his ass around here no more. Stupid cracker. White people ain't done crap for us but try to keep us down, then going to come into our neighborhood. Bump that," Isaiah proffered.

Derrick stood by the passenger door while Isaiah walked to the driver's side and fumbled for his keys.

"Are we still going tonight?" Jordan asked.

There was a party that night at a house widely known for dealing drugs. Cars made brief stops in front of the house throughout the day and night. Someone would step off the porch and communicate with the occupants of the car and make the deal. If the seller didn't have the merchandise in his pocket, a quick wave toward the house would send someone else to retrieve it. All manner of people stopped. It was a veritable picture of the great American melting pot. People of every race and socioeconomic background seemed accounted for. College students, blue-collar workers, and white-collar workers all came shopping. Sometimes people would stop to buy drugs with their young kids in the backseat. Neighbors cringed at the sight of cars stopping in front of the house at all hours of the night. Despite their animus toward the dealers, the neighbors remained silent out of fear.

"If you guys can come up with some gas money, we'll go get something to eat and then hit the party," Isaiah said.

"I made a little money last week," Jordan stated. "I can chip in."

"I might be able to get some," Doug said.

"I might come up with some too," Derrick added.

"That's cool..." Isaiah replied. A group of three girls approaching on the sidewalk distracted him. The other boys turned to see what had captured Isaiah's attention.

Derrick stepped aside and held a hand to his chin as the girls reached the car. He licked his lips and scanned the girls from head to toe.

Aliyah Gaines, a pretty girl who walked between her friends, cast a glance and a smile at Doug as she passed him.

"What's up, baby?" Isaiah asked loudly. The girls ignored him and kept walking. "Hey, y'all want to go with us tonight?"

The girls continued to walk, murmuring among themselves.

"Hey, girl," Derrick called out.

"Girl, I'm talking to you," Isaiah bellowed again as he looked directly at Aliyah.

"You better watch out," Jordan began, "that's Doug's bitch."

"What?" Isaiah asked, seeking verification.

"Yeah, he likes that girl," Jordan confirmed.

"No, I don't," Doug said quietly. His friend embarrassed him. Doug had tried to keep his two-year crush on Aliyah a secret. He only told Jordan while they were playing video games once. Now Jordan had betrayed Doug's trust.

"Man, don't be getting hung up on a bitch," Isaiah advised.

"I don't care about that ho," Doug said, immediately feeling regretful for referencing a girl he was fond of in such a derogatory manner. Nonetheless, he was confident he had gained cool points and looked tough in defusing the situation.

"I gotta get going," Jordan advised. "I'll see y'all tonight."

"What time are we meeting?" Doug asked.

"Be here at about eight o'clock. You better have some money for me," Isaiah announced. "Don't show up with empty pockets."

"I got you," Jordan replied.

"You too, Doug," Isaiah said directly. "I don't care if you have to steal it."

"I'll bring some money," Doug told him.

Isaiah and Derrick got in the car and drove away as Doug and Jordan walked in opposite directions.

Doug traversed the fractured sidewalk, passing boarded-up houses and empty people until he reached the entrance to the housing project he called home. Two-story brick buildings made the place resemble a compound of some sort. Reminders of Doug's circumstances were everywhere. People pried open utility boxes on the buildings and tangled coax cables dangled from them, the handiwork of those trying to steal cable TV. Gang graffiti decked the walls of buildings in various places. The community dumpster overflowed and people left bags of garbage beside it. A few of Doug's neighbors sat on their stoops, watching others suspiciously. A loud car started as Doug walked past, spooking him. The driver cranked up the radio and blared rap music as he sped away. Doug gave a wave to Mrs. Thorpe, the retired lady next door, as he climbed the handful of steps to his front door. Mrs. Thorpe was one of the kinder souls in the projects. She sometimes invited Doug and his mother to eat dinner when she knew times were lean and the cupboards might be bare.

Doug entered the apartment and closed the door behind him. He locked the front door immediately, as was his habit in an area where he heard sirens frequently. Doug paused for a moment in the living room, listening for his mother. The apartment was small and modestly appointed and furnished. A few pictures of Doug and his mother, a short woman with an average build, hung on the wall. A nearby end table was home to a picture of the two of them with a smiling older man. Doug couldn't hear his mother, but he knew she was in her bedroom. He hastily made his way to the kitchen to tend to his busted lip.

After pulling a paper towel from the roll, Doug moistened it and applied it to his lip. He winced and hissed when he felt the sting again. He pulled the paper towel away momentarily and saw it had a smudge of red on it.

Awards and certificates bearing Doug's name adorned the refrigerator. The appliance was a trophy case of sorts that displayed scholastic accomplishments. Sadly, not a single thing contained a date for the most recent school year. Doug was prone to getting into trouble last year, as he did during a field trip to the Civil War battlefield at Bentonville. Doug paid little attention during the trip. His mind was on Aliyah rather than the battlefield or structures that surrounded it. A teacher made him sit on the bus after getting into a scuffle with a classmate.

Doug held the paper towel to his lip as he sauntered back into the living room and sat on the couch. As Doug took a seat, his mother exited her bedroom and walked into the living room. His mother wore a red shirt with a name tag. Doug knew it was the uniform for her part-time job. Knowing he would be free from the watchful eye of his mother for the evening delighted Doug. He was careful not to show it outwardly. Wanda worked a steady job during the day but took a part-time evening job to supplement her income. She had always been a person who saw the glass as half-full. She was determined to create a better life for herself and Doug. Lately, she wanted nothing more than to get Doug back on the right track and away from the negative influences he was now associating with.

"Where have you been?" Wanda asked as she fastened a button on her knit shirt.

"I was just hanging out down at the park," Doug answered as he tried to conceal the paper towel.

Wanda noticed the blood on Doug's shirt.

"What happened to you? Is that blood on your shirt?" Wanda asked. "Did you get into another fight?"

"No, I was playing basketball, and a guy ran into me," Doug replied.

"Don't you lie to me," Wanda warned. "You've been hanging out with Isaiah again, haven't you?"

"What? Come on, mom," Doug pleaded.

"You don't listen to a thing I say. I've known Isaiah since he was little. He's nothing but trouble," Wanda began. "His mama didn't do anything but sit around and smoke that junk. She hardly raised that boy. I'm not letting you go down that same path."

"They're my friends, mom," Doug declared.

"Friends don't get you into trouble and fights all the time, Doug," she told her son. "Friends help you in positive ways."

"They do help me in positive ways," Doug insisted. "You don't know."

"Oh, I don't know? I'm looking right at you, holding a paper towel to your busted lip, wearing your bloody shirt. That doesn't look too positive," Wanda told him.

Doug pulled the paper towel away from his mouth and averted his eyes to the ground for a moment. His mom was hitting close to the mark.

"How many times were you suspended because of those boys?" Wanda asked. "Huh? You used to be an excellent student. Then you started getting kicked out of school. Heck, you even got in a fight when you went on that field trip. I know you can do better because you have done better. You still have a bright future, Doug."

Doug's brow furrowed as he outstretched his arms.

"Look around, mom," Doug said angrily. "We live in the projects. You call this a bright future?"

"Where you live isn't an excuse for acting like a fool, Doug," Wanda stated. "You are who you choose to be. I'm working myself to the bone so maybe someday we won't have to live in the projects. I told you about that house I'm working toward. I'm working hard for that."

"Exactly," Doug stated firmly. "You're working yourself to the bone and we got nothing. We got a busted up car, a busted up TV, and I sleep on a mattress on the floor."

"It isn't like you can't live without a TV. You can read a book or something," Wanda insisted. "At least you're not sleeping on the ground."

"I'm just saying, look at the hand we've been dealt," Doug said.

"Just because you've been dealt a rough hand doesn't mean you give up," Wanda told him. "I wish you could see the opportunities you have, son. If you had to walk in someone else's shoes for a while, then you'd know. You have so much more opportunity than my dad did."

"At least you had a dad," Doug stated bitterly.

Wanda paused, enduring the bite of his words, before composing herself.

"Yeah, and I miss him all the time. I wish he was still here. Maybe he would be able to talk some sense into you. I know it's been hard for you since he passed away, but it's been hard for me too," Wanda told him.

"At least he was there for you," Doug replied, throwing another harsh verbal spear at his mother.

"He was there for you too," Wanda said. "I'm sorry your father isn't around. But you're not like him. And you're not like these so-called friends. You are not a thug. You are not a gangsta. You are my son and I want you to be better than that."

"I'm not trying to be a thug, but I ain't no punk either," Doug declared.

"Boy, I swear... oh my, look at the time," Wanda said, almost panicking as she looked at the clock on the wall. "I have to get going. I'm closing tonight so I'll be home late. There's a plate for you in the fridge. Just put it in the microwave for a couple of minutes."

"I know," Doug assured her.

"Stay home tonight. I don't want you out with those trouble makers," Wanda advised.

Wanda grabbed her purse and keys and leaned over Doug.

"I love you," she told him as she kissed him on the forehead.

Wanda double checked to ensure she had her keys and phone before stepping toward the door.

"I'll see you tonight," she said before exiting.

Doug spent the evening lounging on the couch and watching the television he previously complained about. He sat back with his feet propped up on the coffee table, next to his empty plate.

Doug had once been a stellar student, winning ribbons for his science and history class projects. Doug respected his mother. It wasn't easy for Wanda to raise him alone and Doug understood the sacrifices she made. But events in his life and outside peer pressure brought about unwelcome changes in Doug. The passing of his beloved grandfather and pent up teenage angst related to an absent father were contributing factors in Doug's conversion. Doug's studious ways did not endear him to other kids in the projects who sought street cred more than anything. Like so many sixteen-year-old young men, Doug became more concerned about how he was perceived in the neighborhood than his studies. Doug was soon under the influence of some local mischief-makers, getting into fights and being suspended from school.

Doug noticed the time and quickly got up from the couch. It was almost eight o'clock. He dashed into his mother's room and pulled open the top drawer of her dresser. After pushing some articles of clothing aside, Doug removed a small wooden cigar box. He opened the box, removed some cash, and placed it back in the drawer. Doug shoved the money into the pocket of his jacket as he ran out of the room.

Doug walked the familiar route to the park. The dark of night allowed some of the more nefarious happenings of the neighborhood to remain in seclusion. Nevertheless, Doug knew some dastardly and repugnant things resided in the shadows, and he remained vigilant as he strolled along.

As Doug neared the park he encountered a tall man walking in the opposite direction. Like Doug, the man kept his hands in his jacket pockets. The two met near a row of bushes at the edge of the park property. Doug looked beyond the man but didn't see his friends.

"Hey, young brother," the tall man said. "Can you help me out with a couple of dollars? I just want to get myself a hamburger or something to eat."

"No, I don't have anything," Doug said as he continued to walk.

The tall man turned and followed Doug.

"Man, I was just asking for a little help," the man stated. "Why you got to be like that?"

Doug turned to face the man.

"I said I don't have any money," Doug said sternly. "Now, step off."

"Man, I know you got some money," the man asserted.

"Dude, my boys are going to be here any minute. You better be gone if you don't want to get stomped," Doug warned the man.

The thin man quickly pulled his hands from his pockets and was holding a pistol. The man clobbered Doug on the head, sending him whirling toward the bushes and leaving him befuddled and nearly unconscious. By the time Doug landed on his back beside the bushes, the man was standing over him. He leaned over and held the end of the gun inches away from Doug's face.

"Give me the money," the man demanded.

Doug was disoriented but tried to crawl away from the man. The robber stood up and looked around before turning his attention back to Doug. He hit Doug with the pistol again. Doug rolled over onto his back and tried to ward off unconsciousness, but he was dazed and soon found himself barely able to move. The bandit rummaged through Doug's pockets as he went limp and could not resist. The thin man removed the cash Doug had taken from his mother's dresser and stuffed it in his pocket. He looked around again to ensure the coast was clear before stepping away. Doug peered through barely open eyes and could see the blurry silhouette of his assailant revealed in the pale illumination of a distant streetlight. The man ran down the street and disappeared, leaving Doug in the darkness behind the bushes. The pummeling created a mental fog that clouded his senses, and Doug slowly drifted off into oblivion.

2

Tomorrow Was Yesterday

Doug laid motionless and unconscious in the middle of a dirt road flanked by tall grass. He was shirtless, wearing only baggy tan pants with a string for a belt and a pair of old shoes. It was a strikingly beautiful day aside from the sun hiding behind a cloud. Soaring pine trees stood in the distance beyond the fields of grass. Doug slumbered, unfazed by chirping birds and buzzing insects. The clouds parted and shadows moved, allowing the sun to shine on Doug's face. The full force of the stifling summer heat and the dazzling sunlight caused Doug to stir. He slowly opened his eyes and lifted his head. Doug squinted as he tried to adjust to the brightness of the day. He managed to lift himself further until he was sitting. He wiped the sleep from his eyes and looked at his legs. Astonished to see the pants he was wearing, Doug then peered at his bare arms. He looked around at his surroundings. It was all entirely unfamiliar. Doug stood up gingerly, confused by where he was and what he was wearing. He wiped the dirt from his hands and arms, then brushed his hands off on the coarse material of the pant legs.

"What in the world?" Doug wondered to himself. "What's going on?"

Doug stared into the distance, watching the trees and grass sway with a gentle breeze. He turned in a slow circle, looking for any signs of people. He was completely alone. Doug was perplexed. How did he end up in the middle of nowhere with different clothes on?

"Hey!" Doug yelled, cupping his hands over his mouth.

Doug looked around again, but there wasn't another soul in sight. He could only conclude that his friends were playing a trick on him. Doug vaguely remembered the assault and robbery. Perhaps Isaiah, Derrick, and Jordan found him after he blacked out and moved him.

"Isaiah! Derrick!" Doug called out.

There was no response.

"Jordan! Come on out! You guys stop playing!" Doug demanded.

He paused and scanned the area again. It was still quiet, save for the rustling of windblown grass.

"This isn't funny! You play too much!" Doug hollered. His mounting frustration was becoming clear.

Something in the distance was kicking up a dust cloud. A vehicle was slowly approaching. Doug could picture his friends laughing in anticipation of the expression on his face. His annoyance with the prank began to subside as he imagined the reaction of his friends. But Doug's demeanor once again turned to puzzlement as he saw the vehicle more clearly as it advanced toward him. A horse-drawn wagon slowed as it got closer to Doug. Four other men mounted on horses rode alongside and behind the wagon.

Cleveland Hubbard sat on the wagon and held the reins firmly. He was a portly man and slightly disheveled. His thick beard was moistened with dribble from his mouth full of tobacco. A large hat helped to shield him from the hot sun. Cleveland yanked back on the reins, bringing the wagon to a halt as it reached Doug. The other riders also stopped.

Doug was baffled. Were these men in on the gag? Did his friends drop him off at the site of a reenactment of some sort?

Cleveland spat to the side of the wagon and stared at Doug.

"Hey, what's up?" Doug asked.

"What's up?" Cleveland replied, looking skyward for a moment. He was confused by the question.

"Yeah, you know," Doug answered, "hello. How are you doing?"

Nathaniel, one of Cleveland's sons, is the spitting image of his father when he was young. He sat confidently on his horse, looking intently at Doug.

"He don't talk too bad, Pa," Nathaniel said to his father. "Maybe somebody educated him a little."

"It could be," Cleveland responded.

Doug gave them a confused expression, failing to understand their meaning. No matter, he still needed to get to the bottom of this fiasco.

"This might sound kind of stupid, but can you tell me where I am?" Doug asked. "I think my friends have played a joke on me."

Cleveland looked at Nathaniel and his other son, Reuben, with a puzzled look of his own.

"You don't know where you are?" Cleveland questioned. "Did you get lost, boy? Did you run away?"

"I mean I didn't get lost, I just…" Doug didn't know how to finish the sentence and was uncomfortable with Cleveland's tone. "I don't know what happened. My friends must have played a prank on me. I'm sure they'll be here in a minute."

"Who do you belong to, boy," Cleveland asked pointedly.

"What?" Doug replied hotly. "I don't belong to anybody, except my mama."

Cleveland looked at Nathaniel and Reuben and nodded. Nathaniel dismounted his horse calmly.

"Who is your master?" Cleveland asked.

Doug grimaced at the question.

"Master? Man, what the hell are you talking about?" Doug inquired.

Reuben climbed from his horse and grabbed a rifle. Doug retreated slowly, taking a couple of steps backward as Nathaniel and Reuben flanked him.

"What is this?" Doug asked. "Y'all better stop tripping."

"Check him," Cleveland instructed. "See if he's been branded."

"Branded?" Doug replied in bewilderment. "What are you talking about?"

Nathaniel and Reuben looked at Doug, scrutinizing every part of him.

"He ain't got a mark on him, Pa," Nathaniel reported.

"Well, I guess that makes you mine then," Cleveland asserted.

"What?" Doug questioned, shocked by the absurd remark.

Before Doug could utter another word, Nathaniel reached out and grabbed his arm. Doug jerked his arm away quickly and forcefully.

16

"Get your damn hand off of me," Doug warned.

Reuben stepped around Doug, cutting off any escape route through the field. The move expanded Doug's field of view, allowing him to see behind the wagon. Doug stood aghast at what he saw. Three shirtless black men were shackled together in a single file line and chained to the back of the wagon. Three black women attired in raggedy dresses were gathered in the wagon. Two young children, a boy and a girl as young as seven years old, sat in the wagon with the women.

Doug turned to run away and bumped into Reuben. He sent Doug to the ground with a vigorous jab with the butt of the rifle. Doug tried to get back to his feet but Nathaniel hit him again with his rifle. The blow nearly knocked the young man unconscious again.

"Get some shackles on him and put him in the wagon," Cleveland ordered. "We'll take him with the rest of them."

Doug writhed on the ground, hardly able to move, let alone resist. Nathaniel and Reuben placed Doug's wrists in iron restraints. The two large men lifted Doug by his arms and legs and carried him to the rear of the wagon. They hoisted him higher and put him in the back among the women and children.

Cleveland cracked the reins and yelled. The wagon began to move as Reuben and Nathaniel climbed onto their mounts.

Doug stared at the men in chains who followed the wagon. He found it difficult to keep his eyes open. Laying on his back, Doug turned his head to observe the women and children around him. The other occupants of the wagon sat silently and stared back at him.

"What is happening?" Doug asked so quietly that it was barely more than a whisper. His eyes became heavy and Doug fainted; he found himself aimlessly floating in a sea of unawareness.

A gentle tapping on his cheek awakened Doug. He opened his eyes to see Nathaniel leaning over him.

"He's awake," Nathaniel said to Reuben. "Let's get him on his feet."

The two men dragged Doug from the wagon before he could even sit up.

They helped Doug become steady on his feet before leading him away from the wagon. They guided their captive toward an intersection with many people standing around. Doug gazed upon the scene, dumbfounded by what he saw. People dressed in clothes that almost seemed ancient. Horses and wagons stood nearby. There were no paved roads. Doug was pulled toward an area where the shirtless and bound men huddled with the women and children. A sign was posted on a nearby wall. Doug read the sign as he was navigated past it. He was shocked and certain he read it incorrectly. Doug looked back at the sign to read it again.

"Negroes for sale at auction this day," read the bold headline of the sign. The date on the sign featured the year 1864.

Doug began to struggle, jumping and trying to escape the grasp of his captors.

"No! What is happening?" Doug screamed as he grappled for his freedom. "This isn't happening! Let me go! This isn't real!"

Reuben thrust his knee into Doug's stomach, causing him to fold over. Cleveland ambled over as Doug dropped to his knees. Reuben raised a fist above Doug.

"Don't bruise him," Cleveland insisted. "We won't get as much for him if you bruise him. Put him with the others."

The men dragged Doug and placed him beside Mary and her nine-year-old daughter, Alberta. Doug remained on his knees after the kidnappers released him and walked away. He was in a state of shock. Doug knew this couldn't be real. But he felt the ground beneath him, the wind as it blew over him, and his heart pounding in his chest.

Mary poked Doug on his shoulder and motioned for him to stand up.

"You better stand up. They not like for you to act that way," Mary advised Doug. She didn't speak very clearly due to a lack of education. Nonetheless, Doug could understand her.

Mary kept a firm grasp of her daughter's hand as she bent over and patted Doug gently on the shoulder.

"It's gonna be okay," Mary advised him. "I bet we go to a better place than this. It's gonna be better. They don't want to beat you right now. Better not give them a reason to."

Doug stood up and wiped a tear from his eye.

"What's going on? How did we get here?" Doug asked her.

"I was bought by Mr. Hubbard when I was a little girl. Now he selling me," Mary said.

"This can't be real," Doug said again, trying to convince himself it was part of an elaborate prank. "Maybe I'm dreaming."

"You not dreaming," Mary stated. "You be here breathing, don't you?"

Mary hushed Doug before he could reply as she noticed Cleveland and Nathaniel approaching. The vile men lead the slaves away and lined them up beside a small stage. A well-dressed man walked back and forth in front of Doug and the others, making an initial inspection. Oscar Wilson was looking to purchase and wanted the best value for his money. He stood before Mary and examined her more closely. After looking her up and down, Oscar reached out and placed his hands on her cheeks. With his thumbs, he pried her mouth open easily and began a more thorough analysis. Doug could not believe he was seeing another human being undergoing such scrutiny to be acquired like an animal.

After completing his review of Mary, Oscar sidestepped to stand before Doug. Oscar grabbed Doug's shoulder and turned him halfway around. Doug was too shocked to offer any resistance.

"He hasn't a scratch upon him," Oscar stated as he observed Doug's back.

"Oh, no, very obedient this one," Cleveland stated. "I don't recall ever needing to strike him."

A young boy nearby began beating a drum and an auctioneer stepped onto the small stage.

"Gentlemen, welcome!" the auctioneer began. "Today we have a fine selection of healthy slaves for your consideration. These slaves are from nearby counties and some as far away as South Carolina and Virginia. Each is well-versed in proper etiquette and has proven their worth in the field or kitchen. First up for bid is this adult woman."

An auction worker grabbed Mary by the arm and pulled her forward. Mary did not resist and complied with the direction. She held firm to

Alberta's hand, drawing her daughter closer.

Oscar Wilson immediately raised his hand to stake his claim.

"I'll pay twenty-five dollars!" Oscar called out.

"I hear twenty-five! Who will give thirty?" the auctioneer asked.

Silas King, another sharply dressed man in the crowd raises his hand.

"I'll give thirty-five!" Silas declares.

"Thirty-five! We have thirty-five!" the auctioneer announced.

"Forty!" Oscar offered.

"There's forty!" the auctioneer noted.

"Forty-five!" Silas extended.

"Fifty!" Oscar retorted.

"I hear fifty! Is anyone willing to pay fifty-five?" the auctioneer asked. "Fifty is the number! Do I hear fifty-five?"

The auctioneer paused and scanned the crowd but no hands were raised.

"Sold for fifty dollars to the gentleman!" the auctioneer yelled, settling the process.

Two of Oscar's farmhands progressed toward Mary with shackles. Mary clutched Alberta's hand tightly.

"Put your hands out," ordered one of the farmhands.

Mary disobeyed the order, refusing to let go of her daughter's hand.

"I said put your hands out," the farmhand directed more sternly.

Mary pulled her arms close and refused to relinquish her child's hand.

The farmhand grabbed Mary by the hair and gave a hard yank. Mary yelled in response but would not let go of Alberta.

"I said put your hands out! Don't make me tell you again!" the man warned.

"Please, sir," the auctioneer interjected. "Perhaps there is a better solution. Would you be interested in purchasing the little one, my good man?"

"No, thank you," Oscar said nicely.

"I'm sure she will prove as good a servant as the mother in time," the auctioneer submitted.

"I have no use for her," Oscar stated.

An auction worker grabbed Alberta by the arm and tried to pull her away from her mother. Oscar's farmhand continued to pull Mary in the opposite direction. The men were locked in a tug of war, trying to pull mother and daughter apart.

"No! My baby!" Mary screeched frantically.

"Mama!" Alberta howled in reply. "Mama, no!"

"Baby!" Mary yelled in desperation, her hand like a vice on her daughter.

The men gave all of their efforts but still could not wrest Alberta from Mary.

"Pull them apart already!" Oscar shrieked.

An abolitionist stood near a crowd of angry spectators. The man was short, thin, and even frail in appearance. He looked sorrowfully at the two men prying Alberta and Mary apart. It was as if the men didn't know, or care, that they were trying to break apart a mother and daughter. The bond that held Mary to Alberta was a mother's love, and that is not easily broken. Even as the auction worker slapped her face and pulled her hair, Mary refused to surrender her grip on Alberta's hand. The abolitionist could not hold back any longer. The terror of the scene washed over him like a huge wave.

"Let them be!" the abolitionist cried loudly.

The outburst drew the ire of a large man in the crowd.

"Silence you!" the large man ordered.

The farmhands continued to struggle and the abolitionist was nearly emotionally broken by the commotion.

"Just give him the little girl too! Let them be together for pity's sake!" the abolitionist begged.

"Be quiet!" the large angry man blared again.

Mary's grip on Alberta's hand began to slip. The humidity and violence made it almost impossible to hold her daughter.

"Please, God, no!" Mary pleaded as her hand slipped a little more.

Another farmhand approached carrying a large wooden staff. The man drew back the club and swung hard, striking Mary's abdomen. She crumpled over and dropped to her knees and elbows. The other farmhand dragged Alberta away by the arm and hair.

"Mama, no!" Alberta cried as she was pulled away, her heels dragging the ground.

Mary remained on the ground, wailing uncontrollably. Her hand filled with tears as she wept unceasingly. The farmhand lifted Mary onto her feet but she could barely stand.

"This is a moral outrage!" the abolitionist declared.

"Utter another word and I'll see you run through!" the angry onlooker warned.

The abolitionist was irked to be the target of such scorn and threats. Witnessing Mary's dogged attempt to keep her daughter, and the savagery that unfolded, left the abolitionist incensed. A twinkle of righteous indignation gleamed in his eye as he sarcastically tipped his hat to the crowd and walked away at a brisk pace.

Another farmhand assisted in pulling Mary away. The malicious grant no warmth or compassion to the weary and distressed, even at the loss of a child.

Alberta kept her arm extended, reaching for her mother as she was lead away. She did not avert her eyes from her sobbing mother until she was completely out of sight. The men moved Mary toward a wagon behind a building. They turned the corner, and then she was gone.

As things began to settle, an auction worker grabbed Doug by the arm and led him to the stage. Doug was still in a state of pure shock and confusion. It was as if a dark magic spell had been cast on him.

"Here is a fine, young, hardworking lad. As you can see, he is quite clean and contains no scars. His teeth are as healthy as you will ever see," the auctioneer described. "Shall we start the bidding at seventy-five?"

John Cooper removed the tobacco pipe from his lips and held it aloft.

"I'll give seventy-five!" he offered.

Among the crowd were three men who represented the same employer. Earl Downing was the oldest, a polite and genteel man, if not quite refined. He was charged with inspecting and purchasing slaves for the Cobb family. His party included Philip McKay a farmhand and overseer who would help with the transport of newly purchased slaves. Philip was a sturdily built man, but not enormous. The smallest of the men was Lester Clay, another overseer. He was short in stature, not much bigger than teenage Doug. While lacking in size, Lester was intimidating in appearance. He had hair that was the color of the sun. It looked as though his head was ablaze. Lester stood still as a stone with a fixed angry expression on his face.

"Eighty-Five!" Earl declared.

"Ninety!" John Cooper rebutted.

"Ninety-five!" squawked Arthur Kerr, a portly man entering the contest.

"One hundred!" offered Earl.

Arthur gritted his teeth, seemingly surprised by the offer. John Cooper gnawed on the tip of his pipe, debating internally. After a distinct chomp, John raised his pipe again.

"One hundred and five!" John proclaimed.

"One hundred and ten!" Earl asserted without hesitation.

John Cooper returned to deep thought, biting persistently on his pipe again.

"Do I hear one hundred and twenty?" the auctioneer asked. "One hundred and twenty?"

John Cooper stopped nibbling on his pipe and said nothing. No other hands went up.

"Sold for one hundred and ten dollars!" the auctioneer affirmed.

Auction workers removed Doug from the stage and led him to an area where Lester took possession of him. After double-checking his bounds, Lester and Philip guided Doug toward a wagon. Doug looked at his surroundings as he was escorted to the back of the transport. It seemed so real. He wondered how it could be real.

3

Taken Away

E arl kept the horses at a slow pace as they pulled the wagon. Alberta sat in the back of the wagon and stayed close to Minnie, an elderly slave woman. Doug walked behind the wagon, the last in line with two other men shackled to the buggy. Lester and Philip rode alongside on horseback.

Doug found himself dazed and bewildered. None of it made sense. He lightly tapped his fist on his forehead as he plodded along, hoping to bring himself back into the reality he had always known.

"Come on, wake up," Doug whispered to himself. "Somebody hypnotized me or something."

Doug struggled to keep pace with the wagon. The day was hot, and he was exhausted. Lester's horse galloped quickly until it was beside Doug. Drained and weakened, Doug stumbled and fell. Doug's fall pulled down the man in front of him and the wagon pulled them both through the dirt.

"Whoa, Earl!" Lester yelled.

Earl pulled back on the reins and brought the wagon to a stop. The man in front of Doug quickly climbed back to his feet. Doug struggled to even get on his knees.

"Get up, boy!" Lester bellowed.

Philip trotted over on his horse and stopped next to Doug.

"On your feet," he encouragingly told Doug.

"I'm so tired," Doug replied.

"I said get up!" Lester howled.

"Lester, can you check on the women?" Philip asked. "Maybe see if Earl needs anything."

With a growl, Lester pulled the reins, and the horse stepped away. Philip observed Doug, who remained on the ground, breathing heavily.

"God, I can't go any farther," Doug confessed.

"Yes, you can," Philip began. "The sun's going down. We'll stop soon and get some rest."

Doug slowly got to his feet. Once he was steady and composed, Philip rode away. Philip signaled to Earl and with a snap of the reins, the party was on the move again.

The small convoy created a silhouette against a beautiful sunset. The sun designed a kaleidoscope of orange, yellow, and violet in the sky as it retreated slowly behind the horizon. They were running a losing race against the night. The men decided they should stop and set up camp and brought the group to a halt.

The glow of a crackling fire illuminated the horses grazing nearby. It provided a small amount of light in the tent where Minnie and Alberta were sleeping. Earl laid on the ground near the tent, keeping guard as much as sleeping.

Doug sat on the ground with his back against a wagon wheel. Lester attached a short chain from the wagon to the shackles that bound Doug. He secured the other slave men to different parts of the wagon.

"Wouldn't want to see you run off now," Lester said sarcastically as he completed his work.

Once Lester stepped away, Doug tried to lie on his back. It was uncomfortable because Lester chained his wrists to the wagon on his right side. This caused Doug to lay awkwardly, with his left arm across his chest. Doug adjusted what he could and tried to make the most of it.

Lester moved to the campfire and laid on a blanket near it. Philip positioned himself on a nearby blanket. Lester made himself comfortable and soon both men were fast asleep with their hats sitting atop their faces.

Doug laid quietly and stared up at the sky. Stars became more luminous and plentiful as the fire slowly dimmed. He wondered if somewhere in the universe's vastness there was a tear in space and time itself that had transported him here. Doug fought hard to keep his eyes open, but exhaustion consumed him. He fell asleep and was soon as peaceful as the night itself.

In the morning, Lester, Philip, and Earl moved about, working to ready horses and break camp. A small plume of smoke rose from the embers of the campfire. Doug opened his eyes and looked at the scene. He tried to sit up but was quickly jerked back by the chains prohibiting his movement. Doug looked around and winced in the morning's brightness. He could make out all that was happening around him and was despondent. He was awake, but still in a nightmare. Doug shook his head in disbelief as a tear ran down his cheek.

Philip knelt beside Doug and worked to disconnect his bindings from the wagon.

"Man, what is going on?" Doug asked desperately.

"Won't be long now," Philip replied, almost disregarding the question because he didn't understand why it was asked.

After getting Doug on his feet and in line with the other slave men, Philip went to help Minnie put Alberta in the back of the wagon. Once Alberta was aboard, he delicately helped Minnie into the wagon. Philip waited for the old woman to get seated and stable before telling Earl to move the carriage.

"Ya! Let's go!" Earl shouted.

The wagon moved, and it tugged Doug along with it. Doug was too busy contemplating what was happening to think about the exhaustion. Lester was watching him vigilantly, and Doug wouldn't give the man the satisfaction of seeing him fall.

The slave buyers led their bounty along a smooth, narrow dirt road toward the entrance of a plantation. A two-story house with a large front porch stood in the middle of a sprawling yard of short green grass. Smaller buildings and cabins were in place a short distance away. A gin house and barns were also in view. Closest to the house was a building that served as an outdoor kitchen.

Doug breathed heavily and stared at the house as they dragged him toward it. Sweat ran down his body and fatigue was clear on his face, but he remained upright behind the wagon. In the distance, he could see slaves toiling in a field.

A thin man in his early fifties walked onto the porch and watched the approaching wagon. Joseph Cobb stood erect, proudly wearing a suit that was as meticulous as his nicely groomed beard. His wife, Edith, soon joined him. She was a beautiful woman, radiant and more youthful than her forty-five years would affirm. Edith was confident and self-assured of her standing in the home.

They stood patiently on the porch, enveloped in the shade of a few large oak trees nearby. Joseph stood stiffly until Earl brought the wagon to a stop a short distance from the front steps.

"Morning, boss," Lester said before climbing from his horse.

"Good morning, Lester," Joseph replied.

"You look lovely as always, Mrs. Cobb," Lester said as he tipped his hat to Edith.

"You're too kind, Mr. Clay," Edith said with the slightest of smiles.

Philip and Earl arranged the slaves in a line before the wagon. They stood shoulder to shoulder as Joseph stepped off the porch.

"We found a few good ones at auction," Lester began. "I think they'll work out well."

"Let's see what you've brought," Joseph said as he stepped toward the slaves.

Joseph strolled in a slow and deliberate march in front of the slaves, gazing at each as he passed before them. Doug averted his eyes to the ground as Joseph walked to him. He was still in a daze about what was happening to him.

Edith smiled as she descended the steps and walked toward Alberta and Minnie. While the other slaves stood stoically, Minnie tenderly held Alberta's hand, offering comfort to the young girl.

"Have you done kitchen work before?" Edith asked Minnie. There was a hint of sweetness in her voice. She was not condescending to the older woman.

"Yes, ma'am," Minnie began. "I worked in the kitchen at Mr. Jennings' house for a lot of years. I can make cornbread, beans, cook a ham…whatever you want ma'am."

"That sounds splendid," Edith replied.

Edith bent over and brought her face closer to Alberta's. The little girl stood as close as possible to Minnie.

"And what is your name?" Edith asked Alberta.

"Alberta," the little girl replied concisely.

"Well, Alberta, I'll bet you know your way around the kitchen also," Edith said.

"Yes, ma'am," Alberta replied. "I used to help my mama…"

The girl cried. The devastation of being ripped from her mother's arms the day before was still fresh. Such wounds take ages to scab over and never fully heal.

Edith reached over Alberta's shoulder and rubbed her back to soothe the heartbroken girl.

"There, there. Let's find you ladies some proper clothes for housework," Edith said.

With a steady hand on Alberta's shoulder, Edith led the girl and Minnie toward the house.

While his wife tended to Minnie and Alberta, Joseph made a last inspection of the male slaves.

"Get some clothes for these men and put them to work," Joseph said to Lester. "I need them picking in the south field."

"Yes, sir," Lester replied.

Joseph walked toward the house as Lester and Philip began moving the slaves again.

Doug stood before Lester with the other slave men. A group of men and women picked cotton in the field behind them. Lester handed each of the men a large sack that draped to the ground. Doug watched as the other slaves situated the bags for work. Each man placed a long strap attached to the bag over his head and shoulder so it hung across his body. In this way, they positioned the opening of the bag just above the waist and beneath the chest. A slave could then carry the bag with him as he picked the valuable crop. The men beside Doug were familiar with the bags. Doug watched the other men but hesitated to place the bag on himself.

"Boy, you better put that on and get to work," Lester said ominously. "That field won't pick itself."

"Look, sir, I don't know what's going on. Something is wrong," Doug told him.

"You're right," Lester replied. "Something is wrong. You're standing here bickering instead of being in that field working. Now move before you get lashings."

"I don't understand what is happening," Doug tried to explain.

"What's there to understand?" Lester questioned. "You put the sack over your shoulder and you fill it with cotton. Now git!"

"This must be a bad dream or something," Doug started, "I, I…"

"Did you fall and hit your head or something?" Lester interrupted. "Now you best get to work or you really won't know where you are."

Doug realized he was pressing his luck and hastily put the sack over his shoulder as the other men had done.

The new slaves joined the others in the field. A large basket was positioned at the front of the rows. Once a slave had filled their sack with cotton, they emptied it into the basket. After unloading the cotton, the slave returned to the row to fill the sack again. The overseers expected roughly two hundred pounds of cotton from each slave on an average day. Collecting less meant being punished with several lashings.

Doug had never picked cotton in his life and looked like a fish out of water. He stood while the surrounding men stooped over, picking cotton from the lower branches on plants that stood about five feet high.

"Hey, man, can you show me how to do that?" Doug whispered as he leaned over to the man in the row beside him.

The man gave Doug a brief, confusing stare in reply. Lewis had been a slave his entire life. The notion that a young black man didn't know how to pick cotton was preposterous. He was sure Doug was pulling his leg. Lewis resumed his work as Doug watched him.

Noticing that Philip was observing from a distance, Doug picked at the plants. Unaware of what he was doing, Doug pulled the cotton and the boll from the stem. During some attempts, he even pulled off part of the stem itself. At least he looked busy, he thought.

The plants in the row to the left of Doug rustled and moved as if a dinosaur was walking through the field. Doug stood up so he could see over the plants. He wondered if a farm animal was meandering across the terrain, such was the commotion and disturbance in the row. Peering over the plants, Doug witnessed the broad back and shoulders of the largest man he had ever seen.

The man stood erect and wiped the sweat from his brow. He was nearly six feet, seven inches tall and over two hundred and fifty pounds. He towered over everyone around him, like a lone tree standing in the field. The size of the man amazed Doug. The giant took a deep breath before crouching over to pick cotton again. Once he snapped out of his trance, Doug also resumed picking.

Lewis looked back at Doug and observed him for a moment. Doug moved past plants with cotton on them to look as if he was keeping pace with the other slaves. Lewis watched Doug pull an entire branch off of a plant. In frustrated disbelief, Lewis scampered back down the row a short distance to meet Doug.

"Watch me," Lewis said.

"Did you see how big that man was?" Doug asked.

"That's Vernon," Lewis told him. "He don't say much. Now watch what I do."

Doug watched as Lewis grabbed the cotton at the base, twisted it, and pulled it away from the boll. Lewis repeated the action a second time before motioning for Doug to try. As Doug pulled at the cotton, Lewis glanced to his left and noticed an overseer walking down the row. Lewis quickly scurried back to his previous spot.

Henry Bowman, the youngest overseer in the Cobb family's service, hurried down the row toward Doug. He was in his early twenties and had a thin but muscle toned frame.

"You're leaving a lot of unpicked cotton behind," Henry said to Doug.

"I'm sorry, I don't know..." Doug began. "I don't know if I feel too good."

Henry examined Doug's face.

"You don't look ill," Henry said.

Henry noticed several stems laying on the ground along Doug's row.

"You're tearing these plants up," Henry stated. "You need to be a little more careful. Watch me."

As Lewis had done, Henry grasped the cotton at its base, gave it a turn, and plucked it from the boll.

"Do it just like that," Henry instructed. "Go on, let me see you do it."

Doug grabbed the cotton and mimicked what Henry had done.

"There you go," Henry said approvingly, "that's it."

Henry watched Doug remove cotton from a few more bolls.

"You've got it," Henry assured him. "Now try to catch up with the others. You don't want to get Lester riled up."

Doug continued at a steady pace, working more meticulously than he had before.

Henry casually walked back down the row.

Henry was the youngest of five sons born to Edmond and Camilla Bowman. The family had a modest tract of land but owned no slaves. They grew most of their food but could not harvest a large crop for profit. Henry and his brothers worked as overseers and laborers at other farms and plantations to help provide for the family. Henry had not seen his oldest brother in almost a year. Jasper Bowman joined the Confederate army and left the simple family farm behind. His mother had not received a letter from him for quite some time, and Henry could see the worry on her face every day.

Knowing her other sons were working nearby helped ease her mind.

Henry didn't spoil the slaves, but thought it ineffective to be spiteful toward them. Occasionally, he was even known to treat a slave kindly. Both Henry and Philip drew the ire of Lester and the other overseers and free workers for their sometimes amiable treatment of the slaves. There was enough sorrow in the world with the ongoing war sending innumerable men to their deaths daily. Henry saw no point in adding to the despair.

Like many homes of the day, the Cobb family located the kitchen in an outbuilding separate from the main house. This arrangement was especially helpful during the hot summer months. Keeping the kitchen in an isolated building helped keep the house cooler and reduced the risk of fire. The house still contained fireplaces throughout to heat the home in winter, but for daily cooking, the detached kitchen was ideal. The kitchen had an additional room reserved for the weaving loom.

The dominant feature of the kitchen was the large fireplace with a movable metal arm used for hanging pots over the fire. A big table stood in the center of the room, covered with items to be prepared - baskets of vegetables, loaves of bread, and meats. Iron skillets and pots hung on the wall.

Hilda, a slave woman in her mid-twenties, was a kitchen mainstay. She had primarily worked in the kitchen and house since Mr. Cobb purchased her about eleven years earlier. Hilda moved about the kitchen like a bee in a field of flowers, spending a moment in different places as she worked to prepare supper. She kept the door propped open, hoping a breeze would find its way into the sultry confines of the kitchen.

Edith led Minnie and Alberta across the yard to the kitchen. Hilda immediately stopped what she was doing once the other women arrived.

"Supper will be ready in a little while, Missus Edith," Hilda advised.

"You're doing fine, Hilda," Edith replied. "There's no reason to rush."

Minnie and Alberta stood to one side and looked around the kitchen. Alberta noticed the loom in the next room.

"It looks like we need more wood in here," Edith observed. "Alberta, can you help Hilda gather some wood?"

"Yes, ma'am," Alberta replied.

"Come, child," Hilda said as she extended her hand to the little girl.

Edith pointed to the pots and pans on the wall as Minnie watched. Hilda and Alberta quickly left the room.

A large stack of firewood sat a short distance from the house and kitchen. Slaves stacked wood high enough that it was easy to grab and not at risk of toppling over. Keeping the stack supplied and replenished was the job of Henry and a small group of slaves.

"Hold out your arms, child, and I'll give you some to carry," Hilda said.

Alberta extended her arms. Hilda removed one of the smaller pieces of wood from the stack and placed it across Alberta's outstretched arms. The young girl's arms dropped, but she brought them up again.

"Can you carry another?" Hilda asked.

"Yes, ma'am," Alberta replied.

Hilda scanned the pile for another small piece of wood. Once satisfied with her selection, she placed it in Alberta's arms. The girl curled her arms upward and secured the load. Hilda grabbed some wood herself, and she and Alberta made their way back toward the kitchen.

As night crept in, the field slaves gathered at the gin house where they stood in line to hand in their baskets of cotton. Doug rubbed his dirty fingers to soothe the pain coursing through them. Besides the constant pinching action, the sharp pointy edges of the boll nicked Doug's fingers several times.

Torches and lanterns brightened the night. One by one, each slave handed his or her basket of cotton to Earl, who determined if it was heavy enough by feel. If he considered the basket was too light, he would weigh it to be sure.

Lester stood by a nearby tree, slowly tapping a curled whip against his leg. Henry and Philip also stood to the side and watched the proceedings.

Upon reaching the front of the line, Doug gave his basket to Earl. The man gripped the basket, which was light compared to the full baskets other slaves had turned in. Some baskets were even overflowing.

"Boy, what have you been doing all day?" Earl asked him.

"I did the best I could," Doug began. "I've never picked cotton before."

Earl let out a spirited laugh.

"Never picked cotton before, he says," Earl announced, still laughing.

Lester grinned and chuckled at the joke as he gripped the whip tightly.

"Give him a break, Earl," Philip interjected. "He just traveled from the auction last night and wasn't in the field all day."

Earl gave a slight snarl as he handed the basket to Daniel behind him. The charitable dismissal angered Lester.

"Where are you going?" Lester called to Doug.

Doug stopped and looked at Lester, who was walking toward him. Philip stepped in front of Doug.

"Just go back over yonder, Lester," Philip told him.

"He has to get lashings," Lester replied. "They have to know there is accountability. You go soft on them and they will get lazy."

"He ain't picked all day, Lester," Philip stated again. "Now you can't punish a man for doing less work when he didn't work a full day."

Lester spat at Philip's feet before turning around and walking away. Henry stood grinning from a distance.

"What are you smirking at?" Lester bellowed.

Doug stood still and watched the other slaves walk in the same direction, like a flowing river of humanity. Vernon placed his enormous hand on Doug's shoulder and nudged him along. Guided by Vernon, Doug followed the slaves to an area where small cabins stood close together. The cabins were nearly identical to one another, with a chimney on the side and a single door on the front.

At Vernon's insistence, Doug stepped inside a one-room cabin where he met Florence and Maurice, a married couple in their late forties. Maurice started a fire and once it was burning, he sat upon a rickety chair beside a small wooden table. Florence placed a pot of vegetables on an arm that swung into the fireplace.

"Hi," Doug said as he gave a brief wave to anyone who was paying attention.

"Howdy," Maurice replied.

Doug stepped toward a bed in the cabin's corner. The bed looked shaky, held up on legs that appeared to be nothing more than heavy sticks. A larger bed was in another corner of the structure.

"Is it OK if I sit here?" Doug asked, pointing to the smaller bed.

"I suppose you can," Maurice said. "It's your bed."

As he sat down, Doug gave out a sigh of relief. His legs and feet ached after a long day in the field. Doug laid back on the bed and peered at the ceiling. The mattress made of hay was pleasant compared to the rough ground he slept on the night before. The confused mind races and struggles to comprehend things. Doug still didn't understand what was happening to him or how. Despite the deluge of activity in his mind, Doug soon strayed off to sleep. Exhaustion overpowered his relentless mind.

4

The Thirsty Dirt

A gentle hand atop his head caused Doug to stir as he slept.

"Mom," Doug whispered before opening his eyes.

"It's time to wake up," Florence uttered.

Doug sat up in the ramshackle bed and observed the room. He tapped his forehead again in disbelief that he was still in this strange place and time. Doug rubbed his sore hands and noticed the bruises on his wrists from the shackles he had worn the day before.

Florence placed a plate of cornbread on the table and poured water into a cup.

"Come, sit," she advised Doug.

Doug got up from the bed and stretched before sitting across the table from Maurice. The residents of the cabin sat in silence and ate their simple breakfast.

The sound of a horn blowing broke the peaceful silence. Maurice, Florence, and Vernon arose almost in unison. Uncertain of anything going on around him, Doug followed the others.

The first rays of the morning sun were reaching over the horizon, pushing back the veil of the night. The slaves gathered near the fields in the dim twilight of dawn. Doug yawned and tried to shake off the effects of disrupted sleep. Doug scanned the group, looking over the collection of human beings huddled near him. The variety of slaves was staggering. Young and old, short and tall, sturdy and frail, stood side by side. As he continued to survey the lot, a beautiful young woman captured Doug's gaze. She bore a noticeable resemblance to Aliyah, which made Doug yearn for his old life all the more.

Cecelia was beautiful, with skin so smooth it defied the circumstances of her life. High cheekbones and piercing brown eyes accentuated her attractive face. Her athletic build was delicate and hardy all at once.

Enthralled at the sight of something so alluring and unusual, yet familiar, Doug could not turn his eyes away from her. She stood like a sculpted masterpiece illuminated by the ever brightening sun as if nature itself was casting a spotlight upon her.

Cecelia tilted her face toward the sky, smiled, and closed her eyes, escaping the abhorrent reality of her life for a moment. As she brought her head forward, Cecelia looked at Doug. He disconnected his gaze from her and directed it to the ground. A few seconds later, he glanced back at her. She smiled at Doug and he averted his eyes again. After a few anxious moments, Doug looked around, playing it cool and trying to save face. Yet again his eyes met Cecelia's, and she giggled. Realizing he could not feign ignorance again, he smiled back.

Smiles faded from every face as the overseer and drivers arrived. Philip and Henry began handing out sacks to everyone. Lester stood a scant distance away with his two friends, Thomas and Daniel. Lester watched the group, almost hoping for some transgression. Something was irritating Lester, not that it took much to bring him to that state.

Homer, a slave around the age of forty, scampered toward the group as he fastened the last buttons on his shirt. He tried to move carefully to avoid kicking a pine cone or stepping on a piece of a fallen tree limb. Homer's efforts to avoid detection were in vain. Lester had spotted him.

"Homer, get over here!" Lester commanded, the whip already clenched in his right hand.

Homer halted and almost fell to the ground as he shuddered with fear. He turned to face Lester, his shoulders raised toward his ears in anticipation of what was to come. Homer held his hands up, palms toward the angry overseer, silently pleading for mercy before uttering a word.

"Didn't you hear the horn, Homer?" Lester asked him.

"I heard it Mister, but I fell back asleep," Homer said. "I was dog tired. I worked hard yesterday."

"Everyone else worked hard too. I worked hard, but I'm here," Lester countered condescendingly.

Homer stooped lower as he approached Lester until he was on his knees and clasping his hands as if praying.

"Please, Mister, I ain't never been late," Homer pleaded. "I work real hard. I ain't never been late a day in my life."

The tears streaming down Homer's cheeks did little to placate Lester.

"Get off your knees, Homer," Lester directed. "Show some self-respect."

"Please, Mister, I won't be late no more," Homer stated. "I swear I won't."

"Get him up," Lester instructed Thomas and Daniel.

Each man grabbed one of Homer's already raised arms and lifted him. Frozen with fear, the man was almost dead weight. Homer wept and continued to implore Lester for clemency.

"Please, sir, I won't be late again, I swear," Homer cried.

"I ain't got time for laggards," Lester said.

"Please, Mister," Homer begged almost in a whisper.

"Drag him over yonder and get his shirt off," Lester ordered.

Thomas and Daniel dragged Homer toward a slave cabin. The slave's feet kicked up a slight cloud of dust as they pulled him over the dry sandy soil. Lester uncoiled the whip until it dangled at his side and touched the ground.

Doug watched as they dragged Homer away. The sight of it appalled him. Philip stopped handing out sacks.

"Come on, Lester," Philip began. "He was only a couple of minutes late."

"Tend to your work, Philip!" Lester barked. "I'll see to mine."

Doug saw Thomas and Daniel pull Homer behind a slave cabin. Lester began a slow walk toward them as if he was savoring what was to come. The whip dragged the ground like a viper, slithering toward its prey.

Doug cringed as he listened to Homer's pleas for mercy. The man begged as if his very life was at stake. The crack of the whip soon interrupted

Homer's appeal. Doug heard many agonizing sounds in his housing project and the surrounding neighborhood. Sometimes gunshots rang out. He overheard arguments and fights. He heard the horrible sounds of domestic violence. The night frequently reverberated with the sound of police sirens. But he had never heard sounds so excruciating and ghastly as he heard that morning. The sorrowful wailing and sobbing of a man beaten so harshly jarred Doug to his core.

Homer's yells and howls continued even after the whip fell silent. Lester emerged from behind the slave cabin, shaking his right hand as he held the whip with the other. Thomas and Daniel soon followed him. Thomas threw Homer's shirt onto the steps of the cabin.

The master only gave slaves two shirts each year. The overseers didn't want to befoul a good shirt with the blood of a beaten slave. If a slave were to put on a shirt with fresh wounds, the blood would cause the shirt to adhere to the lesions. Removing the shirt after the blood had dried would reopen the cuts and be painful.

The men walked toward the fields, leaving Homer to stagger behind them. Homer wiped his eyes and tried to catch his breath. Doug saw the fresh lacerations on Homer's back. Blood oozed from cuts in thin lines and followed the contours of Homer's body. Doug watched Homer kneel to retrieve a sack, wincing from the stinging pain in his back as he did. A few drops of blood fell from his side and moistened the parched dirt.

"Get to work now," Philip called out, snapping Doug from an almost trance-like state.

Doug and the other slaves moved to the end of the field and began the tedious and onerous work of the day.

The kitchen was abuzz with activity as the slave women prepared breakfast. Minnie stirred a pot as Hilda prepared a serving platter. Edith handed Alberta a different platter full of bread to carry.

"OK, come along ladies," Edith instructed.

Alberta and Hilda followed Edith, who carried a basket to the house herself.

Joseph sat at the head of the table. His twenty-seven-year-old daughter, Margaret, accompanied him. Joseph cracked a slight smile when his two young granddaughters entered the room. Margaret moved back home after her husband, Samuel, joined the Confederate army. Her oldest daughter, Caroline, was only seven and Charlotte was five. Trying to care for the girls alone seemed unnecessary with her parents so close. Margaret felt safe in the two-story, eight-room house where she grew up. Her mother's guidance and help in raising her children proved invaluable. Minnie would also assist with caring for the children.

Margaret tried to put on a brave face for her children, but she was anxious about the fate of her husband. Letters from Samuel became less frequent. The most recent registered a noticeable melancholic tone. The terror of war had eroded any remaining measure of contentment from him. With each letter, he seemed less like the man he once was. Margaret prayed that the war would end soon and the love of her life would return, whole, in body and spirit.

Edith and the slaves entered carrying breakfast. The women placed the various items on the table and Edith grabbed a plate and handed it to Hilda.

"Hilda, serve the children while I get my husband's plate," Edith said.

"Yes, ma'am," Hilda replied as she took the plate.

Edith and Hilda placed food on plates. Young Alberta lifted a large pitcher of water and tipped it to fill a glass. The pitcher was heavy, and the girl seemed to struggle with the first few glasses. After serving food and drink, Hilda and Alberta stood with their backs against a wall. Edith sat down.

Caroline reached to hug her grandfather as Margaret lifted Charlotte onto a chair. Margaret hugged Charlotte and kissed her head. Alberta gazed at this display of affection, and her eyes glistened with tears. The youthful slave girl had known this kind of nurturing devotion and love days before. She trembled and her heart ached at the sight of an interaction she may never know again.

Hilda leaned over and put her left hand on Alberta's shoulder.

"Hush child," Hilda began. "Don't let them see you like this."

Hilda used her apron to wipe the tears from Alberta's cheeks. The family gathered at the table was oblivious to the nearby slaves and their doings. They were as familiar and banal as a picture on the wall or a lantern on a table.

"There you are," Hilda whispered as she caressed Alberta's face. They returned to their upright posture and watched the table.

"Caroline, would you lead us in grace, please?" Edith asked her grand-daughter.

"Yes, Grandma," the child replied.

Caroline held her hands together in front of her face and closed her eyes. The other members of the family bowed their heads, as did Alberta and Hilda.

"Dear God," the little girl began, "thank you for our blessings, and please bring Daddy home. Amen."

Margaret's eyes gleamed with moisture as she smiled at her eldest daughter.

"That was very nice, Caroline," Joseph said.

"Ladies, that will be all for now," Edith said to Hilda and Alberta.

Hilda nodded her head politely and led Alberta from the room.

The slaves walked around the side of the house toward the kitchen. Hilda stopped and knelt before Alberta. She lifted the hem of her apron and tenderly wiped the remaining tears from Alberta's face.

"It's OK, child," Hilda said in a comforting voice.

"I miss my mama," Alberta said, choking back her sorrow.

"I know you do, baby," Hilda said. "Me and Miss Minnie will take care of you. And Missus Edith, she is a real friendly lady."

"What if mama forgets me?" the girl asked, causing another flood of tears.

"Oh, baby, your mama ain't never going to forget you," Hilda said as she searched for a dry section of her apron. "Don't worry. Mamas never forget their babies."

Once Alberta had regained her composure, Hilda took her by the hand and led her to the kitchen.

The sun was almost directly overhead, and the fields simmered with exhausted human beings. Drops of sweat fell from Doug in rapid and consistent succession. A puff of dust rose with every staggering step he took. Doug was far behind the slaves in other rows. Vernon walked back to meet Doug, then pretended to pick cotton beside him. Vernon reached across the plants and tapped Doug on the shoulder. Doug lifted his heavy head and observed Vernon. The enormous man reached into his sack and removed a handful of cotton and motioned toward Doug's bag. Doug looked puzzled.

"What?" Doug asked as he lifted his sack and looked into it.

Vernon reached across the row and placed his cotton into Doug's sack. Doug stood still in a state of confusion. Vernon placed another handful of cotton into Doug's sack, then another, and several more. After practically doubling the volume of cotton in Doug's sack, Vernon raced back to his place in the row. Doug returned to picking cotton as Philip walked toward him. A slave woman carrying a bucket of water walked behind Philip. Doug stood up as they approached.

"You look like you could use a drink," Philip said.

The woman dipped a large ladle into the bucket before handing it to Doug. He drank from the ladle earnestly. So considerable was his thirst that he questioned not the source of the water.

"You're kind of lagging," Philip uttered.

"I'm still learning," Doug began. "I've never done this before now."

"Won't too many people around here believe that," Philip said.

The slave woman placed the ladle into the bucket.

"Get some to Vernon and Lewis," Philip ordered.

The slave woman walked away as Lester sauntered over.

"What is going on over here?" Lester asked.

"It's fine, Lester," Philip stated. "I'm taking care of it."

"He's way behind the others," Lester noted.

"He's still getting accustomed to a different farm," Philip began, "that's all."

"It's like any other farm," Lester replied. "It's no different from the last farm he was at."

"I've never worked on a farm," Doug interjected.

Lester snorted.

"This one is a piece of work," Lester said.

"Isn't he though?" Philip replied.

"Well, I have to give him twenty lashings," Lester declared. "We have to speed him up. Can't have no loafers."

"I said I'm taking care of it," Philip asserted.

Lester sighed in frustration.

"I know how you take care of things, Philip," Lester said. "You pamper them. You go easy on them. They won't learn nothing that way. They ain't like me and you and you can't treat them like they are."

"Don't you have something else to do, Lester?" Philip asked.

Lester bit his bottom lip and sighed again. Philip's efforts to redirect irked him. Lester stared into the distance behind Philip, too angry to look the man in the eye. Suddenly he tilted his head slightly and looked more intently into the expanse beyond the cotton field. A shirtless black man exited the woods into an open grass field. The man slowly traipsed across the field, trying to avoid detection and not hurt his bare feet.

"Get the dogs!" Lester yelled to Thomas and Daniel.

Lester ran off in pursuit of the curious man as Daniel and Thomas gathered the hunting dogs.

The shirtless man looked behind him for a moment. He saw Lester bearing down on him and heard the baying of the hounds beginning their hunt. He quickened his pace, sparing no concern for his tortured feet. The man headed for the thick woods on the other side of the field as fast as he could. But the tuneless howling of the dogs grew louder. The tree line stood nearby. The four-legged mongrels darted past Lester and made haste toward their mark. The frightened man made it a short distance into the woods before realizing the dogs would overtake him. He attempted to climb a tree to escape the beasts, but his wounded feet betrayed him. The man was barely two feet up the tree before the lead dog snapped its jaws on his leg. The animal tugged and yanked on the man's leg, tearing his pants made of coarse fabric. The pain surging through his leg drained him of any eagerness to struggle. The man bellowed and shrieked as the dogs chomped and nipped at him. Lester, Daniel, and Thomas arrived, and it almost relieved him.

"Get back here!" Thomas hollered.

The dogs surrendered their quarry and returned to the field.

"Come on out of there now," Lester called to the man.

The man staggered from the trees. Blood oozed down his leg, landing on the dusty ground he was standing upon.

"Ooh boy, it's hot," Lester said. "Come on over here in the shade and get out of the sun."

The men moved to the inviting shade offered by a sturdy oak. Lester looked the man over.

"You don't look so good," Lester began. "What are you doing out here?"

"Um," the man began, "my master sent for me to go to the Ferguson farm to get a new ax handle."

He was nervous.

"Oh, he did?" Lester asked.

"Yes, sir," the man replied.

"And what's your name, good sir?" Lester asked him.

"My name is, Auston," the man offered.

"Who is your master, Auston?" Lester queried.

"Uh, my master is Mister Hargrove," Auston stated.

"Jeremiah Hargrove?" Daniel asked.

"Yes, sir," Auston replied.

"Where's your pass?" Lester asked.

Auston paused, thinking of a reply. A slave without a master's written pass was subject to violence by virtually anyone who found him or her. Many owners offered rewards for the return of any wayward slave. It created an incentive to hunt down and apprehend runaways. Auston knew he found himself in perilous circumstances.

"I think it got lost when I was in the woods," Auston answered.

"Why were you in the woods instead of taking the road?" Lester questioned.

"Uh, Master Hargrove told me to hurry, so I thought it would be faster if

I went through the woods," Auston offered.

Lester looked at Auston from head to toe again, noticing the man's wet pants and lack of shoes.

"Why are you all wet, and what happened to your shoes?" Lester asked.

"I stumbled into the big creek and lost my shoes when I was trying to get out," Auston submitted. "I might've lost my pass there too."

"And you said you're going to the Ferguson farm?" Lester challenged.

"Yes, sir," Auston said again.

"Boy, we know you're lying," Thomas interrupted. "The Ferguson farm is in the other direction. You're a runaway."

"That's OK, Thomas," Lester said. "Ole Auston here looks like a good fella."

"Yes, sir," Auston spoke up. "I am real good. Real good."

"What are we to do with you, Auston?" Lester asked.

"Please don't take me back," Auston requested.

"Well, we have to figure out something to do with you," Lester said. "Maybe you could work for us."

"Uh, yes sir, I'll work for you," Auston offered. "I work hard."

"Yeah, but you ran away from your master," Lester said.

"You might run away from us," Daniel added.

"Oh, no, I wouldn't do that," Auston said. "Mister Hargrove whips me almost every day. I just couldn't take no more. But you is good folks, I wouldn't run away."

"Can you dance?" Lester asked.

"Dance?" Auston asked, confused by the off-the-wall question.

"Yeah, me and the guys like to be entertained," Lester said. "Can you dance and entertain us?"

Auston looked at the men with a puzzled look upon his face.

Lester began stomping his foot and clapping his hands.

"Come on, dance," Lester told him.

Daniel grinned and began clapping his hands.

"Dance," a smirking Thomas ordered.

Auston moved his feet slowly, picking them up and putting them down again. He held his arms out and nodded his head along with the rhythm of the clapping. An expression of agony crossed his face as pain shot through his injured feet and legs. Drops of blood spattered across the ground. Auston tried hard to continue the performance through the pain as the men laughed. Lester unfurled his whip and cracked it at Auston's bleeding feet.

"Come on," Lester mocked. "Dance! Move those feet!"

Unable to continue, Auston buckled under the pain whisking through his feet. He fell to the ground, exhausted and aching.

"OK, get him up," Lester ordered. "Bind his hands."

Thomas and Daniel lifted Auston from the ground. Cold with fear, the enslaved man could hardly find the strength to stand on his own.

"Stand up!" Daniel barked as he jerked Auston's arm.

The two men tied a rope around Auston's wrists.

"Please, mister," Auston pleaded. "Don't take me back. Mister Hargrove is the cruelest man I have ever known."

"Oh, I think we can change that," Lester uttered. He nodded his head, signaling toward a robust branch overhead.

Thomas tossed the rope over the limb and pulled hard on the other side. He lifted Auston onto his tiptoes. Auston was dangling more than standing on his own. Daniel stood beside Thomas and grabbed the rope to help hold Auston in place.

"Please, mister, I won't do nothing wrong. I'll work real hard. Please don't hurt me," the slave begged.

His cries for mercy fell silent on Lester's ears. Lester began whipping the man with a ferocity and malice that suggested hatred. Lester spared a stubborn barn animal such barbarity, but not the slave. Lester gnashed his teeth and almost growled as he beat the man. Most times the whip met its target, but sometimes it missed, splitting the skin on Auston's side. Lester flailed so wildly that he could no longer aim. Auston screeched and squealed and cried as if beseeching God for leniency. The whip fell from Lester's hand, so he stepped forward and began punching Auston.

Doug observed in stunned disbelief as Lester and his thugs brought Auston near.

"Go get a collar," Lester instructed Daniel. "And get me a horse."

Moments later an adolescent slave boy led a horse to Lester, and Daniel arrived with a collar. The collar was a form of both punishment and prevention. Four long spikes protruded from it in different directions. Each of those spikes had two smaller spikes on the end. Overseers placed a collar around the neck of a slave that was disobedient or attempted to run away. Running through the wilderness was impossible with the collar on. The long spikes would collide with trees or become ensnared in the brush. Most slaves couldn't swim, but even if they could, the heavy collar made it unwise to try crossing a body of water.

The appearance of Auston shocked Doug. Hardly any place on his back was free of abrasions. His cheeks were puffy and one eye was so swollen it was nearly closed.

Thomas and Daniel affixed the collar to Auston and bolted it around his neck. The battered slave almost collapsed from the weight of the apparatus. Lester climbed onto the saddle, holding the end of the long rope fastened to Auston's wrists.

"I'll be back shortly," Lester stated before enticing the horse to move.

As Lester pulled him behind the animal, Auston almost fell. Auston moaned and worked to stay on his feet as the heartless man tugged him away.

Doug looked around. The other slaves observed only momentarily before returning to their work. They seemed almost apathetic, oblivious to the terrible event that had occurred. For them, the daily clamor of crying and screaming slaves was as common as bird songs.

As Lester turned onto the road, a man astride a horse arrived at the Cobb farm. The horse galloped toward the house before coming to an abrupt stop. Noah Bowman virtually fell from the horse. He sobbed while clenching a piece of paper in his fist. His frail emotional state was antithetical to his rugged appearance. Seeing his brother in this way, Henry dashed toward the house.

Henry grabbed his brother's shoulders, attempting to ease the young man's grief.

"Noah, what's wrong?" Henry asked.

Noah continued weeping. He choked back tears, and though he tried mightily, he could not deliver a coherent word.

"Get hold of yourself!" Henry demanded. "What's the matter? Is Mama OK?"

Unable to articulate his grief, Noah pressed the letter to Henry's chest. Henry grasped the letter and unfolded it as Noah wiped tears and tried to gather himself. Henry read the message.

Dear Mrs. Bowman,

The sad duty is passed to me of informing you of the death of your son, Jasper Bowman. He fell near Petersburg when we met the enemy in a dreadful struggle. He was my friend and requested that I write to you if he were to meet his end. I hope it gives you some measure of comfort to know he relinquished his life in service to his great country and her noble cause. In keeping my promise, I thought a few words from a friend who was with him at the last might be valuable to you. Your son was a fine man and never uttered an unrestrained word to anyone, even during our most grim days. May God now grant you relief and compassion.

Henry's knees buckled and he fell to the ground. A torrent of tears fell onto the soil. Noah placed a hand on his brother's shoulder. Henry tried to gather himself as he rose to his feet. He looked at the letter again, as if hoping the message would change upon a second reading. But grief struck him again like a lightning bolt. He reached out for Noah. The two brothers embraced and wept together.

The commotion distracted Doug, and he paused his work to observe the scene in the distance. Several feet away, Philip also observed the happenings at the house. Thomas meandered over to Philip. The two men engaged in a brief conversation before parting ways.

"What happened?" Doug asked Philip as he walked past him.

Philip stopped and looked at Doug.

"You're a nosy one, aren't you?" Philip asked.

"There's a lot of screaming and crying around her," Doug said.

"Their brother was killed in the war," Philip told him before walking away. "Back to work."

As Doug returned to his task, he noticed Cecelia working two rows over, parallel with him. An older slave man, around sixty years old, walked past Doug in the next row. The man carried a partially filled basket of cotton. He wore a straw planter's hat with a red band. Vernon approached the man with a sack full of cotton. The old man put the basket on the ground and Vernon emptied the contents of his sack into it. The four slaves were now close together across the three rows.

Vernon adjusted the empty sack on his shoulder before bending over to lift the basket.

"Put that down!" the old man protested as Vernon carried the basket to the end of the row.

"He's just trying to help, Charles," Cecelia said to the old man.

"I don't need no help," Charles replied. "I ain't useless. He carries that for me and Mr. Cobb might want to sell me."

"Master Cobb will not sell you, Charles," Cecelia stated.

"I ain't taking that chance," Charles said. "They done sold my wife and daughter. Now my grandson is all I got."

Charles turned his head for a few fleeting moments. He looked thoughtfully at a young man several rows over. The youth appeared to be about Doug's age.

Vernon placed the basket on the ground and walked back down the row. Although hot, tired, and sweaty, Charles lifted the basket and made his way toward the end of the row. Doug found the sight of an older man doing such hard labor bothersome. In the world he knew, Charles would be retired, relaxing, and enjoying the fruits of his labor. He turned to notice Cecelia looking at him. Doug moved his stare in a different direction briefly, then looked back at her. Cecelia grinned and allowed a brief laugh. Doug didn't know if he was more amazed by her beauty, or that she smiled in such reprehensible circumstances.

The ringing of a bell caused Cecelia to turn her attention toward the kitchen. It was time for lunch. Doug walked along the row, following the other slaves. They gathered around a large pot where Minnie served them each a bowl of potatoes. Hilda and Alberta carried food to Philip, Thomas, and the other overseers and drivers.

Doug found some shade behind the kitchen building and sat on the ground there to eat. As soon as he sat down, Cecelia walked over and sat beside him. Big Vernon joined them moments later.

"This is all we get for lunch?" Doug asked as he pushed the potatoes around the bowl.

"Oh, this is good," said Cecelia. "Where I was before, old Master Paul used to put some cornbread and buttermilk into a hog trough and we had to eat from that."

Maurice walked over to the small group and sat with them. Having eaten already, he wanted nothing more than to get off of his feet for a while.

Doug looked at his food, then observed his surroundings again. He still couldn't believe it was real. How could it be real? But he could feel the breeze. He could detect the scents emanating from the kitchen. He could hear the noise the wooden spoon made as he moved it in the bowl.

"Do y'all remember being somewhere else before you were here?" Doug asked the group.

"I told you I used to be at Master Paul's," Cecelia said, taken aback by Doug's question.

"No, I mean, somewhere normal," Doug stated.

"This is normal," Cecelia replied.

Maurice and Vernon chuckled.

"Weren't you somewhere else, where you weren't a slave?" Doug asked Vernon.

The quiet giant shook his head.

"You don't say much," Doug commented.

"He don't really say anything," Maurice said.

"He can't talk?" Doug asked.

"They didn't teach him much," Maurice said. "He was at an awful place before this."

"This is a bad place," Doug said.

Vernon nodded his head.

"He still tells you what he thinks," Maurice said. "I understand what he means."

"I was somewhere else before this, someplace very different," Doug said. "I thought maybe you had been too."

The noise of a horse dashing down the road interrupted the conversation. A courier brought the animal to a halt in front of the house and dismounted. He handed an envelope to Edith before hastily climbing upon the animal's back again and riding away. Edith examined the envelope and saw that it was addressed to Margaret. She turned to locate her daughter, who was sitting on the front porch. Edith walked up the steps and handed the envelope to Margaret. A sense of dread came over Edith. She nudged her granddaughters toward the front door.

"Minnie, please take the girls inside," Edith instructed the elderly slave woman.

"Yes ma'am," Minnie said as she guided the girls into the house.

Margaret opened the envelope and removed the letter. She unfolded it and read as Edith stood close by her side. Seconds later, Margaret let loose a terrible cry as she fell into her mother's arms. Both women fell to their knees on the porch. Margaret buried her head into her mother's shoulder. The war raging between the states brought forth its ruin upon another family. The war created untold numbers of widows and orphans every day. They were the uncounted casualties of the blood-soaked fields across the country. The war seemed far away from the Cobb family home. But the reach of the conflict was vast. It spared not the hearts of brothers, wives, sons and daughters, mothers and fathers.

The slaves returned to their endeavors among the rows. Doug's pace was slow and steady but quickening. He walked along the rows and picked the fluffy crop as if motorized. Doug still couldn't see through the fog in his mind. He continued down the row, hoping that the next step would take him home. The sun crawled toward the horizon, giving some respite from the heat.

Torches and lanterns illuminated the gin house. The drivers and overseers eagerly received the product of the slaves' toil. Doug stood in line with his basket and made his way toward the door of the gin house. One by one, the slaves presented their allotment to Earl. Fear of a less than expected weight kept their hearts racing.

Earl snatched the basket from Doug when he stepped forward. He didn't even weigh the basket.

"This must be less than ninety pounds," Earl said incredulously.

"I haven't..." Doug began before Philip stepped forward.

"He's a raw hand, Earl," Philip stated. "He is used to doing other work. He'll get the hang of it."

Philip moved Doug away from the gin house door, using his body to shield the young man from Lester's gaze. Even the reward money received for the return of Auston had not calmed the angry man.

Charles walked toward the gin house carrying a large basket of cotton. The weary man tripped and fell forward, landing on the basket and spilling its contents. He hurried onto his knees and began placing cotton back into the basket, disregarding his hat, which had fallen off.

"Oh my," Charles said. "I'll get this right up."

Lester was walking toward him before he landed. Robert, Charles' grandson, dashed out of line to aid his grandfather. Robert grabbed handfuls of cotton and hurriedly put them in the basket. He glanced at the approaching overseer with a look of desperation. The whip unrolled. Robert jumped in front of his grandfather as Lester reared back.

The leather strap cracked the air as it bit Robert. The two slave men fell prone on the ground, with Robert shielding his grandfather. Lester struck again and Robert cried out.

"Get him off!" Lester blared.

Philip stepped forward and stood beside the fallen men.

"Lester, now listen..." Philip said.

"I said get him off!" Lester declared. "Do it or I'll rip 'em both to shreds."

Philip reached down and helped Robert to his feet and pulled him away. Robert tried to jerk away, but Philip held him back.

"Don't make it worse," Philip told Robert.

"Get over here," Lester directed Charles.

The old man crawled on the ground toward the spot where Lester pointed at his feet.

"Look at all that good cotton covered in dirt," Lester said. "That ain't really cotton in that basket. That's Mr. Cobb's money."

Charles reached Lester's feet and stayed on his knees. Lester lifted a foot and pressed it on Charles's back. He pushed Charles to the ground until his belly and face were in the dirt.

"You need to take better care in your work, old man," Lester said.

"Yes, sir, I'll try to be more careful," Charles said.

The old man tried to depict a placid demeanor. He had known this cruelty most of his life. But his legs quivered, betraying efforts to hide his fear. Lester raised the whip and struck down upon Charles's back. The man's legs kicked as the hurt raced through his body. Lester hit him again, and the man convulsed in pain once more.

Robert tried to jerk away from Philip but couldn't.

"Don't," Philip said. "You'll only make it worse for him."

Lester stepped on Charles's hand and struck him again. The old man yelled out as best he could. Age and a scarred back conditioned him to temper his anguish. Lester increased the force of his blows, hoping to provoke a heightened reaction.

"Stop it!" Doug yelled as he stepped away from the line of slaves.

Vernon reached out and grabbed Doug's arm before he could move too far. Vernon's huge hand almost wrapped around Doug's thin arm and held the young man back with ease.

Lester hit Charles again and again. The old man fell prone on the ground and did not move or cry out. The whip sent drops of blood sailing through the air. The man's back was covered in blood that dripped onto the ground beneath him.

"He's going to kill him!" Doug hollered, looking around at the other slaves who dared not move. "Stop!"

Seeing his victim unresponsive, Lester finally relented. He coiled the whip and walked away. Robert dashed to his grandfather and carefully lifted his head and rolled him over. Charles winced and moaned as pain covered him.

"Grandpa," Robert called to Charles.

The old man uttered something indiscernible. Others gathered around and helped Charles to his feet. Florence retrieved the man's hat. With the aid of his grandson and Maurice, the man limped toward the slave cabins.

Doug was an emotional wreck. This was barbarism unlike any he witnessed in the projects. Vernon led a sobbing Doug back to the cabin.

Doug practically crumpled onto his flimsy bed in the cabin. He buried his face in the crude pillow and let the tears flow freely. Florence saw the distressed young man and pitied him. She leaned over Doug and tenderly rubbed his head.

"It's all right," Florence said calmly.

The gentle touch of a caring hand did little to allay Doug's sorrow. The steady thrum of heavy rain soon overwhelmed the sound of the young man's weeping. The rhythmic sound reverberated throughout the cabin. The leaky cabin obliged the persistent rain and allowed it entry at various places. A small puddle formed near the end of Doug's bed. Doug lifted his head and viewed the floor as his tears descended, joining those of God.

Outside the heavy rain pelted the ground. Farmers had prayed for rain, but the thirsty dirt did not need this bounty. The tears, blood, and sweat of the oppressed, the widowed, and the heartbroken sated it that day.

5

The Second Birth of Lester Clay

I t is often said we are a product of the times in which we live. Every generation has its societal norms, cultural influences, and conventional wisdom. However, we can't ignore the impact of individual experience. A series of seminal moments comprise a person's life. These events shape and mold us. Some happenings prove more crucial than others. Those consequential incidents steer us in a particular direction when we stand at a crossroads.

Sometimes we forget that reaction is a choice.

Morning dew clung to every surface on a foggy morning at the Clay homestead. A compact house stood in the middle of a field. A forest of tall pine trees bordered the pasture on three sides. A dirt road cut across the front of the meadow. A few hogs roamed a cramped fenced-in area. A scant distance from the house stood an unfinished barn. It was little more than a frame. A decrepit and nearly crumbling slave cabin occupied a plot near a garden.

A slave couple in their mid-twenties hustled to the barn and gathered a few tools - a saw, a hammer, and an ax. Harriet was three and a half months pregnant and showing a little. Being with child afforded her no alleviation of the misery that characterized slavery. The owners made her work with little regard for her health or safety.

Before the slaves finished collecting tools, the door of the house opened and a stocky man stepped forth. He lifted a strap of his suspenders over his right shoulder while clasping a box of nails with his other hand. The man looked groggy and irritable. He walked briskly to the barn.

As he approached, Harriet carried the ax toward a pile of wood.

"Good morning, Master Peter," the slave man said.

"Tell your wife to go feed the chickens, Abraham," Peter said as he watched Harriet swing the ax. "She can cut wood after that."

"Yes, sir, I'll tell her," Abraham replied.

Peter extended his arm to hand the nails to Abraham, but he fumbled the box. Peter tried to grab the box before it hit the ground, but he knocked it up into the air, flipping the box and sending nails flying. The contents of the box descended to the ground and scattered in every direction. Abraham dropped to his knees and quickly began gathering the nails.

"Yeah, pick those up," Peter said.

Abraham didn't reply to the crotchety man. Peter turned toward the house and left the slaves to their work.

"Lester!" Peter yelled as he casually walked toward the house.

An eight-year-old Lester Clay scurried out the front door of the house and raced toward his father.

"Bring my rifle," Peter directed.

Young Lester pivoted back toward the house. He moved around his mother, Rhonda, who was exiting the home. Rhonda carried a basket toward the small garden. Lester reemerged moments later carrying a long rifle. The boy displayed an ungainly walk as he lugged the big gun.

"Come over here," Peter told him.

"OK, Pa," Lester replied.

Peter led his son to the hog pen. The animals moved about, sniffing the air in expectation of a meal. Peter took the rifle from Lester and examined it. After loading it, he handed the weapon back to the boy.

"Now aim it at the big one," Peter ordered.

Young Lester looked puzzled. He held the rifle low and watched his father.

"Raise it and point it at the big one," Peter said again.

Lester looked at the animal with a hollow expression, blinked, and looked back at his father. Peter snatched the gun away from Lester.

"Like this, boy," Peter growled as he demonstrated how to aim the gun.

He placed the rifle back into the hands of Lester and helped him hold it up.

"You hold it and point it at the hog," Peter started. "Just look down the barrel and when you see the animal in front of you, pull the trigger."

Lester tucked the butt of the rifle against his shoulder and peered down the barrel. Peter helped him hold the barrel steady.

"Go on now, boy," Peter said. "Shoot."

Lester adjusted his grip and closed his left eye. The animal before him was oblivious to the threat. The hog continued to smell the environment and forage.

"Pull the trigger, boy," Peter advised.

Lester held his pose, unable to shoot. Peter released the weapon, and the barrel dropped to the ground.

"What's wrong with you?" Peter asked.

"I can't do it, Daddy," Lester said.

The father rubbed his head in frustration.

"You have to do it," Peter told him. "This is how we eat."

"I don't want to hurt him," Lester told his father as the sprightly animal looked directly at him.

"You're gonna do this," Peter said before delivering a swift whack to the rear of Lester's head. "Now lift that rifle and aim."

Lester arched his back and raised the gun. He struggled to keep the weapon aimed.

"OK, now be steady," Peter informed him. "Once you have him in your sights, pull the trigger."

Lester aimed the gun that wobbled in his unsteady hand.

"I can't do it," Lester said. "He's my friend."

"It's not your friend," an exasperated Peter said. "It's our food. Its whole reason for living is to feed us. The hogs, the chickens, Abraham and Harriet, everything on this farm lives to take care of us."

Rhonda stopped picking vegetables for a moment and wiped her forehead with her sleeve. She glimpsed her son and her frustrated husband before returning to her work.

"Raise it again and aim," Peter ordered Lester.

Lester lifted the weapon and pointed at the hog again.

"Now shoot," Peter directed.

Lester continued to hesitate. The boy's eyes moistened as he aimed the gun. Unable to shoot, he lowered the rifle. Lester sniffled and dropped his head.

"What's wrong?" Peter asked. "Are you going to cry?"

"I can't kill him, Daddy," Lester replied.

"Stop your sniffling," Peter demanded.

Lester took a deep breath and tried to compose himself. Peter shook his head and then looked toward the barn. Through the fog, Peter could see Abraham hammering nails as his wife chopped wood a short distance away. Peter grimaced as he watched.

"You better shoot that hog before I get back," Peter told Lester.

Lester watched his father walk away with a vigorous step. He turned his attention back to the hog and tried to muster the fortitude to end the animal's life.

Peter stepped around the partial wall Abraham had completed and walked across the floor of the barn. He said nothing to Abraham as he walked past him. Peter stepped between two vertical boards that made up part of the barn's frame and continued toward Harriet.

The woman gripped the ax and prepared to chop another log. Before she could swing, Peter grabbed a handful of her hair and yanked her to the ground. Harriet landed on her back with the ax beside her. She looked up at the angry man, confused and wondering what infraction she had committed. Peter lined up a kick to her belly. Before he struck, Harriet rolled onto her side and absorbed the blow to her back. The woman held her tummy and got to her knees. She picked up the ax as she rose to her feet. Peter snatched the ax from Harriet's hands. With his other hand, Peter grabbed her hair again and dragged her to the barn.

Abraham stopped his work on the underdeveloped structure as Peter threw Harriet to the floor.

"I told you to feed the chickens!" Peter howled.

"No, sir," Harriet began. "You didn't."

"I know for a fact I did!" Peter yelled.

Harriet looked confused and terrified.

"You didn't, Mister," she said.

"Are you calling me a liar, you wench?" Peter questioned, growing angrier with each breath.

"I forgot to tell her, Master Peter," Abraham pleaded. "I was picking up the nails, and I forgot."

"I'll feed'em," Harriet said as she held her arms up to protect herself.

Lester fought with his emotions as he stared at the large hog. He couldn't bring himself to kill the animal. He turned his attention to the commotion at the barn. He could hardly see what was happening. The fog and partial wall Abraham built obscured the participants.

Peter kicked Harriet again, but she deflected the strike with her hands.

"Please, Master Peter," Abraham petitioned. "It's my fault. I forgot to tell her."

Peter turned and smacked Abraham in the face.

"Be quiet!" Peter commanded.

The slap knocked Abraham back a step.

Using the handle of the ax, Peter unleashed a barrage of strikes upon Harriet. She turned her hips and raised her hands to obstruct every blast and protect her unborn child.

"Please, sir," Abraham said. "The baby."

Peter stood erect and began kicking Harriet again. She continued to shield the child she carried. A firm kick landed on her elbow and Harriet yelled out as her arm flopped to the floor beside her. As Peter prepared another kick, Abraham raised the hammer, then quickly brought it down upon the head of the vile assailant. At the sound of a dull, loud crack, Peter instantly dropped the ax.

Lester held the gun in the hog's direction but left the barrel touching the ground. The sound of a heavy thud drew the boy's attention to the barn. He glared through the fog to see what made the dreadful sound. All he could see was his father's feet protruding from behind the incomplete wall. Lester began walking to the barn slowly, dragging the rifle with him.

Abraham stepped around the pool of blood forming around Peter's head. Abraham crouched to help his wife to her feet. She yelled in pain as he placed her injured arm over his shoulder.

Rhonda observed her son moving toward the barn. She dusted her hands on her apron and followed him.

Lester arrived at the barn as Harriet was getting to her feet. The boy walked around the wall and stood before his dying father.

"Now, I didn't want to do it," Abraham said to the child. "I couldn't let him kill my child."

Lester dropped to his knees while holding the barrel of the rifle.

"Daddy?" the crying boy called out.

Abraham continued to hold Harriet steady as they slowly stepped off the floor of the barn. The slaves slowly began walking across the pasture, toward the tree line in the distance.

Lester cried harder as the time between his father's breaths increased. The boy's face suggested conflicting emotions. He appeared distraught one moment, and furious the next. He rose to his feet and lifted the rifle. Harriet and Abraham were halfway across the pasture, two translucent figures in the fog.

The distressed boy raised the barrel of the rifle and aimed at the slaves. The end of the gun swayed slightly as Lester set his sights on Harriet and Abraham. Overcome with anger, Lester closed his eyes and yanked the trigger. Every bird in the field took flight at the crack of gunfire that echoed through the air. The projectile hit the ground ten feet behind the slaves, leaving only a sprinkle of airborne soil to prove its existence.

Rhonda came running to the barn. She glanced at her son before noticing her husband. Life was fading from him quickly. Rhonda screamed and dropped to her knees beside Peter. The woman sobbed and moaned, helplessly pleading for a miracle. Lester kept his eyes on the slaves as they vanished behind a curtain of timber and fog.

Seeing his father bloody and battered at the feet of the slaves changed something in Lester. An acute hatred fell upon Lester's heart that day. Like a glowing ember that descends on a field of dry grass, a single moment can spark loathing and resentment in a person's soul. If left untended, the fire can spread quickly, destroying all that it touches. The wildfire can be difficult to contain, and nearly impossible to extinguish.

6

The Sacred Unknown

Charles lay on his side as Cecelia gently washed the wounds on his back with a wet cloth. Lucille, a slave woman in her early twenties, sat at the table and fed her baby. Robert rubbed his grandfather's head. The burning logs in the fireplace dimly lit the cabin interior. The red lines on Charles's back glistened and reflected the light. The man moaned softly and seemed to be somewhere between sleep and consciousness.

"It's OK, Grandpa," Robert offered, trying to encourage his only family.

The horn blew, and Robert and the women got to their feet. Cecelia offered a reassuring touch to Charles's shoulder.

"I'll check on you in a little while," she told the old man.

Robert held the cabin door as Lucille exited with her baby on her back. Cecelia followed.

The slaves gathered by the field. Doug stood beside Vernon, Maurice, and Florence, watching Cecelia as she approached.

"How is he?" Doug asked Cecelia.

Cecelia glanced at Robert, who was standing close by.

"He's got the fever," Cecelia told Doug.

"What does that mean?" Doug asked.

Cecelia took Doug by the arm and led him away.

"It means he's sick," Cecelia replied. "Real sick."

"Can't they get a doctor?" Doug asked.

"They're not going to get a doctor for a slave that old," she replied.

"Everyone grab a sack," Henry directed.

Philip and Lester stood near the slaves and watched. Gathering sacks and baskets, the slaves walked through their morning routine.

"Where's the old man?" Lester asked.

"He's sick," Doug replied.

"He ain't too sick to work," Lester said as he took a step toward Charles's cabin.

"He's got the fever," Cecelia said. "He can't get out of bed. He's still bleeding."

"See what you did?" Doug asked angrily.

"Boy," Lester began, "you better learn your place."

Lester altered his path and moved in Doug's direction. Before he got far, Henry stepped in front of Doug and handed him a sack.

"Get to work," Henry said.

Doug glared at Lester as he turned and walked to the field.

"Ought to take him out and put him down like an old dog," Lester callously said.

Cecelia took hold of Doug's arm and led him to the field. The slaves were soon going about the business of harvesting the crop, and Lester and his associates watched closely.

As the sun moved overhead, the slaves moved deeper into the field. Doug hustled in a futile effort to keep pace with the others. The appearance of Doug's industriousness benefited from Vernon placing some cotton in his basket now and then. Doug was not the only one having difficulty. Robert's thoughts were on his grandfather, and it affected his work. Periodically, Cecelia, Florence, or Lucille would sneak to the cabin to check on Charles.

When Florence returned from the cabin, Maurice went to her.

"How is Charles?" Maurice asked.

"He doesn't look good," Florence said. "I don't think he will last the day."

"Dang that, Lester," Maurice rebuked.

"Why don't they get a doctor for him?" Doug asked again.

"He's too old," Maurice reminded him.

The heat and humidity of the day pressed on the slaves like an unseen, heavy boot. Infrequent drinks of water barely sustained the weary people laboring in the fields. As badly as he wanted to stop, Doug would not risk the ire of Lester, or give the man the satisfaction of his suffering.

Cecelia stepped out of her row and met with Lucille. Cecelia carefully lifted the baby boy from Lucille's back. With the baby secure in the arms of Cecelia, Lucille made her way to Charles's cabin. Cecelia moved to the end of a row, within reach of a shadow cast by a tall tree. She rocked the six-month-old baby boy and tried to keep him comfortable.

Lester walked the perimeter of the field, like a beast stalking prey. He noticed Cecelia holding the baby and went to investigate. Lester grinned as he approached Cecelia. You might think he was out for a stroll, if not for the setting.

"Cute kid," Lester said as he stopped before Cecelia. "Where's Lucille?"

"She went to see to Charles for a minute," Cecelia replied.

"She better get back quick," Lester warned.

"I'll get back to work," she said.

"It's OK," Lester said. "Rest for a minute. I'm not a difficult man."

Cecelia cradled the baby in her arms and gazed into the field, refusing to look at the hateful lout.

"One day, you'll be out there picking cotton," Lester said as he rubbed the baby boy on the head.

Cecelia displayed a furrowed brow for a moment. Lester slid his hand off the baby's head and onto Cecelia's shoulder.

"You have smooth skin," Lester said as he stroked her arm.

Cecelia did not acknowledge the comment and stood as if she was alone. Henry observed the scene from afar.

"You look a little different from the others," Lester told Cecelia, as he brushed several strands of hair from her forehead.

"Everybody's a little different, Mr. Lester," she said.

The sound of a closing door distracted Lester before he could respond.

Lucille walked toward the field and paid no attention to the overseer.

"Hey," Lester called. "How is the old-timer?"

"He's dead," Lucille shot back with a scowl upon her face.

Lucille continued toward the field, in the direction of Robert and Doug. Lester removed his hat and ran his fingers through his red hair.

"Darn it all," he said before placing the hat back on his head.

Lester walked into the field as Lucille met Robert. Cecelia followed. They watched as Robert nearly collapsed from grief. Doug and Vernon reached out and kept Robert on his feet. Lucille offered the heartbroken youngster a gentle caress on his cheek.

"Are you sure he's dead?" Lester asked Lucille upon his arrival.

"Yes, sir," she began. "He's gone."

"Well, he was old," Lester started. "He wasn't worth that much, anyway."

"Wasn't worth that much?" Doug exclaimed more than asked. "He was a human being."

"Boy," Lester stated angrily. "I've about had it with you."

Cecelia stood behind Lester and nodded her head at Doug, warning him to be silent. Tears streamed down Robert's face.

"Ain't no sense in all of this blubbering. Go on and bury him over yonder," Lester told Robert. "Big 'un, go help him."

Vernon started toward the cabin.

"You're going to make him dig a hole and bury his grandfather?" Doug asked incredulously.

"Well, you can do it then," Lester ordered. "Go fetch a shovel from Henry and get to it."

Lester spat at Doug's feet and walked away.

Vernon carried the lifeless man from the cabin. Doug and Vernon followed Maurice as he moved toward a small meadow flanked by trees. Robert looked up from the rows of cotton and sobbed at the sight of his deceased grandfather.

Maurice stopped at a spot and thrust his shovel into the ground.

"I guess this is about right," Maurice said. "I don't think there is anyone here."

"You don't think anyone is here," Doug stated. "What do you mean?"

"I mean, I don't think anyone is buried here," Maurice replied. "The rest is over that way."

Maurice motioned to the field immediately behind them.

"There are people buried there?" Doug asked.

"Yeah," Maurice said.

Doug looked over the pasture. If he had not been told, he would never have surmised it was a graveyard.

"There're no markers," Doug said. "How do you know who's buried where?"

"Don't nobody know," Maurice said. "Only those who remember where they buried them."

Fading memories and nature would conceal the graves of the slaves. Future generations would rediscover many of the resting places of the forgotten. While erased from history and memory, the occupants were once cherished by loved ones.

"Better get this done before Lester comes back with the lash," Maurice advised.

Doug snapped out of his trance-like state and jabbed the shovel into the ground.

When the hole was finally finished, Vernon gently placed Charles into the grave.

"Should we say some words?" Doug asked.

"What words would you say?" Maurice asked.

"I don't know," Doug said. "Maybe a brief prayer or something."

Doug bowed his head.

"God, please watch over Charles as he comes to you. This life wasn't good to him, so I hope Heaven is as great as they say. Please be with his grandson," Doug said and paused. "Give him peace. And Lord, please send me back home."

Maurice began putting dirt in the grave. Doug hesitated and peered into the hole with a blank expression on his face. Vernon took the shovel from Doug and lightly pushed him aside. A pensive mood hung over the proceedings.

After they filled the hole, Doug stepped to the tree line and gazed upon the ground. He picked up a rock about the size of a grapefruit and placed it at one end of the freshly dug grave. The simple marker wasn't ideal, but it would have to suffice. Doug couldn't bear the thought of leaving the man in an inelegant state like the other abandoned but dear souls in the meadow. With the stone in place, the three men trekked back to the barn, ceding Charles to the hereafter.

Doug and the other men returned to the field after turning in the tools. Doug winced from the pain in his fingers. He went about the monotonous fieldwork, but his mind could not escape the nearby pasture. Maurice and Florence engaged Robert in conversation while being mindful of the whereabouts of Lester. Doug spotted Lester far away and moved to join the discussion.

"It will be all right," Florence said to Robert as Doug arrived.

Robert sniveled but tried to hold back his emotions.

"Are you OK, man?" Doug asked.

Robert could only afford a sniffle and a nod in response.

"I'm sorry for your loss, man," Doug said to Robert. "I lost my granddad a while back. I miss him all the time. Now more than ever. I know it hurts."

"Were you with your grandfather at the farm where you were before?" Florence asked Doug.

"Uh, yeah, I guess you could say that," Doug told her. "At least for a while. He's been gone about a year."

"That Lester," Robert said as a tear streamed down his cheek. "I should kill him."

"Don't talk all foolish like that," Maurice warned. "Your grandpa wouldn't want you to talk like that."

"He took the only family I had left," Robert replied.

"You still got us," Maurice said.

Florence noticed Lester in the distance. The fiend turned away from his conversation with Thomas and Daniel and watched the slaves.

"Better get to working," Florence told the others.

Without verifying her concern, Maurice resumed harvesting cotton.

Robert wiped the tears from his eyes before gathering the bolls again. Doug followed the example of the others and resumed the plodding, tedious work in his row.

The slaves toiled away beneath the scorching sun and melancholy that hung over them. Then something happened that astonished Doug. It began with a single person humming. Doug could not tell who began the murmur, but others joined in and the thrum of the voices gradually increased. He could not believe his eyes and ears. These tormented and exploited souls were singing. Doug marveled at the sight of men and women laboring under the lash of an oppressor, yet raising a melodic chorus to Heaven. The harmony arose until one could not hear even the cicadas over it. Doug doubted not the purpose of the ballad. A somber tone distinguished the song, and he knew it was for Charles.

"Look at 'em," Lester said to Thomas and Daniel. "They're as happy as can be. I wish all them invading Yankees could see this."

Lester's associates smiled and nodded in accord like obedient dogs.

The singing continued for hours, serenading the sun as it crept across the sky.

The slaves lined up to turn in their baskets of cotton. As always, Lester stood nearby with the whip at the ready. One by one the men and women turned in their baskets, tense with fear.

Doug stepped before Earl and handed over his basket. Earl took the offering and shook his head. Earl looked at Lester.

"It's OK, Earl," Lester said. "I pulled him out of the field to dig a grave."

Earl waved Doug aside, and the young man walked away and stood beside Maurice, Florence, and Vernon. Robert stepped forward and handed his basket to Earl. The thin man handed it to Henry, who placed it on a scale.

"Looks like about two hundred pounds," Henry said to Earl.

Earl looked at Lester again. Lester waved to Earl, as if calling him over. Thomas and Daniel grabbed Robert and pulled him from the line. The men dragged Robert to Lester and threw him to the ground. Philip stepped forward.

"Show some pity, Lester," Philip protested. "He lost his grandfather today."

Tears welled up in Robert's eyes, and only he knew if they were from anger or fear. Henry jumped from the gin house and walked to Robert quickly. Henry cast a menacing stare at Lester as he helped Robert to his feet.

"Have you no mercy?" Henry asked.

Once on his feet, Robert joined Doug and the others. Henry returned to the scale in the gin house. Cecelia provided her basket to Earl, who shook it before handing it to Henry.

"Feels light," Earl said.

"Two hundred," Henry said.

"Did any of y'all pick any cotton today?" Earl asked sarcastically.

"I told her to help with one of the youngsters today," Lester said. "She's fine."

Earl gave a dismissive smirk and Cecelia went about her way. Lucille stepped forward with her baby on her back and turned in her bounty. She appeared exhausted. Earl held the basket for a moment.

"What is this?" Earl asked. "Another light one. I swear none of y'all did any work today."

"I worked hard, mister," Lucille said.

"Weigh this," Earl said as he handed the basket to Henry.

"One hundred and forty pounds," Henry called out.

"I worked hard," Lucille stated. "I had my son on my back."

Lester motioned again, and Thomas and Daniel seized Lucille and pulled her away.

"I was looking after Charles. I worked the best I could," Lucille pleaded.

"She was taking care of the old man," Philip said to Lester.

"Yeah, but nobody told her to do that," Lester replied.

"Please, I worked as hard as I could," Lucille appealed.

"Get the child off her back," Lester ordered.

Daniel removed the little boy and set him on the ground nearby. Thomas threw Lucille to the ground, where she landed on her hands and knees. Lester stepped to her and unwound the whip.

"Please, Mister," she begged. "I ain't no lazy person! I worked hard!"

Henry exited the gin house again and walked toward Lester with a quick step. Lester turned and struck Henry with the whip. It sliced through the sleeve of Henry's shirt, causing him to jump back and grasp his arm.

"Stay out of my business, Henry!" Lester warned.

The brute turned his attention back to Lucille and smacked her so hard with the lash she fell from her hands and knees.

"No!" Doug bellowed. "Stop it!"

Maurice quickly covered Doug's mouth with his hand. Florence put her arm around Doug's shoulder and squeezed tightly. Lester hit Lucille again.

"That's enough, Lester," Philip said.

"Stay out of this! I'll say when she's had enough!" Lester yelled.

The whip chastised the woman repeatedly. Lucille reached out to her crying child sitting on the ground nearby. Lester raised his hand to strike her again, but Philip caught his wrist and stopped the blow.

"You've given her a lesson," Philip stated. "Now let her be. They aren't any good to Mr. Cobb if they cannot work."

Lester jerked his hand away and rolled up the whip.

"Let this be a lesson to all of you, in case you be laggard!" Lester trumpeted. "And some of y'all need to learn this isn't a charity! This is a working farm!"

Lester spat on the ground near Lucille before walking away. Robert and Vernon helped Lucille to her feet as Maurice lifted her crying baby from the ground. Maurice gently handed the boy back to his mother. Florence placed a reassuring hand on Doug's back as she led him back to the cabin.

Maurice tightened some string around the straw that made up Doug's mattress.

"There you go," Maurice said. "That should make it more comfortable for you."

Doug sat on the bed, relieved to be off his aching feet. Florence sat at the table, dropping pieces of bacon into a pot. Maurice and Vernon worked on starting a fire.

Doug checked his dirty and scratched hands. He tried to comprehend the world around him. He wept and placed his face in his hands, then turned his back to the others in the cabin. Florence got up from the table and hung the pot over the fireplace. After seeing Doug in emotional distress, Florence sat on the bed beside him. She placed her arm around Doug and rubbed his head with her free hand.

"There, there," Florence said. "It will be all right."

"I don't know what's going on," Doug replied. "I miss my mom."

"I was even younger than you when I was taken from my mama," Florence told him.

"I don't know what I'm doing here," Doug said. "I don't belong here."

"We all belong here," Florence countered. "We belong to Master Cobb. You'll feel better after you get some food, child."

Florence got up and moved to the fireplace. She held her throbbing back as she stirred the pot. Doug placed his head in his hands again.

A lone window allowed an infinitesimal amount of light into the cabin during the night. Florence and Maurice were fast asleep on the larger bed while Vernon occupied the floor. Doug tossed and turned on the straw bed with only a coarse blanket beneath him. Even sleep brought no alleviation from suffering in a slave's life.

7

A Hollow Kindness

A gentle shake from Maurice awakened Doug. The exhausted young man slept through the morning horn. Doug sat up quickly and felt a pain in his lower back.

"Ouch," Doug uttered as he reached for the source of the ache.

Doug planted his feet on the floor and rubbed the sleep from his eyes.

"God, I'm still here," Doug said with dismay.

"Where else would you be?" Maurice asked.

"Home," Doug responded.

"You are home," Maurice told him.

"No, this isn't home," Doug said with certainty in his voice.

"Eat this," Florence directed Doug as she handed him some cornbread and a cup of water.

Doug hastily devoured the paltry breakfast before following the other slaves to the field.

The kitchen was also abuzz with activity early in the morning. Edith directed Minnie, Hilda, and Alberta in their tasks. Minnie cooked eggs in a pan while Hilda scooped potatoes into a bowl. Edith handed a pitcher of water to Alberta.

"Carry that and go with Hilda to the dining room," Edith instructed. "I'll be along in a moment."

Edith turned her attention back to the table as the servants left the kitchen. After leaving the kitchen, Hilda stopped for a moment to address Alberta.

"No matter what you see, you keep a straight face," Hilda said. "If you see those little girls with their mama, don't let it get to you."

"Yes, ma'am," Alberta replied.

"Remember, you got me, and Miss Minnie now," Hilda said. "We're gonna take care of you."

The girl satisfied Hilda with an understanding nod. The two slaves continued on their way to the house.

Hilda and Alberta entered the dining room to find most of the Cobb family seated at the table. Joseph sat quietly and observed his granddaughters who played among themselves. Margaret stared blankly in a passive stupor. Hilda placed the bowl on the table, then took Joseph's plate and served some potatoes.

"That looks good, Granddaddy," Caroline said.

"It sure does," the man replied.

Alberta stood at the end of the table next to Joseph and took his glass. She carefully poured water into it. The girl lost her grip on the pitcher and quickly acted to avoid dropping it. But in her effort to recover the pitcher, she knocked over Joseph's glass, spilling its contents onto his lap. The mishap etched a look of exasperation on the man's face. Alberta stood frozen, stunned, and expecting retribution. Joseph clenched his fist as if ready to crash it upon the slave girl's head.

"Oh, child, look what you did," Hilda said as she dropped to her knees. "You done got water all over Master Cobb."

Charlotte and Caroline chuckled at the scene. A tepid smile appeared on Joseph's face and he relaxed his hand. Few things pacify the embittered heart like the laughter of grandchildren.

"Be more careful, girl," Hilda said to Alberta.

"It's fine," Joseph stated. "I needed a bath, anyway."

Edith entered the room and quickly placed a platter of eggs on the table.

"My goodness, what happened?" Edith asked.

"I'm sorry, ma'am," Alberta said.

"It's all right," Joseph said. "It was an accident."

"Come on, Alberta," Hilda said as she tugged on the girl's arm.

Alberta dropped to her hands and knees to help Hilda clean up the mess. Once the slaves vanquished the spill, they got to their feet and continued serving breakfast.

"Aren't you going to put on some dry clothes?" Edith asked Joseph.

"It's already hot outside. This feels kind of nice," he said with a smile.

The little girls laughed again. After they finished serving breakfast, Hilda and Alberta stood against the wall.

"Thank you, ladies. That will be all," Edith said.

The slaves exited the room as the family bowed their heads to pray.

The slower pace of life in the South has long been established. The air, heavy and burdened by stifling humidity, impedes everything that tries to move through it.

Unhindered by clouds, the sun took no pity on the forlorn creatures struggling in the field. Everyone inched along their row and Doug clambered behind the others. Lester, Earl, Daniel, and Thomas relaxed under the shade of a tree.

"Oh, she's hot today, I declare," Earl said as he wiped the sweat from his brow.

"It sure is," Lester replied. "Ain't been this hot in a good while."

Lester fanned himself with his hat as he watched the field. The heat exhausted and overwhelmed Doug. He ambled in the field and breathed heavily, almost as if he was panting. Doug fell forward and landed on his knees. He remained there, seeking some respite in the meager shade of the plants that flanked him.

"Look at that loafer," Lester said as he stared at Doug.

Earl joined Lester in his walk to the field. Doug wobbled back to his feet when he saw the approaching enforcers.

"What's wrong with you?" Lester sneered.

"It's so hot," Doug responded.

"It's late summer," Lester said. "It's going to be hot."

Doug placed his hands on his knees and leaned forward. Lester directed a firm kick to Doug's backside, launching him forward. Doug landed in the row. He could feel the heat radiating from the sandy soil. Doug got back on his feet as quickly as possible. He brushed off granules of dirt that stuck to his sweaty skin.

"Well, get to it!" Lester commanded.

"I just," Doug started. "I just need a drink of water."

"You can have a drink when I say you can have a drink," Lester barked.

"It's so hot," Doug said. "I'm thirsty."

The frustration was evident on Lester's face. He looked around purposely until he spotted Lewis in the neighboring row.

"Hey, you!" Lester called. "Lewis!"

The weary slave man ran as fast as he could through the muggy air. Lewis stopped and removed his hat before Lester and Earl.

"Go over yonder and fetch the water bucket," Lester ordered.

Lewis dashed away to retrieve the bucket of water and returned in short order, trying hard not to spill the valuable contents.

"Give me that," Lester said as he snatched the pail away from Lewis.

Lester removed the ladle from the bucket and dropped it on the ground. He positioned his feet about shoulder-width apart and gave the bucket a heave, tossing the water into the air. Doug could hardly brace himself for the impact of the instant deluge. The wave hit him in the face and descended his body, providing Doug some relief to accompany the shock of the deed. Doug exhaled deeply and absorbed the temporary satisfaction the water brought.

Lester bent over and ran the bucket across the ground, scooping up some dirt.

"Here, have some more," Lester said as he tossed the dirt at Doug.

The soil hit Doug's wet face and body, forming a thin layer of muck. Doug spit a tiny amount of the substance from his mouth and rubbed his shirtsleeve over his eyes and face. Lester tossed the bucket away and placed his hat atop his head.

"Now get back to work," Lester demanded.

Doug removed some additional mud from his face and resumed picking cotton. Lester and Earl walked away, rejoining their compatriots beneath a canopy of leaves. Henry and Philip joined them, withdrawing from the merciless sun.

Lester peered across the field, observing the menagerie of persecuted people that tended to the crop. He saw Cecelia carrying Lucille's baby on her back again. Without saying a word to his cohorts, Lester walked away in the direction of the lovely slave woman.

"Where ye off to now, Lester?" Daniel asked.

"I gotta check on something," Lester replied as he continued on his way.

"I bet he's going to chat with that mulatto woman," Earl mumbled.

As Earl suspected, Lester went directly to Cecelia.

"Why you got the little one on your back again?" Lester asked her.

"Lucille can't carry him today, so I told her I would," Cecelia stated.

"Why can't she carry him?" Lester wondered aloud.

"Because her back is all cut up," she replied directly.

The state of affairs didn't bother Lester, and he offered no reply.

"It's too hot out here for a baby, Mr. Lester. Maybe one of the house slaves can watch him," Cecelia pleaded softly.

"Just set him down over yonder by that tree," Lester replied.

"I worry something might happen to him if I leave him unattended," Cecelia countered.

"Oh, he'll be fine," Lester said. "Ain't no critters going to come close to the field with all these people around. You can check on him from time to time. I don't mind."

"Thank you, Mr. Lester," Cecelia said.

Lester walked with Cecelia to the nearest tree. She placed the baby on a soft sandy spot and looked him over. The little boy seemed content.

"See, he's just as happy as can be. He'll be fine," Lester said.

"Yes, sir," she replied.

Something about Cecelia mesmerized Lester. Perhaps it was her natural beauty or that he found her exotic. Her previous owner was also her father. Maybe her parentage helped temper his deeply rooted animosity toward the slaves. They stood quietly and Lester stared at Cecelia. She shifted her eyes away from him and looked down at the baby. A rare breeze lifted her curly hair slightly off her shoulders.

"I better get back to work," Cecelia said as she turned away.

Lester offered no reply. He fixed his eyes on her as she walked back to the field. She walked confidently, her back straight and her chin up. Cecelia's posture defied the overbearing sun and her standing in the world.

After snapping out of his trance-like stance, Lester slowly sauntered around the perimeter of the field. The sun didn't grant leniency to Lester, but he occasionally found asylum in the shade of a tree. Even the most sweltering day could not dissuade Lester in the earnest pursuance of his commission. Aside from Cecelia, the slaves did not differ from any beast of burden in his eyes.

Doug found himself beside Robert and Maurice in the adjoining rows. Robert wore his grandfather's hat with the red band. The group trudged through the field, enduring the pummeling from the sun. Sweat dripped from the men as they hunched over, picking the precious cotton. Doug wiped the sweat from his eyes with the sleeve of his shirt and looked up to locate Lester. The wretched man slowly made his way around the field but would periodically stop to talk with his friends lounging beneath the tree.

"Hey," Doug called to Robert once he was sure Lester was preoccupied.

"What?" Robert responded.

"Don't y'all ever think about taking him out?" Doug queried his peer.

"Take him out?" Robert replied in confusion. "He's already out here."

"No, I mean jump him, knock him out," Doug said. "There's way more of you than there is of him."

"You talking about fighting Lester, you must be dumb," Robert said to Doug.

"You should have an uprising and take them all down," Doug suggested.

"Now you listen here," Maurice said as he stood up slightly to face Doug. "You better stop talking like that. If Lester overheard you saying such things, he would wear out the strap on you."

"He can't whip all of you at the same time," Doug said.

"You talk like you aren't here with us," Robert told Doug.

"I just don't belong here," Doug replied.

"Oh, you belong here, just like the rest of us," Maurice said.

"We should fight back, that's all," Doug said.

"You need to stop talking like that," Maurice warned him again.

"Look how he treats people," Doug countered. "He killed your granddad."

Robert scowled at Lester. He didn't need a reminder, but Doug was pushing the right buttons to stir his anger and resentment.

"We should all revolt and get out of here," Doug proposed.

"You stop that foolish talk right now," Maurice scolded. "You're going to make trouble for everyone with that talk. Listen to you and every white man for a hundred miles would be looking for us."

Maurice noticed Lester on the move again.

"Best get back to work," Maurice advised. "No more of this talk."

Lucille's baby sat quietly, basking in the shade of a protective tree. The child smiled as he beheld the things and happenings around him. A flock of birds flew overhead. A tall weed shook in a quickly passing breeze. He saw the big white house sitting majestically several yards away. A peculiar little creature that seemed to float in the air as it zipped and hovered about caught the boy's attention. The insect was slender, with a tiny midsection that separated two noticeable segments of its body. It flew with two lengthy and narrow wings. Long legs hung beneath the critter as it lingered in the air. The abdomen of the bug tapered almost to a point at the end. The wasp was dark brown with some faint yellow on its legs. The stinging insect came close to the little boy, moving up and down as if attached to a string. Astonished by the bizarre insect, the child reached out for it. The wasp zoomed and whizzed around the boy, evading his grasp. The tot extended his arm as far as he could but just missed clutching the unsafe prize. The wasp landed on the sandy ground just inches from the boy. The wasp's long wings stood almost vertical as it moved on the ground in short, jerky pulses. Lucille's son leaned forward and lunged at the tiny predator. The wasp took to the air, and the baby grasped only sand.

After the wasp was out of sight, the little boy looked about, searching for a new point of interest. He soon noticed his exhausted mother toiling in the field. The baby sent forth a burst of laughter and clapped his little hands. Instinctively, he got on his hands and knees and began to crawl to her. The child moved swiftly toward the cotton field. When his hands touched the scorching sun-baked dirt, the boy halted. He pushed back and sat up, placing part of his body back in the shade. The little boy examined his hands, trying to understand the cause of his anguish.

The baby boy wasn't the only one trying to escape the broiling ground. A tan viper slithered along the ground about twenty yards away. The contrasting dark brown marks on its back helped it blend in among the soil and old sticks on the ground. The snake's forked tongue flicked repeatedly. Its somewhat triangular-shaped head moved slightly left and right as it navigated quietly through the isolated patches of grass closer to the field.

Lucille's baby slapped the ground and babbled loudly. The boy was fussy, tormented by the sun on his legs. The muscular, thick-bodied snake kept moving toward the child. The tot kicked and cried. The inability to reach his mother frustrated the boy. The serpent crept closer to the babe's thrashing, chubby legs. The discontented child was clueless about the approaching threat, now less than two feet away. The viper's progress halted suddenly. Lester had the snake by the tail. Before the animal could strike, Lester pulled it away swiftly and tossed it into the air. The snake landed several feet away and dashed to taller grass and the tree line.

By the time Lester turned around, Lucille and Cecelia had already raced to the baby. An exhausted Lucille lifted her child and examined him. The crying boy didn't have a scratch on him. Lester removed his hat and took a bow, thinking the rescue made him seem magnanimous despite his barbarism. Cecelia took the baby from Lucille and scurried off toward the kitchen.

"Hey!" Lester hollered. "How about a little gratitude?"

Cecelia rounded the corner of the kitchen and stood at the entryway. Edith was inside conducting affairs related to cookery.

"Ma'am, I am sorry to interrupt," Cecelia began.

"What seems to be the trouble?" Edith asked, noticing the agitated and anxious slave woman.

"Could someone keep an eye on the baby?" Cecelia inquired. "It's too hot for him in the field. He's just a baby, ma'am."

"Oh, of course," Edith replied as she sighed.

Edith stepped to Cecelia and held out her arms.

"Thank you, ma'am," Cecelia said as she passed the child to Edith. "I best get back to the field."

Cecelia departed and was quickly out of sight.

"Come with me, Alberta," Edith instructed.

Edith led the young slave girl in the direction of the house.

Cecelia encountered Lester before she was out of the shadow of the kitchen.

"You listen to me," the ruffian said as he grabbed her face. "Don't go around me like that again."

Lester squeezed Cecelia's cheeks so hard that her mouth puckered like a fish. Her body went stiff with fearful anticipation. His fetid breath hung in her face and was made more extreme by the humid air.

"The Cobb's might own you, but I oversee these fields," Lester declared. "As far as I'm concerned, these fields and everything in them belongs to me. Do you understand me?"

Cecelia tried to nod her head despite his constraining hand on her face. Lester slowly released his grip and tenderly ran his thumb across her bottom lip. Cecelia quivered with dread as Lester caressed her cheek with the back of his fingers.

"Am I not good to you?" Lester asked in a soft voice.

"Yes, sir, you're good," Cecelia responded while a single tear cascaded down her cheek.

"OK, off you go," Lester said calmly.

Cecelia departed and collected her confidence as she made her way back to the cotton field.

Edith guided Alberta onto the front porch of the Cobb home. Two rocking chairs sat empty to one side. Margaret sat quietly, almost catatonic in another chair on the opposite side of the porch.

"Sit here," Edith advised, pointing to one of the rocking chairs.

Alberta hesitated for a moment.

"It's all right," Edith encouraged Alberta. "You can sit there. This should offer plenty of shade."

Edith held the baby while Alberta climbed onto the chair. Once Alberta settled, Edith placed the child on her lap.

"There you go. Now you watch the baby and if you need anything, the ladies and I will be just around the way."

Edith stepped off the porch and was quickly around the corner and out of sight. Alberta gently rocked the chair, much to the delight of the little boy sitting on her lap. Margaret was silent, oblivious to the world around her. She held a folding fan on her lap but didn't use it, as if she was defying the stifling heat.

Caroline and Charlotte exited the house. The slamming of the front door broke the tranquility of the afternoon. The girls stood beside their mother and observed her inscrutable face. Margaret did not look at her daughters or acknowledge their presence. Caroline leaned over the side of the chair and hugged her mother's neck. Margaret reciprocated the gesture with a few gentle taps on the girl's arm, but did not turn to see her.

Charlotte followed her older sister to the other side of the porch. The girls stood before Alberta and stared at her without saying a word. Alberta disregarded them and looked across the yard while she continued to rock the baby boy. The failure of the slave girl to acknowledge them left Caroline perplexed. This was a slave girl who helped serve their meals. How could a slave be indifferent to them?

"What are you doing?" Caroline asked.

"Missus Edith told me to sit here and watch the baby," Alberta replied.

"You're in our chair," Caroline said directly.

Alberta glanced at the empty chair beside her.

"You're not supposed to sit in our chairs," Carolina advised.

"No," young Charlotte said to bolster her sister's edict.

"Missus Edith said for me to sit here," Alberta mentioned again.

"You can't sit there," Charlotte said, her voice increasing an octave.

"But Missus Edith…" Alberta began.

"Oh, get up!" Margaret yelled as she jumped from her chair.

Alberta jumped to her feet in sudden consternation and clutched the baby tightly against her. Margaret stomped across the porch and struck Alberta in the face with a swift, open-handed slap. The young slave girl's head swung to the side as she absorbed the force of the impact. Alberta kept a protective grip on the baby. Feeling helpless, Alberta composed herself and looked at Margaret.

"She said you don't sit in that chair," Margaret barked. "It's bad enough these girls have lost their daddy. Now they have to suffer the indignity of a little black wench sassing them!"

"I'm sorry, ma'am," Alberta said, bowing her head as a tear ran down her cheek.

"You can sit down there on the bottom step," Margaret said while pointing at the porch steps.

Alberta immediately walked down the steps and sat on the bottom one. She hugged the baby and wiped the tears from her face. Margaret placed Charlotte on the chair and Caroline climbed onto the one beside it. Having restored the peace of the day, Margaret returned to her chair.

Evening afforded no lull in the heat and humidity. The sultry, lingering hours of the day continued the onslaught on the drained slaves. Just a remnant of their threadbare fortitude endured. Doug stopped to draw a deep breath and looked up at the sun. He silently demanded it hasten its journey to the horizon. Alas, the clockwork of the universe does not concern itself with the wants of a single earthbound creature.

Lester, Earl, Thomas, and the other taskmasters monitored the field. The ceaseless bludgeoning of the sun only riled Lester all the more. Florence worked a row between Maurice and Cecelia. Florence was almost staggering and huffing. The suffocating heat of the day levied an insurmountable blow to the woman, and she collapsed. Maurice clambered out of his row and over the plants. He kneeled beside Florence and held her head off the ground. She was dazed and didn't seem to know what happened. Cecelia began fanning the woman with the hem of her dress.

"Are you all right, Florence?" Maurice questioned, his words laced with worry.

"What... why am I... did someone..." Florence muttered incoherently.

"What in the world is going on?" Lester blared as he made his way toward them.

"Come on, Miss Florence," Cecelia pleaded. "You got to get up."

An apprehensive Doug watched from a nearby row.

Maurice helped Florence sit up by the time Lester arrived.

"What's she doing?" Lester questioned. "You taking a break?"

"She just got hot, boss," Maurice said. "She'll be all right."

"Is nobody going to work today?" Lester griped.

The angry overseer grabbed Maurice by the arm and pulled him away from Florence. The woman slowly got to her feet.

"See, she's fine," Maurice said.

"Earl, Thomas, take her over yonder," Lester ordered while pointing to a flat patch of ground near the field.

Lester's subordinates went for Florence, but Maurice stepped in front of her and clutched his wife in his arms.

"Please, mister," Maurice begged. "She just got dizzy. It's as hot as the devil's house today. Please don't whip her."

"Fine," Lester scoffed. "You can take her lashes for her."

Lester nodded at Earl and Thomas. They grabbed Maurice securely and dragged him away. The husband and wife held hands until they were finally tugged apart. An uneasy Florence looked on with fear for her husband.

Earl and Thomas pulled the shirt off the man's back. Even from dozens of feet away, Doug could see the scars that crisscrossed Maurice's back. The men forced Maurice to the ground, and the slave gave no resistance. Flat on his stomach, Maurice turned his head to see Lester nonchalantly walking toward him. The whip dropped to the ground. Lester stopped and looked eagerly over his prey. It was an occasion that only malice could relish.

Florence bellowed after the first strike hit her husband's back. Lester struck again and again. Maurice winced at each blow but did not utter a sound. Doug and Robert looked on in silent anguish. Maurice's reticence frustrated Lester. The cruel man whipped harder and faster to satisfy his spitefulness. No matter how hard Lester whipped, Maurice refused to give the man a single tear or shriek.

"Stop!" Doug yelled.

Lester stopped swinging and turned to look at Doug. One end of Lester's mouth turned upward. He held the whip in his left hand while he shook his right arm, preparing it to return to the vile task. Lester averted his gaze to the sobbing Florence, who gasped for air as she cried. Lester turned back to Maurice. He took a deep breath and held the whip high over his head. Lester delivered a devastating blow to Maurice's back. Lester raised his arm and prepared to smack the slave again.

"Supper time!" Philip yelled.

The announcement distracted Lester. He saw Edith walking from the kitchen and lowered the whip. The fiend casually walked away, leaving Maurice bleeding on the ground. Florence dashed to her husband. Doug, Robert, and Vernon quickly joined her. The men helped Maurice to his feet as Florence showered him with tenderness. Florence examined her injured husband. Maurice paused for a moment to steady himself. Seething resentment of Lester smoldered within Doug.

Nightfall brought deliverance from the blistering heat and Lester's whip, at least for a short time. Florence saw to her husband's wounds, gently washing them with a wet rag. Doug and Vernon sat on a pine log outside the cabin. Cecelia and Robert approached, and Doug rose to his feet.

"Do you want to sit down?" Doug asked Cecelia.

"No, thank you," she replied. "How is Maurice?"

"He's pretty scratched up, but he's a tough old guy," Doug answered. "I think he'll be OK."

"Sometimes I think Lester won't stop until he kills us all," Cecelia stated.

"I'm telling you, we could take him out," Doug said.

"The sun got to you good today, talking like that," Cecelia said.

"Well, we should do something," Doug declared. "We can't just keep going like this."

"We should run away," Robert interjected.

"Yeah," Doug said. "We should run away."

Vernon shook his head in disagreement.

"Where would you go?" Cecelia asked.

"Home," Doug answered.

"You are home," she replied.

"No, no, I'm not," Doug said. "I think if I went far enough, I could end up back home. I just need to get away from this place and I'll get home."

"It doesn't matter where we go as long as we get away from Lester," Robert added.

Doug nodded in agreement with Robert.

"You better stop talking like that," Cecelia advised.

Vernon got up and walked into the cabin.

"I better go too," Cecelia said.

"Goodnight," Doug told her as she walked away.

Robert nodded at Doug.

"I'm telling you," Doug said. "We could do it. We could get away from here."

Robert departed, leaving Doug alone. Doug stared searchingly at the night sky. The sight of so many stars left him spellbound. Doug wondered if somewhere in the vastness of those celestial bodies his mother was thinking of him. If he could not escape this place, could she find him?

8

Behind Unrelenting Despair

I t was another hot day, but the slaves that toiled in fields of Bentonville yearned for freedom more than water. Nonetheless, Doug would not decline an offer of refreshment. With her baby on her back, Lucille dipped a ladle into a bucket of water and handed it to Doug. He eagerly drank the water and dipped into the bucket again. Lucille spotted Lester walking toward the kitchen. After another hasty drink, Doug scooped more water from the bucket. Once he was finished, Lucille snatched the ladle from him.

"Got to save some for everybody," Lucille said. "Lester see you drinking like that you'll be in trouble."

"I'm not worried about him," Doug responded.

"You better be worried," Lucille said before departing.

Doug resumed picking cotton, and the hum of singing slaves slowly ascended around him. Doug cracked a slight smile and silently rejoiced in the moxie of the slaves to sing in the face of oppression. Earl lifted his arms and moved his hands slowly as if conducting an orchestra. Thomas and Daniel joined Earl in laughing and mocking the fortitude of the slaves.

The women in the kitchen were deeply involved in the business of preparing lunch. Hilda stirred a large pot that hung over the fireplace. Minnie chopped potatoes on the large table in the room. Edith collected some of the potatoes and dropped them into the pot. Alberta entered the kitchen carrying an armful of logs. Edith grabbed one of the logs from Alberta and added it to the fireplace.

"You can put the rest over there, Alberta," Edith said, pointing to a stack of logs in the corner.

The young girl knew where to put them. She was already stepping to the pile before Edith offered instruction. After leaving the firewood in place, Alberta looked into the adjacent room where the weaving loom was kept. She stared at the contraption, mesmerized by it. Alberta stepped into the room and slowly walked toward the empty loom.

"Step away from there, child," Hilda instructed.

Alberta ignored the order and kept looking over the apparatus. Hilda's focus on the room drew Edith's attention.

"Get away from there, girl," Hilda said. "You don't know how to use that."

"I could do it," Alberta replied as Edith appeared in the doorway.

"Well, I'm sure you can," Edith said.

The young girl cracked a smile. Hilda rolled her eyes and returned her concentration to the hanging pot.

"Here, let's have a seat," Edith said as she sat at the loom. Alberta took a seat beside the woman.

"Now put your hands here and your feet there," Edith advised as she demonstrated.

Following Edith's lead, Alberta moved her hands back and forth, producing nothing with the loom but the smiles on their faces.

Lester appeared in the doorway and observed the lesson.

"With a little practice I think you might be very good," Edith said to Alberta. "Perhaps one day I'll show you more."

"You know, I once saw this traveling show in Raleigh where a man had a monkey that played a tambourine," Lester interjected.

"What are you trying to say?" Edith asked. "I'm sure I don't know what you mean."

"Just saying I would be careful teaching them too much, Mrs. Cobb," Lester said. "Best if they don't learn much at all."

"I'll manage the affairs of my own kitchen, Mr. Clay, if you please," Edith replied.

"Sorry, ma'am, I mean no offense," Lester said.

"State your business, Mr. Clay," Edith insisted. "We're quite busy as you can see."

"It's mighty hot today," Lester began. "Me and the boys are going to have our lunch under the shade of the big oak between the house and the south field. Would you mind having it brought to us there?"

"Be patient, Mr. Clay, and I'll see to it that a pot of stew is brought to you as soon as possible," Edith said.

"Thank you, ma'am," Lester said hospitably before turning and leaving.

Alberta and Edith got up from the loom, and the young girl followed the matriarch into the main kitchen area.

"Gather the potatoes she has cut up, Alberta," Edith said, pointing to the table.

"Yes, ma'am," Alberta said before gathering the potatoes from Minnie.

"I have to go to the house for a moment," Edith stated. "Will one of you please carry a pot of stew to Mr. Clay and his men by the tree?"

"Yes, ma'am," Minnie replied.

"Are you certain, Minnie?" Edith asked. "It may be burdensome."

"Yes, ma'am. I can manage," Minnie confirmed.

"All right then. Just don't hurt yourself," Edith advised.

Lester stood between the kitchen and the tree where his friends waited. He watched the field like a hawk. He turned his head momentarily, distracted by Edith walking to the house. Lester pivoted his attention back to the field. He noticed Cecelia and Doug conversing. Lester stood quietly for a moment, allowing this infraction to proceed. The two slaves burst into laughter and Lester's patience was at an end.

"Hey!" Lester bellowed. "Get back to work!"

Lester's howling startled Doug and Cecelia, and they flung themselves back into picking cotton. Lester resumed his slow, businesslike stroll to the enormous tree. His friends beside the tree began chuckling. Lester looked at them and cracked a smile. Earl and Thomas motioned with their hands as if beckoning Lester to come to them. Lester stopped and titled his head like a confused animal. He couldn't understand what they found so hilarious. Lester looked down to make sure there wasn't a stain on his shirt, and that his fly was closed. The men continued to laugh and Daniel clapped his hands and whistled as if calling a dog. Unable to comprehend what was so humorous, Lester looked around. He instantly saw what they were laughing at.

Minnie labored to carry a heavy pot. The old woman clasped the handle of the pot tightly and took slow shuffling steps toward the men. Lester joined in the jeering and waved to the old lady.

"Come on, old woman," Lester hollered. "I'm hungry!"

"I'm going to die of starvation by the time she gets here!" Thomas cried.

Minnie quickened her pace, and the iron pot swayed. The kindly old woman stumbled and fell to the ground, spilling the stew everywhere. Some recently boiled cuisine splattered onto her dress and apron. The contents of the pot made a muddy mess where Minnie's hands landed as she braced herself against the fall. Minnie wiped her hands on the apron and remained on her knees, embarrassed and dismayed by the accident.

"Now doesn't that beat all get out?" Lester said as he stood nearby.

The overseer walked to the old woman and stood over her. Earl joined him shortly.

Minnie fought back tears as she beheld the mess around her.

"What are we supposed to eat now, you old buzzard?" Earl asked.

The old maid was afraid to speak and sat in silence. Lester grabbed a handful of Minnie's hair and jerked her head back, forcing her gaze upward.

"He asked you a question, old-timer," Lester scolded. "You expect us to eat this? Huh?"

"Maybe she wants some," Earl added.

"Do you want some?" Lester asked. "How 'bout it, old woman? Why don't you try it?"

Lester scooped a handful of the mud and spilled food. He lifted the soil mixed with pieces of potatoes and carrots to Minnie's face. He rubbed his hand across the woman's face and cheeks.

"How does it taste?" Lester taunted as he smeared the awful mixture.

Minnie discharged a small amount of mud from her mouth after Lester removed his hand. Her face was filthy and a few fragments of food stuck to the mud on her cheeks.

"What's the matter?" Earl asked. "Don't you like your own cooking?"

Alberta exited the kitchen to see the men laughing as they hovered over Minnie. The young girl raced to Minnie and helped her to her feet.

"Did anyone tell you to help her up?" Lester asked angrily.

"She's an old woman," Alberta said without prevarication.

"I didn't tell you to sass me either," Lester growled.

The angry man searched the ground until he spotted a sizable stick. Lester retrieved the limb and walked toward Alberta with haste.

"Someone should teach you some manners, you little..."

"Put that stick down!" Edith called out.

She hurried to Alberta and Minnie.

"I'm just trying to keep them in line, Mrs. Cobb," Lester replied.

"I must remind you, you are an overseer of these workers," Edith stated. "It is not your place to admonish them without good cause. Now please be the gentlemen I know you are and pick up that pot and hand it to the girl."

"Yes, ma'am," Earl replied before picking up the pot.

Lester stood motionless, but Edith's castigation obviously annoyed him. Earl gently handed the pot to Alberta. The women started back to the kitchen.

"What about lunch?" Lester asked.

"I'll have some cornbread brought to you," Edith replied.

"Feed us like a damn slave," Lester murmured as he turned around.

"I beg your pardon?" Edith asked.

Lester paused and looked at Earl.

"What did you say?" Lester asked as he punched Earl in the arm.

"I didn't say anything," Earl replied, applying a hand to the pain in his arm.

Edith helped Minnie wipe her face as the women walked back to the kitchen. Lester and Earl rejoined their companions by the tree.

Doug witnessed the demeaning episode from afar. He stood like a statue, scowling at the men dawdling in the shade of the oak. Doug was broken out of his trance when Philip and Henry arrived.

"It's not time for lunch just yet," Philip said. "Better get back to work."

Doug turned his angry glare back to Lester.

"You're just looking for trouble," Henry warned Doug.

"I'm not worried about him," Doug haphazardly announced as he turned to look at Henry and Philip.

"Don't go messing with Lester," Philip warned.

"I said I ain't worried about him," Doug stated. "He better worry about pushing me too far."

"I hope he didn't hear you say that," Henry said as he averted his eyes.

Doug glanced over his shoulder and saw Lester making his way to the field. Philip tipped his hat to Doug before walking away with Henry.

Lester ignored Doug as he walked past. His mark was Cecelia.

"Cecelia, come with me," Lester ordered. "I have something for you to do up by the gin house."

The tired woman stood up and followed the vile man without question.

Lester led Cecelia to a barn near the gin house. A cotton press, a contraption that resembled a giant corkscrew, stood next to the barn. The apparatus was used to compress cotton into bales which were eventually loaded onto wagons for transport to market.

Lester opened the door to the barn and walked inside. Cecelia followed.

"Pull that door closed," Lester said to Cecelia after she entered.

"Can we leave it open a little?" Cecelia asked. "It might catch a breeze. It's so hot."

"I don't want a bunch of dust blowing around in here," Lester replied.

Cecelia closed the door and walked to the middle of the room. The barn was partially filled with bales of cotton. Lester walked around the room slowly and leisurely, occasionally touching a bale as if inspecting it. He took a seat on a bale and removed his hat, displaying his red hair.

"Have a seat," Lester said as he patted the cotton bale beside him.

Cecelia walked over and took a seat. Lester leaned forward and rested his arms on his knees as he held his hat.

"What is it you want me to do, Mr. Lester?" Cecelia asked with no emotion.

"Oh, I thought we might sit here for a spell and get you out of the sun," Lester said.

"I think everyone would like to get out of the sun," Cecelia responded.

"Well, the rest of them ain't like you," Lester said. "I guess you might say because of your white father, you aren't half bad."

Lester let out a boisterous laugh and gently nudged Cecelia with his elbow.

"Get it, ain't half bad?" Lester asked as he continued to laugh. "Just one-half of you is bad."

Lester continued to laugh heartily. His colorful outburst of ebullience was unfamiliar to Cecelia. That his exuberance came at her expense dismayed her. Even so, the sight of Lester in high spirits was an acceptable reprieve from his cruelty. Lester's laughter wound to a close, and he composed himself once again.

"The fact that you are different is why I treat you differently," Lester said. "I hope you can see that."

Although confused, Cecelia gave an agreeing nod.

"I don't pull everyone out of the field to spend time with me," Lester told her. "I go a lot easier on you than I do the others. Today I could have strung you up from a branch and whipped the skin off your back for laughing and carrying on with that boy in the field, but I didn't. I didn't because I'm gracious and kind."

Cecelia sat stoically, unaccustomed to being alone with an overseer.

"Well, ain't ya got nothing to say?" Lester asked.

"I don't know what to say, Mr. Lester," Cecelia replied.

"You're right," Lester said. "Sometimes words aren't necessary."

Lester leaned back and placed his hand on the bale behind her.

"I've been good to you," Lester claimed. "It's only proper to show gratitude when someone has been charitable to you."

His words fell upon her like cold water, and she felt a chill race up her spine.

"I am grateful, Mr. Lester," Cecelia said before drawing a deep breath.

"Well," Lester began, "Why don't you show me?"

He lifted his hand from the bale and caressed her back tenderly and slowly.

"I better get back to the field before Mr. Cobb wonders where I am," Cecelia said before promptly standing up.

As she tried to step away, Lester grabbed her arm with the swiftness of a snake strike. He stood up casually, relishing the gratification to come. With both hands, he held her wrists and felt her quickening pulse. Cecelia was fearful and panicking, but Lester only sensed arousal.

"That old man won't miss you," Lester said. "He doesn't even know how many slaves he has."

Lester held her hands and examined them.

"Such soft hands for having labored so much," Lester whispered.

The scoundrel kept a tight grip on Cecelia's hand with his left hand. He calmly ran his right hand up her arm until it came to rest on her shoulder. Lester gave Cecelia's shoulder a gentle, almost affectionate squeeze. Cecelia trembled for a moment as a shiver hurried through her.

"It's all right," Lester whispered as he moved his hand again. "I'll be gentle."

He placed his hand on the back of her neck, lightly at first, then firmly as he felt her pull back.

"Look, I'm offering you the chance to show me some respect and appreciation," Lester said. "You should consider it an honor that I even touch you."

"Please, Mr. Lester," Cecelia said loudly as she instinctively recoiled in horror.

Cecelia retreated from the goon with such force that she tripped and fell. The thud of the slave woman hitting the floor coincided with the opening of the barn door. Henry entered and found Lester lingering over Cecelia, who was prone on the ground.

"What happened?" Henry queried.

"She was helping me move some bales, and she fell," Lester deceitfully replied.

Lester's explanation was met with an expression of incredulity.

"You brought this little woman to help move cotton bales that weigh hundreds of pounds?" Henry asked bitingly.

"Just go mind your own business, Henry," Lester advised.

"Come on, Cecelia, they need you in the field," Henry said.

"She's gonna stay here with me," Lester replied.

"I don't know what you're doing in here, but it has nothing to do with cotton bales," Henry said positively. "Now come along, Cecelia."

"She ain't going nowhere," Lester growled. "If you know what's good for you, you'll turn around and walk out that door. Ain't nothing in here that concerns you."

"Cecelia, let's go," Henry said defiantly.

Lester removed the whip that rested on his belt. The fiend tapped it against his leg, a not so cryptic warning to Henry.

"Enough nonsense, let's go, Cecelia," Henry uttered as he stepped toward her.

Lester moved between them and scowled at Henry, his fists clenched tightly.

Suddenly Philip entered the barn. He stopped and observed the scene.

"What's going on?" Philip asked.

"Oh, nothing," Lester determined. "Nothing at all."

Lester knew he was outmatched and stood down.

"Well, lunch is ready. I'm sure y'all are hungry," Philip said.

"Come on, Cecelia," Henry said.

The slave rose to her feet, adjusted her dress, and serenely walked to the door.

"We can finish this up later, little miss," Lester said before she exited.

Henry and Philip gave one last glancing look of disdain before departing.

Nightfall brought relief that another agonizing day was at an end. But it also summoned anxiety among the slaves. Less than satisfactory results brought forth the sting of the overseer's whip.

Vernon stood in line several places behind Doug. Vernon jumped out of line and walked toward Doug, hoping to place some cotton in his basket.

"Get back in line, big boy," Lester warned Vernon.

Vernon jumped back to his place behind Lucille. The line moved, and the night remained quiet. The slaves had done excellent work that day. In a short time, Doug stood before Earl. The man took the basket of cotton, looked inside, and gave it a shake.

"What is this?" Earl asked. "Where's the rest of it? Have you been sitting under a shade tree all day?"

"Like you?" Doug replied.

Earl sneered at Doug.

"So that's how it is then?" Earl said. "This one has a mouth on him."

Earl turned and nodded at Lester. Thomas and Daniel grabbed Doug and moved him from the line. The two men yanked on Doug's shirt until they ripped it off.

"Hey, man, what are you doing?" Doug asked angrily.

Lester strolled over with the whip in hand. Thomas gave Doug a shove but failed to knock him down. Doug spun around to face Lester. The man lifted the whip so Doug could see it.

"You ain't hitting me with that thing," Doug warned.

A taunting smile appeared on Lester's face. Doug dashed forward and shoved Lester in the chest.

"I said, you ain't hitting me with that," Doug declared. "I ain't some old woman you can pick on."

The slaves looked on with unfaltering stares. Doug's audacity amazed some; others thought him deranged.

"Get some rope, Daniel," Lester instructed.

Daniel ran to the gin house several feet away and retrieved two lengths of rope. Daniel and Thomas flanked Doug.

"Hold your hands out," Lester ordered.

"I won't," Doug said boldly.

Lester raised his arm and cracked the whip near Doug, causing him to jump back. Doug collided with Thomas, who tried to grab him. Doug shoved Thomas away and prepared to fight, but a punch to the head from Daniel blindsided him. The sucker-punch nearly rendered him unconscious, and he staggered down to his knees. As Doug tried to gather himself, the men pounced on him and began fastening the ropes to his wrists. Doug shook off the fogginess in his head and regained his composure, but it was too late. The men lifted Doug onto his feet.

"Take him over yonder against the tree," Lester commanded.

Daniel and Thomas walked toward a thick tree and dragged Doug with them. Doug tried to resist, but it was futile. The men walked past opposite sides of the tree until they pulled Doug against it. The rough bark pressed into Doug's skin as they pulled him tightly against the tree. Lester stood behind Doug, looking him over and taking his time.

"Look at you. You ain't got a scratch on you," Lester said. "That's the last time anyone will tell you that."

Lester took a step back and lifted his arm above and behind his head. He delivered a vigorous blast to Doug's back. Doug cried out as the pain ran through his body, causing his knees to buckle for a moment. The bark scraped Doug's body as he slipped, urging him to stand up. Thomas and Daniel pulled tighter on the ropes. Lester delivered several more ferocious blows in hasty succession. Blood oozed from the cleanly opened skin on Doug's back. Tears flowed down Doug's cheeks as he cried out again. His legs were becoming weak and the bark bore into him as he shifted against the tree.

Lester raised his arm again, but Philip stepped between him and Doug.

"That's enough, Lester," Philip said.

"Will you get out of the way?" Lester pleaded.

"He's cut up good and he can barely stand up. He's had enough," Philip petitioned.

"Stay out of it, Philip," Lester advised.

"He's no good if he can't work," Philip stated.

"Tomorrow is Saturday," Lester said. "He only has to get through tomorrow and then he can rest up on Sunday."

"Just stop already," Philip demanded.

"I'm thinking you love these people. You and that one over there," Lester said as he pointed to Henry. "Y'all go easy on them. Heck, if it was up to the two of you, they'd all be sitting under a shade tree sipping tea all day. Is one of them your bastard or something? Huh, is it this one?"

Lester rolled up the whip as he walked away. Daniel and Thomas dropped the ropes and returned to the gin house. Florence, Maurice, Robert, and Cecelia ran to Doug. Cecelia worked feverishly to loosen the ropes as Maurice and Robert helped Doug stand. After turning in his basket, Vernon helped the others take Doug to the cabin.

Doug laid on the bed as Florence dipped a rag into some water and gently dabbed it on his back. The young man winced and emitted a muted cry of anguish. Maurice scooped some pork from a pot over the fireplace and placed it in a bowl. He returned the ladle to the pot and shuffled to Doug's bed.

"That ole Lester is a wicked man. You have to watch what you say around him. I don't think he likes his own mama. He's as mean as a snake," Maurice said.

"Any man that beats on helpless people is a coward," Florence offered. "That's what Lester is."

"Don't let him hear you say that or you'll be laying here like the boy," Maurice cautioned.

"Sit up now," Florence said.

Maurice and Florence helped Doug sit up on the bed. Doug leaned forward to cope with the pain. Maurice lifted a spoonful of food to Doug's lips. Doug reluctantly consumed the offering.

"This will make you feel better," Maurice said as he scooped another bite.

"You need to get some rest," Florence added.

Vernon sat quietly in the corner, eating his supper. The kind couple continued to care for the injured Doug. Even as war and enslavement were the norms of life, compassion still existed in the world.

When considering the condition of his people, Desmond Tutu once wondered if the world could see the human beings behind the unrelenting despair. One might contemplate the same about those who inhabited the farms and fields throughout Bentonville.

9

An Unspoken Oath

Joseph Cobb stood on his front porch and scrutinized the wet temperate morning. Heavy rain fell from ominous, swollen, jagged, dark clouds. The treetops moaned as the wind pushed against them, and water cascaded down branches and leaves. Lester stood off the porch near the bottom step as if in defiance of the dismal weather. The rain pelted the brim of his hat and made a dull rhythmic beat. Joseph peered into the distance. He could barely see the slaves standing where they gathered.

"The day is a mess, but I'll get work out of 'em," Lester professed.

Joseph stood in quiet contemplation for a moment.

"No, I think not," Joseph said. "They'll drag the sacks and baskets through the mud. It's not a day for working. Besides, if they work today, some of them might get sick, then I'd lose two or more days of work. Best to keep them inside, I think."

"Whatever you say, Mr. Cobb," Lester replied.

"Go tell them to get inside and keep dry. Then you boys head on home yourselves," Joseph said. "I'll see you on Monday."

Lester pinched the front of his hat and tipped it slightly, causing rainwater to pour as if from a spout. Lester turned and walked toward the slaves huddled together in the downpour.

As Lester approached the slaves, he appeared in the gloom like a haunting specter. The slaves could not fear him more if he were an apparition.

"Get back inside! No work today!" Lester yelled. "Mr. Cobb doesn't want none of y'all to get sick! I don't want to see any of you until Monday!"

The slaves briefly stood in a state of confusion before moving to their cabins. Lester walked back to the house. Doug stopped at the cabin door and watched Lester and the other free hands and overseers as best he could. In mere moments, they all mounted their horses and rode away into the bleakness of the day.

Doug stepped inside the cabin and immediately removed his wet shirt. He placed the shirt over a small post on his bed. Large red spots clung to the back of the shirt, a testimony of the beating the night before. Doug grabbed his only other shirt and put it on before sitting on the bed. The young man looked out the open door. The wind blew in such a way that it did not allow rain to enter the door. All the slaves in the cabin gawked at the moving picture framed by the doorway as if it hypnotized them. The thrum of the rain on the roof beckoned the slaves to drowsiness.

A gleam appeared in Doug's eyes, and they widened. He rubbed his chin as if thinking hard about the solution to a math problem before getting up and suddenly bolting from the cabin.

Doug splashed through puddles around the area as he made his way to Robert's cabin. Doug knocked on the door before opening it and stepping inside. Robert, Lewis, Lucille, and Cecelia sat without speaking.

"Robert," Doug called. "Come out here for a minute."

"It's raining," Robert answered. "I'm not standing in the rain 'less I have to."

"Come on," Doug pressed him. "It's important."

Robert sighed as he stood up, put on his hat, and followed Doug through the door. The two young men walked to one side of the structure and stood close against the wall, shielding themselves from the rain as much as possible.

"It's now or never," Doug said to Robert.

"What?" Robert wondered aloud.

"We have to make a run for it. We have to get out of here," Doug said.

"In the rain?"

"Think about it," Doug said. "We're not working today, and tomorrow is Sunday. That gives us almost a two-day head start."

Doug could see Robert thinking, but it wasn't quite sinking in.

"They won't even know we're gone until Monday morning," Doug said.

It was clear from Robert's expression that he grasped Doug's concept. Robert smiled and nodded his head.

"Where are we going to go?" Robert asked.

"We need to get to Durham and find my mom," Doug replied.

"Your mother might not be there anymore," Robert stated. "She may not be alive."

"We just need to head that way," Doug said. "If we get to Durham, or just go far enough, maybe we can get away from all this."

"OK, I'm with you," Robert said.

"Cool, let's go," Doug replied.

Doug peeked around the side of the cabin and looked to the house. There wasn't a soul in sight. The two young slaves casually walked toward the road, keeping the cabins between themselves and sight of the master's house as much as possible.

Inside her cabin, Cecelia peered out the window and saw Doug and Robert departing. Cecelia shook her head in disbelief at the risk they were taking.

The rain drenched Robert and Doug by the time they reached the road. Robert followed Doug as he traversed the wide muddy pathway for a couple of miles. The runaways said nothing as the rain pummeled them. The driving rain forced Doug to keep his gaze upon the ground, only able to see a few feet ahead. Occasionally Doug would look up for a few seconds to see the lay of the land. They didn't fear being seen on the road. Who in their right mind would be out in such weather?

Doug turned to confirm that Robert was still close behind him. He could see his companion following about six feet behind. Doug looked into the distance behind them and stopped so abruptly that Robert almost walked into him. The two young men could no longer see the Cobb farm. But

Doug noticed something that stood out amid the dull and trivial details of the gloomy day. The torrential rain softened the surface of the dirt road, causing their feet to make distinct impressions in the mud. Doug squinted to shield his eyes from the rain as he observed his surroundings. Fields of tall grass with trees in the distance flanked the road.

"We have to get off the road," Doug stated.

"What's wrong?" Robert asked.

"Look," Doug said as he pointed at the road behind them.

The fugitives stood in the rain and stared at the breadcrumbs marking their path.

"Someone might be able to track us," Doug said.

Doug scanned the area for any means of escape that might camouflage their escape route. The landscape looked almost identical in every direction. Doug looked at the sky, searching for the sun, but the reference point he sought was hidden behind thick clouds.

"Let's go this way," Doug said as he set out across a soaked meadow toward the closest tree line. "Hopefully, the rain will wash away our tracks."

With unwavering trust in his companion, Robert followed Doug across the grassy field and further into the unknown. The knee-high grass and twisted shrubs slowed their progress. Rain already added misery to the young men's journey. In the field, they had to contend with plants that seemed to clutch and ensnare them. They remained undaunted, buoyed by the faint hope of freedom that swelled with each laborious step.

Eventually, Doug and Robert reached the forest, where the tall pines deterred the growth of the smaller plants that hassled them so. The shelter offered by the canopy of the trees was negligible, but the escapees could walk a little easier at least. Doug and Robert meandered through the woods, sidestepping trees and ducking under low branches, but kept heading in the same general direction. The soothing hypnotic tone of raindrops on leaves induced silence in both of them.

Thoughts of home drifted into Doug's mind. On such a messy day he would sit comfortably on the couch, playing a video game or watching a movie with his mom. Oh, how desperate he was to be there now. Doug hoped he would soon cross some mysterious line of demarcation and suddenly find himself back home.

As Doug and Robert walked along, the sound of a new instrument gradually arose in the symphony of nature. It was the distant noise of rushing water. The friends quickened their pace in the sound's direction. Minutes later they found the source of the roar. A fast-moving river, bulging with rainwater, blocked their way. Doug stepped closer to the bank and examined the small river. Several small branches passed by as the swift current carried them away. Little whirlpools formed in places where the water abruptly ran into an obstacle.

"I don't see any way to get across," Doug said.

"I can't swim," Robert replied.

Doug spent another moment in contemplation as he stared at the surging river.

"Come on," Doug said. "Let's walk beside it and see where it goes."

As the two allies turned to walk, the soil beneath Doug suddenly gave way and slid into the turbulent waterway. As he fell, Doug frantically grabbed at the embankment, but the effort was futile. Doug slid against the exposed southern red clay dirt, which was instantly wet and slick. In a flash, Doug was in the clutches of the angry river.

"Oh, no!" Robert cried. "Doug!"

Robert ran along the tree line, chasing Doug as the water swept him away. Doug fought to stay above the water, but he submerged every few seconds. Each time Doug went under, Robert feared he would not emerge. Robert was tense with fear as he struggled to keep up with Doug and the current.

Doug looked for any hope when he resurfaced. He saw Robert drifting farther behind. Doug managed to stabilize himself and keep his head above water, but he was still at the mercy of the river. Then, as the water spun him around, Doug saw hope for deliverance. The limb of a stout tree hung low over the water. As Doug drifted under the branch, he reached up as high as he could and grabbed it. But salvation was ephemeral. The river was furious and resentful that day and would not give up its spoils easily. The strong current wrested Doug from the safety of the tree and carried him away again. The brief stop helped Robert close the distance between them, but he couldn't reach Doug in time.

Fate would grant Doug another chance. Ahead of him, a tree protruded from the side of the bank. The tree was a little more than a foot in diameter but looked sturdy. It hung out over the water before curving upward. Doug paddled hard to get closer to the tree as the tide hurriedly carried him away. The water tried to whisk Doug past the tree, but with all the strength he could muster, he hooked his left arm around the tree. Before the current could pull him off, Doug swung his right arm over the other side of the abnormal trunk and embraced it tightly. Doug's forearms scraped against the wet coarse bark of the tree. The young man's body was too focused on survival to notice the pain.

Robert saw Doug clinging to the tree and threw off his hat as he raced toward the water's edge.

"Hold on, Doug," Robert pleaded.

"Help, Robert," Doug implored. "I don't know how long I can hang on."

Despite his own fear of the raging beast that tried to claim his friend, Robert made his way to the edge of the water. Robert grabbed every tree he could reach as he inched closer to Doug. Robert searched the ground for a robust fallen limb, but none he saw would suffice. He knew he had to get closer to reach Doug. Keeping a firm hand on a neighboring tree, Robert stepped onto the tree that held Doug. Robert leaned forward to reach Doug, but his foot slipped off the tree and into the water. The current tried to pull Robert down, but his solid grip on the next tree kept him safe. After placing his foot back on the tree, Robert extended his right hand.

"Grab my hand, Doug," Robert told him.

"I'm afraid to let go," Doug said.

"You have to try," Robert urged. "Reach out and take my hand. I'll pull you up."

Tired and hesitant, Doug slowly inched along the tree and moved closer to Robert. Doug readied himself and reached for Robert. Robert quickly snatched Doug's hand and pulled him to shore. Once Doug was against the bank, Robert backed up and dragged him from the water. Doug crawled away from the edge of the water and rested on his knees and elbows.

"Thank you," Doug said as he panted.

"You would have done the same for me," Robert replied.

"You know I would," Doug stated.

The two friends sat and leaned against a tree and relaxed as heavy rain continued to fall. Once he caught his breath, Robert looked to his right and saw his grandfather's old hat sitting on the ground. He jumped up quickly and ran to retrieve it. Doug composed himself as he watched Robert return. Robert brushed a small amount of mud from the hat and held it so the rain could wash it clean.

"I'm glad you have your grandpa's hat," Doug said.

"It's all I have left of him," Robert replied. "It makes me feel like he's still around."

"Like you still have a physical connection to him," Doug added.

"Yeah, I suppose so," Robert replied. "I'll keep it for the rest of my life."

"My grandpa used to wear an old bucket hat," Doug said.

"Your grandpa wore a bucket on his head?" Robert replied with a smile.

"No, that's what it's called," Doug said, smiling himself. "It looked like a bucket made of fabric. He had it forever. It got a hole in it once, and he asked my grandma to sew a patch on it. He always wore it fishing. Sometimes he just wore it because he knew it cracked me up. I sure miss him."

"I miss my grandpa too," Robert said as his gaze descended reverently on the hat.

"I guess we should keep going," Doug said as he got to his feet.

"Yeah," Robert replied.

The absconding slaves followed the river, being mindful to keep a safe distance from the water.

The young men walked for another hour in the unrelenting rain. Wet clothes chafed them and hunger only added to the misery. Robert and Doug exited the small forest and stood near a muddy road. There was nothing on the other side of the road but a large pasture as far as they could see. Doug observed the scene and peered into the fog. The rain and gloom of the day created a kaleidoscope of gray, brown, and green.

"Which way should we go?" Robert inquired.

"I'm not sure," Doug said. "Can't see too far away. But that means people will have a harder time seeing us. Maybe we should keep following the river for a while."

The fugitives continued on their way beside the river which now ran along the edge of the vast pasture. Each step took them farther away from captivity, but hunger was closing in on them. They ambled through the muck of mud and wild grass, lumbering toward distant freedom. The soothing sounds of falling rain and rushing water enticed them to stop and rest. But Doug and Robert couldn't stop. Safety was fleeting for runaway slaves.

Doug stared at the ground as he followed the river's path. He daydreamed of home, but he was also soaked, miserable, and uncomfortable. Doug stopped when he felt a firm tug on his shirt. He turned around to see Robert pointing into the pasture. Robert held a finger to his lip, signaling Doug to remain silent. Doug squinted as he peered into the murkiness of the day. Through a veil of rain and fog, Doug saw a cottage with a small front porch. A rocking chair gently tilted back and forth, like a lone sentinel guarding the homestead.

"Do you think anyone is home?" Doug whispered to Robert.

Robert touched Dough's shoulder and pointed behind the house. A neatly stacked pile of wood stood between the cabin and a well-tended garden.

"Oh my gosh," Doug said. "Some food."

Doug and Robert slowly crept along the edge of the field while keeping a watchful eye on the cabin. They were meticulous with each step on the squishy ground, cautious to be as silent as possible. But fear amplified the sucking and sloshing sound in their minds. They bent their knees and lowered their profiles as they got closer to the backyard.

The young men reached the corner of the garden and dropped to the ground. The woodpile obstructed the two slaves' view of the house. Doug was starving, but he didn't know what he was looking at. They were all just plants to him. Robert observed the garden attentively. Robert pushed back some leaves and spotted cucumbers on vines laying on the ground. He plucked one and handed it to Doug.

As Robert harvested another cucumber, the sudden sound of a slamming door startled the young men. Robert and Doug quickly ducked behind the woodpile. Doug tried to slow his breath. He could hardly hear the rain over the pounding of his pulse in his head. Doug carefully peered around the side of the woodpile and couldn't believe his eyes. He hurried his head back out of view.

"Oh, no," Doug said with a look of pure dread on his face. "It's Lester."

Stunned, but needing to see for himself, Robert peeked around the stack of timber. He saw Lester walking to an outhouse with long but delicate strides. Lester wore bib overalls with one shoulder unfastened. Doug peeked around the pile of wood in time to see Lester enter the outhouse. The young men returned to the cover of the wood simultaneously.

"Let's go before he sees us," Robert said as he stood up.

"Wait," Doug directed.

Robert looked down at Doug, confused by the delay. Why would he want to remain in the lion's den?

Doug stood up and grabbed an ax that leaned against the woodpile. He gripped the handle of the implement tightly and glared at the outhouse.

"What are you doing, Doug?" Robert asked. "Let's go."

"Wait a minute," Doug replied. "We can take him out."

"What?" Robert asked incredulously. "Are you crazy?"

"Think about it," Doug said. "We can kill him right now, just like in that old movie with Clint Eastwood and Morgan Freeman. One of us opens the door, and the other can hit him in the head with this ax."

"I think the hunger is getting to your head. We're trying to get away from him," Robert expressed.

"I know," Doug said. "But think of everyone at the farm. He won't be able to hurt them anymore."

"Do you really think things will be easier for them if you kill Lester?" Robert retorted.

"He won't be around to beat and torture them," Doug said. "Think about what he did to your grandpa."

"I do think about it," Robert replied sternly. "I think about it every day. But killing Lester won't make anything easier for nobody. They'll just replace him with another Lester, or maybe worse. You act like you ain't never seen it, but there are people in the world even more hateful than Lester."

"Come on," Doug urged.

"No, Doug," Robert said earnestly. "You kill him, and every white man for a hundred miles will look for us. Now let's go before he comes out of there."

Doug picked up the cucumber with his left hand and kept the ax in his right. The two escapees continued on their way swiftly and quietly. Before Lester exited the outhouse, Doug and Robert made their way across the pasture and back into the safety of the woods.

Once they were out of harm's way, Doug and Robert walked casually. The rain stopped, but their wet clothing left them feeling miserable. They walked on a soft carpet of decaying branches and leaves. The swollen river still ran swiftly but seemed less angry.

"Look at that," Doug said as he examined the ax handle. "He carved his initials into the handle."

He showed Robert the letters LC etched into the wood handle.

Doug and Robert happened upon a spot where the ground sloped gradually to the river's edge, creating a tiny beach. The spongy sandy soil displayed animal tracks made of two oblong indentations beside each other.

"Check it out," Doug said, pointing to the hoofprints. "Deer tracks."

Doug looked around but saw no deer. He walked to the edge of the water and placed the ax on the ground beside a rock about the size of a watermelon. Doug dropped the cucumber next to the ax before creeping closer to the water. He placed his right foot in the water and felt it push against the back of his leg, just below the calf.

"Don't fall in again," Robert warned.

"I'm OK," Doug answered. "It's not as bad as it looks."

Doug cupped his hands and gathered some water, then tossed it onto the nearby rock. He repeated the process a few more times.

After finishing, Doug stepped out of the water to grab the cucumbers. He returned to the water and rinsed the dirt from the bounty. Once cleared of dirt, Doug returned the cucumbers to the rock.

Doug kneeled beside the rock and held a cucumber on its flat but bumpy surface. Holding the ax in his other hand, Doug chopped the cucumber into sections.

"There you go, Robert," Doug offered. "That might make it a little easier to eat."

Robert reached down and grabbed several pieces before Doug placed the other cucumber on the rock. Doug hacked again as Robert gobbled the thick slices.

Once Doug finished chopping both cucumbers, he and Robert sat beside the rock and rested while they ate.

"My mom used to slice these up and put them in a salad," Doug said.

"What's a salad?" Robert wondered aloud.

"It's something you eat before the main meal," Doug answered. "Some people eat it as the main meal. It's a bunch of vegetables in a bowl, like lettuce, tomato slices, pieces of carrot. I like to put pieces of boiled egg in mine."

"You and your mama must have had a nice master to give you all that to eat," Robert said.

"No, it wasn't like that. My mama was the master," Doug replied with a chuckle.

Robert looked confused.

"Do you mean you have a white father, like Cecelia? Or is your mama..." Robert stumbled over his words and stopped talking. Doug's remark made little sense to him.

"No," Doug uttered. "It's hard to explain."

The free men finished eating, and Doug lifted his arms over his head and yawned.

"Maybe we better get going," Doug suggested.

The two teenagers rose to their feet and embarked on their journey once more.

The fog lifted, and a light breeze whisked past Doug and Robert. It sent a chill running up Doug's spine, but he welcomed whatever help the gust might offer to dry out his clothes. The leaves and branches of the trees rustled in the wind. The forest was comparatively quiet now, not like the cacophony of the rain and river before. They had been walking in the woods for hours. Doug and Robert hid from the world among the tall Carolina pines, and they hiked as though on a leisurely stroll.

"How long before we get to your mom?" Robert asked.

"It might take a couple of days," Doug replied. "I'm not sure."

Heavy, wet clothes encumbered Doug, and he didn't want to think of how long the journey might be.

"Do you think your mother will still be there? They might've sold her," Robert cautioned.

"I'm not worried about that," Doug said.

"You should be," Robert advised. "She could be in a whole other state if her master sold her."

"My mother isn't owned by anyone," Doug told Robert. "Things are different where I come from. I'm not sure how I got here, or why I'm here. But I'm not supposed to be."

"How is it different?" Robert asked as he stepped over a small tree that fell years ago.

"Black people aren't slaves where I come from," Doug said.

The expression on Robert's face changed to one of wide-eyed astonishment.

"You tell some stories," Robert said, laughing at the absurdity of Doug's statement.

"No, I'm telling you, it's different," Doug replied. "There aren't slaves back home."

Robert was at first incredulous, but fascination and hope tempered his skepticism.

"You mean nobody will make us pick cotton?" Robert asked.

"Nope. You don't have to pick cotton if you don't want to. Heck, you get paid for your work where I come from," Doug said.

"What?" Robert asked, still doubtful yet captivated by Doug's claims.

"Oh yeah," Doug said confidently. "You can use that money to buy nice clothes. You don't have to wear these old rags."

Robert displayed an enchanting smile. He was eager to hear more about this magical place.

"What else?" Robert asked eagerly.

"Well, you can go to school," Doug added.

"Really?" Robert asked in disbelief.

"Yeah," Doug confirmed.

"What do they teach you?" Robert asked. "Could I learn letters and numbers?"

"Yeah, man. You can learn all kinds of things," Doug said.

Robert looked at Doug quizzically, silently urging him to say more.

"Some people that look just like me and you get paid millions of dollars to sing. People pay money to watch black people play sports or act in a movie. You can eat just about whatever you want," Doug stated.

"I could have salad?" Robert asked excitedly.

"Yeah, if you want," Doug replied. "But a lot of stuff is better than salad."

"It sounds better than what I see in my dreams," Robert said with yearning in his eyes.

"Oh, it ain't perfect. There are still a lot of things to do to make it better," Doug said without equivocation. "But it's a long way from this."

The friends continued their journey to freedom as the woods grew dim. Through the treetops, they saw the approaching sunset decorate the sky with brilliant shades of orange blended with red and yellow. Twilight would soon beckon the moon and the boys grew weary.

The crowd of trees that hid Doug and Robert during the day was now a hindrance as they tried to make their way in the dark. While they were tired and all manner of things impeded their progress, they pressed on. Their first steps on the journey constituted an unspoken oath to endure any hardship together.

Doug listened to the trickling of the river on his right and moved slowly and carefully among the pines. He nearly stumbled over a fallen tree more than once, but navigated the forest with the help of the river. The shroud of blackness slowly lifted as Doug and Robert reached the edge of the woods.

Exiting the forest was like a curtain drawing open on a grand stage play of creation. The young men stood in a vast field. Doug looked at the sky. Thousands of stars spanned the heavens, reaching from horizon to horizon. In the dark rural setting and absent from the pollution of the city, Doug saw more stars than he ever thought possible. The night sky was awash with exquisite hues of blue, black, and purple. On a formless void canvas, God created a masterpiece.

Doug pulled himself free from the hypnotic grip of the scenery and checked his surroundings. Far away, trees surrounded the enormous field. The river shimmered in the moonlight. A road sliced through the middle of the field ahead of the runaways.

"Let's take the road for a while," Doug insisted.

Doug and Robert walked toward the road at a slow pace. Hunger and fatigue burdened them.

"We have to find more food," Robert said.

"I know. A cucumber isn't a hearty meal, is it?" Doug asked, half-joking.

Doug and Robert were several yards from the road when Doug suddenly stopped. He rested the ax on his shoulder as he sniffed and examined the air.

"Do you smell that?" Doug asked.

Robert sniffed the air deeply.

"Yeah," Robert replied. "Something smells good."

Doug looked around, hoping to locate the source of the delightful aroma. The mouthwatering scent of something delectable was riding the wind like a boat on a river. Doug last smelled something so delicious while standing in his mother's kitchen.

The hungry young men moved hastily but cautiously to the road. About two hundred yards ahead, on the other side of the trees, Doug saw the orange and yellow glow of a campfire.

10

Scarce and Cherished Riches

Doug and Robert scampered across a bridge and took cover behind some trees. They saw a portly man tending to a campfire in a field beside the road. A spit made of tree limbs held a hanging pot over the fire. The light of the fire revealed a covered wagon attached to a pair of horses. The rotund man stirred the contents of the vessel before sitting on a wooden crate.

"What do we do?" Robert asked Doug in a whisper.

Hunger and the smell of food clouded Doug's judgment.

"It looks like he's alone. We can sneak up on him and take some food," Doug said as he held up the ax.

"I told you if you kill a white man, every one of them for a hundred miles will be after us," Robert replied.

"We won't hit him unless we have to," Doug said.

Robert looked uneasy and didn't respond.

"Come on, man. We got to survive," Doug stated.

"Okay, but don't hurt him unless he makes us," Robert insisted.

"All right," Doug said. "We'll stay on the road, so we don't make too much noise, then sneak up behind him."

Doug and Robert moved along the road slowly and quietly. The surface was wet but surprisingly firm. The thought of accosting the white man and confiscating his food made Doug squeamish, but he couldn't stop now. He was hungry, and the smell of food in the air enticed him like a Siren's song. Doug couldn't hear his footsteps over the rhythmic thumping in his ears, keeping perfect time with his quickening heartbeat.

It seemed like an eternity passed before Doug was behind the overweight man. Only a few more steps and Doug would be upon him. The plump man leaned forward and reached for the cauldron dangling over the fire. Before the man was off the crate, Doug charged forward and jabbed the tip of the ax handle into his back.

"Don't move," Doug ordered.

"All right, all right," the large man said, his voice shaking as he instinctively lifted his hands in the air.

Robert stepped into view while Doug kept the ax handle pressed firmly against the man's back.

"We don't mean you no harm, sir," Robert said nervously. "We just want something to eat."

The reply that came was jarring and unexpected. The click-clack of a rifle being primed to fire froze Doug and Robert like statues. Doug noticed a second crate beside the fire. A tall, burly man stepped forth from behind the wagon. The flicker of the campfire caused shadows to dance about the man's face beneath the brim of his hat.

"Toss that ax," the hulking man said.

Doug removed the ax from the fat man's back and cast it aside. The implement landed near the fire.

"Luke, why don't you pull up a couple of chairs for our guests?" the tall man said to his companion.

Luke stood up and retrieved two crates from the wagon. He returned quickly and placed the boxes beside the fire opposite the others.

"Have a seat," the armed man instructed.

Doug and Robert moved slowly, keeping their eyes on the rifle. Luke seated the slaves, then returned to his crate. The towering man remained standing with the repeating rifle pointed at the interlopers.

"What are your names?" the tall man asked.

Doug answered quickly, but a jumpy Robert spoke so hastily he inter-

114

rupted Doug.

"Well, Robert and Doug, what are you doing out here by yourselves?" the muscular man asked.

Doug and Robert looked at each other before speaking.

"Um, we got lost," Doug answered.

"Did you get lost, or did you run away?" the strapping man challenged.

The boys looked at each other again.

"We ran away, sir," Robert replied. "Please, mister, we didn't mean no harm. We're just hungry, that's all."

"Do you reckon your master is out looking for you?" the tall man asked.

"No, sir, not yet," Robert said. "It's been raining all day."

Doug ricocheted between anger and fright. Robert was peeling away the veneer of their plan, and he didn't know what these men would do.

"Please, mister, can we have some food before you take us back?" Robert pleaded.

"What do you think, Stephen?" Luke asked his friend. "Can we spare some food?"

"I suppose we can," Stephen replied.

Luke retrieved bowls from the back of the wagon and returned to the hanging pot. After stirring the stew a few times, Luke scooped some into a bowl and handed it to Robert. The young man grabbed the bowl and ate impatiently.

"There you go," Luke said as he handed a bowl to Doug.

Doug inspected the food before slowly grasping the spoon. He stirred the food as he watched Luke fill another bowl and hand it to Stephen.

"I'll get some in a bit," the tall man responded.

Doug watched Luke sit down and take a bite. Assured the food was safe, Doug had a taste for himself.

"You're scarfing that down like you haven't eaten in a week," Stephen said to Robert.

"This is good," Robert offered between bites.

"How long have you been on the run?" Luke asked. "You look like you've traveled a thousand miles."

"We only left this morning," Doug replied.

"Who is your master?" Stephen asked.

"I don't know," Doug answered.

"Do you have any brands on you?" Stephen queried.

"No, sir, Mr. Cobb doesn't brand us," Robert said.

"Cobb?" Luke asked, seeking verification.

"Yes, sir. Mr. Cobb is our master," Robert confirmed.

"I wonder if that's the Cobbs over near Bentonville?" Stephen wondered aloud.

"I think they're telling the truth," Luke said to Stephen. "Cobb doesn't brand his slaves."

"I guess that means y'all can sell us if you don't take us back," Doug said frankly.

"Take it easy," the towering, athletic man said before sitting down.

Stephen rested the rifle across his legs.

"We're not going to return you to your master," Luke advised.

"And we will not sell you," Stephen added.

"You ain't?" Robert asked in disbelief.

"We're abolitionists," Luke said.

"You guys are abolitionists?" Doug asked incredulously.

"Yes," Luke replied.

"Like you work on the Underground Railroad?" Doug pressed.

"We're on our way to a station house with supplies now," Luke stated. "I helped a young man escape from the Cobb farm some time ago. He was about your age at the time."

Robert couldn't hold back an excited smile. Doug was wary and expressionless.

"Where were you boys headed?" Stephen asked.

"We are going to find his mama," Robert said, still smiling.

"Oh yeah, where is she?" Luke asked.

"She's in Durham," Robert answered.

"Oh, you're a long way from Durham," Luke replied.

"Are you going to help her escape captivity?" Stephen inquired.

"She isn't a slave," Doug said.

He worried Robert said too much already.

"Not a slave?" Luke responded with puzzlement. "Is she hiding out waiting for you?"

"No, she isn't a slave. Never has been," Doug said.

"He does tell some stories," Robert asserted. "He said they pay black people lots of money to sing where he came from."

Doug lowered his head toward the bowl as if trying to hide in it.

"Tell them about salad," Robert added. "He said they get all kinds of good things to eat. I can't imagine it's better than this right here."

Robert gleefully ate another bite. Doug was not willing to take the strangers' comments at face value. Robert displayed the enthusiasm of a disciple. Doug wondered if Robert truly accepted the men were abolitionists or just ardently wanted to believe it.

"If you're going to Durham, you're heading the wrong way," Stephen added.

"What?" Doug asked.

"If you came from the Cobb farm, you've been going in the wrong direction," Stephen said.

"Oh, man, no way," Doug said. "I have to get to Durham."

"Well, Durham is in the other direction," Stephen said.

"Maybe they came from a different farm," Luke offered. "Which direction did you boys come from?"

"We came from over yonder," Robert said, pointing down the road.

Robert remained still as he looked into the surrounding darkness. The others turned to see what captured the young man's attention and saw a pair of small, glowing objects approaching. The clip-clop of hooves on the boards of the bridge soon followed.

"Hush, don't say a word," Stephen instructed Doug and Robert.

Three men on horseback advanced toward the group. The outsiders stopped just off the road and didn't dismount from their animals.

"How do you do?" Edward Black asked.

Edward was a clean-cut man, wholesome in appearance, with neatly combed hair. He was clearly the leader of the uninvited guests, and you would have known it before he spoke a word. His companions were Linus Hammond and Jeffrey Brown. Linus was a large, imposing man, but not as stout as Stephen. Jeffrey was smaller than the other two, with unkempt curly hair and a few missing teeth that he unabashedly displayed with a smile.

"Oh, we're doing fine," Luke said. "I hope you are."

"Doing just fine, thank you," Edward replied. "Y'all haven't seen a couple dogs wander past this way, have you?"

"No, sure haven't," Luke answered.

"They got a whiff of something down the road and took off into the trees. Thought maybe we'd find them over this way on the other side," Edward said.

"Some night for hunting, with it raining all day and such," Stephen replied.

"We thought the weather might have spooked some deer or possum maybe," Linus responded.

"Weather like that can flush out runaways too," Edward added. "You can make a right smart a money returning a fugitive to his master."

"You fellas catchers?" Stephen asked.

"The best there is," Jeffrey added excitedly, before wiping spittle from his mouth.

"It's not our primary occupation," Edward interjected. "But we've been known to round up a few wayward rascals."

Edward kept his head still as he stared at the fire, but the almost jittery movement of his eyes betrayed his attempt to seem disinterested in his surroundings. He was quietly appraising the situation. Edward noticed the unrestrained black youngsters, but also the muscular man gripping the rifle.

"Where y'all headed?" Edward quizzed.

Neither Luke nor Stephen answered immediately.

"We're headed to Goldsboro with some supplies for General Baker's troops," Stephen replied after the uneasy pause.

"You don't say. You hear that, boys? These fellows are pitching in for the cause," Edward said as he turned to his associates.

"Just one wagon," Linus noted acerbically.

"Every bit helps," Luke added.

"That's right," Edward replied.

Stephen adjusted his grip on the rifle. He found Edward's surveying stare disquieting.

"I couldn't help but notice they don't have any shackles on them," Edward said, pointing at Doug and Robert.

"They might try to run off," Jeffrey said with a sneer.

"No, they know better than that. I can part a man's hair from a mile away with this popgun. They know they wouldn't get far," Stephen countered.

"I don't doubt that a bit," Edward stated.

"There's an ax on the ground right by that one," Jeffrey said. "Careful, he might pick it up and hit ya."

Almost simultaneously, the group turned to observe the ax on the ground near Doug's feet.

"Pick it up, you," Stephen instructed Doug.

Doug glanced around the group before leaning forward slowly and grasping the ax. Part of him wanted to swing the weapon, but Doug knew the attempt would be futile.

"Now hand it over to Luke," Stephen told him.

Doug stood up and gently handed the ax to Luke, then sat back down.

"See, no problem at all. We keep them in line," Luke said.

"Yes, sir, you have them trained well," Edward uttered.

The conversation halted for a few restless moments. A clear sense of apprehension idled around the men.

"I hope you find your dogs. If you keep going down this road for a few miles, it will turn to the right and cut through the woods. Maybe your dogs came out down there," Stephen suggested.

"Thank you. I think we'll do that," Edward responded.

While Stephen's recommendation was polite, the uninvited guests got the message. It was time for Edward and his men to move on. Edward tugged on the reins, and the horse moved back to the road. Linus tipped his hat to the men as he withdrew. As a parting testament to his boorish behavior,

Jeffrey spat on the ground before trotting away. Stephen monitored the trespassers until they were out of sight.

"Go on and finish eating," Luke advised Doug and Robert.

The two exhausted young men earnestly dug into their bowls once again.

Stars gleamed overhead as if light perforated the midnight sky. The horses grazed and rested in the field near the wagon. Stephen threw a large canvas cover on the ground several feet from the fire.

"You can sleep on that tonight. Sorry, we can't offer you better," Stephen said to Doug and Robert.

"You're welcome to come to the station house with us in the morning. We can get you started north on your way to freedom," Luke offered.

Robert turned to his companion, exhibiting unmistakable delight. Doug's face held a sober expression.

"Thanks, but we need to go to Durham," Doug said plainly.

"What?" Robert asked in disbelief. "They can help us."

"We don't know that," Doug whispered. "For all we know, they might try to sell us."

"Come on now. Look at what they've done for us," Robert pleaded.

"People will be nice to you just before they stab you in the back," Doug asserted. "You have a lot to learn about the world."

"You don't even know if your mother is in the same place. How could you know?" Robert asked.

"Look, I appreciate the offer, but we have to go toward Durham," Doug said again.

"Suit yourself," Luke said. "I wouldn't advise two runaway slaves to go to Durham, but you do what you must."

"Please, Doug. This is our chance to be free," Robert argued.

"Trust me. If we get where I'm trying to go, you'll be freer with me than with them," Doug countered.

"OK, Doug, I trust you," Robert vowed.

Trust.

One of life's scarce and cherished riches is trust. We don't always find the rare and precious treasures in life. Now and then, someone gives us such a gift. We decide to treasure that offering or discard it like rotten fruit.

Stephen tossed long lengths of rope to Doug and Robert.

"Wrap those around your wrists," Stephen ordered.

Doug and Robert looked back at him with wide eyes.

"You want us to tie ourselves up?" Robert asked.

"No, just wrap it around your wrists and then toss the long end under the wagon. That way, if those catchers come this way again, they will think you're tied up," Stephen explained.

"How do we know you won't tighten the ropes on us during the night?" Doug asked.

An annoyed Stephen tapped the rifle against his leg.

"You don't. You'll just have to trust us," Stephen told them.

Trust.

There it was again. A stranger was asking for something they had not earned. Robert was quick to trust the men, but Doug was reluctant. Despite his hesitance, Doug did as Stephen instructed and crawled onto the canvas. Robert took a place beside him.

"Go on and get some shut-eye," Stephen advised Luke. "I'll take first watch. I don't think they'll come back this way, but better to be safe."

"I agree," Luke said as he stretched out on another canvas tarp and pulled a blanket over his ample torso.

Doug stared at the shimmering sky and listened to the dull hiss and snap of the fire. He fought to keep sleep away. Although they fed him, Doug did not trust the men. Did the men protect him from the slave catchers, or were they only preserving a prize for themselves? Sleep inched closer, and Doug blinked his eyes rapidly, hoping to ward it off. Doug surveyed the sky and thought about his mother. He tried to find the resemblance of her face among the shades of color, twinkling stars, and shapes on the moon. Soon Doug drifted off to sleep, as men do when clutching pleasant thoughts.

11

A Prison That Binds the Soul

Doug opened his eyes slowly and met the morning. He yawned before rolling onto his back, relieving the pressure on his sore shoulder. After pausing for a moment to wake fully, Doug attempted to sit up. The rope suddenly halted Doug's progress, and he fell back to the dirt. Doug tugged on the ropes he loosely wrapped around his wrists the night before, but the binds limited his movement. His eyes followed the rope until Doug saw the knot constraining him to the side of the wagon. Doug twisted around and got to his feet, then yanked on the taut rope. Even with added leverage, Doug could not slacken the threads that held him.

"Good morning," Stephen said after emerging from behind the covered wagon.

Doug's face displayed a somewhat panicked look.

"I think the ropes got tangled up during the night," Doug said.

"No, I tightened them," Stephen explained.

"What?" Doug asked.

"You didn't really think we were abolitionists, did you?" Stephen asked.

"I knew it!" Doug yelped.

Robert awakened in a jerk and rose to his feet. He quickly recoiled in the rope's grasp.

"What's happening?" Robert wondered aloud.

"They're going to sell us at auction," Doug told his friend. "I told you!"

"You're not going to auction," Stephen said. "We already have a buyer."

Luke appeared from the back of the wagon with a rifle on his shoulder.

"Stephen is going to loosen your ropes and then you're going to get in the back of the wagon, nice and easy-like," Luke instructed. "Do you understand?"

"I won't do it," Doug said. "You can't sell me like an animal! I won't do it!"

"Then you'll be dead," Luke said as he lowered the rifle and pointed it at Doug.

Doug looked at the weapon and knew the man was telling him the truth. The young man said nothing in reply.

"Go ahead, Stephen. He hears what I'm saying," Luke said.

Stephen untied the ropes from the wagon and pulled the young slaves to the rear of the primitive carriage.

"Climb in," Luke ordered.

Robert and Doug reluctantly climbed into the wagon and sat on a large wooden box. Stephen climbed in behind them and tied the ropes to a metal loop on the floor of the wagon.

"You come out of there before we get to Fayetteville and we'll shoot you," Stephen warned.

Stephen unrolled a canvass door at the back of the wagon, concealing the stolen men. The two thieves climbed onto the front of the wagon and with a snap of the reins, the horses pulled away.

Doug and Robert swayed in the back of the wagon as it rocked along the bumpy road. Doug leaned forward and began working on the tangle that secured him to the loop.

"What are you doing?" Robert asked.

"I'm trying to get loose," Doug said.

"Stop," Robert insisted. "Didn't you hear what they said? They'll shoot us."

"We can untie ourselves, then jump out the back and take off running," Doug said.

"You can't outrun that gun," Robert informed Doug.

Doug continued to work on the rope. Robert grabbed Doug by the shoulders and pulled him back.

"Stop it before you get yourself killed," Robert said sternly.

A frustrated Doug took a seat on a box opposite Robert.

"I knew we couldn't trust them, but oh, no, you wanted to go with them," Doug said. "Well, guess what? Now you're going with them. This is all your fault."

"Don't say that. You wanted to steal that man's food," Robert retorted.

"I wasn't the one sitting there grinning like an idiot when they said they were abolitionists," Doug said sharply.

"Don't get mad at me for having hope," Robert replied.

"You can't put hope in people like that," Doug responded. "You have to watch out for yourself. You can't trust nobody."

"I trusted you and look what that got me," Robert stated.

"If you listened to me, we wouldn't be in this mess," Doug said.

"I did listen to you," Robert noted. "That's why I'm here. You said we should run away and now here I am in the back of this wagon."

"Don't blame me for this," Doug replied angrily. "I'm not the stupid one here. You can't even read. I should have escaped by myself."

Robert paused for a moment, absorbing the verbal gut punch administered by Doug's degrading words.

"Maybe I can't read, but it don't mean I'm stupid. I don't know if you can really read. You say you can, but you might just be saying that. Either way, thinking you're smart didn't help you when you fell into that river. If stupid old me hadn't been there, you would have drowned."

"Man, don't even talk to me," Doug said dismissively. "I should have left you at the farm."

Robert withstood Doug's scorn and lowered his head. The two young runaways sat in uncomfortable silence.

After sauntering along rugged dirt roads for a few hours, the wagon came to a stop. Light poured into the back of the wagon as the assailants rolled up the door. Doug squinted as he watched Luke and Stephen remove a large box from the wagon.

"Just sit tight," Luke advised. "We'll have something to eat shortly and then be on our way again."

"I have to go to the bathroom," Doug said.

"I'll bring you out one at a time. Once you're done, you go back in the wagon," Stephen declared.

Stephen looked after the slaves as Luke prepared food. Once Robert and Doug were secure in the wagon again, Stephen joined his associate around the fire for food and rest. When the food was ready, Luke handed each slave a plate of pork and cornbread and a metal cup of water.

"There you go boys, eat up," Luke said as if trying to seem charitable.

Luke returned to the fire as Doug and Robert hastily grabbed the food and drink. They ate hurriedly and spoke not a word to each other. Doug shoved food into his mouth faster than he could chew and swallow. Doug reached for his drink to help wash it all down, but in his urgency he knocked the cup over, spilling the water on the floor. He placed his hand on his forehead, annoyed by his own clumsiness.

Robert stopped eating and gently reached for his cup. He extended his hand across the area between them and offered the drink to Doug. Doug picked up his cup and held it next to Robert's mug. Robert tilted the cup and poured some water into Doug's vessel. Doug nodded before taking a drink and swallowing his food.

"Thank you," Doug said.

"You're welcome," Robert replied.

The slaves continued their meal, albeit more slowly than before.

"I'm sorry for what I said earlier," Doug offered. "It was mean and uncalled for. You're not stupid, Robert."

"It's all right," Robert responded. "I'm sure a lot worse is waiting for me where we're heading."

"I appreciate what you did for me at the river," Doug said. "We have to support one another, lift each other up. That's what my grandfather used to say. We have to lift each other up, not tear each other down."

The youngsters continued to eat their food and sat in somber meditation about their fate.

Once they had rested for a while, Luke and Stephen loaded the box onto the wagon. Soon Doug and Robert were rocking and wobbling with the movement of the wagon again.

The thieves traveled for another three hours before arriving in Fayetteville with their living plunder. Luke rolled open the door of the wagon, allowing in the scant remaining light of the day. Stephen climbed in and untied the two slaves.

"Come on out, nice and slow," Luke warned Doug and Robert.

The young men climbed out carefully and stood behind the wagon. Stephen took the rifle from Luke and kept it aimed at Doug and Robert.

"I'll go fetch them," Luke said before walking away.

The bandits stopped near the market square of the town. The Market House, a two-story brick building, stood in the center of the square. A series of arches provided access to a public market in an open area beneath the Market House. Doug watched wagons and their cargoes pass through the square and understood he was nothing more than a commodity in the eyes of his captors.

Luke returned shortly with six other men, one of them nicely dressed in a tall hat and a cane in hand.

"Here they are, gentlemen," Luke said as he handed some money to Stephen. "It's been nice doing business with you."

Two men grabbed Doug by the arms and dragged him away. The men who held Doug followed the man with the tall hat. Doug turned to see the other three men taking Robert in a different direction.

"Robert!" Doug called out.

"Doug!" Robert cried back.

"Wait, where are you taking us?" Doug asked his detainers.

"I don't know where they're taking him, but you're headed to South Carolina," the man with the hat answered.

"Robert, wait!" Doug yelled.

The farther they dragged him from Robert, the greater the sense of fear increased in Doug. In desperation, Doug pulled one arm free from his holders and tried to run. The other brute held fast to Doug's arm. Doug punched the man, but he would not relinquish his grip. The other lout regained his hold on Doug's arm just as the man with the hat approached. The man grasped his thick shiny cane tightly and whacked Doug against the leg. Doug buckled and fell to his knees. The saddened slave remained on the ground as he watched Robert disappear into the back of a wagon. A shriek of outright despair emanated from Doug. The noise was an indescribable expression of pain, the kind of babble that seems unintelligible, yet fully illustrates the agony of the soul.

"Get him to the holding pen," the man with the tall hat ordered. "He can wait there until the boat arrives."

The repugnant men pulled Doug along an alley before stopping at a tall iron gate. The gate squeaked ominously as it opened. They led Doug into a courtyard at the rear of a two-story brick structure. Doug saw other slaves in gated pens adjacent to the right wall of the courtyard. The fiends led Doug to a narrow passage at the back of the building. The men guided Doug down some stairs to a dingy hallway. Moisture clung to the walls of the dank, shadowy passage. A lone lantern hung from the ceiling, illuminating a sturdy door. One of Doug's captors used a large key to unlock the door before pushing it open. The men shoved Doug into the room and forced him to sit on a bench along the right wall of the room. They fastened chains on his wrists and ankles, then attached the binds to a metal ring anchored to the floor. Doug observed his temporary prison, a room made almost entirely of old red bricks. There was no window in the room. The men exited the chamber and pulled the heavy door closed. A sense of finality washed over Doug as he heard the click of the lock. Doug sat silently in the darkened room, the only light entering through a thin space between the bottom of the door and the floor. Doug stared into the bleak emptiness in front of him as the minutes torturously ticked away, and he felt hopeless and utterly alone.

The scene before Doug was unchanged for what seemed like an eternity until a shadow passed across the light at the underside of the door. Doug heard a door open down the hall and the rattling of keys followed.

"I think it went in there," a voice said in the hall.

More shadows appeared beneath the door and a clank came from the lock. The door swung open slightly on old hinges. A broad beam of light formed a pathway on the floor, leading directly to a rat in the opposite corner.

"There it is!" a man with a long goatee said.

The two men awkwardly stumbled into the room and went after the rat. The rat moved about rapidly, running back and forth and avoiding the men. Curiously, the animal didn't exit through the open door.

Doug watched the men fumble in their attempts to catch the rat. The light coming from the hall helped diminish the darkness around Doug. He looked at his feet and examined the irons gripping his ankles. Doug heard a noise to his left and turned to see a rat appearing from a hole in the wall. The animal moved around Doug's feet and a second rat exited the hole directly after the first. Another rat followed that one, then another, and another. A parade of rats withdrew from the hole and scurried about at Doug's feet. Doug kicked as much as the chains would allow, hoping to drive the rats away. It seemed like seventy-five rats thronged about the young slave's feet.

"Hey!" Doug called out. "There's a bunch over here."

The men continued their farcical pursuit of the single rat that danced around the brightly lit portion of the floor as if they didn't even hear Doug.

"Hey! There's a bunch of rats over here!" Doug barked again.

The men stopped and looked at Doug.

"I don't see nothing, do you Bart?" the bearded man asked.

"Na, I don't see nothing neither, Russell," Bart replied.

The odd men resumed their silly hunt of the lone rat.

"They're all over the place!" Doug decried. "Help, get them off of me!"

Bart and Russell stopped again and stared at Doug with annoyed expressions.

"We ain't got time for them rats," Russell said.

"Yeah, can't you see this rat?" Bart asked.

"We have to deal with this rat. Them rats over there ain't important. This rat is the real problem. You stop worrying about them rats. If you ain't gonna help with this rat, just keep your mouth shut and don't say nothing," Russell advised.

The light coming in the door seemed like a spotlight on the men and their target. Doug and the dozens of rats around him remained shrouded in dimness and obscurity.

"Oops, there he goes," Bart said as he watched the rat scurry out of the room.

Bart and Russell gave chase and slammed the door closed behind them. The rats continued to move around Doug and a few climbed his legs.

"Hey! Get these rats off of me!" Doug yelled.

Doug shrieked and howled and flailed about to rid himself of the critters creeping around and on him. Doug heard people stampeding down the hall. The door flung open and Bart and Russell walked back into the room.

"What is going on in here?" Bart asked loudly.

"The rats," Doug said.

"What rats?" Russell challenged.

Doug glanced at his feet and saw nothing.

"They were just here, a bunch of them," Doug stated.

"You think you're funny," Russell said.

"No, I don't know what happened. They were here just a second ago," Doug proclaimed.

"He's playing games with us. I think he needs to learn some manners," Bart said.

"Go fetch the driver," Russell ordered.

Bart dashed from the room and left the door open.

"You think you can holler and we'll just come running?" Russell asked.

"No, I swear, there were rats," Doug repeated.

"The only rat I see is you," Russell hissed. "All you have to do is what we tell you. But you can't do that. You have to be one that tries to think on your own. Well, we'll fix that."

Bart returned in the company of a thin black man in his early thirties.

"Get him ready," Russell told the others.

Bart and the slave driver lifted Doug onto his feet and swiftly pulled his shirt up, exposing his back. The men spun Doug around so he faced the wall before pushing him to his knees. Bart forced Doug to place his hands on the bench, then he planted his heavy boot on the chains that linked Doug's cuffs. Bart handed a long, thin wooden pole to the driver.

"Get to it and don't spare your arm," Russell directed.

Doug turned his head as far as he could toward the men behind him.

"Please, you don't have to do this," Doug stated.

"Yeah, we do," Russell said. "You need to learn. You only do what we tell you to do. You only think what we tell you to think."

The driver struck Doug on the back with the pole, causing him to scream. The black man hit Doug again and again. Doug yelled and tried to catch his breath between blows. Doug could hardly move, thus he consumed the totality of each stroke. The beating stopped and Doug gagged as he tried to collect himself.

"What are you stopping for?" Russell asked.

Doug barely held his head up.

"Please stop," Doug implored the men.

"It looks like he's getting the message," Bart said.

Doug beseeched the other slave to stop beating him.

"Please don't hurt me anymore, man," Doug appealed.

"Be quiet you," the driver replied before he hit Doug again.

The driver hit Doug on the legs, the rear end, and his back. The assaulter tired and stopped again.

"Why are you hurting me, brother?" Doug asked in a low voice.

"You not acting right," the driver replied. "You act right and this won't happen."

"That's enough, get him up," Russell instructed.

Bart and the driver lifted Doug back onto his feet and pulled his shirt down. The men escorted the driver out of the room. Russell offered a last word of warning before exiting.

"I don't want to hear another sound out of you. I don't care if there are a thousand rats," the man said.

Russell slammed the door shut, encasing Doug in blackness again. Doug moved onto the bench and stretched out on his side. Isolation and excruciating pain drew over Doug like an eclipse that blocked out hope and pity. Doug attempted to keep fear at bay by thinking about his mother and grandfather. He yearned for the reassuring touch of his mother's hand.

After sitting in the darkened room for an hour and a half, Doug could make out basic features. Being able to see the wall and bench on the other side of the room settled Doug's nerves a little. Doug couldn't sleep but rested as best he could in the damp, musty chamber. Anxiety pounced on him again when he heard footsteps in the hall. Doug sat up as the door swung open with a loud squeak.

"On your feet," Russell ordered Doug. "Time to go."

"You get to go on a boat ride," Bart added. "Ain't you the lucky one?"

The men led Doug up the narrow passage and out into the street. The thoroughfare was full of people moving about, many of them in the same direction Doug was being taken. After marching for a mile, they brought Doug to the banks of the Cape Fear River, where a riverboat awaited. Nicely dressed people lingered around waiting to board the ship. The men took Doug to a ramp near the back of the boat. Doug gazed upon the immense paddlewheel as he walked up the ramp. A pair of tall smokestacks reached into the air near the bow of the vessel.

Bart and Russell escorted Doug to the bowels of the ship and placed him in a room with dozens of other slaves. Overseers shackled together the men and women in the room. The human chain grew longer each time the villains added an enslaved person. Soon the room was full of slaves lined up against the walls, three and four persons deep.

"Have a pleasant trip," Bart said before he slammed the door closed.

Doug could barely hear the click of the lock over the men's laughter. Doug looked at the expressionless faces in the room. The condition of bondage was as customary to them as breathing. The sight only hardened Doug's resolve. He had to get free. Moments later, Doug felt the ship move and heard the splashing of the paddlewheel.

There was an open area in the center of the room, but Doug couldn't move to it while tethered to the other slaves. A lantern hung from the ceiling and illuminated the room. Shadows moved around the place with the gentle rocking of the boat. Doug lifted his hands and examined the shackles. He tried to pull them apart, twisted and turned them, and banged them together. The endeavor was useless, and Doug remained harnessed to the other people in the room.

"Come on, let's work together and free ourselves," Doug said to the others.

Nobody replied to Doug. He continued to struggle with the binds to no avail.

"Hey," Doug said to the man next to him. "If we work together, maybe we can get free."

Doug yanked on the chain, jerking the man's arm toward him.

"You pull that way, and I'll pull this way. Maybe something will come loose," Doug told the man.

Doug tugged on the chain again. The man took no action and Doug shook his arm again.

"We have to work together," Doug insisted.

"Leave me alone," the man replied.

Doug wiggled and pulled on the chains again, but only grew more frustrated.

"Ugh, I have to get free," Doug trumpeted as he contended with the manacles.

"You're already free," a soft, familiar voice stated.

Doug looked around the room in disbelief.

"Who said that?" Doug asked urgently.

Doug looked across the room and saw two slaves move apart as far as they were able. A distinct figure appeared in the faint light of the corner. The man wore a bucket hat that concealed his eyes in the dimly lit room. A short salt and pepper beard clutched the man's face.

"Grandpa?" Doug asked with more than a hint of bewilderment in his voice.

"You're already free, son," the man said.

Doug lifted his hands again and discovered the shackles were on the floor. Nothing restrained him to another person. Even more perplexed, Doug stared at this man that was recognizable and strange at the same time.

"You go make me proud now," the man with the pleasant voice said to Doug.

Doug moved to the door of the room and turned the handle. The exit was unlocked and opened easily. Doug looked at the man in the hat and motioned for him.

"Grandpa, let's go. Let's get out of here," Doug stated.

"I can't go with you, but I'll see you again one day," the man replied.

The people in front of the man stepped toward each other and concealed him again.

"Grandpa," Doug called.

There was no reply. Doug poked his head into the hallway, but there was no sentry. The hall was empty.

"Come on, let's go," Doug said as he waved to the others.

The people in the room did not respond to Doug's overtures, remaining in the room as if they didn't even see him.

"Let's go," Doug pleaded again. "You don't have to stay in there."

"Leave us be," said the man who earlier urged Doug not to bother him.

Discouraged and confused, Doug cautiously crept down the passage. He stopped at each intersection and looked for watchmen before progressing. The corridor was weirdly quiet save for the noise of the boilers and engine. Apart from the enslaved people, there wasn't another soul to be found in the lower levels of the boat.

Doug discovered a staircase where moonlight cascaded down like a waterfall. He approached warily and slowly made his way up the steps. As Doug neared the top, he heard a train of voices that sounded like a grand procession on deck. Doug peeked through the open doorway and observed the merry scene at the bow. Well-dressed men and women lingered and conversed cheerfully in what seemed like a small gala. Doug wondered if he should retreat to the levels below. The emptiness behind him suggested Doug could roam about the belly of the ship to his heart's content, so long as he stayed there. To reach freedom, Doug would have to risk being seen.

Doug tiptoed onto the deck of the ship, and slowly but hurriedly moved toward the stern. Upon seeing the rotating paddlewheel, he realized he couldn't jump off the back of the ship. Doug moved a short distance toward the bow, far enough to feel confident that he could avoid the paddlewheel. Doug grabbed the handrail and lifted his leg over. On the other side of the railing, Doug prepared himself for the jump. He gazed into the river below, uneasy about what lay beneath its inky black surface.

"Don't do it!" a man cried out.

Doug turned to see a sharply dressed man with a long mustache. The man stood about twenty-five feet away with his arm outstretched.

"You'll plunge to your death. Please, don't do it," the mustached man said.

"I'm getting off this ship," Doug replied.

"The wheel will pull you under and pummel you," the man proclaimed.

"I can jump pretty far. It won't get me," Doug boasted.

Other well-dressed partygoers approached and stood behind the man.

"If you survive the fall, you won't last long on your own. The world is a dangerous place for you," the man stated.

"This ship is a dangerous place for me," Doug countered.

"Trust me, I know what's best. Climb down from there and stay here with us. We'll take care of you," the man promised.

"You'll take care of me?" Doug questioned. "How? Give me a little bread to eat, maybe two shirts to wear? And when I don't do what you tell me to do, then I'm no good to you anymore. Then what?"

"Stay here with us where it's safe," the man suggested again. "It's safer here with us on the ship."

"I have to be free," Doug said.

"Is not safety more imperative than freedom?" the mustached man challenged.

Doug looked at the murky water. The pleading nobleman's eyes were full of longing as he waved Doug back over the rail.

"What is safety without freedom?" Doug asked.

Doug didn't wait for the man's reply. He jumped from the ship and plunged feet first toward the river. Doug pierced the water like an arrow.

Water splashed on Doug's face, and he sat up with great haste. Doug's heart raced as he tried to make sense of his surroundings. Stephen stood over him with a cup. Robert sat beside the fire with Luke. Doug checked his unbound hands.

"Sorry about that," Stephen said. "We couldn't wake you. It seemed you were having a mighty unpleasant dream. Let's have some breakfast."

Doug sat for a moment and calmed his breathing.

The strongest shackles are often unseen, and self can be an inescapable dungeon.

12

The Wisdom of Old Men and Trees

Doug and Robert helped the abolitionists break camp after breakfast. They finished the work in no time. After loading the final crate, Luke leaned against the wagon and rested.

"Thanks for your help, fellas," Luke said as he tried to catch his breath.

"You're still welcome to come to the station house with us," Stephen offered. "It's not too far away."

"You'll be on your way north in a couple of days," Luke added.

Robert stared at Doug with his eyes laden with hope.

"I appreciate it," Doug started. "But I really need to get to Durham and find my mom."

Robert's smile straightened a little.

"What about you, Robert?" Luke asked.

Robert peered at Doug.

"Come on, Doug. They can take us north," Robert said.

"I have to get home," Doug replied. "My home isn't in the north."

"You don't know if your mother is still there," Robert stated.

"She is," Doug said. "I just know it."

"Well, how about it?" Luke asked Robert.

Robert looked northward beyond the wagon, then glanced at Doug. He faced the ground and wrestled with his thoughts.

"You can go with them if you want to," Doug said. "But my mom's place is a lot better than where they'll take you."

Robert stared at the ground for another moment before lifting his head.

"Mr. Luke, Mr. Stephen, I sure do appreciate your kindness. I would love to go with you, I swear I would, but I can't let Doug go all on his own," Robert said.

"I admire your loyalty and courage," Stephen replied with a smile.

"If you're going to Durham, head west," Luke said. "Keep the sun at your back and stick to the trees."

Stephen handed each young man something wrapped in cloth and tied with a string.

"Here's a little pork and cornbread for your journey. It isn't much, but it'll keep you from getting too hungry," Stephen stated.

The abolitionists climbed onto the wagon, and Stephen grabbed the reins.

"Good luck to you, boys," Luke offered as the wagon pulled away.

Doug picked up the ax he stole at Lester's homestead, and the two runaways were on their way again.

Doug and Robert stayed near the edge of the woods, as Luke advised them to do. The young men welcomed the sun and light breeze the day offered, a pleasant alternative to the rainy muck they traveled in the previous day.

"I sure hope you know how to get to Durham," said Robert.

Doug wasn't sure he could find the city, but felt if he went west he might eventually cross an unseen border between the nightmare and home.

"We'll get there," Doug reassured his friend. "We just need to keep going west."

Doug and Robert continued to follow the tree line and walked at a slow, almost casual pace. The serenity of the day made it easy for Doug and Robert to keep fear and anxiety at bay. There was neither a callous man nor ravenous beast in sight, not even a foul scent on the wind. Doug watched a squirrel race up a tree while a tiny chipmunk foraged on the ground. It was a delightful day and Doug felt home couldn't be too far off.

The boys alarmed a dove as they neared, and the bird swiftly took to the sky. Robert watched the bird soar over the treetops and glide as easily as a leaf on a breeze.

"I wonder what it's like to be a bird and fly," Robert thought aloud. "You wouldn't have to touch this rough dirt and sharp grass no more. You could go anywhere you want. Instead of picking cotton, you could hide in the clouds."

"Someday, people will touch the clouds," Doug told Robert.

"What?" Robert replied doubtingly. "Are you saying people fly where you come from?"

"Yeah," Doug said with conviction.

"What? People don't have wings, Doug," Robert pointed out.

"No, they fly in airplanes," Doug stated before realizing Robert had no concept of an airplane. "It's a machine."

Robert's confusion was obvious, and Doug grappled with finding a logical explanation.

"It's like a wagon with wings and it flies," Doug explained.

Robert laughed and snorted at the thought. Doug could only smile himself as he realized how absurd it must have sounded to his companion.

"I can see a wagon flying through the air and flapping wings," Robert said, still laughing.

"Well, it doesn't work exactly like that, but you have the idea," said Doug.

The partners continued on their way. Robert watched the bird vanish into the glorious blue beyond, and he never felt so free.

Doug and Robert walked for several miles. The midday sun hovered directly over the young men when they happened upon a large fallen tree at the boundary of the meadow and the woodland. The thick tree provided a perfect spot to sit and rest while indulging in the forest's shade. The travelers sat quietly and ate their plain food. Doug looked around him and examined the terrain. The tree line ended a short distance ahead, which would leave them walking in the open again. Despite the risk, Doug looked forward to savoring the beauty of the day.

A thick oak tree stood beside the boys. It was much larger than the surrounding trees, as if lording over them. Doug grabbed the ax and rose to his feet. He stood in front of the tree and studied its broad trunk.

"Watch back," Doug advised Robert.

Robert pushed the last bit of cornbread into his mouth and stood up, then moved behind Doug. Doug extended his arm toward the tree, like a football player preparing for a kick. Once he determined the angle, Doug raised the ax over his right shoulder and hurled it toward the tree. The ax missed the tree completely and came to rest on the ground behind it.

"What are you doing?" Robert asked, somewhat startled. "Did you see a snake?"

"No. I just wanted to see if I could make it stick in the tree," Doug replied.

Doug retrieved the ax and returned to Robert.

"Let me try again," Doug said as he positioned himself once more.

Doug stared at the tree as if he could intimidate it before slinging the implement at the wood again. The handle hit the tree, and the ax bounced back to the ground.

Doug moved to fetch the ax again.

"I'll do it," Robert asserted.

"OK, try it," Doug said as he handed the ax to Robert.

Robert lined up in front of the tree, took his time adjusting his feet and shoulders, then heaved the ax. The edge of the blade struck and chipped a little bark away from the tree.

"Oh, almost!" Doug exclaimed.

Robert smiled in delight at the result of his first attempt.

Doug recovered the ax and scampered back to Robert.

"Here, try again," Doug said as he passed the ax to Robert.

Robert slung the ax again and watched it ricochet off the tree before sticking into the ground. The boys burst into chuckling again.

"You're supposed to stab the tree, not the ground," said Doug with a toothy smile.

The boys spent at least half an hour taking turns throwing the ax. They didn't get the ax stuck in the tree a single time. The lack of success didn't matter. Neither young man could remember the last time he laughed with such exuberance. The youngsters knew they couldn't stay and play all day, although they wanted to. They had to be on their way. Doug's mom was waiting.

Doug and Robert meandered across a large, grassy field, almost leisurely. The lower humidity of the day made for pleasant traveling conditions, despite the sun having free rein over a cloudless sky.

"I hope everyone back at the farm is all right," Robert said. "I sure am going to miss Lucille."

Doug lifted his hand to cover his smile.

"Oh snap, you like Lucille," Doug replied, laughing as he would with Isaiah and the fellas at the park in Durham.

"She's nice," Robert replied, slightly annoyed by Doug's reaction to the revelation.

"She has a baby, though," Doug noted. "Where is her baby daddy?"

"The daddy was killed before the baby was born. Got kicked in the head by a mule one day," Robert informed Doug.

"Dang, that sucks, yo. But hey, she's available then. Tell the truth," Doug uttered, grinning ear to ear. "You tapped that ho."

"I tapped a hoe on the ground when Lester made me work in the vegetable garden," Robert replied in complete blindness to urban slang.

"No, I mean a ho, like a woman," Doug told him.

"You call women hoes where you come from?" Robert asked.

"Yeah, but not like you mean. A ho is what we call a woman. If you have a woman, that's your ho, your bitch," Doug said.

"That sounds dumb," Robert stated.

"It's slang, like ho is another way of saying whore," Doug explained.

"Why would you call a woman you like a whore?" Robert asked. "That don't make no kind of sense. I would never call Lucille a ho or a whore, or anything like that. I wouldn't talk to any woman that way. My grandpa would've hit me upside my head for being so disrespectful."

"It's all right, man," Doug responded. "It's just the way people talk where I come from. At least a lot of people do."

"It doesn't sound like people are very nice to each other there," Robert added.

Doug reflected on the comment that hit pretty close to the mark.

"Sometimes they can be," Doug said in a solemn tone.

Doug realized how his words resonated with Robert and he felt an urge to show contrition.

"I'm sorry, man," Doug offered. "I wasn't trying to be disrespectful to your girl."

"It's all right. She isn't my girl," Robert replied. "I may never see her again."

"Don't worry, there are plenty of chicks, I mean girls, where we're going," Doug assured Robert.

"What about you? Haven't you ever liked a girl?" Robert asked.

"Uh," Doug began, hesitant to answer honestly. "There was a girl back where I come from that was pretty nice."

"Tell me about her," Robert urged. "What was she like?"

"Well, she's pretty and nice," Doug said. "She's kind of quiet, but not afraid to speak her mind. Oh, and really smart. We used to be in some classes together, back when I got good grades. My grandpa liked her. He said she kept herself up and didn't dress like a floozie. Grandpa used to tell me I better not come home with a girl who has the word juicy tattooed on her neck. I don't think he was joking, even though he laughed about it. He thought every woman should be like my grandma."

"She sounds nice," Robert commented. "I never knew my grandma, but my grandpa never forgot her. He never got with another woman after she was sold."

"I didn't know my grandma either," Doug said. "She died before I was even a year old. My grandpa talked about her sometimes. He would tell a funny story about her and laugh, but then get sad. He never married again, said he wouldn't find another one like her."

Robert removed the hat from his head and looked over it, brushing off a tiny clump of dried mud.

"My grandpa would be so happy to know I'm gonna be free," Robert said. "I wish he was going with us."

"He's still with you, man," Doug assured him. "I feel like my grandpa watches me. Sometimes I swear I hear him scolding me when I do something bad. I'm glad my mom has all his old pictures."

"What's pictures?" Robert inquired.

"Well, it's like," Doug floundered for a moment in his effort to find a description. "So you see that tree way out in the field?"

"I see it," Robert replied.

"Now take your hands like this," Doug said as he cupped his hands and touched the tips of his fingers together. "Now hold them up so the tree is in the middle of your hands."

Robert mimicked Doug and extended his arms before him toward the tree.

"That's it. Now imagine if you could take what you see in your hands with you anywhere. You could put that scene in your pocket and carry it with you, but it's not bigger than it looks now," Doug explained.

"I can't put no tree in my pocket," Robert said as he chortled at the thought.

"No, you're not putting the tree in your pocket," Doug explained. "It's like a painting. You can hang it on the wall, or keep a small one with you."

"Oh, I understand," Robert replied, wide-eyed.

"Any time you want to remember this place, or this day, you can look at a picture. You can look back in time because it doesn't change. Years from now that tree will be different, but you could still see it like it is now. I know what my grandpa looked like when he was young because of pictures."

Robert darted off and raced toward the tree.

"Where are you going?" Doug petitioned to know.

"To the tree," Robert called back.

Doug chased after him.

The tree stood alone in the vast field, like the gatekeeper of a magical realm beyond. Rays of sunshine burst through the clouds and pointed to the tree as if drawn to it like Robert. The grass, gently blown by the wind, seemed to part and clear a path for the delighted boys.

When Doug reached the tree, he found Robert standing beneath it with a gigantic smile.

"Look, apples," Robert said, pointing to the fruit dangling from the limbs above them.

Doug looked at the inviting fruit, then observed the ground under him as he savored the shade of the tree. Wind and gravity had scattered apples on the ground beneath the tree.

"Look at all this," Doug said as he bent over to grab an apple.

"Nah," Robert responded. "Don't mess with that. I'll get us some good ones."

Robert climbed the tree and made his way to a branch about six and a half feet off the ground. His belly rested against the rough bark as he pulled himself along the tree's extremity to reach a couple of plump, luscious apples. Robert extended his arm, but could not reach his reward. The young man grasped the branch with both hands and shook it. But the tree would not surrender its bounty.

"Let me see that ax," Robert instructed.

Doug stood beneath Robert and lifted the ax so the handle was easily reachable. Robert grabbed the tool and pulled it to him. Doug took a few steps back while Robert extended the ax toward the apples.

"Be careful," Doug advised.

One swift swipe of the ax and an apple fell. Doug moved quickly to retrieve it. Robert inched a little farther on the branch, like a giant caterpillar. He accomplished the mission with another swing of the ax. Robert cautiously climbed down from the tree as Doug collected the other apple.

The two escapees stood together and ate, staring in the direction from which they came. Doug stayed in the shade and pondered the path ahead as he surveyed the steps behind. Such an open and beautiful expanse didn't exist in the urban desert formed of concrete and brick he called home.

"I wonder how old this tree is," Doug contemplated openly.

"I don't know," Robert answered.

"Think of everything it has seen," Doug said.

"A tree can't see nothing, Doug," Robert insisted. "It ain't got no eyes."

"I know that. Maybe it sees a different way," Doug replied. "Maybe it sees things we can't."

The runaways remained in thoughtful silence, lost in reverie, and enjoyed the breeze and serenity around them. Doug took another bite of the crisp, firm apple and checked his surroundings. He pivoted to face the tree and witnessed a breathtaking sight. Unable to speak, Doug gently touched Robert on the shoulder and pushed him around. Robert turned slowly, and his eyes widened when he saw a deer standing on the other side of the tree. The boys beamed in subdued astonishment at the sight of the regal animal standing approximately thirty feet away. The deer was about six feet tall and weighed around two hundred pounds. A narrow band of white circled the animal's muzzle just behind the nose. A set of prominent antlers adorned the buck's head, like a crown befitting the majesty of the creature. The animal lowered its head and snatched an apple, undeterred by the gawking defectors a short distance away. Being frozen in wonderment rather than fear was a new thrill for both of them. Doug and Robert watched the deer with smiles fixed on their faces. When the deer finished eating, it raised its head and looked across the field. The animal stood motionless for a moment before trotting away in the same direction Doug and Robert were going.

The refugees stepped around the tree and watched the deer stroll away. The creature stopped midway across the field and looked back at Doug and Robert. It sniffed the air before bounding from the field with haste.

"That was so cool," Doug said excitedly. "I've never seen one so close."

Robert couldn't bring himself to speak. The smile on his face wouldn't move, and it restricted his ability to talk.

"Come on," Doug said as he bent over.

The boys searched the ground for apples that were in good condition for eating. After collecting a few pieces of suitable fruit, the boys continued their journey, following the deer's path.

Doug and Robert walked for miles. The sun was low in the sky and blinding them, so Doug knew they were going in the right direction and evening was nigh. The young men saw trees in the distance. While they enjoyed the splendor and sense of liberation the pastureland afforded, Doug and Robert required the safety of the forest.

As they approached the woods, the boys encountered an old nemesis. A narrow river crossed their path. The water's edge was several feet down an embankment with a smooth, gradual slope. Robert looked at the trees beyond with yearning and disappointment on his face simultaneously.

"How are we going to get across?" Robert asked.

Doug examined the waterway. Muddy water flowed through the channel, and it moved slowly despite the heavy rain of the day before. Large branches and dead leaves collected against a fallen tree in a bend of the river about twenty yards to Doug's left.

"We can swim across," Doug proposed.

"I can't swim," Robert replied.

"It's probably not too deep," Doug suggested.

"It doesn't have to be too deep to drown in," Robert countered without a morsel of sarcasm.

"Let me check it out," Doug recommended.

Doug traversed the embankment easily, stopping at the river's edge. He watched the flow of the water, studying it and planning his means of attack. Doug began by placing his right leg in the water. He felt a modest push against his calf, but nothing threatening or distressing. Once he was confident in its safety, Doug stepped into the river. The water reached his waist after several steps. Doug turned to see Robert standing above him at the top of the small hill.

"See, it's all right," Doug said. "It's really not that deep."

"Keep on going. You ain't no way across that river yet," Robert stated.

Doug moved farther out, hoping he could install some confidence in his comrade. Doug stopped when the water reached his chest and he was standing in the middle of the river.

"It only comes up to here," Doug called back to Robert.

"Let's go around and find a bridge," Robert advised.

"It's fine. You can walk across," Doug said. "It's really not too deep."

Robert silently fought his dread and remained at the top of the embankment.

"What if something goes wrong?" Robert asked. "I can't swim."

"Well, I'll teach you how," Doug offered. "It's easy."

"How you going to teach me when you almost drowned?" Robert responded.

"That was different. It's not storming now," Doug said, trying to strengthen his friend's courage.

Robert didn't answer. He remained steadfast in his appeal to find a route around the river. Doug moved closer to the bank and into shallower water.

"You can do it," Doug said encouragingly.

"I can't. Let's find a bridge," Robert implored.

"Are you chicken or something?" Doug teased.

Doug slapped the water, causing it to splash toward Robert, but it didn't get far up the embankment. Doug challenged Robert's bravery and made noises that mimicked a chicken, hoping to goad his buddy into the water. Both young men smiled as Doug slapped the water harder and sent the spray flying toward Robert.

"Are you afraid to even get wet?" Doug asked in a heckling way as he whacked the river again.

Robert laughed heartily as the water landed harmlessly on the side of the embankment.

"Come on, get a little closer," Doug challenged.

Laughing, Robert descended the small hill and stood at the water's edge. The boys grinned at each other in a playful standoff to see who would flinch first. Doug swiftly moved his hand, but stopped before striking the water. Robert turned quickly but cut short his retreat once he realized Doug didn't make contact.

"Ha, fooled you," Doug declared.

Robert chuckled and tiptoed closer to the river again.

"Come on, you're right there. Just jump in," Doug suggested.

"I ain't getting in there," Robert said as he snickered.

"Chicken," Doug declared again as he splashed Robert.

Robert turned and dropped the ax before charging up the embankment to escape the reach of Doug's aquatic bombardment.

"Bok, bok, bok!" Doug jeered while he watched Robert race to the crest of the small ridge.

Robert stopped when he reached the top and looked across the field. Something instantly erased the smile from Robert's face. The young slave stood like a mime depicting a ghost story. He was stiff with fear and his mouth hung open, but neither word nor sound escaped.

"Robert, what is it?" Doug earnestly wanted to know.

The scared youth turned toward Doug with a face that expressed sheer terror.

"Doug, it's those slave catchers."

13

Tangled Wilderness

The terror upon Robert's face asserted the sincerity of his words.

"It's those slave catchers, Doug," Robert repeated. "They have dogs."

Doug listened attentively and heard the howls of the approaching dogs.

"What are we gonna do, Doug?" a panicked Robert asked.

"Come on, Robert. We have to get across the river," Doug stated.

The wailing of the dogs intensified as Robert rushed towards the waterfront.

"I'm afraid, Doug," Robert confessed.

"Just jump in. I'll help you," Doug urged.

Robert breathed deeply, heaving air as he struggled in panic's grasp.

"Calm down, Robert," Doug advised. "Get in the water. Let's go."

Robert observed the river, then glanced back at the field. Should he risk drowning or being maimed by the dogs, he wondered? It was an impossible choice.

"Doug, come on," Robert said. "We can run and find a bridge."

"Get in here," Doug insisted.

The dogs drew near, but Robert's heart pounded so hard he could barely hear them.

"Doug, let's go," Robert pleaded. "Help me."

"I'm trying to help you. Jump in the water. I'll get you," Doug promised.

"Don't leave me, Doug," Robert begged.

"I won't. Now come on, let's go," Doug insisted.

Robert stood by the water and tried to muster enough bravery to dive.

"Please Doug, help me," Robert asked again.

Two surly dogs emerged and descended the hill. The first vicious animal clamped onto Robert's backside, causing him to lurch back in pain. Robert's hat flew from his head and landed in the water.

"Doug! Help me!" Robert squealed as he tried to escape the clutches of the beast.

"Jump in the water, Robert!" Doug replied.

"I can't!" Robert bellowed. "It hurts!"

Doug forced his way towards the shore, but the other dog turned its attention to him and snarled. Robert struck his attacker, and the dog released its grip, only to seize his hand. Robert pulled his hand from the mouth of the brute, scraping his skin. The terrified slave went up the embankment a short distance before the dog snatched him from behind again. Robert screamed out in pain but ascended the hill, dragging the dog with him.

"Doug, help!" Robert cried.

"Get in the water," Doug said loudly, but beneath a yell.

"Don't leave me!" Robert shouted.

Robert's calls for help drew the awareness of the other dog. Overpowered by fear, Doug instinctively lowered himself into the water and lifted his feet off the slimy bottom. Doug kept his eyes on Robert while he slowly drifted away beside the old straw planter's hat. Robert kicked the dog holding him and got to his feet. The young man turned to his left and fled along the river, still in Doug's view. The dogs were upon Robert quickly and dragged him to the ground. Doug could still hear the cries of his companion when he reached the fallen tree partially blocking the river. The old hat came to rest against the numerous branches gathered by the tree. Doug maneuvered around the logjam and took cover behind it. The many spaces between the branches made it possible for Doug to see Robert while he remained hidden. Watching the dogs tug and pull at his friend tormented Doug's heart. The screams resounded through the air like the sick call of a wounded wild animal. Despair and helplessness stayed Doug's hand, and he did nothing.

Only seconds passed before the slave catchers arrived. Doug recognized them instantly. As Robert suggested, the men were the same fiends they encountered in camp with Stephen and Luke. All three dismounted their horses and approached Robert, who was still on the ground.

Linus, the largest of the men, pulled the dogs off of Robert.

"Get back ya dumb animals!" Linus blared.

A dog bolted and returned to the riverbank.

"Jeffrey, go fetch the dog," Edward ordered.

The slovenly man ran after the filthy dog. The dog stood at the water's edge and barked loudly. Jeffrey descended the embankment and grabbed the dog.

"What are ye hollerin' at ya mangy dog?" Jeffrey asked.

The dog stopped barking and drank from the river. Jeffrey spotted Lester's ax on the ground and picked it up. He held the ax with one hand and grabbed the rope around the dog's neck with his other hand, which he then used to pull the animal back up the hill.

"Looky here," Jeffrey called out as he traipsed back to his companions. "He had an ax."

Linus grabbed Robert's shirt and nearly lifted him with one hand. Robert was a little unsteady on his feet after the assault.

"Well, isn't it nice to see a familiar face," Edward said cheerily. "I say, where is your master?"

"I don't know," Robert answered while wincing.

"You don't know?" Edward asked. "How can that be? Answer me truthfully. Did you run off?"

"Yes, sir. I got loose from my ropes in the middle of the night and run off," Robert said.

"Where is the other slave? Did you not see fit to set him free also?" Edward inquired.

"No, sir," Robert answered. "He wouldn't have helped me, so I didn't help him."

"Well, I regret to inform you that your little adventure has concluded. We intend to return you to your master forthwith and collect a generous reward for the return of his property," Edward said.

Jeffrey kept the dogs restrained as Edward and Linus tended to Robert. It was anyone's guess who slobbered more, Jeffrey or the dogs.

"Linus, might I have the use of your belt momentarily?" asked Edward.

The large man unbuckled his belt and pulled it from around his waist, and handed it to Edward. The man in charge wrapped the belt around his hand two times and secured a tight grip on it.

"Oh dear me, where are my manners?" Edward scolded himself. "My name is Edward Black, and what might your name be, sir?"

"My name is Robert, mister," the frightened young man answered, trembling.

"Excellent. It is nice to make your acquaintance, Robert," Edward replied. "I think we can dispense with the formalities now."

"You don't have to beat me, Mr. Black," Robert explained. "I won't be no trouble."

"Oh, but I do, I'm afraid," Edward replied.

"Please, mister. I done been all chewed up by them dogs. I'm hurt awfully bad," Robert said.

Robert's groaning pleas for mercy fell mute upon Edward's ears.

"Allow me to explain. You have already run from your master. Therefore, it is reasonable to assume you might also flee from me. I take no pleasure in this. But I must take measures to encourage your obedience," Edward explained. "Linus, would you be so kind as to remove the gentleman's shirt?"

Linus pulled Robert's shirt off his shoulders, exposing the upper portion of the slave's back. The large man pushed Robert to the ground so that he was on his stomach. Linus placed his enormous foot on Robert's lower back, pinning the boy's arms behind him.

Without saying a word or warning, Edward flogged Robert repeatedly.

Doug heard his friend's painful cries. The horror of it all marred the beauty of the picturesque place, as if it defiled nature itself. After Robert's cries went silent, Doug listened closely for a sign of Robert's condition. The sound of Robert murmuring as Linus lifted him from the ground saddened and encouraged Doug at the same time. Robert was battered but still alive.

The thugs secured Robert's hands with a rope, the end of which Linus held while sitting atop his horse. The goons trotted away with their prize, leaving the field to the vagaries of the quickly approaching dusk.

Doug waited until darkness shrouded the world before crawling out of the river. He hauled himself up to the closest embankment, sneaking through the mud and leaves before resting on his belly. Doug propped his head on his fists and wept. There was nothing he could have done to help Robert, he told himself, and now he was alone. Doug bit his shirt sleeve to stifle the sound of his crying, fearful the hooligans were still waiting nearby.

Tired of watching the muck, Doug turned around and sat on the hill among the trees. The young man breathed deeply and tried to calm down. Doug listened to the soothing sound of the river and watched as time and water passed him. He had a million thoughts but couldn't pull them together into a coherent plan.

The world is an enchanting place filled with wonder and inspiration. But it can be a frightening, tangled wilderness of misery, sorrow, and hardship for the lost and lonely. Doug wondered if he should keep going or turn back. Few things are as daunting as the unknown. Inconceivable dangers, the likes of which Doug could only presume, riddled the way forward. Doug sat in quiet contemplation for an hour, pondering his next step. He noticed that Robert's hat remained stuck against the debris in the river and rose to his feet to retrieve the precious heirloom. Doug rinsed the mud off himself as he waded into the water to get the hat. He fanned himself with the hat to dry it a little and enjoyed the small wet gusts across his face. Doug fixed his gaze on the solitary tree in the field and the wheels turned in his mind. The brutal slave hunters would surely draw the truth from Robert one way or another and return him to his master. Doug feared Lester would send a party to look for him. Aware of the risk, Doug darted across the field and the game was afoot. He had to return to Bentonville before Edward extracted the truth from Robert. If he could make it back to the Cobb farm before sunrise, the slave masters wouldn't know he left.

The restless night kept Doug on edge as he ventured back to the plantation. He listened and watched intently for any signs of danger, fearful the slavers would backtrack, or scoundrels sharing similar ideas prowled about. Doug begged the world to be silent as he tried to concentrate, but the windblown trees, hooting owls, and chirping crickets would not oblige him.

Doug returned to the road and found a small stack of charred black wood, the last remnant of the abolitionist campsite. Feeling vulnerable in the open, Doug continued to retrace his steps and scurried back to the woods as quickly as he could. The forest filtered out much of the moonlight, and Doug ambled through the shadowy wilderness. Doug's footsteps added to the cacophony of sounds that hampered his ability to focus. Leaves and twigs crunched under Doug's feet no matter how he softened his steps. The melodies of the night echoed, but Doug could hear the trickling of the nearby river that had been his guide throughout the journey. Doug's vision gradually acclimated to the darkness of a thicket the moon seemed powerless to penetrate. The young slave made excellent progress, despite the tedious but consistent pace.

A ruthless enemy tracked Doug during the night, and as the minutes ticked away, it drew closer. Exhaustion nipped at Doug's feet, which ached and throbbed with pain. Doug sometimes reached out and placed his hand against a tree to keep himself steady. He shook his head periodically, trying to snap out of a lethargic stupor. Doug's strides became shorter, his stature slightly hunched over, and his mind more cloudy. Doug stood beside a large fallen tree when the jaws of fatigue ensnared him.

"Just have to sit down and rest for a minute," Doug said softly to himself as he sat on the ground and leaned against the log.

Doug stretched his legs, and the hurting in his feet subsided. He shook his head again, still unable to free himself from the grasp of weariness. Doug laid on his side and placed his arm beneath his head, and rested his back against the tree. The pain in his feet faded to a dull soreness, and a whip-poor-will's sweet lullaby called Doug to sleep. The delightful tune calmed the boy's anxious mind, and he drifted off to sleep, hoping to open his eyes upon his mother's lovely face.

A sprinkle of rain on his face brought Doug to life. He opened his eyes and saw a few lonely clouds passing before the moon, and watched the branches of large trees sway as they attempted to capture the wind. The soft rain felt good on his face. Doug rolled onto his knees quickly and scanned the surrounding woods. He was happy to see the planter's hat close by.

"What time is it? How long have I been asleep?" Doug whispered to himself.

Doug could see the moon was still high. The exhausted young man hadn't slept long, but the rest invigorated him. Recalling that he had to be back at the Cobb farm before daybreak, Doug got to his feet and started on his way. He hoped Robert would remain strong against his captor's wanton brutality. The shower ended as suddenly as it had started. Rain would not impede Doug this time.

Doug's pace accelerated after the clouds disappeared, leaving the immense, luminous moon unhindered. Doug soon noticed Lester's cabin in the field beyond the trees and crouched down to lower his profile. He could not see Lester, but the light of a lantern pierced a window, indicating that the man was at home. Doug remained secluded among the trees while he methodically maneuvered around Lester's homestead. He watched the cabin as much as the path ahead, ready to bolt at the first sign of the contemptible lout. Doug arrived at the road near Lester's house and, crossing it, knew he would expose himself. The young runaway surveyed the way forward and saw another tree line in the distance. Doug checked the cottage a final time and prepared to run. The lantern dimmed, the cabin turned dark, and Doug dashed across the road. When Doug reached the trees, he turned around and looked for danger. The night was quiet, and nothing obscured the serenity of God's creation. Doug was safe.

The fugitive slave meandered through the wilderness beside the river, backtracking the route he and Robert took during their escape. Doug passed familiar sights, the tree that saved his life, the collapsed riverbank, and the field of rough grass. He quickly marched along the road with nervous impatience, knowing that his destination was near.

The moon still hovered high in the heavens when Doug noticed the magnificent oak trees that bordered the Cobb farm. He cautiously trekked toward the slave cabins as quietly as he could. It pleased Doug to find the domain of the slaves tranquil and still. Doug noticed the door of his cabin ajar, and he pulled it gently and entered before carefully walking over the colossus sleeping on the floor. Vernon snorted as Doug stepped over him, but didn't wake anyone else in the cabin. Doug hung the hat on a short post before he crawled into bed. The planks that made up his bed creaked as Doug laid down. His mind raced as he wondered if the slave catchers had returned with Robert. The rickety old bed was comfortable after days of slumbering on the ground. Doug couldn't resist sleep for long. The events of the previous days drained him and Doug drifted off to dream in short order.

14

An Unearned Reward

The clanging of a spoon against a small iron kettle hanging in the fireplace awakened Doug. The young man opened his eyes and saw Florence scooping some boiled corn into a bowl. She placed the bowl before Maurice, who was sitting at the little table. Doug sat up and wiped the sleep from his eyes.

"I think a coyote dragged something in last night," Maurice said before laughing.

"Where did you get to, boy?" Florence asked.

"I was going to run away, but changed my mind and came back," Doug explained.

"You best not be running off by yourself like that," Maurice warned him.

"Come on and eat," Florence said as she placed another bowl on the table.

Doug removed Robert's hat from the chair and sat down. He ate quickly and finished his breakfast moments before the horn blew. The slaves exited the cabin in an orderly fashion and gathered beside the field.

Doug searched for Robert as the slaves converged, but didn't see his friend's face among the other subjugated people. He noticed Cecelia and walked to her without delay.

"Couldn't do it?" Cecelia questioned.

"We ran into trouble. Have you seen Robert?" Doug asked.

"No, didn't he go with you?" Cecelia replied.

"Some bad men caught us, slave catchers," Doug said. "I was able to get away, but they caught Robert."

"Oh, no," a worried Cecelia responded.

Lucille, carrying her baby boy on her back, joined Doug and Cecelia.

"Where is Robert?" Lucille queried.

"Slave catchers caught him," Cecelia answered directly.

"You were fools for going," Lucille said sternly.

The conversation yielded to Lester's arrival. Philip and Henry started handing sacks to the slaves while Lester looked on with an arrogant smirk affixed to his face.

"Y'all got an extra day off, so you should pick twice as much cotton today," the small-minded bigot said without a hint of irony.

"It looks like we're missing one," Earl interjected.

"What? Count them again," Lester ordered.

"I counted twice. We're one short," Earl confirmed.

Lester sighed and counted the slaves himself. He frowned after counting and unwound the whip.

"Who's late?" Lester demanded to know.

The slaves remained quiet, and Doug cast his gaze on the ground.

"Thomas, go check the cabins. Make sure ain't nobody trying to skip out on work," Lester dictated.

Thomas took only a few steps before the squeaking and clattering sound of an arriving wagon distracted the group. Lester stared at the visitors as if mesmerized by the clippety-clop of the horse's hooves. The animal stopped and let out a robust breath as Edward climbed down from the wagon. Linus and Jeffrey stood beside the wagon. Doug took cover behind Lucille and Cecelia out of fear the men would recognize him.

"Can I help you?" Lester grumbled while approaching the guests.

"Good morning, sir," Edward stated. "I'm here to return your property, as any upstanding gentleman would do."

"What might that be?" Lester asked.

"Linus, would you please unload the cargo?" Edward asked. "Jeffrey, please help him."

The large man and dimwitted slob dragged an injured Robert from the back of the wagon. The men guided the stumbling slave to Lester, where they released him and Robert collapsed on the ground.

"Well, there's the one we were missing," Lester said with a sigh.

Lester examined the beaten slave. The rascal could see bruises on Robert's face and the boy's left eye was swollen closed. Blood seeped from beneath the ropes that bound Robert's wrists.

"He looks like a right mess, I declare. He won't be able to work today," Lester fussed.

"We had to take the lash to him, I'm afraid. He put up a horrendous fight. I'm sure he will mend in time and work harder than ever," Edward claimed.

"Where did you find him?" Lester asked.

"He was in the company of two men and another slave. I suspect the men hoped to sell him for their own profit. I sure hope the other slave wasn't one of yours as well," Edward replied.

"I don't think so. We just did a head count," Lester uttered before turning his attention to Robert. "Did someone else run away with you, boy? Did you have help?"

Robert shook his head to imply he didn't receive aid. It was the only way he could communicate in his battered state. Cecelia turned her head and delivered a judgmental look at Doug.

"Now, who must we see about our compensation?" Edward inquired.

"Daniel, take him up yonder to see Mr. Cobb," Lester told his associate.

Before departing, Jeffrey retrieved something from the wagon and rushed it to Lester.

"He had this with him," Jeffrey stated as he dropped the ax on the ground beside Lester and Robert. "He might have stole it from y'all."

Lester kneeled down to pick up the ax while Daniel escorted the men to the house. The vile man picked up the ax and looked it over closely, spotting his initials.

"You bastard. You stole my ax. You came to my home and stole my ax, you thief. Why I ought to...,"

Lester didn't finish his sentence before he began thrashing Robert with the whip.

"You think you can steal from me? You invaded my home, you worthless piece of..."

The dastardly man was untethered from mercy or sanity. He pummeled the frightened young slave without concern for his already ruined form. Robert merely grunted and moaned under the assault, as the severely wounded boy could not offer a more vigorous expression of his anguish.

"Lester, stop before you kill him," Henry pleaded.

"Did he steal something from you?" Lester asked after momentarily pausing the onslaught.

Henry offered no reply.

"I didn't think so!" Lester yelled before he continued the thrashing.

Henry rushed forth and grabbed Lester's wrist as he prepared to strike another blow. The men wrestled over the whip high above Lester's head.

"Stop before you kill him," Henry insisted.

Lester placed his feet in a position that provided leverage, and he threw Henry to the ground. The evil man stood over Henry and glared at him.

"Why do you like these savages so much?" Lester asked. "Maybe you need a little of what they get so you can understand better."

"All right, that's enough!" Philip declared. "Vernon, Lewis, y'all take Robert to his cabin. Lucille, you go tend to him for a bit."

Robert barely made a sound when Vernon and Lewis picked him up. The sight of him proclaimed the suffering his voice could not. Blood trickled down his chin from his busted lip. The bruises were so abundant throughout his body, Robert appeared as spotted as a leopard. His head was so swollen it seemed it may pop at any moment. Watching as they took Robert to the cabin, Doug felt a sense of guilt and shame, knowing he evaded such torture.

"What are the rest of you standing around for? Get to work!" Lester commanded.

The slaves scattered in the fields as Philip helped Henry get to his feet. Lester approached the two hired hands.

"You two best not forget who is in charge around here," Lester warned.

Henry dusted himself off as the jerk walked away.

Doug found it difficult to keep up with the other slaves in the field after his arduous journey and little sleep. Despite fatigue and pain, Doug worked hard to keep pace with the others. He escaped punishment after running away and didn't want to invite it for another reason. Doug focused on his work, but his mind sometimes strayed to thoughts about Robert. He hoped his friend was on the mend and the consequences of their dreaded adventure would soon be a thing of the past.

When the lunch bell rang, Doug ran to Robert's cabin before going to eat. Doug gingerly stepped into the cabin, hoping not to disturb his resting friend. Lucille sat beside the bed and gently washed the dried blood from Robert's body.

"How is he?" asked Doug softly.

"He's hurt real bad," Lucille responded.

Doug stepped closer to the bed, but when Robert saw him through his one open eye, the young man became restless. Robert's breathing deepened, and he tried to speak, but words could not escape his mouth. Robert lifted his arm and turned his face toward the wall as he waved Doug away.

"He don't feel good. Maybe you should come back later," Lucille suggested.

"Yeah, I'll let him get some rest," Doug said in reply before exiting the cottage.

Doug ran to the kitchen, where slaves had lined up for food. After receiving a bowl with a few potatoes, Doug sat on the ground beside Cecelia.

"How is Robert doing?" she asked him.

"He still looks rough," Doug answered.

"What happened out there?"

Doug noticed Henry and Philip standing beside a nearby tree. Lester scowled at the two slaves from beside the neighboring tree.

"I'll have to tell you later," Doug said.

The slaves returned to the fields and worked until nightfall. With a little help from Vernon, Doug presented enough cotton to avoid Lester's strap. Doug was so tired that night he went to sleep without eating supper. He slept as hard as a person could on such a decrepit bed.

In the morning, Doug again dressed in the accoutrements of slavery and reported to the field for work. Doug looked for Robert but didn't see him in the group. He approached Cecelia and Lucille in search of information.

"Where is Robert?" Doug asked.

"He's still laid up in the bed," Lucille answered.

"His face is still puffed up, but he is getting better," Cecelia added.

The conversation was brief. The valuable fluffy white crop needed to be collected from the field. Doug, well-rested and invigorated, picked enough cotton on his own that day to evade discipline.

A coolness uncommon in late summer lingered in the air that night. Doug welcomed the relief after the long, harsh day in the field. Doug retrieved the old planter's hat from his cabin and resolved to return it to his friend. Cecelia met Doug as he neared Robert's home.

"Where are you going?" she asked.

"I'm bringing Robert's hat back to him. I got it out of the river after the slave catchers took him."

"He's sitting up and talking now, but he still looks mighty rough, and sad too."

"Maybe the hat will cheer him up."

Doug led Cecelia into the cabin, where he found Lucille and Lewis sitting next to Robert's bed. Florence wiped Robert's forehead while he sat in bed calmly with his back against the wall. Doug handed the hat to Robert, who took it and examined it without displaying a shred of gratitude.

"I fetched it from the river so I could bring it back to you," Doug stated.

"How did you know I would get back here?"

"I figured sooner or later they'd..."

"You figured what?" Robert interrupted angrily. "Figured they'd beat me until I told them what they wanted to hear?"

"No, that's not..."

"And no matter how bad they beat me, I didn't tell them about you. Even when you didn't help me, I helped you."

"I'm sorry man, I tried to help you."

"You didn't try to help me, you just tried to save yourself."

"Boys, don't argue," Florence interjected. "Everyone is safe now. Calm down and I'll fix us something to eat."

"I got your grandpa's hat. I didn't have to do that," Doug said.

"Do you think my grandpa would want me to have this hat, or be on my way north? We could have gone north with those nice men, but you didn't want to."

"I told you to go if you wanted."

"I wasn't gonna leave you all alone. But you left me all alone at the river. I wanted to go north, but now look at me. You stole Lester's ax, and look at me. I paid the price for what you did. You didn't get hurt, I did."

"Man, forget you. I'm outta here," Doug said before turning and storming out of the cabin.

"Leave. Go on back to that magical place you talk about," Robert ridiculed.

"Hush now," Florence instructed as she handed the damp rag to Lucille. "Y'all shouldn't be mean to each other."

Florence exited the cabin, and Lucille and Cecelia tended to Robert's injuries.

Doug sat quietly on the bed while Florence made supper. When she was done, she placed a bowl on the table for Doug.

"Come eat now, and get that frown off your face," Florence advised.

Doug, Florence, Maurice, and Vernon all sat in silence and ate. The flickering flames in the fireplace caused shadows to dance on the walls. Maurice eventually breached the tranquility when he dropped a spoon into his empty bowl with a clatter.

"That was delicious, Mammy Lou," Maurice said.

Vernon erupted with a raucous laugh. Maurice cracked a smile. The merriment infected Doug, and he too began giggling.

"Why did you call her, Mammy Lou?" Doug asked with a huge smile. "Is that her real name?"

"No," Florence insisted. "He calls me that because he thinks it's funny, even though he knows I don't like it."

"I'm sorry, Mammy Lou," Maurice said, and his smile grew wider on his face.

Florence pursed her lips and shook her fist at Maurice, jokingly threatening him. Vernon and Doug continued to laugh.

Robert returned to the field the following day. Doug saw him struggle through the pain even as the bruises slowly disappeared and Robert's left eye opened. Robert actively tried to avoid Doug throughout the week, keeping a row between them in the field, and choosing to eat away from Doug. Robert even told Lucille and Lewis to keep Doug out of their cabin.

"I didn't do anything to him," Doug thought to himself. But he felt ostracized by several of the other slaves, an outcast even among those miserable souls.

Doug hid his feelings. He was a forlorn spirit, as hollow as a shell cast upon the beach by an indifferent ocean. At quiet times, during the middle of the night when the moon kept lonely vigil over the Cobb farm, Doug would cry. He yearned to see his mother. Oh, how he missed the loving embrace of his Wanda.

15

Of Strong Children and Broken Men

Doug felt a gentle grip on his shoulder as Maurice shook him from sleep. The young man opened his eyes to find an empty chair and a full bowl waiting for him. Doug sat up quickly and pulled on his shoes.

"I thought you were going to sleep all day," Maurice said with a chuckle.

Sunday, the lone day of rest for slaves, had come again. Once upon a time, Doug would dismiss a quiet, relaxing afternoon, but now he realized how precious a day could be. The slaves breathed easier, absent the threat of Lester's whip. A noticeable sense of tranquility pervaded everything around them as the slaves tended to their own affairs.

Maurice fastened a length of string to the end of a sturdy stick while Doug ate his breakfast. Florence took a seat at the table across from Doug.

"Don't you be gone till dark now," Florence said to Maurice. "Those fish won't be good eating if you leave them sitting out all day."

"You're going fishing?" Doug asked. "Where?"

"At the pond over past the trees. You're going with me," Maurice said as he picked up another stick.

"Don't y'all ever have church on Sunday?" Doug asked.

"Reverend Steve used to come preach to us until Lester told Mr. Cobb it was going to make us revolt," Florence answered.

Maurice tied a small hook to the end of the string and finished the

164

modifications of his homemade fishing poles.

"Eat up now; we got some fish to catch."

After Doug finished eating breakfast, he and Maurice exited the cabin. Maurice gingerly handed a fishing pole to Doug while keeping hold of a bucket and his own pole.

"Don't let that hook snag you," Maurice cautioned.

Doug took the stick and carefully twisted the string around it and held the hook securely. Maurice greeted other slaves as he passed their cabins. Robert sat on a pail next to Lucille, who sat in the cabin's doorway and tended to her child. Cecelia stood beside her housemates.

"Robert, you want to go fishing?" Maurice asked.

"No, sir. I ain't going nowhere with him ever."

Doug furrowed his brow and kept moving.

"Something sure made y'all bitter while you were away," Maurice quietly said to Doug as they moved along.

"He's mad at me because the slave catchers got him. But I tried to help him. It's not my fault he was too scared to get in the river."

"Well, he was afraid of the water as much as he was those slave catchers," Maurice noted.

"I was gonna help him," Doug repeated. "I fell in the river the day before, so maybe that freaked him out and made him more scared."

"Y'all need to make peace. A lot of people hate us, Lester most of all. Don't do no good for slaves to hate each other."

Doug and Maurice walked past the field of buried slaves, now overgrown with weeds and cluttered with small branches and sticks blown down by storms. The only spot of bare ground in the field was the last resting place of Charles. Doug and Maurice walked past a grove of trees and down a small hill where a large pond sat placid and still. The men laid their poles and the bucket on the ground and Maurice pulled a big spoon from his shirt. He crouched on the ground and started digging and pushing aside clumps of soil.

"There's a good one," Maurice said as he held up a pudgy worm.

He handed the worm to Doug and combed through some more dirt until he found another. Maurice got to his feet and retrieved the poles, handing one to Doug. The young man followed Maurice to the bank of the pond. Doug watched as Maurice placed the worm on the hook, but found the task too disgusting to attempt on his own. After he had finished, Maurice observed Doug holding the fishing pole in one hand and the worm in the other.

"You have to put the worm on the hook. Ain't you ever been fishing?" Maurice asked.

"My grandpa took me a couple times when I was little, but he baited my hook."

"Here, let me show you how."

Maurice secured the worm on the hook properly and handed the pole back to Doug. With their worms on the hooks, the slaves were ready to fish. Maurice pulled his arm back and cast his line into the water. Doug attempted to the do the same but his line landed in some tall grass along the bank.

"You just point your arm where you want to go," Maurice said to Doug as he watched the young man pull the line back.

Doug stepped a little closer to the shore and cast the line out again, keeping his arm extended this time. The hook landed in the water with a plop and a cork bobber rolled over the little wave it made. Maurice sat down on the bank and Doug followed his lead.

Doug absorbed the surrounding scenery and breathed deeply the fresh air. Tall grass grew around the large pond, except in places where captive men and women or wild animals pushed it down in pursuit of fish to eat or water to drink. The wind pressed against the standing grass, causing it to sway elegantly. Given the state of the world around Doug, the scene was more beautiful and serene than it had any right to be.

Doug noticed a great blue heron quietly enter the water near the other side of the pond. The long-legged bird slowly waded into deeper water, moving gracefully in search of an unsuspecting fish. The animal extended its long neck and stood about four feet tall as it scanned the pond diligently. Doug stared in amazement as he watched the wily hunter stalk its prey. Without moving its lower body, the bird struck the water with its beak and snared a large fish. The aquatic predator swallowed its breakfast whole, followed it with a gulp of water, then began the search anew. The creature mesmerized Doug, as herons didn't visit the projects.

A tug on the line jerked Doug from his trance. He pulled on the pole and tried to stand, but slipped and fell. Doug clambered to his feet and gripped the fishing pole tightly, determined to land the fish.

"Hang onto it," Maurice told Doug.

Doug instinctively looked for a reel for an instant before tugging on the line again.

"Pull it back," Maurice advised.

Doug yanked again, and the tension in the line relaxed. He dragged the line from the water and discovered a bare hook.

"Ah, it got away," Maurice said, sounding mildly disappointed.

"I almost got one."

"Come on, let's find another worm."

Maurice quickly located another worm and placed it on Doug's hook. The men cast their lines again and sat down.

"Didn't your daddy ever take you fishing?" Maurice asked.

"Nah, he wasn't around."

"Was he sold when you were little?"

"No, he just wasn't around. He... well, it's a long story. He left me and my mom."

"That must have been hard for him. It ain't no easy thing to leave your child."

"It was pretty easy for him. He left when I was two."

"He up and left you, but he wasn't sold? Did he go north on the railroad?"

"I don't know where he is."

"That don't make no sense. I could see if he sent you north to freedom, but I can't understand why he would run off and leave you behind."

"He didn't care about us. He wanted his own freedom. He didn't want the burden of helping my mom raise me."

"That's a shame. Boys are too wild. Fathers teach boys how to control themselves. A father has to show his son how to be a man, like my daddy did for me. A father shows a boy how to treat a woman."

"My mom said my father treated her like dirt. He used to slap her, even if she was holding me. It's probably better that he left."

"I don't understand how a man gives up on his child. A man's children are his promise to the future. A man who gives up on his children is giving up on his own destiny, giving up on the hope of a better world. You always want your children to live in a better world than you did."

Maurice's words caused Doug to recall something his mother used to say.

"It is easier to build strong children than to repair broken men," Wanda would say, quoting Fredrick Douglass. She offered the wisdom whenever Doug thought she expected too much of him. Doug sometimes wondered if his father's parents failed to raise a strong child, or if his father neglected their best efforts to put him on the right path. Whatever the reason, Doug felt he paid the price for it.

"Sometimes I think about all I missed out on," Doug said with regret. "He missed all my church league games, Christmases, birthdays, my first steps, my first day of school... all of that."

"School? Boy, what are you talking about? They don't let us go to school."

"Oh, I've been to school. I can read, do math, all kinds of stuff."

"You must have bumped your head when you fell in that river. You can't read."

"I can," Doug insisted. "Almost everyone can read in the... I mean, where I come from."

"You was in the sun too long. They don't let no black people read."

"Someday they will. One day, lots of black people will learn to read. A black man will even become president someday."

Maurice touched Doug's head and turned it to the side as he chuckled.

"Do you have a hole in your head, boy? President? You done lost your mind."

Doug giggled as he ducked Maurice's hand. Suddenly, Doug's line jerked and moved toward deeper water.

"I got another bite!" Doug exclaimed.

"I'll be you sure do. Give it a little tug real quick."

Following Maurice's instructions, Doug drew back on the line. Maurice placed a sturdy hand on Doug's back.

"Now get up slow and walk him back."

Doug rose to his feet and gradually stepped back from the pond.

"Pull the line toward you a little," Maurice suggested.

Doug retreated until a gorgeous fish emerged from the water and wriggled on the end of the line. Maurice collected the fish while Doug flashed the biggest smile he could bear.

"I caught one!" an excited Doug declared.

"Yeah, you did, and it ain't a bad one either."

Maurice held the fish up so Doug could admire his catch a little longer before placing it into the bucket.

"OK, let's get some more," Maurice proposed.

"Can you help me with the worm again?"

"Sure I can."

Doug beamed as Maurice attached another worm to his hook. The two slaves cast their lines back into the pond and sat on the shore. The surface of the pond glistened in the sunlight. Doug understood as he watched the heron grab another fish that the most enjoyable part of fishing is typically the company you keep and the conversations you have.

The slaves busied themselves with various tasks around their cabins, gathering firewood, cleaning potatoes, and sweeping floors. Doug and Maurice arrived with five fish in the bucket, which Maurice cheerfully held high. Florence wiped her hands on an apron as she approached her husband and his young helper.

"Let's cook these up," Maurice suggested.

"I caught three of them," Doug proudly announced.

"Good," Florence said before patting Doug on the back. "Let's get these cleaned up, and we'll have them for supper."

Robert observed the trio from the steps of his cabin where he tended to Lucille's boy while she and Cecelia ripped apart greens and dumped them into a pot. Robert's face was expressionless, but inside he seethed at the sight of Doug's happiness. It seemed unfair that Doug would have a smile on his face after all that Robert endured on his behalf. At least Robert thought so. He remained stone-faced as he watched Doug go to his cabin with Maurice and Florence. Once they were out of sight, Robert focused on the baby once again.

A cozy fire flickered in the fireplace and illuminated the cabin as the slaves finished supper. Plates of bones served as the centerpiece of the small table where Florence and Maurice sat. Maurice leaned back in his chair, rubbed his belly, and emitted a sigh that bore witness to his hearty appetite. Doug stood up from the bed and placed his plate on the table with the others.

"Thank you, Miss Florence," Doug said. "That was great."

"You're welcome, Doug."

Vernon walked into the cabin with a grin on his face that suggested mischief was afoot. The enormous man removed a few loose bricks from the fireplace and revealed a book hidden behind them. Vernon took the book out of hiding and looked longingly at the cover. It is such sorrow to hold something precious in one's hand and have it be unattainable. Vernon could not read.

"Fool, put that thing away," Maurice ordered.

"Let him look at it," Florence stated.

"He can't read it."

"Oh, leave him be. He likes to hold it and look at it."

Vernon thumbed through the book and marveled at the pages filled with words he couldn't decipher. It amazed him that anyone could write so many words. Doug noticed the title as Vernon continued his childlike fascination with the book.

"That's *Moby Dick*," Doug said. "It's a classic."

"How do you know if it's a classic if you've never read it?" Maurice asked with a chuckle.

"You're right. I've never read it, but I've heard it's a classic. It's about the captain of a ship who lost his leg to a giant whale, and he wants revenge on it."

Maurice laughed again.

"You just making that up. You don't know what that book's about," said Maurice.

"OK, let's all find out what it's about. Let me see that, big man," Doug said as he carefully took the book from Vernon.

Doug sat on his bed, opened the book, and observed the words bathed in the soft orange glow of the fire.

"*Moby Dick* by Herman Melville," Doug began. "Call me Ishmael. Some years ago—never mind how long precisely—having little or no money in my purse, and nothing particular to interest me on shore, I thought I would sail about a little and see the watery part of the world."

The other bed creaked and moaned as Vernon sat down and leaned in to listen to Doug read.

"Are you making up a story, or can you really read that?" Florence asked.

"Oh, he's telling a story. You know they don't teach us to read," Maurice replied.

"I'm really reading it. That's what it says," declared Doug.

"Go on, read some more," Maurice insisted.

Doug continued reading, "Whenever I find myself growing grim about the mouth; whenever it is a damp, drizzly November in my soul; whenever I find myself involuntarily pausing before coffin warehouses, and bringing up the rear of every funeral I meet; and especially whenever my hypos get such an upper hand of me, that it requires a strong moral principle to prevent me from deliberately stepping into the street, and methodically knocking people's hats off—then, I account it high time to get to sea as soon as I can."

Florence smiled proudly while Maurice shook his head.

"Well, I'll be. I think the boy might know how to read," Maurice said.

"I told you I did," Doug stated.

"You better not let Lester catch you reading," Florence warned.

"Why? Why should I be afraid to read?" Doug wondered aloud.

"It's against the law to teach slaves how to read," Florence said.

"Nobody here taught me to read. I learned in school and from my mama reading to me," Doug stated emphatically.

Maurice burst into laughter again.

"Oh, boy, you got some good ones. I done told you they don't let us go to school."

"Lester doesn't want you to learn to read because he's scared. Knowledge is power, but he only knows how to hit people. He's a bully," Doug said.

Doug paused as a wave of clear thinking crashed down upon him. He remembered the kid in the park he assaulted with Isaiah. He recalled how his grades slipped. Doug had abandoned knowledge to be a tough guy and a bully. Doug looked at the faces in the room, those tortured souls who never learned to read, knowing he had taken it for granted. Florence and Maurice got up from the table. She walked to Doug and rubbed his head as Maurice gathered the dinner plates.

"Just you be careful," Florence suggested. "I don't want to see you get hurt anymore. Don't let Lester find you reading. But you have a gift. Don't let it go to waste. Do good things with your schoolin'."

"I'll do good things. I promise."

Vernon grew impatient and pointed at the book. Doug read the story to his friends until the hour was late.

"We better turn in. Back to the fields tomorrow," Maurice finally suggested.

The slaves of the Cobb farm were soon fast asleep, dreaming of white whales, a man with a wooden leg, and freedom.

16

A Quenchless Feud

Doug slogged through the field with the other slaves. He sheepishly extended a greeting to Robert, who sneered in reply. The days grew slightly cooler, but the work was no less rigorous and taxing on the servants. Doug struggled but mostly kept pace with the other slaves.

Alberta grappled with a heavy bucket of water as she carried it to the field. The young girl felt the piercing stare of Lester upon her and periodically glanced in his direction to see if he was still watching. Alberta reached Doug and placed the bucket on the ground between two rows.

"You want some water?" Alberta asked.

"Thank you," Doug replied as he lifted the ladle from the pail.

Doug hastily emptied the ladle before he noticed Lester and Earl glaring at him. Doug scooped more water from the bucket and drank slowly, in an act of blatant defiance. He kept his eyes on Lester and Earl while water that glistened in the sun ran down his chin and neck.

"You sure are thirsty," Alberta commented.

"What's your name again?" Doug asked.

"I'm Alberta," the young girl answered.

"You're usually at the house. What are you doing out here?"

"Mister Lester said he needed someone to carry water, so Missus Edith told me to help."

"Where do you sleep at night?"

"I has a bed in the attic with Miss Hilda and Miss Minnie."

Doug noticed that Lester and Earl were still watching and clearly growing impatient. The insubordinate slave dipped the ladle into the bucket again. Alberta glanced at the supervisors before turning her attention back to Doug.

"You better stop. You gonna get in trouble," she cautioned.

Doug reached into the bucket for yet another drink, disregarding the girl's warning. Lester had seen enough. With Earl close behind, Lester strolled over to the slaves.

"You've had enough to drink, ain't you, boy?" Lester asked calmly.

Doug dipped the ladle, retrieved some water, and drank again. After he consumed the water, Doug let out an exaggerated sigh, as if expressing satisfaction. Lester smirked and shook his head, but his growing anger was unmistakable. Doug lowered the ladle into the bucket again, then raised it toward his lips. Lester smacked the ladle from Doug's hand before pushing the young man to the ground. The brute unfurled the whip as he stepped around Doug. Before Doug could get to his feet, Lester wrapped the whip around his neck and began lifting him. Doug grasped at the strand around his neck and kicked his feet, fighting for breath as Lester dragged him away from the field. Earl attempted to grab Doug's feet, but the defiant slave kicked the man in the head, sending him careening back and tripping over the water bucket. Being wet and muddy only incensed the man, who swiftly climbed to his feet and stormed after Doug. Earl kicked Doug and belted him in the stomach as Lester released the whip around his neck. The combination of being choked and gut-punched caused Doug to buckle over, and he fell onto his hands and knees, groaning and gasping for air. The heartless reprobates showed Doug no quarter. As Doug tried to catch his breath, Earl kicked him in the ribs, sending the young man onto his side grimacing. Lester delivered four blasts of the whip across Doug's right arm and leg. Doug remained on the ground, writhing in pain as Lester wound the whip into a loop and placed it back on his hip. Philip arrived on the scene, followed closely by Henry.

"Not one word, Philip!" Lester shrieked.

"I have no words to give, Lester."

"You! Pick up that pail and go fill it with water before you get what he got!" Lester shouted as he pointed at Alberta.

The young girl hastily recovered the bucket and ladle before racing to the well near the main house. Lester tugged his pants up and strolled back into the field. Earl looked over his wet, filthy pants and delivered one last kick to Doug for good measure before walking away. Doug laid on the ground clutching his midsection, trying to compose himself before attempting to stand.

"You OK, Doug?" Philip asked.

"I'll be all right," Doug replied with a cough.

"You know, there's courage, and then there's foolishness."

"I ain't gonna let him push me around. I'm going to stand up for myself."

"There's a time and a place to make a stand. This isn't the time or place."

"It's always the right time to stand up for yourself. I ain't no punk."

"So you're going to make a stand by constantly pushing Lester to beat you to a pulp? There are better ways to make a stand, more honorable ways."

"Man, what are you talking about? It's not honorable to let a man beat you down. Keeping people in chains isn't honorable."

"And you think you're going to change that by antagonizing Lester?"

"You don't know what you're talking about."

Philip and Doug noticed Lester observing them from the other side of the field.

"Get yourself together and get back to work," Philip advised before walking away.

Doug stood up, brushed himself off, then returned to the field. He was sore and angry, but Doug retrieved his sack and began picking cotton without showing his pain. He could not thwart the attacks of his armed oppressor, but Doug vowed to deny the man the enjoyment of breaking his spirit.

The sun inched closer to the treetops, a sight Doug was glad to see. The pain of vigorous fieldwork and the beating sustained at the hands of Lester and Earl were taking their toll on Doug in equal measure. Even the melancholy yet calming sounds of singing slaves did not lessen his anguish. Doug did not know the words but hummed along with the singing as best he could.

The plants to the left of Doug rustled as someone plucked cotton from the other side. Doug stood up to take a restful breath and stretch and saw Robert singing beside him. Doug wondered if Robert was still angry. Over two weeks had passed since they returned to the Cobb farm separately.

"Sounding good," Doug said to Robert.

Robert continued to collect cotton and sing and ignored Doug.

"Robert, what's wrong?"

"Stop talking to me," Robert responded.

"What did I do? Why are you so mad? I tried to help you."

Robert stood up and faced Doug.

"You don't help nobody. You get people hurt. You only care about yourself."

"I tried to help. All you had to do was get in the water."

"We could have been on our way north. But you didn't want to do that. People get hurt around you, Doug. Heck, you get hurt around you. Look at you. Just leave me alone."

"Fine then," Doug retorted. "I don't need you no how."

"Lester watching," Robert informed Doug after spotting the man looking at them from afar. "You better get back to work before you get beat again."

Without saying another word, the young men returned to their work.

That night, as almost every night, the slaves lined up to turn in the bounty of their labor. Vernon handed his basket to Earl, and the slave driver nearly fell over.

"I swear, boy, you sure are stupid, but you can pick a wagonload of cotton in a day. Get out of here," Earl said.

Vernon walked away, and Cecelia stepped forward. Lester usually stood a short distance away and watched the slaves, but he moved to stand next to Earl as Cecelia turned in her harvest. Lester's proximity made Cecelia uncomfortable, and she timidly lowered her head and handed her basket to Earl. The ogre tilted his head to the side and bent his knees so he could look upon her face.

"What's wrong, darling? You ain't worried, are you? I'm sure you picked quite enough cotton," said Lester.

"No, sir," Cecelia replied, keeping her head down.

Lester placed his index finger under Cecelia's chin and raised her gaze to him.

"It's all right," Lester said. "You don't have anything to worry about. Earl said you picked enough cotton, didn't you Earl?"

"Yeah, I guess I did," Lester's slightly older companion answered.

"You look prettier all the time. Do you know that?" Lester asked, but Cecelia gave no reply. "Don't you think, Earl? Ain't she pretty?"

"Sure, boss."

"Remember, I said you ain't half bad?" Lester said with a snicker.

Lester stroked Cecelia's cheek with the back of his hand. Doug stood behind her, ready to turn in his cotton, and grew agitated at the sight of Lester's demeaning behavior. Cecelia remained tense and demure as the disgusting lout touched her.

"Maybe if you're lucky, I might just have my way with you someday. Heck, maybe Earl will share his bed with you. Would you like that?" Lester asked.

Lester's remarks appalled Cecelia, and she did not respond. Doug had seen enough. He cleared his throat and stepped forward energetically, lifting his basket to Earl.

"I did good, sir. I picked lots of cotton," Doug announced.

Doug's interruption distracted Lester, so Cecelia seized the opportunity to scamper away.

"Get out of my sight," Earl instructed.

Doug didn't dawdle and evacuated the area with a brisk pace so that he caught up with Cecelia.

"Are you all right?" Doug asked her.

"Yeah. Thank you for that."

"No problem."

"I can sweat and bleed and crawl in the soil all day in the field and I don't feel as dirty as when that man touches me."

"He's a pig and something needs to be done about him."

Once they reached the slave quarters, Cecelia and Doug parted ways, going to their respective cabins.

Doug sat on his bed, picked up *Moby Dick* and continued the tale of Ahab's quest for revenge, much to the gratification of the others. Florence and Maurice sat at the table, mesmerized by the story as the fire crackled. Vernon sat on the floor while leaning against a wall, his eyes heavy as sleep enticed him.

"I, Ishmael, was one of that crew; my shouts had gone up with the rest; my oath had been welded with theirs; and stronger I shouted, and more did I hammer and clinch my oath, because of the dread in my soul. A wild, mystical, sympathetical feeling was in me; Ahab's quenchless feud seemed mine. With greedy ears I learned the history of that murderous monster against whom I and all the others had taken our oaths of violence and revenge," Doug read.

Florence watched Doug read and flip the pages with a prideful smile. A single tear streamed down her cheek, and she stood up and exited the cabin. Doug stopped reading and closed the text, keeping his thumb as a bookmark.

"Is she all right?" Doug asked Maurice.

"She goes to pray for our son. You remind her of him. He was only a little older than you."

"Where is he? What happened to him?"

"We sent him north on the Underground Railroad some months ago. Mr. Cobb sent me and my son to work for Mr. Tooley for a little while, as collateral for a loan. One of Mr. Tooley's farmhands said he was an abolitionist. I didn't believe him at first, but after some time, I trusted him. He gave Vernon that book you been reading. He even snuck us some extra food one night. When it came time for him to go, he said he could only take one of us, so Florence and I told him to take our son. Our boy didn't want to go, but we begged him to go. We told him we'd see him again someday. It broke our hearts, but we wanted him to find freedom. We didn't care about ourselves. I guess we felt if he's free, then we free too in some kinda way."

"What's his name? Your son, I mean," Doug inquired.

"Ben, his name was Ben, is Ben," Maurice said with moistened eyes. "Sometimes I dream me and Florence get free, and we go north. We sit in the back of a church, and there's singing and joy, and folks are happy. Up front, we see a man and his wife with three smiling children. The man turns around so I can see his face, and it's my son, it's Ben."

"I hope you see him someday. You know, it isn't going to be like this forever. One day slavery is going to end."

Florence entered the cabin and wiped her face once more before sitting down at the table.

"Go on, Doug. Please read some more," she appealed.

Doug opened the book and continued the story of the crew of the Pequod as Maurice reached across the table and held his wife's hand and smiled at her warmly.

The following day, Doug kept a close eye on Lester while working in the field. Lester's crude banter and behavior with Cecelia perturbed Doug. The man sat beneath a tree, conversing with Earl, Thomas, and Daniel as they ate lunch. Alberta continued to distribute water nearby, serving Homer a much-needed drink. Minnie slowly walked toward Lester and his minions, pushing wrinkles from her apron as she went.

"I come to take y'all's bowls if you're finished," Minnie told the men.

Three of the men raised their dishes and the elderly slave woman carefully collected them with shaking hands, stacking the bowls on top of each other.

"You can take this one too. I don't think I'm going to eat the rest," Lester instructed.

A spoonful of beans remained in Lester's bowl.

"Don't let me catch you eating that last bite," Lester warned. "You don't eat from the same bowl as me."

"No, sir, I won't."

Minnie took the bowl and added it to the stack, which leaned precariously.

The old slave stumbled as she turned, causing the top bowl to topple from its perch. The bowl landed in Lester's lap, spilling a tiny amount of food onto his pants.

"Oh, I'm sorry, sir," a frightened Minnie stated.

The furious man sprang to his feet and huffed like a raging bull.

"I'll clean that right up," Minnie said as she grabbed the bottom of her apron to use as a towel.

Her apology fell on deaf ears. Lester slapped the dishes from her hands, scattering them on the ground.

"You got beans all over my pants, you old hag!" Lester yelled.

"I'm sorry."

Lester shoved the elderly slave to the ground before examining the small spot on his pants. The commotion drew Doug's attention. He wanted to rush to Minnie's defense, but Doug knew running from the field to confront Lester and his sycophants would only mean bigger trouble. One courageous slave remained undeterred. Alberta dropped the ladle in the bucket and ran to Minnie, placing herself between the older slave and the rogue.

"Stop, she's just an old lady," Alberta demanded.

Lester grabbed Alberta by the hair and pushed the little girl onto her knees, and pressed her face in the dirt.

"Don't you sass me, you wench!" the angry man yelled, spitting on the young girl.

"Come on, Lester, let her up," Henry said as he sauntered over.

"How many times do I have to tell you to mind your own business?"

"You're roughing up an old woman and a child."

"Now you see there's your problem, Henry," Lester said as he released Alberta. "You see an old woman and a child. I see an old slave and a young slave. You think they can be like us."

"All I'm saying is you don't have to be cruel to them."

"No, you're saying they can be the same as us. Right here is where they should be, in the dirt," Lester said, pointing at the slaves at his feet. "You and Philip try to be nice to them and think that will make them work hard for you. Go on and believe that. You'll end up with an ax in your back or a hammer in your head, just like my daddy. Keep thinking they're on the same level as you. Let me tell you something, they might be the same as you, but they ain't the same as me."

Lester kicked a bowl and sent it rolling toward the house before he walked away.

"Someone should take that old dog behind the barn and put her out of her misery," Lester called out, looking back at the group.

Life went on in that way for the slaves that dwelled in Bentonville. Day after day, the servants toiled in the fields, or the master's house, then tended to their families by night and kept their secrets. Doug continued the story of Captain Ahab and the white whale, and his own heart filled with a thirst for vengeance that paralyzed his ability to see important things both near and far.

17

The Glowing Horizon

Fall brought cool breezes and gorgeous sunsets that left the horizon aglow with orange, violet, and yellow. The slaves neared the end of the harvest season, but there was always other work to be done. Livestock needed feeding, wood needed chopping, and barns required repairs. The shorter days of autumn pleased the weary slaves. The servants had nearly stripped the fields clean, leaving brown shrubs where fluffy clouds of white cotton once endured. Things changed in Bentonville, but not so much for the captives who inhabited it.

Doug had become accustomed to the grueling routine of his daily life, and it vexed him. He unloaded boards from a wagon and set them on the ground along the long narrow road leading to the Cobb house. Other slaves lifted boards and held them in place as they hammered nails into the wood. The slaves worked hard building a post and rail fence to border much of the property.

The wagon stopped about twenty yards away from the main house. Doug grabbed a shovel and began digging a new posthole next to the road. Maurice, Florence, and Cecelia dug holes several feet away from each other.

Mr. Cobb sat in a rocking chair on his front porch, examining the craftmanship of his slaves. His daughter, Margaret, sat, as she often did, gazing into the distance, wishing to see her husband walk down the road. The woman hoped someone wrote to her in error, and he might yet return to her. But as the months passed, an irrefutable truth slowly took root in her heart. Samuel would never come home.

Lester walked up and down the road and watched the slaves, but he mostly shadowed Cecelia. Henry gave instructions to other slaves a short distance away. Lester checked each hole for depth as he walked by.

"OK, that's a good one. Go fetch another post," Lester ordered.

Cecelia and Florence grabbed opposite ends of a post and lifted it. A sharp pain ran up her back, and Florence dropped her end of the pole. It landed on the ground, bounced, and pivoted, driving a splinter into Cecelia's hand.

"Ouch!" Cecelia barked as she dropped the other end of the beam.

The thick piece of wood fell onto Lester's foot, and he yelped loudly. The angry man limped for a few steps before turning and striking Cecelia across the face with an open hand. Cecelia fell onto her back, still holding her hand. Doug clutched the shovel tightly and took a step toward Lester before Maurice grabbed his arm and held him back.

"Don't think I won't slap your pretty face!" Lester howled.

"I couldn't help it! I got a plank in my hand!" Cecelia declared, holding up her hand.

"Are you sassing me?" Lester asked as he unleashed the whip. The irritable man raised the whip over his head and stared at the injured woman. Cecelia looked at Lester with tearful eyes that beseeched him to stay his hand. Blood trickled down her wrist and dropped onto her dress.

"Let her up, Lester," Henry advised as he walked to the scene.

Lester spun around and flailed the whip wildly. The lash missed Henry but grazed Florence's arm. The woman grabbed her arm but bit her tongue, fearful that an expression of pain would redirect Lester's fury to her.

"Don't you ever swing that thing at me again," Henry warned Lester.

"What's wrong, Henry? You like these devils, might as well treat you just like one of them," Lester said.

Lester cracked the whip again and sent the tip reaching for Henry. The strike missed its mark when Henry jumped out of the way. Henry spotted a shovel on the ground beside him and picked it up.

"All right, Lester, let's see how tough you are when someone fights back,"

Henry said, gripping the shovel and holding it across his chest.

"Oh, you want to see how tough I am, do you?" Lester inquired sarcastically.

"Yeah."

"You really want to see?" Lester asked, flicking the whip on the ground.

"Yeah!"

"Do it," Doug mumbled quietly through gritted teeth.

"Huh, you want to see, do you?" Lester challenged in a yell.

"I dare you! Come on!"

"Hit him!" Doug reflexively hollered.

"ENOUGH!" came a screech that echoed across the farm.

All heads turned toward the house and observed Joseph Cobb as he descended the steps from the front porch.

"Stop this foolishness this instant!"

Henry dropped the shovel and Lester wound the whip. The Cobb family patriarch stood between the men with an air of command that affirmed his dominion over the farm.

"I pay you men to see to the affairs of my farm and oversee my slaves. But you're as crude and senseless as they are. If you men can't work together, I'll find men who can. Now I don't want to see any more of this petty behavior."

"I'm sorry, Mr. Cobb," Henry offered sincerely.

"I didn't mean no trouble, Mr. Cobb. You know I get good work out of them for you," Lester uttered.

"Well, see that you do. Tomorrow's Sunday and I'd like to have at least this portion of the fence done today," Cobb told the men.

Joseph Cobb walked back toward the house. Cecelia got to her feet and worked to remove the splinter from her hand. The slaves resumed digging and hammering as orange and yellow leaves drifted slowly and gently to the ground.

Hours after the excitement of the faceoff between Lester and Henry, Doug and Maurice worked on the end of the fence, far from the house and Lester's watchful eye. Doug held a board steady against a post while Maurice drove nails into it with a hammer.

"Do you ever think about leaving here and going to find your son?" Doug asked.

"I dream about it," Maurice said. "But I don't think about it."

"What do you mean?"

"I mean I don't think about it when I'm awake cause I might do it. Look what happened to you and Robert. I couldn't put Florence through that. Now you listen to me, you better get that kind of craziness out of your head. Talk like that is gonna get you hurt."

"I get hurt every day. We all do. I hate Lester. That stupid man treats us like dogs. I think I'd kill him if I had the chance."

"Don't let that anger and hate get all over you. It will eat you up. You will end up just like Lester."

"No, I won't."

"Listen to you. You hate Lester as much as he hates you."

"I have good reason to hate him."

"You think the reason someone hates makes it better? It don't matter if you hate Lester because he beats us or because of the color of his skin."

"I'm not a racist like he is. I can't be. We can't be. We don't have any power."

"You said a black man will be president someday. Can't get much more power than that. Anyway, a man doesn't need power to hate another man. No matter where a man's hate comes from, it all leads to the same place. Some people got to stop hating or else we just hate each other for all time."

"How can you talk like that after everything he's done? You have every reason to hate Lester and all these people."

"I don't hate Lester. I don't like him much, but I don't hate him. You can't change the heart of a man who hates you by hating him back. Lester's a broken man. Something poisoned his soul and shattered him into pieces. It ain't easy, but you can fix broken men."

"Don't take this the wrong way, Mr. Maurice, but you don't know what you're talking about."

"I know this much. You can't fix a broken thing by smashing it further.

You can't fix a broken man by hating him. A man's heart and spirit are kind of like this hammer. You can use it to tear down this whole fence or use it to build the fence. It's all up to you."

"Some things are broken beyond repair," Doug countered.

"Come on, hold that board steady," Maurice instructed before placing a nail.

Doug held the board in place as Maurice banged on the tiny iron spike. A day's work was nearly done.

Sunday returned, and the slaves carried on their own business. Doug helped Maurice and Florence break up some leafy vegetables. Vernon and Robert played with Alberta, holding her hands and spinning until her feet left the ground. Cecelia and Lucille cared for the baby. Clouds rode gentle winds, which plucked more colorful leaves from their branches. Doug faced the sky, closed his eyes, and took a deep breath.

"Ah, football weather," Doug said with a smile.

"Football weather?" Florence asked.

"What's that?" Maurice also wanted to know.

"Football is a game. People played it this time of year back home. On a day like this, thousands of people would gather at a stadium, a building as big as this farm, just to watch the game," Doug explained.

"There he goes again, talking about that strange place he comes from," Maurice said with a chuckle.

"You should show us how to play," Florence suggested.

"You need a bunch of people," Doug replied.

"Plenty of folks around here," said Maurice.

"Let's see," Doug stated as he looked around.

Doug stood up and grabbed a nearby stick that leaned against the cabin. He ran a short distance away and used the stick to etch a line in the ground. Once it was complete, Doug ran to the other end of the slaves' living area, where he drew another line on the ground. Doug returned the stick to its resting spot and scanned the area for the next object he needed. He dashed to a basket of squash and removed one, then walked to a line he drew on the ground.

"OK, this is how you play football," Doug began. "So you start here, at this end, and you have to carry the football, this squash, to the other line over there."

Maurice and Florence walked to where Doug stood and observed how he tucked the squash between his arm and side.

"You have two teams. One team tries to get the football from here to there, and the other team tries to stop them."

Doug positioned Maurice with his back to the nearby line in the dirt.

"You stand here. You have to stop me from getting the football across that line. You need to tackle me."

"Tackle you?"

"Here, I'll show you," Doug said as he handed the squash to Maurice. "You hold this. What you have to do is run across the line at the other end there, carrying the squash. I'm going to wrestle you to the ground before you get there. That's tackling."

Doug bent his knees and lowered his stance before Maurice, who looked slightly confused.

"OK, hut! Hut!" Doug shouted.

Maurice didn't move.

"That means you hiked the ball. You run with it."

Maurice took off in a slow trot. Doug scampered after him and wrapped his arms around the man's waist before gently taking him to the ground. The other slaves laughed, humored by the rules of Doug's peculiar game. Maurice rose to his feet and jogged toward the makeshift goal line again.

"Wait," Doug cheerfully said. "You need to line up again and run a new play. Come back here."

Maurice returned to Doug and cracked a big smile.

"I bet you won't take me down next time."

"That's what I like to hear. But we need more people to play. Who wants to play?" Doug asked, looking for volunteers.

Cecelia jumped to her feet with a gigantic smile on her face and bounced over to join the huddle. Homer promptly engaged in the fun as well. Robert slowly strode over and kept a stoic profile. Even Florence lined up across from her husband. Doug moved around the group, getting everyone into position. He bypassed Robert, clearly able to see the resentment that simmered behind his expressionless eyes. Once everyone was in place, Doug lined up at quarterback.

"OK, when I hike the ball, everyone on this side moves toward that line over there, and the people on that side stop the person with the ball," Doug explained. "Are you ready?"

"I'm ready," Florence and Cecelia said almost simultaneously.

"Hut! Hut!" Doug called out before stepping back with the squash.

The slaves moved about the area as clumsily as children in bumper cars.

"Here you go, Miss Florence," Doug said as he handed the squash to her.

Florence took the squash and held it carelessly in her hand, and fast-walked toward the goal line. She smiled widely as Maurice skipped to intercept her. Maurice wrapped his arms around his wife, lifted her feet off the ground, and spun her around slowly.

"So she's down now," Doug said.

"She's not down. Maurice picked her up," Cecelia disputed.

"No, I mean…" Doug struggled to find the words to explain the rules. "Each time you run a play, run with the ball, the squash, it's called a down. You have four downs to go ten yards. Then you get a new set of downs."

Doug had the attention of the slaves, but they all conveyed bafflement.

"Let's go. Everyone line up again," Doug told the group.

The participants lined up again and got set.

"Hut! Hut!" Doug called out.

Doug watched his teammates move about and scanned the field for an option.

"Quarterback sneak!" Doug hailed as he tucked the squash under his arm and darted through the crowd. Doug quickly found himself with nothing but open real estate before him. Robert ran as hard as he could and closed the gap. The collision was violent when Robert threw his total weight behind the tackle. Doug dropped the squash, and it rolled away as the boys crashed to the ground. Robert immediately jumped to his feet, cracking the slightest smile that betrayed his vacant demeanor. Doug remained on his back, examining his scraped elbow. Florence cast a disapproving look at Robert that sent an unmistakable message. Feeling instant remorse, Robert extended his hand to Doug. The young men clasped hands, and Robert helped Doug to his feet.

"Thanks," Doug offered.

"Uh, huh," Robert replied before walking away.

Everyone gathered at the new line of scrimmage.

"I almost pulled a Cam Newton on y'all," Doug laughingly told them.

"I don't know what a Cam Newton is," Homer stated.

"Cam is a person. He was a great player for my favorite football team, the Carolina Panthers," Doug informed Homer.

Vernon joined the huddle, towering over everyone.

"Let's go again," Doug said.

Doug lined up with the squash and examined the defense. He could hardly see the field around Vernon. Doug noticed a figure sitting atop a horse next to a tree a short distance away. It was Lester. The cruel man lifted a bottle to his lips and took a long sip. Doug committed to enjoying the game. It was Sunday, after all.

"Hut! Hut!" Doug shouted again.

Doug clutched the squash and took off again, but he didn't get far. Vernon reached out his arm and without taking a step, grabbed Doug by the shoulder and stopped him in his tracks. Shocked by the suddenness of his apprehension and the strength of Vernon's grip, Doug dropped the ball. Vernon released his grasp on Doug and bent over to claim the squash. The enormous man stood still, uncertain of what to do next.

"Dang, you're strong," Doug started. "I fumbled, and you recovered. You have a chance to score. Run to the line at the other end."

Vernon wasn't sure of the rules as Doug explained them, but he lumbered toward the goal line and Doug gave pursuit. Cecelia laughed as she clutched Vernon's arm, and the gentle giant dragged her along with him. Homer snatched one of Vernon's legs, but he barely slowed the man. Doug jumped on Vernon's back and tried to pull him down, but the titan carried the young man like a child. Doug slid off Vernon's back and grabbed the man's other leg. The slaves laughed as Vernon dragged Homer and Doug across the goal line.

"How you supposed to pull him to the ground?" Maurice questioned.

Doug got to his feet and dusted himself off.

"You scored a touchdown," Doug said. "Spike it. Throw it down."

Doug demonstrated the celebratory move which Vernon cheerfully duplicated, busting open the squash when he threw it to the ground.

"Um, we need another ball," Doug said with a chuckle.

Doug dashed toward the basket to retrieve another squash, but he halted abruptly and his smile vanished, as it did from every face among the slaves. Lester walked toward them from the opposite goal line. The slaves stood detached from joy, the elation they felt moments prior gone in a twinkling moment.

"Oh, no, don't stop on my behalf," the brute began. "Keep laughing and acting like a bunch of savages."

The green glass bottle he held in his hand clanged against the metal gun on his hip.

"Cecelia, come over here," Lester said as he summoned her hither with the hand that held the bottle.

The frightened woman reluctantly walked to the hateful strongman. She stopped before him and cringed as he looked deeply into her eyes. Lester even kept his eyes upon her as he took another drink.

"Have a drink," Lester offered as he extended the bottle to her.

Cecelia meekly shook her head from side to side.

"It's all right; have a drink."

"I don't want no drink, Mr. Lester."

"You know nobody else is going to have this chance, don't you? I told you, you're different from them."

"I ain't thirsty, Mr. Lester."

"If you say so. Maybe one of these days you'll show a little gratitude for the special treatment you get," Lester uttered before walking away.

Lester's words were like an odious insult to Cecelia, but she dared not respond. He walked among the slaves, looked them over, assured of his jurisdiction over the anxious and disheartened people. Lester stepped into a cabin and observed the squalid living conditions of the captives. He removed the lid from an iron kettle hanging in the fireplace, then quickly dropped it back into place.

"You live like animals. Heck, I've seen hog pens tidier than this," the ogre said.

Lester stood in the doorway and faced the slaves, searching their ranks for a suitable candidate.

"Lucille, get in here," Lester ordered.

The anxious woman handed her son to Florence before stepping into the cabin with Lester. He swung her around to make her also face the doorway. Lester handed his bottle to Lucille, which she clasped with both hands.

"Don't drop it now," Lester warned as he removed a knife from his belt.

Lucille's breathing sped up as Lester pinched the cloth on the shoulder of her dress and cut it. The fabric fell away, revealing the flesh of her bare shoulder.

"Thank you," Lester said as he plucked the bottle from her hands. "You stay right here."

Lester stepped out of the cabin and stood just outside the door.

"OK, big boy, get in there and make me one just as big and strong and dumb as you are. Ain't no sense in Mr. Cobb buying new slaves when we can make them."

Vernon didn't move.

"I said get in there, now get."

Vernon stood like a statue. Exasperated by the behemoth's failure to comply, Lester stepped behind Vernon and delivered a swift kick to the back of his leg, which had no effect.

"Get in there!" Lester shouted.

Vernon didn't budge. In a fit of frustration, Lester threw his bottle at the cabin wall, breaking it to pieces. Tears flowed down Lucille's face.

"Please don't Mr. Lester," Lucille pleaded.

"Be quiet! You ain't nothing but a sow!"

"Please stop," Doug asked in a moderate tone.

"Don't make me tell you again! Now get in there and put a baby in her belly before I go fetch my whip!" Lester howled as he kicked Lester repeatedly.

"Lester, stop it!" Doug yelled.

Lester glared at Doug. The brutish man's expression left no doubt about his state of mind. Lester displayed the comportment one might expect of a lunatic. Furious at Doug's outburst, Lester reached for his pistol. As Lester clutched the weapon and prepared to pull it from the holster, the front door of the main house slammed shut with a bang. Joseph Cobb scurried down the steps and set his course directly to the slave cabins at a lively pace.

"What is all this caterwauling over here?" the slave owner loudly demanded to know.

The slaves did not answer, but simply parted their ranks to reveal Lester's presence.

"Lester, it's Sunday. Why are you here?"

"I was riding by, and I heard a loud commotion. They were out here hooting and cackling like a bunch of wild animals. I wanted to make sure everything was all right."

"Well, I thank you kindly. Come along and I'll walk you back to your horse."

The slaves resumed their previous tasks as Lester and Mr. Cobb walked away.

"I didn't mean to intrude on you, Mr. Cobb. If you don't keep them on a short leash, they might revolt."

"Oh, it's fine Lester. I appreciate you stopping by and checking on things."

"They were laughing and carrying on. I had to make sure your family was all right. I told you about what happened to my father. You think you have them under control and then one day they just up and bite the hand that feeds them."

The men stopped by Lester's horse, and Joseph Cobb stared at the horizon.

"I fear I may lose them all anyway," Joseph stated.

"Now, Mr. Cobb, why would you say a thing like that? You know me and the fellas are going to keep them under control. They ain't going anywhere."

The older man sighed and smirked in disappointment.

"Sherman has taken Atlanta. They will surely re-elect Lincoln in the north and this war will continue," Mr. Cobb said. "I'm afraid it does not bode well for the Confederacy."

"Don't be disheartened, Mr. Cobb. Our boys will soon repel Sherman's aggression and send him right back to that tyrant Lincoln with his tail between his legs."

"Time will tell I suppose."

The ringing of a bell at the house interrupted the men.

"Won't you stay for supper?" Mr. Cobb asked.

"No, sir. I appreciate the invite, but I need to be heading home. I'll see you in the morning."

Lester mounted his horse, pulled on the reins, and began the journey home. Joseph Cobb took a slow, meandering walk back to his house.

The day bid farewell to the inhabitants of Bentonville with another dazzling sunset. Doug stood outside the cabin and gazed upon the horizon that glowed with brilliant shades of orange and yellow. He marveled at the way nature could display the most sublime and remarkable scenery, even as men were cruel to each other.

Far to the south, the sun did not illuminate the horizon. War fires raged in the cities and homesteads of the South. The flames kept the darkness at bay, except that which dwelled in the hearts of men. Step by step and day by day, the source of those fires drew closer to Bentonville.

18

Uncle Billy Takes a Walk

Telegram sent to General Ulysses S. Grant from General William T. Sherman in Allatoona, Georgia:

"Until we can repopulate Georgia, it is useless to occupy it, but utter destruction of its roads, houses, and people will cripple their military resources. By attempting to hold the roads we will lose a thousand men monthly and will gain no result. I can make the march and make Georgia howl."

On November 15, 1864, General Sherman began his March to the Sea. An army of over 60,000 men tore across the land like locusts, devastating farms, factories, and railroads in its path. Instead of relying on supply lines, the man affectionately known as "Uncle Billy" by his soldiers, sent groups to plunder the countryside. He hoped the tactic would feed his army and terrorize the Southern populace, diminishing its support for the war.

The Hopper farm in rural Georgia was abuzz with activity on an early December day. Kitch, a tall man dressed in a long-sleeve white shirt, swung an ax down and split a small log in one swoop. He tossed the pieces of timber onto a pile while his ten-year-old son, Moses, lifted another log and placed it on the stump. Their master's nine-year-old son stood to the side and watched.

"Stand back now, Moses," Kitch warned his son as he raised the ax above his head.

After splitting another log, Kitch tossed it toward the pile of broken wood but missed.

"I'll get it," the master's son declared as he raced to retrieve the piece of lumber.

"Thank you, George," Kitch said.

Moses set another log for his father and stepped away. Kitch swung the blade, and father and son repeated the process.

"Kitch, how long are you going to chop that wood?" George asked.

"As long as I live," Kitch replied with a smile and a wink.

George and Moses laughed at the grinning man.

"You always say that about everything," a giggling George said.

George's mother, Catherine, walked past carrying an empty basket.

"George, you let them be. They've got work to do," Catherine informed her son.

"I'm helping, mama," the young lad answered.

"They don't need your help," Catherine stated as she continued toward a garden.

"I won't get in the way, mama," George replied.

"Kitch, when you're done chopping that wood, go fetch some hay and feed the sheep," Catherine ordered.

"Yes, ma'am."

Catherine walked to the large vegetable garden where Nan, Kitch's wife, was on her knees harvesting carrots, pulling them from the ground, and placing them in a basket.

"I'll take those, Nan," Catherine said as she placed the empty basket on the ground and took the full one. "Fill that one too."

"Yes, ma'am," Nan softly said.

Catherine carried the basket of carrots to a large white house that stood at the center of the picturesque property. She walked through the beautiful foyer of the house and entered the kitchen at the end of a hallway. Catherine's daughter, Clara, sorted potatoes with the help of a young slave woman named Patty, the matriarch of another slave family owned by the

Hopper household. Catherine placed the basket of carrots on the table before opening a cupboard and removing a box with a lid, about the size of a modern lunch pail. Mrs. Hopper opened a fine cabinet with shiny silverware. Catherine pulled the valuable utensils from the cabinet and loaded them into the box, then closed the lid.

"Patty, fetch a shovel and dig a hole beside the porch and bury this box," Catherine instructed.

"Yes, ma'am, I sure will."

"If any Yankee scoundrels pass this way, I don't want them stealing my fine silver."

The slave woman accepted the box and left the kitchen.

"I'm going to fetch more potatoes, Mama," Clara said before exiting the room herself.

Kitch used a pitchfork to sling hay into a wagon parked in the barn. Moses pushed hay to the front of the wagon, allowing room for much more. George sat in a loft about ten feet above them, his feet dangling over the side and moving back and forth.

"Hey, Kitch, how long are you going to scoop that hay?" George asked.

"As long as I live," George said, sending the boys into a fit of laughter.

Kitch laughed with the boys as he continued about his work.

"Kitch, when do you reckon Daddy's coming home?" young George asked.

"Oh, he'll be home once the war is over. I suppose it won't be too much longer."

"Do you think he'll remember me? He's been away a long time."

"Of course he will remember you. Fathers never forget their children," Kitch told the boy. "Besides, I don't think anybody could forget a boy like you George, whether or not they're your daddy."

George cracked a smile again and looked down at the wagon, now stuffed with hay.

"Moses," George whispered.

Kitch's son looked up at George, who waved him away. Moses stepped to one end of the wagon and watched the younger boy above him. George pushed himself from the loft and dropped into the hay, and disappeared into it before he jumped up laughing. Moses chuckled as well. George climbed from the wagon and returned to the ladder leading to the loft.

"Come on, Moses," George said as he beckoned the other boy to join him.

Moses looked at his father for a moment, silently seeking permission to join in the fun. Kitch nodded his head in a manner that said, "go ahead." Moses jumped from the wagon and followed George to the loft. The boys plunged from the loft and landed in the safety of the hay as Kitch added more to the pile between leaps.

"Come on, Kitch, you should do it," George urged.

"Yeah, come on, Daddy!" Moses encouraged his father.

"It looks like great fun, but I have to go feed the sheep. Get down from there now."

The boys made one final plunge into the wagon.

"Moses, help me get the mule," Kitch insisted.

"Yes, Daddy."

The young man climbed from the wagon as Kitch led a mule from a stall. Once the animal was in place, Moses helped his father tether it to the wagon.

"Get in, Moses," George advised.

"Go on," Kitch told his son with a grin.

Moses climbed back into the wagon and fell onto the dry yellow grass. Kitch grabbed the reins and walked before the mule, leading it through the open barn doors.

Clara walked to a field far from the house next to a row of dense pine trees near the road. She slowed her pace as she neared. Something moved among the trees. Clara sought to determine what was slithering through the woods as she moved closer to the field. Twenty men wearing blue coats and holding long rifles suddenly burst forth from the trees. They spread out across the land like an out-of-control wildfire. Clara nearly fell when she stopped and spun around to run. One soldier raised his rifle and took aim at Clara as she fled toward the house. The man fired off a round that whizzed past Clara and disturbed the ground before her.

"Halt, you rebel wench!" the soldier yelled.

The shot alerted Patty, who held a shovel and hovered over a hole beside the porch.

"If any of those stinking Yankees try to get in the house, you hit them with that shovel!" Clara ordered as she ran up the steps.

Having only exited the barn moments earlier, Kitch stood in stunned awe at the sight. Another shot rang out.

"Stay down, boys," Kitch ordered as he pushed Moses flat in the wagon.

Patty observed the Union soldiers that scattered across the farm rounding up sheep and potatoes. Two wagons turned off the road and hurried up the driveway. Soldiers deposited their plunder into the wagons before they came to a stop. Patty released the shovel and let it fall to the ground. Amid the chaos, Patty could only think of her two young children, so she dashed toward a far away barn. Patty's husband carried the children from the barn, one in each arm. Soldiers each led three hogs from the barn and tethered them to one wagon.

George raised his head and witnessed the tempest that engulfed his family's home. The boy jumped from the wagon and raced toward the house.

"George, come back!" Kitch called.

The young lad bolted to the house with great haste, as if he could outrun Kitch's words.

Union soldiers continued to raid the farm, dragging anything useful for the army's March to the Sea from barns to the wagons. Nan ran to her husband and son beside the wagon.

"What's happening, Kitch?" Nan asked, her eyes filled with panic.

"I think General Sherman's army is here. Some of them at least."

Patty's family joined Kitch and Nan.

"Lord, I never thought I'd see this happen here," Patty said.

Two soldiers approached Kitch and the other slaves. The men seemed more civilized than their counterparts who ran scattershot and pillaged the farm. The men stood before Kitch and removed their hats.

"You need not fear. We are your friends, friends who have set you free.

Any able-bodied man may come with us if he chooses. We can use you to help build roads, bridges, and tend to the animals. If you have family, please consider remaining with your master. We cannot take care of women and children alongside you," the soldier said to the group.

Nan looked at Kitch. Her face brimmed with expectation and belief.

"Take the time you need to decide. We have work to do. You may join us when we depart if you choose to do so," the soldier said.

"We're free, Kitch. Do you hear that? We're free," Nan said to her husband.

Kitch looked at the tumultuous scene unfolding around him.

"Why you look so unhappy? We're free," Nan reminded Kitch.

"I worry about the boy. Look what's happening," he replied.

"We have our own son to look after. Kitch, we can't stay here. We won't ever be free."

"I know. But think about little George."

"I helped bring that boy into the world. Changed his diapers, cleaned him up. I helped raise him. You think I don't care about that boy? I do. But our boy deserves to be as free as George. We have to go, Kitch."

Kitch watched a soldier set fire to the gin house. Smoke billowed from a barn. Soldiers ran from a smokehouse carrying cuts of meat. Most of the slaves gathered near the wagons, save for Patty, who dug up the silverware she buried minutes before. A few soldiers ran up the steps and barged into the house.

"I know. We will go. I just need to make sure he's all right."

Invading soldiers rummaged through the house, seeking anything of value. A tall bearded soldier rushed to the kitchen entrance, where he met the end of a rifle held by little George Hopper. The soldier froze in his tracks, watching the nervous but angry boy holding the firearm. Catherine and Clara stood behind George, cowering in an embrace.

"Hey there, fella," the soldier began. "You be careful with that thing now. You don't want to hurt anybody."

"You stay away from us. I'll shoot, I swear I will," George warned the man. The rifle shook in his unsteady hand.

"Just take it easy. Calm down, son."

Two other uniformed raiders arrived at the kitchen door and stood behind their comrade. George kept the gun pointed at the men. Despite being afraid and outnumbered, George meant to protect his family.

"Why don't we make a deal?" the bearded man asked as he slowly removed a knife from his belt. "Now, you put down that gun, and I'll give you this knife. Look how nice it is. I got it during battle in Atlanta. It's yours if you want it."

The man held the knife by the blade and extended the handle toward George.

"Stay back!" George cautioned. "Put it on the ground or I'll shoot!"

The unshaven man slowly bent at the knees and placed the knife on the floor.

"Step back before I blast a hole in ya," the boy ordered.

The soldier retreated a couple of steps.

"I mean it, I'll kill you dead if you don't get out of here," George declared.

The standoff continued between the scared, fidgety boy and the battle-hardened soldiers. Unexpectedly and calmly, Kitch appeared from the side and stood in the doorway, placing himself between the barrel of the gun and the Union soldiers.

"Get out of the way, Kitch," George instructed.

"It's all right, George. Put the gun down now," Kitch suggested.

"Daddy said I had to protect Mama."

"I know, and you're a brave boy. But your daddy wouldn't want nothing bad to happen to you."

Kitch grasped the barrel of the weapon and eased it up and away as he kneeled before George.

"It's OK, you can let it go now," Kitch told George.

George kept his right hand on the rifle, which stood vertically between them.

"Let go, George. Just let it go," Kitch directed.

The boy released his grip on the gun and almost fell forward as he wrapped his arms around Kitch's neck. George sobbed and buried his face in the slave's shoulder. The soldiers rushed into the kitchen and emptied bowls of vegetables into burlap sacks. The women screamed, adding to the pandemonium. But the slave and boy were oblivious to it, seeking assurance and comfort among themselves. Kitch rubbed George's back, helping to soothe the wailing George.

"Get out!" cried the bearded soldier as he jabbed Clara in the back.

"Don't you touch her!" warned Catherine.

"I said git!"

Kitch carried the rifle in one hand and kept his other on George's shoulder as he guided the boy out of the house. Catherine couldn't believe her eyes when she saw the condition of her homestead. Barns burned. It appeared as though a stampede of wild animals had trampled the garden. The slaves gathered with the soldiers beside wagons full of food and property. Patty removed the box of silver from the hole in the ground, then tucked it under her arm and ran toward her family by the wagons.

"Patty, you get back here! That was my mother's silver!" Catherine howled.

The disheartened woman dropped to her knees and held her face in her hands. Clara leaned over and hugged her mother as a man carrying a torch approached. Kitch removed his hand from George's shoulder and addressed the bearded soldier.

"Please, sir, not the house. They don't have nothing. You took everything else they have."

Kitch's compassion and concern for the people who kept him in bondage visibly stirred the soldier's emotions.

"Leave the house," the bearded soldier ordered his subordinate.

Kitch handed the man the rifle before walking toward his family waiting beside the wagons.

"Kitch, come back," George called.

Kitch stopped in his tracks, then turned to face his former master's son as a free man. Tears flowed down the boy's face and Kitch walked to him.

"Is everything all right, George?" Kitch asked as he dropped to one knee.

"No. I don't want you to go. Please stay."

"As much as I might want to, I need to watch after Moses and Nan."

"They can stay too."

"You're a good boy, George. The world is changing all around us. Don't you change. You stay the sweet boy you always been."

"Please don't go, Kitch. Stay here," George pleaded again.

"I wish I could, but I want Moses to grow up free, just like you."

"But you're my friend," George said with tear-filled eyes.

"I'll always be your friend."

"You promise?"

"As long as I live."

Kitch drew George to him and hugged the boy tightly. After a minute of the unspoken expression of affection, Kitch rose to his feet and rubbed George on the head.

"You stay good, George," Kitch offered before walking away.

Young George ran to his mother, then wiped the tears from his face with part of her dress. Kitch put his arm around his wife and a procession of soldiers, animals, and free people departed the Hopper farm to join Uncle Billy on his long walk to the ocean.

Thousands of freed slaves followed Sherman's army along the crude roads heading east. Among the Union soldiers, the destitute people found compassion, scorn, confusion, and salvation. Some Union soldiers had never interacted with a black person before the war and their reaction was as diverse as the group marching to the sea. Many former slaves shook a white man's hand for the first time. To the newly free people, some soldiers were heroes, while others were no better than the people who kept them in chains.

An icy reception from many of the Union troops was not the only concern for those at the rear of Sherman's columns. Although decimated in Georgia, the Confederate army still harassed the Yankee intruders. Groups of cavalry engaged Sherman's army in skirmishes along their route. Southerners regarded freed slaves as stolen property and, if captured, returned them to bondage.

The large number of people following the army slowed its march and frustrated Sherman and his officers. Nonetheless, the army found the labor of the once enslaved men to be a valuable resource.

Kitch's feet ached as he walked along the road among the thousands of people and troops. The army moved fifteen miles on a good day. Sherman pushed his men hard. Stopping for too long might bring the quest to ruin. Staying in place put the army at risk of attack and starvation.

"Daddy, I'm tired and hungry too," young Moses told his father.

"I know, son. Try not to think about it. Think about what it will be like in the north."

A soldier on horseback arrived at the back of the column before Moses could reply.

"Uncle Billy needs some vigorous men to clear trees from the road," the man told the group.

Kitch took a step forward before Nan grabbed his arm.

"Don't go, Kitch."

"It will be fine. Y'all sit and rest a spell. I don't mind helping. Maybe I feel like I'm helping win our liberty. I'll be back before long."

Nan looked at her exhausted son, then released Kitch. The husband and father joined a group of stout men who walked to the front of the throng of soldiers and free citizens.

That night, camp bustled with activity. Soldiers without tents relaxed on blankets on the ground. Fires crackled and brightened the landscape. Men fed themselves with the bounty gained by foraging as some slept, exhausted after a long day's march. A handful of hungry erstwhile servants meandered about the camp, requesting something to eat. Moses drew near to a pair of soldiers sharing a sizable chunk of smoked meat. The boy stopped and stared with great expectancy. The largest of the soldiers stopped mid-chew to glare at the child.

"Can I help you with something?" the grumpy man asked.

"I'm sorry, sir. I'm hungry," the famished boy said with a nearly expressionless face.

"Yeah, well, so am I."

A young trooper sat alone about fifteen feet away and watched the scene as it unfolded, cutting his own dinner into pieces. Moses watched the surly men slice the slab of meat and devour it in big bites. The large man stopped eating and looked at Moses again. Juices dribbled down his chin as the sloppy eater shook his head.

"Get from 'round here now," the slob said to Moses. "Can't you see we're trying to eat?"

"Can I please have a piece?" Moses asked. "I don't mean no harm. I'm awfully hungry. We been traveling a long way these past few days."

"Here, you can have this," the brute said as he tossed away a piece of meat.

Moses scampered after the morsel, which landed halfway to the young soldier who watched the spectacle develop. The starving boy hastily picked up the scrap and lifted it to his mouth.

"Stop," the observant serviceman instructed. "Come here."

Moses paused and held the filthy remnant of food with a dejected look upon his face.

"It's all right. Come over here," the young man advised again.

The boy walked to the soldier, heartbroken by the prospect of a lost meal.

"What's your name?" the trooper asked.

"Moses," the boy replied.

"Nice to meet you, Moses. My name is Bernard."

"Hello, sir," Moses sheepishly replied.

"You can call me, Bernard," the young man assured Moses. "Where are you from?"

Moses pointed down the road toward his parents.

"Oh, just down the way. Well, listen, I was wondering if you could help me."

"Yes, sir Mr. Bernard, I'm a good helper."

Moses noticed a red ribbon tied among the laces on one of the soldier's boots.

"Why do you have a ribbon on your boots?" Moses asked.

"Oh, I keep that there to remind me of a girl back home. She wore it in her hair sometimes."

"Back home? Where is that?"

"I come from a town in the hills of Pennsylvania."

"I've never been to the hills of Pennsylvania."

"You'll have to visit sometime."

"Sure, maybe I can come visit you."

"That would be fine. Before you do, I need you to help me."

"Yes, sir, Mr. Bernard, I'm glad to help you. Anything you need."

"Would you trade me that piece of meat you have for this piece of meat I have?"

Moses looked puzzled. He couldn't comprehend why Bernard wanted to trade the meat on his plate for a dirty piece lifted off the ground moments earlier.

"Are you sure you want to do that?" Moses asked.

"Yes, I'm sure. Just put it right there," Bernard said as he tapped an empty place on his plate with a fork.

Moses placed the dirty piece of food on the plate. Bernard stabbed a large pork chop and raised it to the eager boy.

"There you go."

"Thank you, sir," Moses said with a beaming smile on his face.

The boy ran to his parents, chomping on the savory meal as he went. Bernard scraped the piece of meat off his plate, then jabbed a potato wedge and ate it. After eating his meager supper, Bernard laid on a blanket and stared at the sky. He quickly drifted off to sleep and felt, like the stars overhead, he was a point of light amid a world filled with darkness.

December 9, 1864.

The light of the morning sun caused man and beast to stir throughout the camp. Kitch awoke to find his son's head resting on his outstretched arm. The father gently shook his boy. Moses sat up slowly and yawned. Kitch stood up and brushed the dirt from his pants, then helped his son dust off as well.

The caravan was on the move again before the dew evaporated. Weary former slaves and soldiers alike pressed on, knowing that each step they took led them closer to home. Sometimes Moses became too fatigued to walk, so Kitch carried him. The sandy soil covered in fallen pine needles added to the arduousness of the journey, making every step seem like two. Kitch and his family were among a cluster of six hundred freed slaves following a branch of 14,000 Union troops. The group reached a portable pontoon bridge that crossed Ebenezer Creek and came to a halt. An officer addressed the crowd.

"We need about twenty able-bodied men on the other side of the bridge to assist with work on the other side. The rest of you remain here as these men and troops cross."

Nan held Kitch tightly by the arm.

"I know what you're thinking, and I wish you wouldn't," she said to her husband.

"I have to help. These men set us free, Nan. It's only right that I go when they need our help."

"Be careful," Nan pleaded with her husband.

"I'll see you on the other side."

Kitch followed a handful of freed slaves across the bridge with the soldiers. A detachment of armed men stayed back and blocked the bridge. The onetime slaves grew restless as they watched their kinfolk move farther away. Some concerned people tried to push their way past the guards.

"Get back!" a soldier exclaimed. "You can't cross!"

"You can't just leave us here!" Nan shouted.

"Our family is over there!" yelled Patty.

"We can't feed you!" the soldier roared again.

"Them gray coats ain't far behind!" shrieked another woman.

The free people shoved the guards and tried to occupy the bridge, only to be pushed back repeatedly.

"Cut the ropes!" came the order.

A uniformed man hastily dropped to his knees and severed the ropes holding the bridge against the bank. Almost instantly, the bridge drifted away from the shore. To expedite their movement, soldiers on the other side pulled the bridge. The abandoned people screamed in despair.

Kitch looked at the water and saw the bridge moving away, then noticed his wife and son on the other side. His heartbeat quickened and Kitch's soul filled with as much dread as those trapped across the broad swamp.

Nan looked behind her and witnessed the building panic. Confederate cavalry lay behind the helpless people and deep, murky water before them. Stricken with fear and desperate for freedom, some people flung themselves into the water, even though they could not swim. Nan cried and held Moses close as the screams of the destitute rose to a crescendo. Shouting, splashing, and gurgling sounds resonated across the swamp as people thrashed in the water.

Kitch fixed a look of pure horror on his face. He saw his son and wife holding each other. The only thing he wanted at that moment was to have them in his arms. While those on the other side of the wide creek risked their lives to cross to freedom, Kitch defied death for something more important to him.

Nan and Moses looked across Ebenezer Creek and observed Kitch as he jumped into the cold, dark water. Nan raised a hand and covered her mouth to hold in a scream. She knew her husband could not swim. Nan held her son tighter, wishing she could pass any extra strength she had to the boy's father.

Kitch felt his foot touch the bottom and kicked off, propelling him forward. In mere moments, Kitch found himself in deeper water and struggled to keep his chin above the surface. The desperate man inhaled before he went under again. He kicked hard and his head breached the surface once more, where he quickly gulped air again before submerging.

Nan and Moses watched Kitch's head bob in the water while his arms flailed about. The man exerted himself mightily but made little progress. The seconds Kitch spent beneath the surface of the dingy water seemed like hours. Each time the man reemerged filled Nan with hope.

Kitch felt his legs turn to jelly. Fatigue overtook him, and he struggled to catch a breath each time he came up. Kitch kicked his legs and waved his arms frantically. His face emerged from the creek and he opened his mouth, but Kitch captured more water than air. He slipped beneath the water once again and held on to what little air he had. Kitch bobbed up again, spit out the water, and tried to inhale, but only took in more water. The exhausted man gargled and choked when he came up again. Kitch caught brief glimpses of his wife and child through the splashes of water. He had to reach them. They needed him, and he needed them.

Kitch grew more fatigued, and he barely saw his family through the blur of disturbed water. When Kitch tried to secure more air, he was already beneath the surface again. Kitch instinctively spat the water from his mouth, but there was no air to take in. All that surrounded him was the awful, merciless water of Ebenezer Creek. His body gasped for air and water swept into his lungs, pushing out the remaining life-sustaining oxygen. Kitch stared into the emptiness before him, knowing it was the end. He would pay any price to be with his family. And he did.

Nan saw Kitch's body emerge from Ebenezer Creek, floating face down, his arms stretched out above his head. She turned Moses away from the grisly sight and held her son warmly, resting her cheek on his head as she cried.

The Union army kept moving, and soon the shouts of the crestfallen and dispossessed became faint.

Sherman's army arrived outside Savannah the following day. Confederate General William Hardee fled the city on December 20th, surrendering it to the Union army. Sherman wired a message to President Lincoln to present the city of Savannah as a Christmas gift. Soon Uncle Billy would turn his unflinching gaze northward, where destiny awaited.

19

The Veil

Torchlight flickered and illuminated the smiling faces of slaves and masters alike. A long table covered with food far better than the usual fare sat on one side of the slaves' meager courtyard. Edith Cobb handed red ribbons to all the female slaves.

"There you are, Cecelia," Edith said as she placed a ribbon in the enslaved woman's hand. "Won't you look pretty with that in your hair?"

Cecelia and Lucille giggled and smiled widely at each other. Lucille spun around and Cecelia helped her arrange the ribbon in her hair. Doug observed Robert standing a short distance away. The young man was clean and without his late grandfather's hat, revealing to Doug the importance of the occasion. Philip opened a case and brought forth a banjo, which he then inspected. Joseph Cobb stood by with a rare smile on his face, looking proudly at the scene. Best of all, Lester was absent from the celebration.

Christmas was one of the unique times that slaves could mask their anguish through a pretense of joy. The master usually gave slaves a few days free from work and might even permit them a pass to visit family members on other farms and plantations. Some daring slaves attempted to flee once a pass was in hand, knowing the master would not expect them back for some time. Slave owners from nearby farms held joint celebrations so their slaves could interact with one another, and the owners could conduct business.

Henry arrived with a large bag slung over his shoulder. He placed the bag on the end of the table and opened it wide.

"Everyone gather round," Joseph Cobb instructed. "Let's hand out gifts before our guests arrive, lest they want something too."

The slaves assembled in a line before the master and stood silently, many with smiles on their faces. Henry shuffled through the bag and removed packages wrapped in plain paper. Philip and Edith took the packages and began giving them away.

"There you go, Doug," Philip said as he handed a package to the young man.

Philip continued down the line and Doug held the package, bewildered that they would give a slave a gift, even at Christmas.

"Don't be shy; open them!" Edith enthusiastically suggested.

Doug was more reluctant than the other slaves and opened his slowly. It was nothing like the holidays he spent with his mother. Doug finally opened the present and saw what the masters provided: two fresh shirts. The women were each given two simple dresses.

"Thank you, Massa Cobb," Homer said.

"There are your new clothes for next year," the master said, doing his best to seem benevolent.

Doug found it insulting. He saw the items as a means of control, not a gift. Doug knew Mr. Cobb expected gratitude, recognition, and obedience for a paltry shirt. The slave relied on the master for his very existence. The slaves carried their new clothes to their cabins before returning to the yard.

A wagon rattled and bounced as it came down the road to the Cobb farm. The owner of a nearby farm, Jeremiah Hargrove, arrived with his dozen slaves. Homer beamed as he watched the wagon's approach. Doug joined Florence and Maurice around the large table and marveled at different food items on display. After sustaining himself on a rudimentary slave's diet for so long, Doug couldn't believe his eyes. A large turkey and two chickens, as well as apples, bread, and potatoes, adorned the table.

Robert stayed close to Lucille. They tried to hide it, but Robert and Lucille had an obvious fondness for each other. Seeing Robert with a smile on his face brought some peace to Doug's soul. The runaway journey damaged their friendship, but it had not ruined either young man's capacity to care.

Jeremiah Hargrove's slaves gathered near the table. Doug recognized Auston, the runaway slave Lester had beaten months earlier. Auston was thinner and a fresh scar decorated his face. The man appeared thoroughly defeated, too timid to hold his head up, and did so only to offer a cursory glance from time to time.

Homer saw a sweet and familiar countenance among the visiting slaves and a smile spontaneously appeared on his face. He stared at a woman in a pink and white dress as if he couldn't believe his eyes. Homer snapped from his trance when Vernon bumped into him. Seeing the woman was still there, that she was real, Homer trotted over to her almost at a sprint.

"Betty," Homer said jubilantly as soon as he reached the woman.

With complete disregard for propriety, Homer took her hands in his own.

"Betty, is it really you?" he asked.

"Homer," the woman replied.

"Oh, Betty!" Homer declared as he jumped up and down while holding her hands.

The woman remained stone-faced while Homer giddily bounced with joy.

"I can't believe it's really you," Homer said with a grin that extended the width of his face.

A tall man with a baby in his arms walked to them and stood beside Betty.

"Who is this?" the man asked in a deep voice.

The man was as tall as Lester, but a fraction of the size. Still, he towered over most of the people at the gathering.

"This is Homer," Betty stated, and quickly withdrew her hands from Homer's grasp. "Homer, this is my husband, Pompey."

"Husband?" Homer asked as the smile evaporated from his face.

"Yes, her husband," Pompey replied.

The tall man's nose crinkled, and he practically snarled.

"Homer and I lived in the same cabin when I was owned by Mr. Cobb," Betty explained.

Homer stared at the pair in disbelief. Pompey handed the child to Betty.

"It's nice to meet you, Homer," Pompey said as he extended his hand to Homer.

Homer's legs wobbled as he retreated and he nearly fell, but he recovered almost gracefully. The ringing of a bell penetrated the night as Homer disappeared behind the crowd.

"Let's eat, everyone," Edith Cobb called out.

The throng of people gathered around the table and prepared for a feast unlike most they could remember. Doug couldn't help but recall the holiday meals enjoyed with his mom and grandparents and a sense of longing overtook him once again.

The slaves spent the time after dinner schmoozing among themselves. Mr. Cobb retired to the house, having stroked his ego and asserted his dominion over the land and people who lived there. Jeremiah joined Mr. Cobb on the front porch of the house. Doug noticed Homer sitting alone on a stump far from the crowd, sobbing.

"Homer, are you OK?" Doug inquired as he neared.

The man didn't answer Doug's question. Homer lowered his head and covered his face with his hands.

"What's wrong, man?" Doug asked.

Homer tried to compose himself and lifted his head. He pointed at Betty and Pompey.

"That's my wife," Homer said through tears.

Doug turned in time to see Pompey put his arm around Betty.

"What?" Doug replied. "That's your wife? But she lives on another farm."

Cecelia walked to Doug and Homer, carrying Lucille's child.

"Homer, what's wrong?" a concerned Cecelia asked.

"He says that woman is his wife," Doug announced.

"Mr. Cobb sold her to Mr. Hargrove three Christmases ago. She ain't been back before now. She done found her another husband," Homer explained.

"Oh, Homer, I'm so sorry," Cecelia said, freeing an arm so she could rub the man's shoulder.

The sound of Philip's banjo suddenly resounded through the night. The slaves converged on a dance floor of dirt and pine needles. Maurice held his wife's hands and swayed with the upbeat music. Florence laughed at her husband, who was hamming it up. Robert and Lucille couldn't stop smiling as they joined in the revelry. Even giant Vernon slouched over to dance with young Alberta, if not inelegantly. Doug and Cecelia did their best to comfort and console Homer. Edith took Henry's hand and led him to the dance floor. The sounds of happiness only added to Homer's grief, and his head fell again into his hands.

Doug watched the merriment taking place around him. He wondered if it was just a lie, an illusion, or were the people genuinely happy? Tender is the hand of the gardener, who sees joy take root in the sourest of rotten ground. Somehow, despite their suffering, the slaves celebrated. They did not extol some unseen virtue of their condition, as there was none, but proclaimed the hope of tomorrow. Christmas, of all days, was a time to recognize that even the meekest among us could rise to great things.

Florence went to Doug after the music stopped.

"Oh, my, I need to sit down for a minute," Florence declared.

Maurice arrived carrying a chair, which he placed beside Homer.

"There you go, Mammy Lou," Maurice said with a smile.

Florence shook her head with a smirk on her face as she took a seat. Philip began playing another song and the dancing began anew.

"Y'all get out there and dance. I'll hold the baby," Florence offered.

"Are you sure, Miss Florence?" Cecelia asked.

"Yes, hand him here. You have some fun."

Cecelia gave the baby to Florence, then skipped onto the dance floor, where she motioned for Doug to join her.

"Go on, son," Florence told Doug.

Maurice and Florence stayed with Homer and tended to Lucille's little boy while Doug joined the others in the soiree. Cecelia grabbed Doug's hands and swayed from side to side. She looked to her left and saw Lucille and Robert, then led Doug toward them. The foursome danced side by side with smiling faces and quick steps that even the tension between Doug and Robert was helpless to resist. After several minutes of dancing, Lucille and

Cecelia switched partners. Doug danced with Lucille and glanced at Robert, aware of his fondness for the woman. Robert smiled while he danced with Cecelia.

Beaming faces and the sounds of music and cheerfulness abounded in Bentonville. The joyful scene only deepened Homer's sorrow. He wept openly as he watched the love of his life hold the child she had as another man's wife. Maurice placed a tender hand on Homer's shoulder and applied a gentle squeeze.

"I always hoped she would come back," Homer said through tears. "But not like this. Not like this."

Maurice patted Homer's shoulders, unable to find the words to comfort him. Homer watched Pompey place his hand on the baby's head, then lean over to apply a delicate kiss to Betty's forehead. It was more than Homer could bear. He rocketed off the chair and dashed to his cabin.

Lucille and Cecelia moved closer together, bringing Doug and Robert with them. The women pushed Doug and Robert's hands together, then embraced each other, giggling while they continued dancing. Lucille and Cecelia watched Doug and Robert, who stood motionless for a moment with grins affixed on their faces. The tension between the young men broke like a dam holding back an expansive reservoir. A festive night and the guiding hearts of two young women reminded Doug and Robert of the importance of friendship, even if it is sometimes shaken and tested. The young men clenched each other's hands and burst into laughter, then put on a display of exaggerated dancing. All the slaves around Doug and Robert whooped and chuckled at the hilarity of their antics. Cecelia and Lucille grinned, knowing they set a foundation to rebuild trust. Doug and Robert would need to mend fences and heal old wounds, but the icy stubbornness that prevented them from trying had melted away.

Robert released his grip on Doug and took Lucille's hands again. Cecelia returned to Doug and resumed dancing. Alberta sat atop Vernon's shoulders while he danced with Minnie. The old woman mostly stood in place but found herself captured by the music and the wonder of the moment. Music and laughter filled the air and nobody heard Homer's agonizing lamentations for the love he lost. The unhappy man cried alone on a rickety bed in a nearby cabin, enslaved by the ways of the world and a heart that never gave up hope he would one day find his beloved again.

The party was short-lived. After an hour, Jeremiah Hargrove summoned his slaves to the wagon. Betty took a last look at the slave cabins, which were still familiar to her. Her eyes flickered as she gazed searchingly before turning to climb into the wagon.

After their guests departed, the slaves of the Cobb farm returned to their ramshackle homes. Doug crawled into bed and pulled a shabby blanket over him. The soft glow and crackle of the fire set the perfect mood for a Christmas night. Doug knew the festive atmosphere of the night was merely a veil that covered the anguish and misery that existed all around him. Yet on that cold, silent night, Doug understood the meaning of Christmas like he never had before. The world found hope in a lowly manger in Bethlehem. Surely that light could find its way to the darkest parts of the world, Doug thought. The young man drifted off to sleep with thoughts of Christmas with his mother and grandparents dancing in his head.

Heart-wrenching wailing and grieving awakened Doug the next morning. He jumped from the bed and hastily put on his shoes. Outside, Doug found a crying Florence being consoled by her husband. Several people gathered outside the cabin where Homer lived, and Doug moved to inspect the commotion. Lucille cried in Robert's embrace. Cecelia stood near them, holding her hand over her mouth, partially concealing an anguished look on her face.

"What happened?" Doug asked Cecelia.

"It's Homer," she began. "He must have died in his sleep."

"Oh, no," Doug replied, shocked by the news.

Doug felt a chill come over him when he saw Vernon carry Homer from the cabin. The sight of Homer's limp body, his arm dangling awkwardly, left no doubters among the witnesses. The certainty of Homer's death resonated like a crack of thunder.

A procession of slaves followed Vernon as he carried Homer to the field that was the last resting place for so many lost souls. Robert brought two shovels with him and handed one to Doug. The two young men went to work digging a grave while Vernon held Homer. A song of remembrance and mourning rose in the air. Doug and Robert struggled to pierce the cold, hard earth. Sometimes it seemed they only had a spoonful of dirt on their shovels. The tough job provided Doug with plenty of time to think. Homer's body bore no visible fresh wounds. Doug could only conclude that Homer's heart gave up. The previous night took the one thing that gave Homer hope, the return of his long-lost love. Hope is among the greatest of things, but it is fragile. Without hope and meaning to keep them at bay, grief and sorrow took Homer's life as might a slow working poison.

Doug and Robert had dug a suitable tomb for Homer by the time the slaves finished their agonizing eulogy. Vernon laid the dead man in the grave as gently as a mother places a newborn in a cradle. Robert and Doug filled the space with dirt while muffled cries serenaded Homer into the afterlife. After burying the gentle slave, Doug retrieved a large and small rock from near the trees. He placed the larger rock at one end of the grave and grasped the smaller rock in his hand. Applying a good amount of force, Doug scratched the letter H onto the big rock. Once Doug had finished, the slaves spent a final mournful moment with Homer, then returned to their cabins.

At the Cobb house, Caroline and Charlotte dashed down the stairs, eager to see if their Christmas wishes came true. During this time, the slaves of Bentonville yearned for a day when all things would be new.

20

All Things New

Spring arrived, and the world flourished with new life. Flowers dotted the landscape with brilliant colors, and the grass regained its deep green hue. Slaves plowed the fields to prepare for planting season. Other slaves, including Doug, Cecelia, and Lucille, worked to repair fencing around hog pens. The women held boards in place as Doug hammered nails. Vernon worked the plow in the fields. A short distance away, Henry watched Maurice and Robert chop wood. While happy to be free from the grasp of the cruel winter's chill, the slaves knew a hard season was about to begin. Longer days and warmer weather were no better friends to the slave than the plow and the whip. As always, Lester's watchful eye wasn't far away. The brute watched from a nearby fence where he loitered with Earl, Daniel, and Thomas. In the field, Philip walked along the rows and overlooked the men toiling in the dirt.

The wind wore the sweet fragrance of flowers, which made the world seem clean and radiant. Lester watched Cecelia's wavy hair bounce on her shoulders as the breeze drew near to her. Cecelia's alluring smile and exposed neck caused Lester's heart to quiver. Without saying a word, Lester abandoned the company of his friends and walked to Cecelia.

"There he goes again," Earl said with a chuckle.

Lester placed his hand on Cecelia's shoulder and pushed her dress slightly, exposing her skin.

"Cecelia, I have something for you to do at the barn," Lester said.

"But Mr. Lester, I'm helping them with the hog pen."

"They don't need your help."

"I have to hold the plank…"

Lester grabbed Cecelia around the arm tightly and pulled her away before she completed the sentence.

"I said they don't need your help, I do," the lout said as he pulled her toward the barn.

Henry noticed Lester leading Cecelia away, and his brow furrowed.

Lester slung open the small barn door and dragged Cecelia inside. He calmly closed the door and released Cecelia before he walked toward a table holding an assortment of tools.

"What do you want, Mr. Lester?" Cecelia asked, dreadfully expecting an answer she was certain she already knew.

"I want you to come over here by this table."

Cecelia was tense and stiff as a board as she walked to Lester.

"You look nervous as a polecat. You ain't got nothing to worry about. Come over here and sit a spell," Lester said as he pushed aside a hammer and saw and tapped on the end of the table.

Cecelia anxiously walked to Lester and stopped by the table. Lester again tapped his hand on the end of the table and took a step back. Cecelia sheepishly took a seat on the table and lowered her head. Lester stepped forward, pushing her knees apart and placing himself between her dangling legs. The oaf gently grabbed Cecelia's chin and lifted her face to him. Lester caressed her face and placed his hand on the back of her neck, where he could feel how shaky she was.

"It's alright. Relax."

The man slid his hand down, pushed the dress off her shoulder, and continued to fondle her body as he worked his way down her side. His hands came to rest on her knees, where the impish man gave a flirtatious squeeze.

"Mr. Lester, I have to help Lucille and Doug with the hog pen."

"You just sit tight. I thought you might appreciate getting off your feet for a moment. Besides, I've got something else for you to do."

Lester pinched her dress at the knees and gave a slight tug, moving the garment up a bit. Cecelia's breath quickened as the fabric slowly slithered up her legs. When the hem of her dress reached her knees, Cecelia pressed her clothing against the table to prevent it from moving further.

"I need to get back, Mr. Lester."

Lester grabbed Cecelia's wrist and moved her arm away. Cecelia struggled and pulled her hand away from him, but Lester landed a swift smack on her cheek.

"Hey, don't make this rough."

Lester pushed her back onto the table before he started unbuckling his trousers. Cecelia sat up and tried to push Lester aside, but he delivered a harder blow, causing her lip to bleed. Cecelia fell back with her face turned to the door and several stands of her hair covering her left eye. She resigned herself to her fate as she tasted the saltiness of her own blood. Lester grabbed his belt once again and unfastened it, but the door burst open and interrupted him. Startled, Lester scrambled to tighten his belt.

Henry stepped into the barn just in time to notice Lester pushing the tip of his belt through a loop on his pants. Cecelia remained on her back with the dress pulled over her knees and her legs dangling over the side of the table.

"What in the world is going on here?" Henry asked with a scowl on his face. He already knew the answer.

"Well, she was helping me organize these tools," Lester claimed. "Alright, move out of the way, Cecelia."

Cecelia practically drifted off the table. Lester moved around her and shuffled the tools around the table as if forming them into a line.

"Why is her lip bleeding?" Henry inquired.

"Just clumsy. I told her to lift this hammer and she hit herself in the mouth with it."

"Sure, Lester," Henry said doubtingly. "Cecelia, go on back to the hog pen now."

"Yeah, Cecelia, get to work with the pigs. I'll call when I need your help again," Lester added.

Cecelia pulled her dress over her shoulder and hastily exited the barn.

"I know what you were doing," Henry said firmly.

Lester glared at Henry, his face turning a red complexion that nearly matched his hair. His nostrils flared before he let out a deep breath.

"Ah, what do you care?" Lester said dismissively.

"They're people, Lester. They ain't animals for you to do whatever you wish."

"They are animals! They're savages! Maybe that one is a person, but the rest are animals! You don't understand because you ain't never had one turn on you. Treat them like animals or they'll kill you the first chance they get."

"One day you'll have to answer for all of your misdeeds," Henry cautioned.

"When I see God, He can judge me, and I think He will look upon me with favor."

"I doubt Mr. Cobb will when I tell him what I saw," Henry said before turning to leave.

Henry's words sent a flash of panic through Lester. The violent man grabbed the hammer off the table and spun around and swung in one motion, striking Henry on the back of the head. The blow created a horrible dull sound, like an egg cracking, only amplified many times over. Lester did it without thinking, almost instinctively. He simply reacted.

Henry fell forward and revealed Lucille standing in the doorway. The snap and thud of Henry hitting the floor sent a shudder coursing through Lucille and she trembled. Lester inhaled quickly, almost in a gasp.

"Uh, Mr. Earl told me to come fetch Mr. Henry," Lucille said, almost stuttering.

Lester looked at Lucille with blank eyes as he searched for something to say. She started to leave before Lester called out and tossed the hammer onto the floor.

"Wait," Lester beckoned. "I need your help. Henry fell and hurt himself. Come over here and help me."

Lucille reluctantly moved away from the door.

"Close the door," Lester ordered.

Lucille pulled the door closed, then stumbled closer to Lester but couldn't take her eyes off Henry's motionless body.

"Come on over here. We have to help him."

"I didn't see nothing."

"I know you didn't."

Lucille took half steps as she inched closer to the men.

"Come on, help me roll him over," Lester told her.

Lucille knelt beside Henry and averted her eyes as she helped Lester push Henry onto his back.

"Get over there," Lester said, pointing to Henry's head. "We have to stop the bleeding."

Lester looked around the room filled with tools and barrels.

"Use your dress. Press it against the wound."

Lucille's reluctance was obvious.

"Move, he's going to bleed out," Lester said.

Lucille shifted closer to Henry's head but appeared to be shell-shocked by the calamity. Lester grabbed part of her dress and pressed it against the open wound on Henry's head.

"Like this," Lester instructed, as he seized her hands and applied them to the spot.

Henry Bowman's blood oozed onto Lucille's dress, where it created a large patch of red tint on her dirty clothing.

"Wake up, Mr. Henry," Lucille uttered as she eased Henry's head back and forth. "I think he's dead, Mr. Lester."

"I think you're right," Lester said with a sigh.

The murderer looked around the room again.

"OK, he fell and hit his head. Do you understand?" Lester asked the frightened woman.

"Yes, sir."

Lester continued searching the room. There was nothing to indicate a fall or a disturbance. The only uncommon sight in the barn was a dead man, a slave in a bloody dress, and a hammer on the floor beside her.

"No, that won't do. They won't believe he fell and hit his head. But they might believe you did this."

"What? No, sir. I didn't do nothing."

"Yeah, he tried to have his way with you, and you hit him with that mallet."

"No, sir. I didn't hurt Mr. Henry."

"Who do you think they're going to believe? If I say you did it, who do you think they will believe? Me, or a stupid slave woman with blood all over her dress?"

"But, but," Lucille pondered a reply, but she knew he was right. Nobody would believe her. She was just a slave.

"You best stop cackling like a chicken and get going."

"Go where?"

"I don't know. Run through the woods behind the barn. You better get before someone sees you in that bloody dress. I'll tell them you went the other way. Just go, get as far away as you can."

Lucille stood up and froze again. She stared at Lester with tears streaming down her cheeks, her eyes open wide with terror.

"Don't you understand? They're going to kill you if they see you like that. Now get going."

"But I," Lucille began before being interrupted.

"Go! Now!" Lester blared as he raised his hand over his head.

Lucille nearly stumbled to the floor as she turned. She regained her balance and dashed out the door. Lester heard Lucille's footsteps as she ran around the barn. Limbs shuffled and cracked as the terrified slave pushed through the wilderness. Lester removed his hat and fanned himself while looking at Henry's corpse.

"You just had to go sticking your nose where it didn't belong, didn't you?" Lester said as if Henry was still alive.

Lester waited for several moments before leaving the barn. He brushed himself off and adjusted his attire in hopes of evading suspicion. The cowardly man wished for a hard drink to bolster his confidence, but he would have to propel his lie without one. Lester glanced at Henry again before exiting the barn.

Cecelia and Philip held a board in place for Doug when Lester came running.

"Where did she go?" Lester called out.

"What?" Earl asked as Lester approached him.

"Where'd she go?"

"Who?" Earl questioned.

"Lucille! That black wench killed Henry!"

"What?" Earl replied. "Are you serious?"

"Yes, I'm serious!"

Philip released the board and walked to Lester.

"Did you say Lucille killed Henry?" Philip asked incredulously.

"Yes, that's what I said."

"Lucille?" Philip asked again.

"Yes, Philip, Lucille! Can't you hear good?" Lester yelled.

"But, why?"

"I don't know. I was in the back of the barn trying to fetch a saw. When I came around the barrels, I saw her hit him in the head with a mallet. It looked like he might have been trying to have his way with her," Lester lied.

"It doesn't make sense. That's not like him, or her," Philip said in disbelief.

"Go to the barn and have a look for yourself, Philip. Go ask Henry what he thinks."

Earl took off toward the barn in a fast walk and the others followed. Doug and Cecelia stayed by the hog pen.

"I know Lucille didn't kill Henry. Henry stopped Lester from taking my clothes off and attacking me. That evil man killed Henry," Cecelia uttered.

"Where's Lucille?" Doug wondered aloud.

"I don't know, but I'm scared."

Philip ran from the barn and dashed to the house, arriving as Joseph Cobb stepped onto the porch. Lester and Earl exited the barn and walked to the house at a brisk pace.

"What in the world is all the ruckus out here?" Cobb asked.

"It's Henry. He's been killed," Philip answered.

"What? What do you mean?" Cobb pondered openly.

"Somebody killed him," Philip stated.

"Who?"

"It was Lucille," Lester interjected. "She hit him in the head with an iron mallet and took off running like a deer."

"Oh, no. You men go find her. Bring her back here. I paid good money for her. You boys find her before someone else does. Dear Lord, how did this happen?"

"What about Henry?" Philip asked.

"Yes, yes. Philip, you ride and tell his family. God bless his poor mother. She already lost a son to the war," Cobb said.

Earl, Daniel, Thomas, and Lester mounted horses.

"She ran that way," Lester said. "Follow me!"

"We should split up," Earl insisted. "We'll cover more ground."

Lester looked bewildered. He hoped if he led the men in the wrong direction, Lucille might escape and make it far from Bentonville. The heartless man needed Lucille to go far away, where nobody knew her or the name Lester Clay.

"Earl's right," Joseph Cobb suggested. "You'll cover more ground if you split up."

"You go that way," Earl said, pointing in the direction Lester said Lucille ran. "Me and Thomas will go this way."

The horses darted off into the distance, kicking up a cloud of dirt that obscured the men as much as Lester's lies clouded the truth. Doug looked around and took an inventory of the surrounding newness. The green grass, beautiful flowers, little piglets, and recently plowed field proved all things were new in Bentonville. Like a caterpillar, Lester's malice seemed to undergo a metamorphosis, and something uglier and darker emerged from the chrysalis that was his heart.

Clouds rolled in before dusk as if the heavens descended upon Bentonville. The slaves waited anxiously outside their cabins, hopeful for any news about Lucille. Joseph Cobb sat on his front porch and watched as Earl and Thomas trotted down the drive with Lucille in tow. Joseph stood up and stepped off the porch as the men came to a stop.

"Where did you find her?" Mr. Cobb asked.

"She was coming out of the woods a few miles from here. We were on our way back when we spotted her," Thomas said.

"She doesn't look to be in bad shape," Mr. Cobb stated.

"The woods scratched her up a little, but she didn't even try to run when we caught her. She didn't resist at all," Earl offered.

"And get this, even though she has blood all over her, she swears it was Lester that killed Henry," Thomas added.

Mr. Cobb stepped to Lucille and examined her, noticing the bloody spot on her dress.

"If Lester killed Henry, how did you get that blood on you?" Mr. Cobb asked.

"Mr. Lester told me to use my dress to stop the bleeding from Mr. Henry's head," Lucille replied.

"Wait a second, he killed him, but then told you to tend to him?" Mr. Cobb asked.

"Yes, sir. Mr. Lester grabbed my dress and put it on Mr. Henry's head."

"That makes little sense. Why try to save a man if you mean to kill him? Unless he wanted to point the blame," Mr. Cobb paused. "Nah. We'll sort this out. Let's get her to her cabin and see to it she stays there. We'll lock her in if we have to."

Thomas and Earl dismounted the horses and followed a slow-moving Joseph Cobb to the slave cabins, pulling Lucille behind them. The other slaves gathered to greet Lucille. The sound of galloping horses announced Lester's arrival. Lester's eyes grew wide when he saw Lucille. The brute quickly jumped off his horse before Daniel could stop behind him.

"Oh, you found her," Lester said.

"She didn't get far," Earl informed his friend.

"Oh, good," Lester answered.

"You want to know what else?" Thomas asked, knowing he wouldn't wait for an answer. "She says you're the one who killed Henry."

"What? Why you wench! How dare you!" Lester blared as he stepped to Lucille.

The terrified slave moved away from the approaching reprobate.

"Lester, stop. We'll deal with this later," Joseph Cobb ordered.

"Mr. Cobb, you ain't buying any of these lies, are you? Look at her. She's covered in blood."

"I'm not saying I believe her. We'll deal with it later," Mr. Cobb said. "I've lost three slaves the past year. Two died and one ran off. We're going to start planting soon."

Three men on horses raced down the drive and came to a stop before the small crowd. Philip followed close behind them. Noah Bowman quickly climbed from his horse. Claude and Horatio Bowman joined their older brother.

"Did you find her? Is this the one?" Noah asked, looking at Lucille.

Philip got off his horse and united with the group.

"Noah, I'm very sorry about Henry. I truly am," Mr. Cobb said.

"We got no quarrel with you, Mr. Cobb. We only want justice for our brother," Horatio stated.

"This must be her. She's the only one with blood on her. My brother's blood!" Claude declared before striking Lucille in the face with the thick leather handle of a whip.

"Stop!" Doug yelled.

"Did you help her?" Noah asked, turning his attention to Doug.

"No, but if you want justice for your brother, you need to talk to Lester," Doug explained.

"What's he talking about?" Horatio asked.

"Lester killed your brother, not her," Doug insisted.

"Don't listen to that one. He ain't nothing but trouble and a bald-faced liar," Lester contended.

"It's true!" Lucille hollered. "Mr. Lester killed your brother! He hit him with a hammer! I saw him!"

"You're a murderer, Lester!" Doug alleged.

Lester marched to Doug and uncoiled the whip as he went. He struck Doug across the torso, slicing into his shirt. Doug bent over but stayed on his feet. Lester bashed Doug again, knocking him to his knees.

"You're a killer," Doug charged.

Lester hammered Doug again and sent him to the ground, squirming in pain in a fetal position.

"I swear, Mr. Lester killed Mr. Henry!" Lucille announced again.

Doug looked up at Noah while still writhing on the ground and wincing through the pain.

"Lester hated your brother. You know that. I'm sure he said something to you about Lester. Come on, man. Henry told you about Lester, didn't he?" Doug uttered.

"I didn't kill Mr. Henry. That evil man did," Lucille said, staring directly at Lester.

"You can't believe this nonsense," Lester said as he looped the whip. "Just look at the blood on her dress. I ain't got a drop on me."

Noah scowled at Lester for a moment before turning his gaze upon Lucille. The terrified slave looked at Henry's brother with eyes that implored him to find the truth.

"Keep her hands bound," Noah ordered Horatio.

Claude retrieved a rope from a saddlebag and fashioned a noose. Horatio took the rope connected to Lucille's wrists from Thomas and led her away to a sturdy tree.

"Put her hands behind her back," Noah instructed.

"Noah, please be reasonable. You can't just come in here and take my property," Mr. Cobb advised.

"Your property? Your property took my brother's life. What am I supposed to tell my mama and daddy, that we let their son's killer go free because Mr. Cobb didn't want to lose his property?" Noah replied.

"I'm sorry for your loss, I am, but we need to sort this out another way," Mr. Cobb insisted.

"You've always been good to our family, Mr. Cobb, but that don't make up for a lost brother and son," Noah stated.

Joseph Cobb threw his hands up in exasperation. Horatio and Claude placed Lucille's hands behind her back and encircled them with rope. Claude held Lucille in place while Horatio tossed the noose over a high branch and gave it enough slack to reach her neck. Noah took the noose and placed it over Lucille's head, then pulled it snug around her neck.

"Please, I swear I didn't kill Mr. Henry. He was nice to me," Lucille pleaded almost prayerfully through tears.

The slaves inched closer as a group, many of them also crying.

"Stop! She didn't kill him!" Doug yelled.

"She has a little boy!" Robert added.

Florence and Cecelia cried in each other's arms. Maurice held Lucille's tot, trying to shield the boy from the sight of his mother.

"Get over here and help me, Claude," Horatio told his brother.

Claude and Horatio grabbed the rope and pulled, lifting Lucille until her feet dangled about three feet off the ground.

"Hold her there until she stops moving," Noah ordered.

"Noah, please stop," Mr. Cobb asked.

"I'm sorry, Mr. Cobb. This is for my brother."

"Stop! She's innocent!" Doug declared.

Robert sobbed as he watched Lucille's legs kick and her eyes roll back, her mouth open as she struggled for air. Unable to bear any more, Robert lunged forth and moved toward the tree with a determination he had never known. Lester reached for Robert, but the young slave pushed him aside. Philip placed his hand on Lester's shoulder, hoping to keep him still, but the fiend shrugged Philip away. Doug joined Robert in his quest to save Lucille. Lester grabbed Doug and threw him to the ground. Noah watched Robert approach the tree, almost amused by the courage on display.

Robert wrapped his arms around Lucille's legs and lifted her up, putting some slack on the rope. Lucille gasped as she sucked in a huge gulp of air. Robert cried as he fought to keep Lucille up. Noah unraveled a whip and swung hard, striking Robert in the back. The distressed slave crumpled under the pain and slipped, but quickly recovered and lifted Lucille. She exhaled loudly before swallowing more air. Noah hit him again, and Robert buckled, causing Lucille to drop. Robert battled to get to his feet. He refused to let Lucille die. He loved her too much. Noah shook his head in disbelief at Robert's conviction. Robert signaled for his brothers to lift Lucille higher.

Claude and Horatio pulled on the rope and Robert felt Lucille move from his grasp, higher than he could hold her up.

Doug fought to get up, but Lester punched him in the face and knocked him onto his back. Joseph Cobb watched the mayhem with incredulity, helpless to stop it. Vernon walked forward and Noah stepped back without realizing he had.

Robert wept as he felt Lucille's legs elude his grasp. Vernon reached high above Lucille, and with a jump, grabbed the rope above her head. Claude and Horatio jerked forward and Lucille lowered into Robert's arms again. The vengeful brothers pulled hard on the rope but they could not budge mighty Vernon. Robert held Lucille up as Vernon kept the rope slack above her. Lucille fought for every breath with the coarse rope tight around her neck. Noah cracked the whip against Vernon's back, but the giant stood steady. The silent giant growled as he pulled the rope harder and the muscles in his arms expanded against his shirtsleeves, nearly splitting them at the seams. Noah hit him again, but Vernon didn't move.

"Get a horse," Noah instructed.

Horatio let go of the rope to fetch the horse and Claude lurched forward. Lucille descended until her feet touched the ground.

"Don't let go of the rope," Horatio advised Claude.

A loud gunshot rang out as Horatio reached the animal. Edith Cobb approached the chaotic scene holding a long rifle.

"That's enough now, you hear?" Edith warned.

"Mrs. Cobb, this slave woman killed our brother," Horatio stated.

"I'm sorry about Henry. But you can't just come to our house and start hanging our slaves," Edith exclaimed.

"Mrs. Cobb, you have children. Think about our mother," Noah said.

"I have thought about your mama. My heart goes out to her. Now I think it's best you young men go home to her," Edith advised.

"We're going to get justice for our brother," Noah said as he mounted his horse.

"I reckon you will," Edith said. "But not like this."

The Bowman brothers fled the Cobb farm while Edith kept the rifle leveled on them. Lester got to his feet, allowing Doug to stand up. The two combatants faced each other with pure contempt.

"Everyone get to your cabins. No more of this foolishness tonight. You men head home and I'll see you in the morning. There's work to be done tomorrow, and it better get done," Joseph Cobb sternly suggested.

Lester hastily jumped astride his horse and bolted down the long driveway. Joseph put his arm around Edith and walked her back to the house.

"You did good, mama," Joseph Cobb complimented his wife.

The slaves gathered around Lucille. Robert caressed her cheeks while Vernon loosened the rope around her neck. Lucille embraced Robert and reached behind him, gesturing for her child.

Light rain fell as the slaves returned to the cabins. Doug looked up to the heavens, letting the raindrops camouflage his tears. He yearned to be home. The delicate caress of the gentle rain was no substitute for his mother's tender, reassuring hand.

The night sky grumbled with a crash of thunder. A storm was coming to Bentonville.

21

Prelude to Freedom

Lester carried himself the next day as if he didn't have a care in the world. He wore a smile as the scent of spring swept past his nose. Lester behaved as though God whispered in his ear and gave him power over the world.

Doug, Maurice, Vernon, and Robert relished the mild spring weather as they cultivated soil in a field. Alberta and Hilda draped laundry over a wooden frame to dry while Minnie helped Edith in the kitchen. Florence and other slave women fed hogs, and Lucille carried a bucket of water.

A gentle breeze blew through the field. Maurice stood erect, lifted his face to the heavens, and reveled in the wind's kiss. Maurice drew in a deep breath and exhaled slowly.

"Ah, football weather," Maurice said.

"Not quite, but I'll take it," Doug responded with a chuckle.

Lucille arrived with the water bucket and the men dropped their implements on the ground and rested their arms. Robert examined the bruising on Lucille's neck, evidence of the previous night's violence. Lucille winced when Robert tenderly caressed her neck, so he slid his hand to her shoulder and gave her a sympathetic pat. Vernon took the pail from Lucille and gave the ladle to Maurice. The elder slave took a big drink before passing the ladle to Doug. The young man took his time drinking, dipping the ladle, and waiting a moment before sipping some more. Lester watched the group while he relaxed against a nearby tree. The sight of the group laughing and smiling stirred Lester's bitterness.

"Get back to work and stop wasting time with that lying wench!" Lester ordered.

Vernon handed the water bucket back to Lucille, but Doug intercepted it. Doug took another drink, then held the ladle and continued conversing with the other slaves.

"I said get back to work!" Lester blared as he walked toward the assembled slaves.

Maurice picked up a hoe and tapped it on the ground, but Doug, Robert, and Vernon didn't move. Lucille took a step to the side, seeking protection behind Robert and the other men.

"What is this? Y'all think it's Christmas or something? Get back to work," Lester told the group.

"We're just getting a drink of water, Lester," Doug replied.

"You've had plenty to drink," Lester stated as he slapped the ladle from Doug's hand.

"Gosh, won't you let us rest for just a minute?" Doug asked angrily.

"All you've been doing is resting the entire day. Over here laughing and carrying on with that lying Jezebel whore," Lester stated.

"Don't you talk like that," Robert said sternly, stepping forward. "She ain't no liar."

Maurice placed his hand on Robert's shoulder and stopped his progress.

"She is a liar. A murdering liar."

"She is not," Doug insisted. "But you are."

"Ah, what do you know? You didn't see nothing."

"I believe her," Doug said.

"Me too," Robert added.

"So what? Nobody would believe the word of the lot of you over me. I'm Lester Clay. You're just a bunch of savages."

"How many people have you killed, Lester Clay?" Doug asked.

"Not enough like you, that's for sure," Lester replied in an ominous tone. "Now I said get back to work."

"OK, just let me grab another drink real quick," Doug countered.

"No more drinking. No more talking. No more laughing. Just work. Now get to it!" Lester yelled as he grabbed the whip.

"Oh, so you're going to hit me for drinking water?" Doug asked.

"I don't need a reason," Lester uttered as he cracked the whip in the air near Doug.

Vernon stepped to the front of the group with a grimace on his face.

"I don't mind hitting you too, big boy. You better get back to work before you taste the lash," Lester warned.

Vernon stood like a statue staring at Lester. Maurice picked up another hoe and pressed it against Vernon's chest.

"Come on, Vernon, let's get back to work," Maurice advised his quiet friend.

Vernon grasped the handle of the tool and held it in place in front of him. Maurice retreated to a row and began patting the ground with the hoe, then looked up to see who might join him. Robert and Doug did not move.

"I warned you," said Lester, clenching the handle of the whip.

The brute raised the lash and struck at Vernon, tagging him on the arm. The mountain of a man winced but didn't make a sound. Lester hit the giant again, and once more Vernon refused to reward him with a shout of agony. Frustrated and growing angrier, Lester swung the whip high over his head to strike Vernon's face from above. As the whip descended toward him, Vernon raised the hoe, causing the whip to wrap around the handle. With a powerful tug, Vernon jerked the whip from Lester's hand.

"I don't know what's gotten into you, big fella, but you better hand that back," Lester said nervously. He felt naked without his tool of persecution.

Vernon did not move. He continued to stare at Lester. Robert knelt slowly to pick up the whip.

"Come on y'all, let's get back to work," Maurice repeated.

Robert stood up with the whip in his hand. He stepped toward Lester, who extended his arm to receive the whip.

"Yeah, just hand it over," Lester told Robert.

"You was going to get Lucille killed for what you did," Robert said almost in a hiss. "You didn't care if she swung from that tree for what you did."

Robert slowly crept closer to Lester.

"Now listen, you hand that over nice and slow," Lester instructed as he took a step back.

Doug watched, astonished by Robert's boldness and growing indignation. Vernon moved forward with Robert. A feeling of anguish seized Doug, the kind of threatening warning that something bad was going to happen.

"Hey, Robert, let's get back to work," Doug urged.

Robert heard Doug but wasn't listening. He did not want to listen when he possessed the instrument of so much suffering and hardship for the slaves of Bentonville.

"Give it to me!" Lester demanded loudly.

Robert swung the whip and hit Lester on the hand. The man recoiled like a hurt beast. Robert lacked Lester's prowess with the whip, but he delighted in his ability to hurt the man.

"Put that down or I'll whip the skin right off you!"

"With what, this?" Robert asked as he swung again.

Lester cowered as the whip reached for him. Lester's knees buckled when the whip smacked his back. He moved onto his hands and knees to get up, but Robert whacked Lester again, dropping him to the ground. The tyrant trembled and winced in pain and appeared to hold back tears. Robert raised the whip again before Doug stayed his hand.

"Let it go, Robert. He isn't worth it. Don't make yourself like him," Doug urged. "It's going to be better one day, I promise."

Robert glared at Lester for several seconds before coiling the whip and throwing it onto the roof of a cabin. Lester scrambled to his feet and fumed and seethed.

"You can't do this to me!" Lester yelled as he held his stinging hand. "I'll see that all of you are put to death! Do you hear me? Mr. Cobb won't stand for a revolt!"

Lester stumbled toward the house, still clutching his hand. Earl, Philip, and the other hands raced to the scene of the commotion.

"What's going on?" Philip asked.

"They revolted and attacked me!"

The men looked at the slaves, who remained expressionless, as they retrieved garden tools.

"Do y'all want some water?" Lucille asked the men.

The men stood mired in confusion as they watched Lester run away.

"You're all going to die! You hear me? I swear it!" Lester howled as he fled to the house.

Several bangs and pops echoed in the distance. Everyone turned their heads toward the sounds, which repeated.

"Is that thunder?" Daniel asked, looking up at a cloudless sky.

"No," Philip answered. "That isn't thunder."

Joseph and Edith Cobb exited the house and stepped onto the front porch. Husband and wife listened to the crackling far away gunshots. Lester stopped at the bottom of the steps and held up his palm, which was adorned with a red stripe.

"Look what those savages did to me, Mr. Cobb."

Joseph and Edith ignored the raving sadistic lout, listening intently for the alarming sounds from afar.

"Mr. Cobb, the slaves, they revolted and struck me with my own whip."

"Hush, listen," Joseph Cobb replied without looking at Lester.

The Cobbs gazed at the horizon toward the intermittent sounds.

"Mr. Cobb, we have to do something about those slaves."

"Lester, be quiet," Mr. Cobb said firmly. "Can you hear that? There's a battle being fought nearby."

"We might lose it because of old fools like you."

"How dare you?" Edith Cobb uttered with a deep breath.

"Get off my land," Joseph instructed. "And don't you ever come back. You have been nothing but trouble."

Lester walked to his horse at a brisk pace.

"Earl! Y'all come on! Let's get out of here before the Yankees show up!" Lester said as he mounted his horse.

Earl, Thomas, and Daniel held puzzled expressions but seemed to realize the gravity of events unfolding around them. The distant gunfire sounded the alarm for the people of Bentonville, and nothing would ever be the same.

On March 19, 1865, Confederate General Joseph Johnston attempted to prevent Union General William T. Sherman's forces from crossing North Carolina. Sherman hoped to unite with other troops in the town of Goldsboro, North Carolina. From there, the powerful Union army would march north to join General Ulysses S. Grant's forces in Petersburg, Virginia. Together, they would seek to vanquish the mighty Army of Northern Virginia, the largest remaining Confederate force under the command of Confederate General Robert E. Lee.

General Johnston amassed a force of 17,000 troops from soldiers scattered throughout North Carolina. They were little more than castoffs and remnants of other units. Johnston hoped to catch Sherman by surprise and attacked the Union army as it converged on Bentonville. Thus began the largest battle ever fought in North Carolina.

Soldiers from both sides lined up shoulder to shoulder in ranks and marched toward the enemy. Weapons of the time, such as the Enfield rifle, fired slowly and had limited range, inhibiting the effectiveness of individual soldiers. In large groups, the troops became a potent fighting force.

Bernard marched among the ranks and slowly progressed toward the rebels on the other side of the field. His blue wool uniform made him hot in the spring sunshine. The red ribbon twisted in his boot laces brushed the green grass as he stepped. The night he met young Moses near Ebenezer Creek seemed like years ago. Bernard marched beside an older man with a fluffy beard. The man looked weary, with sunken eyes and a wrinkled face. War has a habit of doing that to a man. Despite his haggard appearance, the scowl on the man's face made him seem formidable. War has a habit of doing that to a man.

The line stopped, and Bernard raised his rifle in unison with his colleagues. Clouds of smoke puffed from each barrel as suddenly as the bang of the shot reverberated through the air. Bernard heard a bullet whiz past his head as he knelt to reload his rifle. The projectile struck the man behind Bernard in the abdomen, causing him to crumple to the ground. Bernard removed a paper cartridge of black powder from a case attached to his uniform. He bit the top off the cartridge and poured the powder down the barrel of his trusty Enfield. The young soldier dropped a bullet down the barrel before using the ramrod to finish preparing the weapon. He withdrew the ramrod from the barrel and placed it back in its holder along the outside of the barrel. Bernard cocked the hammer and arranged the firing cap in place. He performed the series of events quickly, but not chaotically. Every motion was fluid and precise. Bernard could load the weapon with his eyes closed by that time.

Bernard aimed the rifle again and pulled the trigger. The hammer slammed down on the firing cap and ignited the powder inside, propelling the bullet out of the barrel. The slug hit its mark, but Bernard didn't watch the man fall. He needed to load his weapon again.

Gunshots rang out, and a cloud of smoke partially obscured the combatants on the other side of the field. A spout of blood erupted from the chest of the man with the fluffy beard, and he dropped next to Bernard. An officer shouted the order to fall back. Bernard looked at the ground and saw the older man press his hand to his chest. Blood oozed from the corner of his mouth and dribbled onto his ear.

"Help me!" Bernard shouted to another young soldier.

The soldier rushed to Bernard. They each took one of the fallen man's arms and started to drag him across the field with the other retreating soldiers. Bernard looked down at the man as they pulled him. The sun made his blood-soaked beard glisten and sparkle like the brass buckles on the man's uniform. The man looked up at Bernard. His dark brown eyes expressed sadness and relief all at once. War has a habit of doing that to a man.

The thunderous boom of artillery joined the crackle of rifles. A large contingent of Union soldiers with three horse-drawn ambulances arrived at the Cobb farm by late afternoon. The slaves flocked to the house to glimpse the men who would surely be their liberators. An officer stopped before the porch of the Cobb house but did not dismount his horse. Joseph got up from his rocking chair to greet the officer.

"How do you do?" Joseph asked awkwardly.

"Rebel troops set upon us a short distance from here. We mean you no harm, but I have wounded men and must commandeer this house to serve as a hospital," the officer stated plainly.

"Of course, bring your men inside," Joseph replied, knowing he didn't have a choice in the matter.

The officer turned his attention to the gathered slaves beside the house.

"You there. Your bondage is broken. I ask only that you render aid to the wounded and assist in the care of my men. When we depart, you may leave as free people."

Maurice gawked at the man. He heard the words but couldn't believe them.

"We're going to be free," Florence said to her husband. "We can go find our boy."

The soldiers scurried about the area, setting up tents and carrying a wounded man inside the house. Other soldiers dismantled the fence the slaves built the previous fall and chopped it into firewood.

Men cleared off the Cobb family dining table and carried it to the front parlor. Soldiers draped a blanket across the table before they brought an injured man into the room. Blood spurted from a gaping wound on the man's leg as they placed him on the makeshift operating table. Edith quickly ushered her granddaughters upstairs.

"Come along, girls, let's go up to our rooms," Edith told the children as she guided them up the stairs.

Doug and the other slaves walked around the front yard and watched the Union soldiers set up camp. Long rows of tents dotted the landscape. Doug meandered past wounded men on cots. One had a bandage around his head. A splint held the next man's leg in place. Another man had a bandage soaked with blood over his knee. Beside that man, another had his arm in a sling. A loud yell of anguish emitted from the house, and Doug's blood ran cold at the dreadful sound, unlike anything he'd ever heard.

The injured man's cries resonated throughout the house. Edith held her granddaughters in an upstairs room.

"There, there, it's all right," Edith told the girls, hoping they would believe her despite the shrieking.

Margaret covered her ears and dashed across the hall to her bedroom. The cries of men in misery made her think of her husband's end, and it tormented her soul. Minnie and Alberta entered the room carrying bowls of stew.

"Thought we should bring you something to eat before them folks ate it all," Minnie said as she placed a bowl on a small table in the room. Alberta positioned another bowl.

"Alright, girls, let's eat, then we'll have a bedtime story," Edith said.

Edith nodded in a gesture of gratitude to the slave women. If she uttered the words of her heart, she would have broken into tears.

Doug reunited with Maurice and Robert when another ambulance arrived. A soldier ran to the back of the wagon.

"You there!" the soldier called to Doug and his friends. "Help us carry these men inside!"

Doug and Robert grabbed a cot holding a man with a maimed leg. A tourniquet prevented much of the man's life-giving blood from escaping. Beneath the band, a narrow bridge of flesh connected the man's lower leg to the rest of his body. Doug and Robert winced at the gruesome sight. The injured man groaned as Robert and Doug carried him to the steps of the house. A doctor waited at the bottom of the steps to examine the wounded.

"Take him to the room on the right," the doctor ordered after a hasty inspection of the frightful damage to the man's leg.

Doug and Robert walked up the steps but quickly stopped as soldiers carried another man from the house on a stretcher. The man's leg was missing below the knee and fresh bandages embraced what remained. The young slaves stared in astonishment as the man went by.

"You two, snap out of it," said a surgeon standing at the house door. "Bring him inside."

Doug and Robert quickly scampered up the steps with the hurt man and rushed him into the parlor to the right. Bloody bandages and strips of cloth littered the floor of the room. An attentive soldier discarded a bloody blanket and wiped a splotch of red from the table. Men lifted the injured soldier from the cot and placed him onto the table. A window was open to the side of the room, allowing in a breeze, which helped to dissipate the fetid smell of the room.

"Thank you, boys. Now please step aside," the surgeon told Doug and Robert.

The slaves exited the house and stood on the porch as they looked at the scene before them. The Cobb farm resembled a military camp. Tents, horses, soldiers, and wagons were seemingly everywhere. Vernon helped four men dig graves next to the Cobb family cemetery. Doug saw five bodies wrapped in white canvass on the ground behind Vernon.

Among the wounded men scattered on the lawn of the Cobb family home was the bearded man who fell next to Bernard. The young soldier knelt beside the man and held his hand. The injured man's breathing became more labored. He searched his coat pocket and removed an envelope, then pressed it into Bernard's hand. The dying man peered into Bernard's eyes, silently asking him to make a vow to see the letter delivered. Bernard knew the man had little time. The young soldier displayed a smile of feigned reassurance, a gesture as strong as a handshake. It seemed like minutes passed between each breath the man took, but Bernard stayed with him until the end. After the man's hand went limp in his, Bernard placed it gently beside him. The bearded man's open eyes gazed past Bernard to a destination in the sky far beyond him. The man died in the embrace of a companion surrounded by the sobbing and wailing of hundreds of others. War has a habit of doing that to a man.

Bernard studied the envelope the man gave him. A smudge of dirt and blood graced the lower right corner. The weight and thickness of the envelope acknowledged a letter inside. The man addressed it to a woman named Rebecca in Baltimore. Bernard wondered if Rebecca was a wife, a cousin, a sister, or the man's daughter. The young man stood up and placed the envelope in his coat pocket, then grabbed his rifle and returned to his tent. He had a promise to keep.

The cannons fell silent when night descended on Bentonville. Doug carried an empty water bucket from the tents and placed it on the ground near the well. Exhaustion covered Doug like a robe. Dried blood stained his hands. He retrieved more water from the well and rubbed his wet hands together to remove the desiccated blood. Doug took another glance at the military encampment before returning to his cabin to sleep. He would hear no crickets or owls that night, only the moans of the hurt and dying. History informs us that sacrifice and bloodshed are often a prelude to freedom.

22

Cost

Morning dew still clung to the grass as soldiers ate breakfast and gazed upon a sunrise that each knew could be his last. Some men read letters from home for the tenth time. One soldier shined his boots, even though he was about to march into battle.

Doug emerged from the cabin in time to see the troops lining up to march to the fight. The young man scarcely rested at all. The shouts of the injured or dying or a man having a nightmare filled the night before.

The slaves gathered near the house and encampment as the soldiers marched away into the icy grasp of destiny. Alberta, Hilda, and Minnie helped Edith cook large pots of cornmeal mush to feed the increasing population of the Cobb farm.

Bernard joined his allies in line before a wide field. An officer on horseback stood before the men, brandishing a sword.

"Today we will see if they have any fight left in them, men! Make them show you their heels!" the officer blared.

Across the field, the Confederate troops set up a mostly defensive posture in shallow trenches with a pine forest at their backs. The stars and bars battle flag fluttered in the breeze above them. The Yanks stepped onto the field and followed their banner toward the enemy. Shots rang out and a line of white smoke floated in the air before the Rebs. Men in front of Bernard dropped like rocks in a pond. The young soldier aimed at the Confederate line and fired. Birds fled in the sky, their songs replaced by gunfire and screaming. Union artillery bombarded the rebel fortifications. The shelling threw earth, wood, and gray-coated men into the air. The Confederates reloaded and fired another salvo at the oncoming Union troops. More men dropped around Bernard, but he pressed forward.

The cannons roared again as a Confederate soldier climbed through a gap in the hastily constructed rampart that shielded the trench. As soon as he stood up, a cannonball the size of a softball struck the doomed man. The projectile tore a hole in the man's torso, shattering ribs and a lung before it exited his body with such force it threw him back into the trench. Like encroaching floodwaters, Northern forces crept further across the field.

Bernard fired his rifle in coordination with the men in his rank. He saw splinters and a man fell back in the trench beyond. A ball got through the entwined branches of the fortifications and hit a man in gray in the shoulder. One of the man's Confederate comrades rushed to his side and wrapped his arm around his shoulder to help him up. A Napoleon cannon sent a twelve-pound cannonball across the field. The heavy round ricocheted off the ground before smashing through the trench defenses. The ball hit the men huddled together, beheading one and tearing an arm from the other.

A roaring chorus of rebel yells filled the air as the Confederates stormed over the barricades and charged their enemy on the field. Bernard knelt, took aim, shot, and felled another soldier in gray. The rebel charge moved fast and Bernard had to step back to reload his weapon, lest they be upon him. He tried to prepare the rifle as he backpedaled, but moving made the task more difficult. Bernard had no choice but to stop and focus on reloading the firearm. He readied the weapon quickly and took down another foe. The men in gray were closing in and portions of the battlefield descended into hand-to-hand combat.

The chaotic battle overloaded Bernard's senses. Men yelled and gunshots rang out in all directions. Blankets of fire exploded from rifles lined up in rows. The screams of stricken men and horses traveled all over the field. A Union soldier writhed on the ground as he tried to hold in his blood, which leaked from a gash in his neck. A rebel soldier crawled back toward the trench, his left foot on the ground six feet behind him. One Confederate rested on the ground and held a brilliant white handkerchief that stood out among the blue, gray, brown, and green of the battlefield canvass. Bernard wondered if the man might surrender, but he did not. Despite being outnumbered nearly three to one, the soldiers in gray still had plenty of fight left in them. The man pressed the handkerchief to his abdomen and watched it turn red almost instantly.

A round struck a nearby infantryman in the head, sending pieces of gray, white, and red matter onto Bernard's blue sleeve and even his cheek. Bernard wiped his cheek with his clean sleeve before attempting to reload the Enfield. Gunshots clacked from so many directions Bernard didn't know which one sent the bullet that struck him. He felt the sting and warmth in his upper right thigh as he reached into a pouch for a powder cartridge. Bernard knelt to load the weapon, but his leg buckled and sent him to his hands and knees. The ghastly yell of a charging Confederate soldier sent a chill through Bernard. He looked up and saw the man bearing down on him. Bernard pressed the butt of his rifle to the ground so it stood vertically, then used it to pull himself up. As the man reached him, Bernard swung the rifle with all his might. The fat end of the rifle struck the man in the head, opening a wide laceration that sent him to the ground.

Bernard felt blood trickle down his leg and into his boot, and it terrified him. He fled toward the rear of the Union line amid the pandemonium and cacophony on the field. Wet with his blood, Bernard's foot slipped inside his boot. He placed his hand over his leg's yawning wound and limped away as swiftly as he could, dragging the gun behind him. A loud shot rang out and a hole in the back of the individual ahead of him immediately confronted Bernard. As the man fell, Bernard turned and saw a Confederate soldier approximately fifty feet away lowering his rifle. Bernard hastily began loading his Enfield as the Confederate did the same. The men shared glances as they checked each other's progress. The Confederate soldier hoisted his gun and rushed at the wounded Bernard. Tense and alarmed, Bernard bobbled the ramrod as he drew it from its holder and it dropped to the ground. As the man approached, Bernard grabbed the rifle's barrel and prepared himself like a batter in baseball. Bernard swung the rifle with all his might once the opponent was within range. The Confederate jumped backward and dodged the blow. The momentum of the swing sent Bernard spinning like a ballerina, but without the grace or agility one would embody. Losing his balance, Bernard fell to the ground on his stomach. The Confederate soldier lunged at Bernard with the rifle's bayonet as he saw an opportunity to finish him. Bernard quickly rolled out of the way and onto his back. The attacker adjusted his direction as he stumbled forward and the blade sliced through the side of Bernard's injured thigh before stabbing into the ground. The abrupt stop caused the long rifle to jerk away from the man and he fell onto Bernard's chest. Bernard tried to push the man off, but the pain in his leg sapped his strength.

The combatants exchanged punches to the face, but the weight of the man over Bernard gave him leverage. The Confederate wrapped his muscular hands around Bernard's neck and squeezed. Bernard pulled in another gulp of air before the enemy's chubby fingers pressed his windpipe shut. That was warfare at its most personal. It is one thing to be cut down by a shot from an unseen distant adversary. Bernard saw the hate in the man's eyes as he tried to choke the life out of him. He could smell the man's foul breath, see the gaps left by missing teeth, and looked closely at the scar on his killer's face. Dying in that manner had a cold, twisted intimacy about it. The Confederate pressed his forearms against Bernard's chest as he strangled him. Slobber hung from the man's lip for a moment before falling onto Bernard's face. Bernard clawed at the man's hands but could not break free from his grasp. The sun shined brightly behind the Confederate soldier. As though death itself, the man's shadow moved over Bernard. The young Union soldier felt dizzy and knew he needed to act soon. He reached up and put his hands on the man's face, then pressed his thumbs on the attacker's eyes. The man leaned back and released Bernard's throat. Bernard inhaled deeply and braced himself for the next attack. The Confederate removed a Bowie knife from a sheath on his belt and raised it high. The sun came over the enemy's head and blinded Bernard, making his assailant appear as a hellish specter.

Suddenly, the Confederate soldier lurched backward and dropped the knife. His mouth opened but didn't emit a sound. The trooper reached over his shoulder as he fell forward, removing himself from the bayonet that impaled his back. The man landed face down beside Bernard, revealing a Union soldier standing over him.

"Help me with this man!" Bernard's rescuer yelled.

Bernard winced as two men hauled him away from the battleground.

The slaves moved about the Cobb farm, helping to care for injured and dying men. Doug carried a bowl of food to a wounded man with a bandaged leg.

"There you are," Doug said to the man in a soothing voice.

The soldier grimaced and hissed in pain as he took the bowl. Doug turned toward the kitchen to fetch some food for another man when he noticed a gruesome sight beside the Cobb family home. Outside the house, beneath the open parlor window, sat a small pile of severed limbs and discarded boots. The view made Doug feel queasy, but he couldn't turn away. Flies flew around the little pile of arms and legs, the remains of the most common major surgery performed during the war. A tall man with rolled-up sleeves walked to the window from inside the house. Doug saw him toss an arm out the window and onto the pile. The young fellow watched in awe, unable to fathom the toll the war had taken on the individuals who fought it, as well as the nation as a whole.

"Hey, Doug!" Robert called out from the other side of the house near the kitchen.

Doug snapped from his trance and looked up at Robert, who was waving him over. Doug jogged over to see what help Robert might require.

"What's up, Robert?" Doug asked.

"Look," Robert said, pointing to a tree where Florence and Maurice stood with Luke, the portly abolitionist they encountered on the road months prior.

"Let's go say hello," Doug suggested.

Luke, Maurice, and Florence turned to face the boys as they neared.

"Well, I'll be," Luke started. "I guess you didn't make it to Durham."

"No," Robert murmured.

Luke's remark irritated Doug, and he feared it might rekindle Robert's hostility after finally breaching the barrier between them.

"You know these boys?" Florence asked Luke.

"Yes, I met them on the road last year."

"This is the man who took our son north," Florence told Doug.

"I remember Maurice telling me about that," Doug replied.

"This is him," Maurice added.

"He said our boy is safe and he's doing fine. He's in Indianapolis. I don't know where that is, but I can't wait to get there," Florence said with a gigantic smile on her face. "I can't wait to see my boy again."

"Calm down, Mammy Lou," Maurice suggested. "It's going to take some time to get there."

"Once this battle has ended, I'll take as many of you as I can with me. There's enough room for at least ten at the station house," Luke stated.

Robert grinned with the same eager look he had when he first met Luke. Florence rested her head on Maurice's shoulder and closed her eyes for a moment, the smile never leaving her face.

The rattle of arriving ambulances diverted the group's attention. Wagons full of hurt men and corpses came to a stop near the tents, and soldiers rushed to unload them.

"We best get back to drawing some food and water for these men," Maurice said.

The slaves lined up outside the kitchen where Minnie, Hilda, and Alberta were frantically cooking and dishing out food. Minnie handed Doug a bowl of grits.

"There ya are," the kind old lady told him. "Make sure them new men get some."

Doug left the kitchen and Robert stepped forward and grabbed another bowl. The medics placed many of the newcomers in tents, beside trees, or on cots on the ground, wherever they could find room for them. Doug came upon Bernard, who sat on a cot with his back against a tree. A belt served as a tourniquet high on Bernard's right leg. Below the belt and above the knee, a messy, bloody bandage encircled Bernard's leg. Doug knelt beside the wounded young soldier.

"Here you go," Doug said as he handed the bowl and a spoon to Bernard.

While attempting to sit up straight, the injured man whimpered in pain. Bernard held the bowl and peered at its contents as he stirred the thick white goop.

"What do you call this?" Bernard asked.

"Folks around here call it hominy, but where I come from, and pretty much everywhere else, they call it grits."

"Grits? Ain't never had grits."

Bernard scooped a spoonful and tasted grits for the first time. He swallowed fast, and his countenance conveyed his displeasure.

"It's rather bland, but I'm hungry so, thank you."

"Yeah, most folks put something in them. Personally, I like salt and butter in mine. Some people put cheese in them. Shrimp and grits is popular, too."

Doug assessed the youthful man before him. The soldier couldn't have been much older than Doug himself. Bernard's leg bled through the bandage. His clothes were dirty and bloody in spots. Bernard's face was young and old all at once. War has a habit of doing that to a man.

"How old are you?" Doug asked.

"I'm eighteen. I'll be nineteen next month. I hope I will," Bernard answered before he looked at his leg and winced.

"Dang, you're not much older than me."

"Well, what's your name, and how old are you?" Bernard inquired.

"My name is Doug. I'm seventeen," Doug answered. "At least I think I am. I might be eighteen now. I don't know. I didn't celebrate my last birthday."

"Me either. It's nice to meet you, Doug. I'm Bernard," the young soldier said, extending his hand.

Doug grasped Bernard's hand and applied a firm grip and a gentle shake. Doug's eye was drawn to Bernard's right boot when he looked at the man's injuries. Despite the blood, half of the bright red ribbon intertwined with the laces of the boot was readily visible.

"It looks like you have something in your laces. Do you want me to get that out for you?" Doug asked.

"Oh, not at all. I keep that there."

"What is it?"

"A special girl back home in Pennsylvania took that out of her hair and gave it to me before I left. When things get hard or we're on a long march and I hang my head, I see that lovely ribbon. It makes me think about her and keeps me going. What about you? Do you have a special girl?"

"Maybe. I don't know."

"Well, you know or you don't, Doug," Bernard said with a laugh, followed by a quick cough that made him frown with pain.

"I guess you could say there is."

"I tell you, I can't wait to get back home and see her pretty face again."

A yell from the house drew Doug's and Bernard's attention. Doug observed Bernard's bandage, which was completely red by that time. Bernard set the bowl of grits aside and swatted away a fly that hummed around his leg.

"Does it hurt?" Doug asked.

"Yes, it does. I'll be honest, Doug, nothing's ever hurt this bad."

Bernard rested his head against the tree and looked around the camp. Men stacked a nearby wagon with the bodies of the dead. A soldier older than Doug and Bernard openly wept and called for his mother. Another man's head was bandaged in a way that covered his right eye. The two young men heard muted cannon fire in the distance.

"Look at it all. How did we let it come to this? So much suffering. Entire families are torn apart. My mother's family is in Bowling Green, Virginia. I have cousins fighting for the South. I've marched past piles of bricks and wood where homes and towns used to be. We've passed orphans crying on the side of the road. It shouldn't take this for you to be free," Bernard said.

"You're right."

Doug looked upon the surrounding misery before the annoying fly returned with backup. Bernard waved them away from his bloody leg.

"Bernard, can I ask you a question?"

"Certainly."

"Why did you join the army at your age?"

"Sometimes I don't know," Bernard said with a chuckle before a solemn expression washed over him. "The greatest man I've ever known is my dad. He read me a copy of the Declaration of Independence when I was younger. My father instilled in me a love of country and a desire to do what's right. Men gave their lives to establish the United States as a free country. Father said we won't fulfill our promise until everyone is free."

"Your dad sounds like a great guy," Doug complimented.

"He is as great as any man, even Mr. Lincoln himself. I can't wait to sit down and talk with him after all of this is over. Everything that is good in me came from him and my mother."

"That's great. I hope you get to see them soon."

"How about you? What's your father like?"

"I don't know. I never really knew him."

"Oh, I'm sorry. Was he sold away from you?"

"No, he just wasn't around."

"What about your mother?"

"My mom is great. She's always been there for me."

"Where is she? I'd love to meet her."

"Well, she's not here."

Bernard cast a confused glance at Doug that dissipated in a moment as pain shot through his leg.

"I can see the wisdom in your eyes, Doug. You've seen things I'll never understand."

"Thank you. That's really nice of you to say. I guess you could say I've seen a lot."

"This war has shown me things I'll never forget. As we marched, I saw slaves who were beaten so badly their backs were crisscrossed with scars. I saw a man with a metal collar around his neck. Nobody should be treated that way. Other men fought so I could be free. It's only right that I be willing to risk my life for your freedom."

"Thank you," Doug said, inspecting Bernard's leg again. "I'm really sorry about your leg."

"I guess I always knew this could happen. If I'm going to lose my leg or even my life, I want it to mean something. If you and your friends are free, it will mean something."

Bernard surveyed the devastation and despair at the Cobb farm. Misery serves as a harsh reminder of man's ignorance. The young soldier pondered once more how the country had degenerated into such chaos.

"This has to be worth it," Bernard uttered as he looked at the bodies in the wagon. "We all have to be better people. It can't be in vain. We have to be worth this."

Bernard grabbed Doug's arm, his eyes welling up with tears as he stared at him.

"You stay a good man. Always be worth it."

"I will, I promise."

"Promise, that reminds me," Bernard said as he dug into his coat pocket. "I made a promise to a man, but it's now your promise to keep."

Bernard removed the bearded soldier's letter, adding his own bloody thumbprint to it, then held it up to Doug.

"A man gave this to me before he died. It needs to get to Baltimore. I vowed I would see it delivered. Just in case I don't make it, I want you to take this. Give it to an officer if I don't return. This is your promise now, Doug."

Doug took the letter and placed it in his lone pants pocket. Soldiers arrived and lifted Bernard's cot. The frightened soldier reached for Doug's hand and clutched it.

"Don't forget me, Doug."

"I won't."

"Be worth this," Bernard said as they hurried him away. "Be worth this."

Doug watched the troopers ascend the steps to the house carrying Bernard. Doug's eyes scanned the farm. He took it all in, the ever-growing pile of limbs beside the house, the men with bloody bandages and splints. The cost of freedom was all around him. Doug understood the price of liberty like never before. Doctor King, Rosa Parks, William Lloyd Garrison, Sojourner Truth, Harriet Tubman, Elizabeth Margaret Chandler, Booker T. Washington, and countless others paid the toll. Battles like Gettysburg, Chickamauga, Spotsylvania, Chancellorsville, Shiloh, and Antietam brought over 600,000 to their end with unprecedented brutality. People risked all for freedom at a bridge in Selma, the deep murky waters of Ebenezer Creek, and a lunch counter in Greensboro. Homer, Charles, and Kitch paid the price. Doug witnessed the cost of emancipation in the blood and tears shed on the cotton fields and battlefields of Bentonville.

As the sun dropped lower in the sky, Robert drew a bucket of water from the well. He carried it to a row of tents where soldiers waited patiently. Robert saw Doug help Vernon dig a grave in the distance. The young man placed the bucket on the ground next to a pair of tired soldiers sitting outside a tent.

"I've got some water for you," Robert informed them.

"Thank you," said one soldier as he lifted his metal cup.

Robert scooped some water from the bucket, then carefully dumped the ladle's contents into the man's mug. The other soldier seemed impatient and not so polite. He leaned forward and dipped his cup into the bucket, then promptly raised it to his lips.

Another wagon arrived at the Cobb farm and Robert turned to view it as it passed. His mouth opened a little when he saw the occupants in the back. Two Confederate prisoners sat flanked by five Union soldiers. The wagon stopped, and the guards pulled the shackled Confederates from the large cart. They led the men to a neighboring tent, and the guards took up posts outside.

"You there, bring that water," the ranking soldier ordered.

Robert carried the bucket to the man, his hands hurting from countless trips hauling the bucket throughout the day.

"Yes, sir. You want some water?" Robert asked.

"Give these traitors a drink," the soldier directed.

Robert peered into the wide-open entrance of the tent. The men sat in chairs, and Robert noticed their bloody clothing. Dried blood bonded one man's hair together, and the other prisoner's arm hung awkwardly at his side. Pure hatred swelled in Robert's heart. Despite the order, he bristled at the idea of giving the men something to drink. They wanted to keep him in servitude. They felt no pity for his suffering, so why should he care about theirs? But almost as quickly as contempt filled him, it faded. Robert recalled his grandfather's admonition against harboring hatred. Maurice wisely reiterated the same view many times. Fostering hate doesn't make you different from the hateful. Love is the polar opposite of hatred because, unlike hate, malice does not motivate it.

"Well, get on with it," the guard instructed as he handed Robert an empty cup.

Robert dipped the mug into the water, then carefully handed it to the detainee with blood on his head. The Confederate grasped the mug with his shackled hands and looked at its contents, examining the water and swirling it around. The prisoner threw the water from the cup upon Robert's face with a rapid upward and forward movement of his arms. Robert paused for a moment to collect his emotions as water dripped from his face.

"I don't want no water from him," the Confederate prisoner declared.

A guard raised the butt of his rifle and prepared to strike the captive in the head.

"Wait, stop," Robert insisted. "He might be bleeding on his head, but something hurt him a lot worse on the inside. His heart ain't right."

"Can I please have some water?" the prisoner with the broken arm asked.

Robert dipped the mug again and filled it with water. He handed it to the other captive, who reached for it hastily with his healthy arm. The parched and exhausted man eagerly drank from the cup.

"Thank you, that will be all," the head of the guards advised Robert.

Robert dried his face with his shirtsleeve as he walked away. He showed goodwill to men who opposed nearly everything about him, even his basic humanity. Robert adjusted the old planter's hat on his head. His grandfather would have been proud.

After they finished preparing the grave, Doug and Vernon returned to the encampment. As they passed the house, Doug stopped in his tracks. Atop the pile of discarded appendages sat a boot with a red ribbon twisted through the laces. Doug fought back tears as an icy chill ran up his spine. The young man walked past the rows of tents, looking for Bernard. Doug didn't find the youthful Union soldier anywhere. Doug returned to the tree where he spoke with Bernard, but he wasn't there either. The despondent lad leaned against the tree and muttered a quick prayer and hoped Bernard was still alive and would soon return to his family. The rising moon illuminated Doug's watery eyes. Luke joined Doug beside the tree and turned his attention to the sky.

"It's amazing, isn't it?" Luke asked.

"What's that?"

"Amid all this death and misery, we can still see the beauty of creation."

"I guess so."

"Look how beautiful the moon is tonight."

"You know one day we're going there. Men will stand on the moon."

"Wouldn't that be something?"

"It will be."

"It seems so far away."

"It is."

"How long do you think it will take to get there?"

"From here? A little over a hundred years," Doug replied with a chuckle, cognizant of the 1969 moon landing.

The men stood in silence for a minute, taking in the majesty of the night sky as the moaning of men drowned out the calls of crickets.

"What's on your mind, Doug?" Luke finally asked.

"I can't believe all of this is happening."

"It is hard to believe. The birth of freedom is seldom a pleasant labor."

"Yeah, but I mean me being here. I just want to go home. I want to see my mom. She told me things I didn't want to understand before, but I understand them now."

"I promise you, Doug, I'll make every effort to get you home once this battle is over."

"Well, just so you know, I'm a long, long way from home."

"I'll do my best," Luke assured Doug before patting him on the back and walking away.

Doug kept his gaze fixed on the moon. It seemed so far away, yet was closer than home.

23

The Hand of Hatred

Tall grass waved gently in the breeze and glistened like golden threads in the afternoon sunlight. Birds chirped, and trees rustled once more in the wind. There was no stench or haze of gun smoke in the air. After three days of fighting, the battlefield fell silent. Heavily outnumbered and outgunned, General Johnston withdrew his Confederate army during the night. Sherman would continue on his course to Goldsboro. The following month, the men would meet again at the home of James and Nancy Bennett, near Durham, North Carolina. Over a few days, the men negotiated the largest surrender of the war, and over 89,000 Confederate soldiers in the Carolinas, Georgia, and Florida laid down their arms.

An officer stood on the front porch with Joseph and Edith Cobb. One of the injured Confederates sat in a rocking chair with his broken arm in a sling. Union guards loaded his spiteful companion into the back of a wagon. The slaves slowly made their way to the house from the slave cabins.

"I thank you for your hospitality. I leave this man in your care. Please see to him until he is healthy," the officer requested.

"We will take care of him," Joseph replied.

"One of my cavalry units is searching the area and may pass this way as they try to rejoin me. They will do you no harm."

"We will show kindness to all who come," Joseph Cobb pledged.

"Then I bid you a good day," the officer said, tipping his hat to the Cobb family.

The officer mounted his horse and led his men down the driveway and onto the road. As the dust settled, the slaves gathered at the steps of the house, many of them with sacks containing their meager possessions. Philip exited the house and stood on the porch beside Joseph. Luke walked to the front of the slaves and looked up at the family assembled on the porch.

"You are not slaves, but any of you who wish to stay may do so. I need help with planting season. You can continue to live in the cabins, and will be provided with food and clothing. No whip shall touch you," Joseph granted.

"I'm taking these to a station house. They will head north from there," Luke said of the group behind him containing Maurice, Florence, Cecelia, Lucille and her child, Alberta, Hilda, Minnie, Vernon, Robert, and Doug.

"I wish you all a safe journey," Joseph stated.

"Thank you. We best be going. It will be dark before we get there," said Luke.

Tears welled up in Edith's eyes. Despite the nature of their relationship, she was fond of the women who worked in her home and kitchen. The slaves turned and started the walk down the long path away from the Cobb farm.

"You're welcome to stay for supper, Philip," Edith offered.

"That would be nice. Thank you," Philip responded.

Vernon lifted Alberta and carried her so she could see over his shoulder. She looked back at the Cobb house and the people congregated there. The young girl smiled and waved. Those gathered on the porch stood in silence and watched the world change before their eyes. The servants of Cobb farm turned onto the road and bid farewell to their old life. Hope burned like a torch that illuminated a dark world. They were slaves no more.

Bright moonlight highlighted the path of the former slaves as they walked along a dirt road. A deep ditch to the right and a large meadow on the left flanked the party. Doug and Vernon assisted Minnie as the rest of the group walked slowly to keep pace with her.

"Oh, boy, my feet hurt," Minnie declared. "How far is this station, Mr. Luke?"

"We still have a way to go, Miss Minnie."

"I might need to stop and rest a spell," Minnie suggested.

"That will be fine. Let's stop for a bit, everyone," Luke recommended.

Vernon got down on one knee and offered his forward leg as a bench. Doug helped Minnie sit on the large man's leg, placing his hand on her back to keep her steady.

"I ain't never walked on a road before. I ain't never been off a farm, less I was carried away in a wagon," Alberta said.

"I can't wait to get to Indianapolis," Florence said.

"Patience, Miss Florence. It's going to take a while," Luke reminded her.

The constant beat of hooves on the road drew the group's attention. Philip raced towards them at breakneck speed. The farmhand pulled the reins and brought the horse to a halt beside them.

"What are you doing? You've got to move fast," Philip said with a sense of urgency.

"Philip, what's wrong?" Doug asked.

"Lester and his boys came by the farm looking for you. They're out for blood. They can't be far behind me. You've got to move!"

"We have to go, everyone," Luke urged as he waved his arms.

"Y'all go on without me," Minnie suggested. "I'll slow you down too much."

"Don't talk all that foolishness, old woman," Maurice stated bluntly.

"Here," Philip declared as he dismounted his horse. "Take my horse."

Vernon, Doug, and Robert help Minnie climb onto the saddle.

"You hold on now," Maurice told her as he grabbed the reins to lead the animal.

The party was on the move again, but hardly quicker than a fast walk.

"You go on. I'll distract them as long as I can," Philip said.

"Wait," Doug stated. "I'll help you."

"Doug, let's go," Florence suggested.

"You'll never make it. I'm going to help Philip buy you some time."

"Come on, Doug. We can make it," Maurice stated.

"Lester's not after Philip. He's coming for us. He won't go after Philip unless he thinks we're with him," Doug explained.

"He's right," Philip agreed.

"Just go, I'll catch up," Doug insisted.

"Follow this road. Look for a house on the left with a lantern hanging from a post near the road," Luke instructed. "It's the station house."

"I'll catch up to you before you get there."

Vernon stepped toward Doug, determined to go with him.

"You stay with them, big guy. They need you," Doug advised.

Vernon nodded in agreement.

"I'll go with you," Robert said, stepping forward.

"Robert, no. Lester will kill you," Lucille pleaded.

"I have to help keep you all safe. I'll catch up with you," Robert responded.

Lucille placed a gentle kiss on his cheek.

"Be careful," she implored Robert.

"Come on," Philip argued. "There's no time to waste."

"Thank you, men," Luke said as he led the others on the road.

Doug, Robert, and Philip darted away to intercept Lester and his underlings.

The larger group was barely out of sight when Doug, Robert, and Philip saw a lantern's light that revealed Lester's crew in the distance. Doug looked to his right and saw a large two-story barn standing in a field, far from a farmhouse.

"Hey, dummy!" Doug yelled, taunting the vile man racing toward them. "Over here! Come and get us!"

Certain that Lester and his men saw them, the trio ran into the field of knee-high grass in the direction of the barn. The sounds of thumping horse's hooves quickened. Doug's heartbeat raced as the fanatics on horseback turned into the field. Doug reached the barn first and yanked on the large door, but it wouldn't budge. A big lock secured the door. A gunshot echoed through the field and a hole appeared in the wood next to Doug. The trio fled around the back of the barn.

"Into the woods!" Doug yelled, pointing to the tree line behind the outbuilding.

The three fleeing men dashed into the thicket of pine trees and disappeared into the isolation within. Lester, Daniel, and Thomas arrived quickly and dismounted their horses. Lester peered into the blackness of the dense forest, squinting, hoping to see movement. He heard a stick break as Doug and Robert trampled it, giving him a general idea of the direction of his prey.

"Daniel, bring the lantern," Lester instructed.

Lester's henchman stepped forward with the lamp and stared into the darkness ahead.

"Let's go," Lester ordered.

The three hunters entered the woods, pushing back the gloom and creating a bubble of light in a murky sea of night and wilderness. The wretched men pursued their quarry like wolves stalking elk. Doug heard the noise the huntsmen made as they stepped on limbs and leaves. Doug looked back and saw the dim glow of the light far behind them. The hunted moved as swiftly and softly as they could, but try as they might, the mangled underbrush betrayed their path with cracking and snapping.

Robert tripped over a large root and stumbled to the ground. The noise rang out like a sonar beacon, and Lester and his men altered their course.

"Be careful," Philip whispered.

The evading party pressed on as quietly as possible. Doug glanced behind him and realized the light was getting closer. Doug searched the ground until he found a sturdy branch felled by a storm long ago. He lifted the limb and heaved it as hard as he could. The branch spun in the air as if doing a cartwheel before striking a tree. Doug saw the jittery movement of the light as Lester's men reacted to the sound.

"Keep going," Doug said softly, urging his companions forward.

Doug, Robert, and Philip quickened their pace while Lester and his henchmen moved in another direction. As they moved, branches hacked at their arms, snagging their shirt sleeves. Every step took them further from their pursuers and closer to liberation. Philip stepped on a fresh limb and a loud snap seemed to reverberate in the forest. Doug felt as though he might pass out as a sense of dread washed over him. A gunshot confirmed Doug's fears. A bullet ripped through the tranquil, crisp night air. Doug heard the impact of the bullet on a faraway tree, which warned that Lester was back on the trail. Doug, Robert, and Philip ran. Thick leaves created an impenetrable canopy over the forest, leaving the moon powerless to brighten a path for the retreating men. A low branch caught Doug just below his left eye. He didn't miss a step. The potential loss of an eye was minor compared to Lester's cruelty. Doug kept running until he felt the ground beneath his feet fall away, sending him rolling down a gradual hill. Doug and his companions came to rest on the bank of a river. The sound of the fast-moving water as it rushed over a large rock gave Doug a sense of peace for a second. Doug shook off the hypnotizing tranquility of the setting and remembered the danger. Doug quickly got to his feet and climbed the short hill. The light bobbed as Lester's crew moved toward them.

"They're coming," Doug warned the others after skipping back down the hill.

"Let's get across the river," Philip suggested.

Doug immediately looked at Robert, who said nothing and stood motionless.

"He can't swim," Doug advised Philip.

"We can help him," Philip replied as he stepped closer to the water.

"I can't swim. I'll drown," Robert stated.

"Come on, there's no time to lose," Philip said.

"You go ahead," Doug said. "We'll find a way across."

An exasperated Philip rubbed his forehead.

"All right, come on," Philip replied.

The group turned right and followed the river. Dim light chased the men and caused barely visible shadows to emerge and shift and stir around them. Doug drew in the earthy smells of the forest as he ran, and the sound of aged leaves rustled beneath his feet. The river took the fleeing men to the edge of the wilderness, where it suddenly stopped before a small pasture. Doug, Robert, and Philip stopped to catch their breath and surveyed the land ahead. A road crossed the other side of the field and beyond that, a two-story wooden grist mill rested on its stone foundation. Soft moonlight poured through the canopy of broken clouds, spreading an extraordinary, delicate white radiance across the ground. The three runners looked back to see the mellow but threatening light of the lantern drawing near.

"Get to the mill," Philip said, leading his compatriots across the field.

The men ran as fast as they could until they reached the mill. A rusty, broken metal padlock hung impotently from a loop in the door. Robert quickly removed the lock and tossed it aside. Robert pulled the door so hard he felt it would come off its hinges. Lester, Daniel, and Thomas reached the edge of the pasture just as their prey dashed inside the mill and hastily closed the door.

"We've got 'em now," Lester said.

Philip examined the door from inside. There was no way to lock it, and it swung open to the outside. Doug looked out a window and observed the ominous yellow glow that emanated from the woods beyond the field.

"I can see them," Doug told the others.

"There's no way to bar the door," Philip imparted, his words marinated in hopelessness. "Quick, hide."

Doug and his friends scrambled up the stairs.

Lester stood quietly in the field and ruminated on his next step. His quarry had trapped itself, making it easy, almost too easy.

"Daniel, go get the horses and bring them around to the mill. When you get there, wait outside in case any of them come out," Lester ordered.

"Sure thing, boss."

Daniel turned back into the woods and used the lantern to illuminate his path. Darkness covered Lester's face like a veil as the light receded into the forest.

"Let's go. Be on your guard," Lester advised Thomas.

Lester walked casually across the field. The mill beckoned him to the hunt.

Doug peered through a small hole in the wall on the mill's second floor and observed Lester and Thomas approaching. A chill ran up Doug's spine as he felt the hand of hatred reaching for him.

24

The Embers of Loathing

Lester stopped outside the mill and listened for any movement inside. All he could hear was water rushing over the top of a dam that stood about ten feet tall beside the mill. Lester pushed the door open slowly and cautiously stepped inside. The brute looked around, peering through particles of dust that floated in the air. A variety of tools and items, including hammers, buckets, and even a few iron kettles, hung from the rafters and walls. Thomas stepped around a table and bumped into the mill crane, a contraption used to change the heavy millstones. The bails on the mill crane, long metal prongs that affixed to the stone for lifting, clanged when Thomas hit them.

"Be careful," Lester said. "They might be waiting to ambush us."

Lester felt along the wall until he discovered a lantern hanging from a wooden peg. He lifted the lantern and shook it. A smile crept across Lester's face as a sloshing sound confirmed the presence of fuel. Lester placed the lantern on a table and withdrew a box of matches from his pocket. He swiped a match against the side of the box and a tiny orange flame burst to life, brightening the area.

Lester raised the lantern with his left hand and gripped a pistol in his right. He held the lamp high, illuminating the space around him as he searched the room for his targets.

Doug hid behind a large hopper on the second floor, where a thick leather belt came through a hole in the floor and connected to a pulley on the ceiling. The hopper looked like a giant pail that tapered at the bottom, feeding corn to the millstones below. Philip took cover behind a stack of barrels on the other side of the room, while Robert hid in a corner behind a large overturned table. Doug listened to Lester's slow, methodical steps beneath him. Doug struggled to keep his breathing calm as terror made every stride Lester took sound like a hammer blow.

"Hold this," Lester ordered Thomas as he handed him the lantern.

Lester grabbed a big iron wheel protruding from the floor near a wall and turned it several times. The sound of rushing water became louder behind the wall. Lester could see the waterwheel start to turn as he watched through a window. Lester turned other wheels in the room and set the millstone turning and belts moving. The hopper beside Doug shimmied, and the mill filled with the droning noise of antique machinery, squeaking pulleys, and creaking wood. Lester retrieved the lantern from Thomas and resumed his meticulous search.

Lester spun quickly after hearing a noise in the far corner beneath the stairs. He inched cautiously toward the sound, holding the gun in front of him. When he reached the corner, Lester kicked over a bucket and watched a rat scurry down a hole in the floor. After inspecting the room, Lester looked up and signaled to Thomas, pointing his pistol upward as if poking the ceiling. Lester tiptoed up the stairs, masked by the noise of the rotating gears, rushing water, flapping belts, and spinning stone. The steps creaked under the weight of contemptible men and bad intentions. Lester paused at the top of the stairs and gazed at the dusty, dim room's obscurity. He advanced into the room slowly. The lantern swayed gently in his grasp, and the moving shadows created a bland kaleidoscopic pattern on the walls.

Doug saw the ghostly shapes rotate on the wall before him. He could almost hear Lester's snarling breath over the clatter of the mill, and it nearly petrified him with fear. Suddenly, the shadows became still.

Lester noticed the table laying on its side and walked slowly toward it, keeping the pistol ready. Robert sprang from the dark corner near the table and lunged at Lester. The monster sidestepped the attack and extended his leg to trip Robert. As Robert fell past him, Lester smacked the young man on the side of the head with the pistol. Robert hit the floor with a loud thud. Robert rolled onto his back and found himself face to face with the end of Lester's gun. The former slave held his trembling hands in front of his face, silently seeking mercy.

"Get up nice and easy," Lester ordered.

Robert carefully got to his feet and kept his hands raised.

"Tip that table back up, then step over here," Lester instructed.

Robert pushed the table back onto its legs, then moved to the middle of the room. Lester placed the lantern on the table and returned his attention to Robert.

"Alright, the rest of y'all come on out. No more running and hiding," Lester said.

Anxiety held Doug tightly in its grasp, and he couldn't move. He barely made out the shape of Philip hiding in the opposite corner.

"Where are they?" Lester asked Robert.

"I don't know," Robert nervously responded.

"You have three seconds to come out before I put a bullet in this one!" Lester shouted. "One!"

Despite his fear, Doug stood up immediately, and Philip followed.

"Get from around there and come over here by him," Lester advised, motioning with the gun.

Doug and Philip walked to the center of the room and stood beside Robert. Thomas remained near the stairs, blocking any escape route from the upper floor. Lester surveyed the trio, pacing as Thomas kept his gun pointed at them.

"Well, well," Lester said, looking at Robert. "You're the one who hit me."

"You hit me in the head," Robert replied while pressing his hand to his ear.

"Oh, I'm going to do more than that."

"Lester, please, stop this," Philip urged. "Let it go."

"I'm not letting anything go. Look at my hand," Lester said as he displayed the contusion on his palm, compliments of the whipping Robert had given him.

"How many slaves have you beaten?" Doug asked calmly. "How many have you killed?"

"As I told you before, not nearly enough," Lester replied.

"Why all this hatred, Lester?" Doug inquired, speaking loud enough to be heard over the various gears and belts turning throughout the mill.

"You want to know why I hate you?" Lester asked rhetorically. "I don't need a reason to hate you. You're no better than the stuff at the bottom of a hog pen. We feed you. Put clothes on your back. Give you a house to stay in. What more could you ask for? You couldn't do that for yourself. I hate everything about you. But then one of you went and killed my father. I saw your true nature."

"Listen to me, Lester. Let's talk," Doug encouraged the vengeful man. "I know what it's like to hate. I've despised people. I've hurt people. Hate can poison your soul. I know because it happened to me. But I saw the cost of that hate. It's in the ground all around us. We can't go on hating each other. Hate can't defeat hate. They're the same. It's like building a levee out of water to protect against a flood. We can't go on like this. We have to be better. We all have to be better. Don't we owe that to the ones who come after us?"

"Listen to this one," Lester said with a chuckle. "He sounds like a poet."

Thomas giggled in reply to Lester's remark.

"He's right, Lester," Philip added. "Pretty wise for a dumb savage, don't you think?"

"Who's side are you on anyway, Philip?" Lester asked.

"I've been on the wrong side for too long."

"Are you willing to die for these devils? You saw what that one did to me," Lester stated, motioning to Robert. "And this other one ain't been nothing but trouble from the minute Earl wasted Mr. Cobb's money at auction."

Lester scrutinized the captives, focusing on Robert and Doug as if he were a predator relishing an impending kill.

"These two stole from me, made me bleed, but here you are, Philip, running with them. Why?" Lester interrogated.

"Someday, when I meet my maker, I want to say I made amends for what

I did," Philip replied.

"Tell your maker these two will be along shortly," Lester said threateningly as he lifted his pistol to Philip's head.

"Wait," Doug interjected, fully aware of how perilous the situation was. "You don't want to do this."

"Why not?" Lester asked as he lowered the gun.

"Because you don't want more blood on your hands. You killed Charles, you killed Henry. That has to be hard to live with."

"I sleep just fine at night," Lester replied.

"You killed Henry?" Philip questioned.

"He wasn't worth spit," Lester declared.

"Wait, who killed Henry?" Thomas asked.

"Lester did," Robert clarified.

"Why?" Thomas queried.

"Because he went poking his nose where it didn't belong!" Lester yelled.

Thomas looked uneasy after hearing the answer. Lester's eyes revealed the feverish rage inside of him.

"He was just like his friend here," Lester said with a scowl as he stared into Philip's eyes. "Always trying to tell me something they know nothing about. Threatening me."

Lester raised the pistol again and pointed it at Philip's head. Doug felt his heart race. It pounded in his ears louder than the commotion of the machinery in the building. Lester placed his thumb on the hammer and prepared to cock the gun. Doug knew they were all facing certain death. He had to act. A surge of adrenaline shot through Doug. While Lester fixated on Philip, Doug rushed the scoundrel and tackled him. The momentum of the charge sent the enemies careening into the table. The force catapulted the lantern into the air. Both men and the table crashed to the floor. The lamp crashed against a thick wooden pillar, breaking into fragments that sent flame and oil cascading onto the wall before landing on sacks and barrels. A fire flared up in an instant.

"Come on, we have to get out of here!" Thomas pleaded.

Doug and Lester rolled on the floor as Doug tried to wrestle the gun away from the hateful man. Lester pulled the trigger and the random shot shattered a window. Doug attempted to thrust his knee into whatever part of Lester he could, but the futile effort missed the mark. Doug labored to free the gun from Lester's grasp while also keeping it pointed away from himself. Lester fired the gun again. The bullet ricocheted off a metal pulley mounted on the ceiling before blasting a hole in a barrel next to Robert.

"Let's go!" Thomas urged again.

"Doug, come on!" Robert pleaded.

Doug's reply was a shout of anguish as Lester landed a punch to the side of his head. The fire spread quickly, sustained by the bounty of wood and burlap surrounding it. Lester kept a solid grip on the gun, but Doug maintained a hand on Lester's arm and pushed it above his head. Lester landed a punch to Doug's face that sent a jolt through the young man's jaw. Doug shook off the pain; he had to restrain Lester's arm that held the pistol. As they rolled around on the floor, they changed positions frequently. One moment Lester was over Doug, and the next minute it was reversed. The warriors neared the fire, so close that Doug's shirtsleeve nearly touched the blaze. The flame flicked like a snake's tongue, sensing a victim within striking distance. They rolled away just before the fire could grab them. Doug landed a punch to Lester's ribs that knocked the wind out of the man for a second. Lester delivered another blow to Doug's head. Doug replied in kind, blasting Lester just below his left eye.

Lester loosed another random gunshot that sent Thomas racing down the stairs. The fire climbed and reached for the ceiling. A metal hook fell from the wall, bringing with it a hammer it held in place.

"Doug, come on!" Robert screamed.

A thick belt ran through a hole in the floor near Doug and Lester. Doug kept his left hand on the gun that Lester clutched in his right. Lester shoved Doug's right arm and pressed it against the fast-moving strap. Doug jerked his free arm away, but wouldn't relinquish his grip on the gun.

The fire seemed to make an audible roar as it streaked across the ceiling at the far end of the room. The flames engulfed half the place and smoke billowed out of the broken window, while also lingering inside.

"Doug needs our help!" Robert said to Philip, squinting as the smoke and brightness of the blaze burned his eyes.

A section of the roof caved in the distant corner of the room.

"We have to get out of here!" Philip argued as he grabbed Robert's arm.

"Doug!" Robert bellowed while being pulled down the steps.

"Come on! We have to go!" Philip demanded.

Doug pulled Lester's hand to him, then bit it hard. The rancid taste of the tyrant's flesh disgusted him, but Doug had to fight with everything he had. Lester screamed and dropped the pistol. Doug climbed over Lester to retrieve the weapon, but Lester gut-punched him again and stopped his progress. Lester reached out to grab the gun when Doug delivered a knee to his groin. Both warriors rolled over and got on their hands and knees, then lunged toward the revolver. Before Lester's hand reached it, Doug blasted him in the side of the face with a hard jab. Lester landed with a thump as Doug seized the gun. Lester quickly recovered and reached for Doug, tackling the young man. The fighters rolled over again before coming to a halt with Doug atop Lester's chest, the pistol's end directed at his face. Doug stood up and kept the gun pointed at Lester.

Lester gazed at the angry young man hovering over him. The flames danced around the room, and the bitterness in Doug's eyes made him look like a demon. Robert ran up the stairs to find Doug aiming the pistol at their tormentor.

"Get out of here!" Robert yelled.

Doug remained like a statue above Lester. He held complete power over the man who had brought misery and even death to so many. Doug quivered with anger and the gun shook in his hand.

"Go on!" Lester howled. "Do it!"

"Part of me wants to pull this trigger!" Doug confessed.

"Go ahead! It's in your character!" Lester howled.

"Killing him won't give you peace, Doug!" Robert offered. "Think about your grandpa and your mom! We need to go!"

Doug coughed, and his eyes seemed to clear as animosity drained from him.

"I'm not like you!" Doug stated. "I'm choosing to be better than you!"

Doug turned away from Lester in a manner that was as symbolic as it was physical. Robert and Doug descended the steps rapidly and dashed toward the door. Wood creaked and hissed. Iron clanged and thudded as it hit the floor. A tremendous groaning sound filled the air, as if the old mill wept in agony as the fire consumed it.

"Hey!"

Doug and Robert had nearly reached the door when they heard Lester. The young men turned to see Lester standing at the bottom of the stairs.

"I'm not done with you yet," Lester declared.

The despot turned to them ominously. As Lester stumbled toward them, the building moaned loudly. Over the din of the flames, a loud break and crack erupted before a massive beam plummeted from the ceiling and slammed Lester across the shoulders. Lester collapsed beneath the weight of the huge board, which pinned him to the floor. Lester barely moved. He resembled a dying fish out of water. Doug and Robert glanced at each other. The fire encroached on the lower floor.

"We can't leave him," Doug said.

Robert nodded in agreement, and the young men hurried to the fallen beast.

"Come on," Doug said as he grabbed the end of the beam.

Robert grabbed the same end as Doug and together they strained as they hoisted the log. The men shuffled to the left and pivoted the obstacle off of Lester's back. The former slaves each grabbed one of their oppressor's arms, then pulled him from the disintegrating building. Lester's feet bounced on the steps as Doug and Robert dragged him outside.

Philip, Thomas, and Daniel watched the amazing scene unfold. Two men scarred by the harshness of whips and hateful words saved the life of another who despised their very existence. Such bitter irony often changes history. It can prevent the burning embers of loathing from becoming a wildfire.

25

Malice Toward None

Once a safe distance from danger, Doug and Robert released Lester and rolled him onto his back. The goon gasped and winced as he tried to collect himself and shake off the pain in his shoulders and back. Doug and Robert coughed as fresh air raced into their lungs. As the ceiling crumbled, the old mill made horrifying groans, as if it were a living thing pleading for death's merciful release.

Daniel and Thomas stood near Philip and watched the fire defy the night. Doug and Robert reached under Lester's arms and helped him to his feet.

"Get your hands off me," Lester said with a cough as he waved the young lads away.

"You're welcome," Doug said flippantly before he took several steps back.

A group of Union soldiers approached on horseback and interrupted the conversation. The assemblage comprised about twenty men, led by a handful of officers. The troopers pulled their horses to a stop when they arrived at the scene of the blaze.

"Dear Lord," the captain said as he gawked at the incinerating structure. "Are you men all right?"

"Yes, sir. We're fine," Doug answered the man.

"We were headed north when we saw the glow of the fire through the trees," the captain added.

"That's where you should go, north," Lester uttered without the slightest hint of decorum.

"I beg your pardon?" The captain replied.

"I said you should just keep going north. You don't belong here meddling in our affairs," Lester said, his voice increasing an octave.

"I don't like your tone. I would advise you to watch your tongue," the captain warned.

"You watch your tongue," Lester responded.

The officer scowled at Lester.

"I say, you must be wallpapered or you're just a bad egg," the officer proclaimed, using the slang of the day to assert that Lester was drunk, or simply a bad person.

"He's a lot worse than that," Doug professed.

"What do you mean?" the officer asked.

"That man's a murderer," Doug charged.

The officer offered a perplexed but curious gaze. Lester replied with a dismissive snicker.

"Who do you say he killed?" the officer inquired.

"He killed his grandfather," Doug explained, pointing to Robert. "And he also killed a man named Henry."

The officer turned his attention to Lester, who reacted with a smug grin.

"You can't believe anything these dogs say. Certainly, you aren't going to take their word over mine. They're liars, I tell you," Lester added.

"You best tell me the truth, boy," the officer sternly told Doug.

"I swear it. He killed those men. Now I know it doesn't count for much to most of you that he killed Robert's grandfather, and that's a shame," Doug stated. "But he also killed Henry, and even the laws of today say that is a crime."

"You bald-faced liar," Lester said. "Don't listen to him. You can't trust them. Why they'd kill you the first chance they got."

"They saved your life," Philip offered in defense of the former slaves.

Lester cast a look at Philip that cursed him most severely without saying a word.

"These young men are telling the truth. Lester there all but confessed to the murder of Henry Bowman. I witnessed his acknowledgment myself, just before he meant to kill the three of us," Philip continued.

"Put this man in binders," the officer instructed a man to his left.

The guard climbed down from his horse and signaled to two other soldiers. Three men approached Lester, two of them held long rifles. Lester retreated slowly in short steps.

"They're all liars," Lester said. "Thomas, tell them."

Thomas surveyed the surrounding scene. The sight of armed troops staring at him, awaiting his testimony, smothered any inclination of lying for Lester.

"It seemed like you kinda said you killed Henry, Lester," Thomas meekly replied.

The soldiers grabbed Lester's arms.

"Get your Yankee hands off me! You have no authority here!" Lester blared as he jerked his arms free.

One soldier raised his rifle high, then swiftly brought the stock to Lester's abdomen. The oaf crumpled and dropped to his knees and gasped for air. The soldiers bound Lester's hands before him, then lifted the rascal back to his feet. Light from the mill fire revealed the shock on Lester's face as the soldiers led him to be the back of the column.

"If there is nothing else, we need to be going," the officer announced.

"I don't suppose you have a couple of horses you could spare," Philip wondered aloud. "We have to catch up to some other slaves, former slaves I mean."

"I'm afraid I can't spare any, but perhaps these fellows can part with one," the officer proposed. "The murderous scoundrel will have no use of his."

Daniel and Thomas hesitated for a moment but realized the Union officer didn't merely suggest they separate with one of their steeds.

"Oh, of course," Daniel said before handing the reins of his horse to Philip. Doug grasped the lead of Lester's horse.

"I'll return them, I promise," Philip vowed. "You can get them at Mr. Cobb's farm tomorrow if you like."

"Sure. I'll just ride with him," Daniel sheepishly said while pointing at

Thomas.

The officer tipped his hat and led his men on a slow trot down the road. One of the last soldiers in line held a long rope attached to Lester's hands. The fiend struggled to keep pace with the horse that pulled him. Doug felt no pleasure in seeing Lester dragged away in the same manner as he'd done to many slaves. While he was glad the man would face justice, Doug knew the world couldn't change for the better if people delighted in the suffering of others.

Robert and Doug watched the soldiers and their prisoner fade into the blackness of the long narrow road, like a nightmare evaporating from memory. Philip climbed atop Daniel's horse, then extended a hand to Robert.

"Here, I'll help you up," Philip offered.

Robert climbed onto the horse and sat behind Philip.

"Now hand me those reins, Doug, and I'll lead the horse for you," Philip said.

Doug handed the lead to Philip, then mounted Lester's horse.

"Hang on men," Philip said before urging the animals into motion.

The men departed at a slow gallop and left Daniel and Thomas alone at the old mill, which burned and crumbled like slavery itself.

Vernon heard horses approaching and moved to the rear of the group to take up a defensive posture. The large man's scowl turned to a smile when he recognized Doug sitting on a fleet-footed horse. Philip brought the animals to a halt and Robert climbed off quickly. Lucille shrieked with joy and ran to Robert, wrapping her arms tightly around his neck. She kissed Robert's cheek and inspected his face for injuries, then drew him near again. Doug embraced Florence as Maurice patted him on the back.

"I'm so happy to see you," Florence said.

"What happened to Lester?" Maurice asked.

"Some Union soldiers took him into custody for killing Henry," Doug explained.

Lucille nearly fell to her knees after hearing the proclamation of her innocence. Cecelia smiled at Doug while holding Lucille's little boy. The young man smiled back at her, a gesture she found as tender and comforting as a hug. The cheerful sounds of erstwhile slaves drowned out the crickets caterwauling in the night.

"I'm sorry to stifle this merriment, but we must continue on our way," Luke informed the group.

"Florence, would you like to ride on the horse?" Philip asked.

"Oh, that big animal might kick me off," Florence replied.

"It will be perfectly fine. I'll keep hold of it at all times," Philip assured her.

"Go on, Mammy-Lou," Maurice suggested.

Philip and Doug carefully lifted Florence onto the horse. The woman clumsily leaned forward before gaining her confidence and sitting straight.

"Ladies, there's another horse if you would like to ride," Philip offered.

Lucille, Cecelia, and Hilda all politely declined the offer.

"Are you sure?" Philip asked again.

"I want to ride the horse," Alberta declared excitedly.

"Come on over and we'll get you up there," Philip said.

Once Doug and Philip positioned Alberta on the horse, the group continued on their journey to the station house.

"It's not much farther now," Luke advised the smiling crowd.

The moon shined brightly over them, lighting a path to liberation.

"I wonder what the future holds for you," Philip speculated aloud as he strolled beside Doug. "What does it hold for all of us?"

"My mom used to tell me you are who you choose to be. So I guess it's up to each of us to decide. The future is what we make it," Doug responded.

"Everything is going to be different. Can we all live together now?" Philip deliberated openly.

"It will take some time, a long time, and it won't be easy, but eventually, we'll get there," Doug offered.

The men walked quietly, each lost in his thoughts and expectations.

After traveling a few more miles, the party arrived at a post with a lantern standing before a two-story house.

"Here we are," said Luke as he led his friends into the yard.

Once the group came to a stop, the men helped the ladies dismount from the horses. Alberta reached for Vernon's finger, something that would make her feel secure in this unfamiliar place. The bruised and battered men and women huddled together and cautiously walked toward the house. The front door swung open and a woman in her thirties stepped out.

"Emma," Luke called as he extended his arms.

The two friends hugged in the yard before Luke turned and presented the freed slaves.

"I hope you have enough beds still," Luke said.

"Of course, there's enough room for all of them," Emma replied.

The woman approached the crowd and extended her arm toward the house.

"Right this way, everyone," Emma said with a smile.

Two black women exited the house and stood on the porch. Alberta stopped in her tracks and stared at the women. The look on Alberta's face painted an expression of puzzlement. A tear left a long, moist line on her face as it raced to the ground. Alberta wiped the tear from her cheek and took a second look at the porch. One woman's face appeared gaunt, eroded by misery and suffering, but Alberta saw a strikingly familiar countenance. The young girl released Vernon's finger and ran to the porch.

"Mama!" screamed Alberta as she dashed across the lawn.

Mary waved her thin arms over her head and scampered down the stairs. Tears flowed as mother and daughter converged in the yard.

"Baby!" Mary cried. "Alberta! My baby!"

Mother and daughter nearly fell over when they collided. Mary embraced her daughter as tightly as the day slave traders pried Alberta from her arms. Alberta buried her face in her mother's shoulder.

"Let me see you," Mary said, almost stuttering from excitement. She lifted Alberta's head and kissed her face. Mary patted Alberta's shoulders and arms before pulling her close again. Mary looked up at the moon as if it was the face of God and shed tears of unmistakable joy and gratitude.

Nearly everyone in the yard felt a joy that heretofore was unknown, the beautiful sight of a slave family reunited. The celebration moved into the house, but Doug and Robert remained in the yard with Luke and Philip.

"I guess I better be getting these horses to Mr. Cobb's place," Philip said.

"I'll help you," Luke offered.

"Thank you."

Philip stepped before the former slaves, shaking each man's hand.

"Good luck to you. I hope you find a place where the world is kind," Philip said.

"Thank you, Philip," Doug said as the man walked to his horse.

"What you men did was incredibly brave," Luke stated. "It takes great courage to put your life and welfare at risk for the sake of others."

"Any of them would have done the same for us," Doug replied.

"Of that, I have no doubt," Luke affirmed. "Maurice and Florence are fond of you both."

"They are some of the kindest people I've ever met," Doug asserted.

"It is amazing that people treated so harshly can be uncommonly warm-hearted," Luke stated.

"I hope you can help them reach their son," Doug said.

"I'm certainly going to do my best. But if you ask me, I would say they have two more sons," Luke replied.

Doug and Robert smiled humbly at the suggestion but knew Luke spoke sincerely.

"Get some rest. Tomorrow we wake up to a whole new world. Soon, we'll be going north," Luke encouraged the young men as he climbed onto a horse.

Doug and Robert watched Luke and Philip ride away before walking to the house. Hot food and a comfortable bed offered a reprieve from the exhausting events of the day.

The slaves gathered around a large table for supper. Doug watched the smiling faces around him. Alberta sat between her mother and Minnie.

"I told you, girl," Hilda said to Alberta, remembering when she informed the young girl that mothers do not forget their children.

Lucille held her son on her lap as Robert leaned over and made a funny face that caused the boy to laugh. Despite losing his grandfather, Doug knew Robert wouldn't feel alone in the world.

Maurice tenderly held Florence's hand, and he knew their thoughts were on their son, Ben. Doug couldn't imagine the joy they would feel when reunited with their boy.

Vernon sat and smiled, simply happy that others were happy.

Doug knew hard days lay ahead. The world would still be unkind. But he dared not diminish their joy or aspiration for the future.

"What's on your mind, Doug?" Cecelia asked as she rubbed his back.

"Oh, nothing. Just thinking about the future, like everybody else," Doug replied, offering her a grin.

"Come on, Mammy Lou, let's get some sleep," Maurice said while standing up.

Florence shook her head at her husband's refusal to abandon his nickname for her.

That night, the former slaves of Bentonville slept on comfortable beds. Doug and Robert shared a room with Vernon. While the younger men each had a small but cozy bed, Vernon still preferred the space the floor provided, although he added an extra pillow for his head.

"This is so soft," Robert declared.

"It is nice," Doug replied as he shifted his head on the pillow.

"I wonder what it's going to be like," Robert thought openly. "Maybe they'll let me ride a riverboat, but on deck where I can feel the wind and the spray of water on my face. Or maybe I'll take a train ride to a friendly little town somewhere. Heck, maybe I'll go to Washington and see Mr. Lincoln and thank him in person. Me and Lucille will get a little house where we can raise the baby. You can come stay with us, Doug. You too, Vernon."

The big man smiled widely, his eyes closed, trying to picture it all.

"Pump your brakes a little, man," Doug suggested.

"What does that mean? Pump your brakes," Robert asked.

"I'm just saying there are still some hard days ahead. Things don't change overnight."

"I'm sure there will be bad times. But you know what? Yesterday I was a slave. Tonight I'm sleeping on the softest bed I've ever felt in my life. Today was better than yesterday. That's what we do. Try to make today better than yesterday. Keep doing that, and the whole world will be better after a while," Robert professed.

"You know what, Robert?"

"What?"

"You're a pretty smart guy," Doug complimented his friend.

"So are you, Doug. I guess I got smart because I have friends like you."

"Thanks, man. Sleep well."

"You too."

Crickets chirped, an owl hooted, and the moon stood over the station house like a guardian angel. The serenity of the night contrasted the mood of the war-torn country. That night, former slaves went to bed with hearts full of hope: hope in a promise hard-earned on the fields of Bentonville.

26

The Second Birth of Douglas Timmons

Doug felt someone shake him and heard Cecelia's voice but kept his eyes closed, cherishing the deepest sleep he had known for as long as he could remember.

"Wake up, Doug," Cecelia said as she gently shook him.

Doug drifted his head back, hoping to deter her efforts to wake him.

"Come on, Doug," she said again, but her voice changed a little.

Doug raised his right hand to his head. It ached.

"Doug, wake up," the changing voice said.

Doug opened his eyes and saw Aliyah Gaines leaning over him with her hands on his shoulders. The young man was flat on the ground, and his head throbbed.

"Cecelia?" Doug asked with a distressed and confused expression on his face.

"Who's Cecelia?" Aliyah asked him.

Doug lifted his arms to his face and examined his shirt sleeves. He wasn't wearing slave clothing and it puzzled him. Doug patted his shirt as if making sure his clothes were real. He watched a bird soar in the blue sky above him.

"How did I get here?" Doug wondered.

"I was hoping you could tell me. We've been looking everywhere for you."

"I was in bed," Doug said before pausing. He searched for words to explain his previous whereabouts but couldn't find them.

"You must have done some serious sleepwalking to get all the way out here," Aliyah said incredulously.

"Where's Robert?" Doug asked, still perplexed.

"Doug, are you OK?"

"Florence? Maurice?" Doug inquired about his friends, baffled by the transition back into the world he had always known. His mind was as dull as a wooden spoon.

"Who are you looking for?" Aliyah sought to know.

Doug touched the sore spot on his head and flinched in reaction to the pain. The discomfort gradually pushed away the uncertainty, much like the sun warms the air and dissipates a morning fog. Visions of Doug's recent life flashed in his head. He recalled the events in Bentonville but could feel the wetness of the grass he laid on, smell the nearby flowers, and hear birds singing their morning songs. The young man remained still as he struggled to decipher reality from dream. Doug seemed stuck between two worlds and he was the son of them both. He closed his eyes and frowned because of the pulsing agony in his head. When Doug opened his eyes again, he saw Aliyah's lovely face, and it pulled him from the tangle of memories.

"Aliyah," Doug said as he tried to shake the sleep and pain from his head. "What's going on?"

"Everybody's been looking for you," Aliyah answered.

Doug looked to his left and saw Jordan standing beside him.

"He's over here!" Jordan shouted.

Aliyah's soft hands comforted Doug, and he didn't want to move.

"Come on, sit up," Aliyah said, gently helping Doug lean forward.

He winced and hissed as he moved and felt the wetness of morning dew on his back.

"It looks like your head is bleeding a little," she observed.

"Some guy hit me," Doug informed her.

"It looked like he knocked you clean into the hedges. We had to pull you out from between those bushes," Jordan said, pointing to the shrubbery near Doug's feet.

"Doug! My baby! My baby!" Wanda exclaimed as she ran to her son.

Doug rose to his feet to meet his mother. A throng of people roamed the park but all Doug could see was Wanda. She wrapped her arms around Doug and squeezed him tightly, causing him to grimace. It was the most painful, welcomed embrace of Doug's young life.

"Oh, my goodness! Are you hurt? I was so worried!" Wanda asked as she took a step back and examined Doug.

Doug fought back tears as he stared at his mother's cheerful face. He had yearned to see her for so long.

"Mom, I," Doug said before stopping. No more words could cross his lips as he struggled to hold back his emotions. He wanted to tell her about the robbery, his grand adventure in Bentonville, and so many things, but his thoughts collide. Wanda drew him in close and rubbed the back of his neck. Doug rested his chin on his mother's shoulder and tears welled up in his eyes.

"It's OK," Wanda said, attempting to soothe her son's restless spirit.

Doug grappled with his feelings a few moments more, then composed himself. He lifted his head and saw with clarity as if a gentle breeze blew away a pall of thick smoke that obscured the world. Doug saw a group of people walking toward him.

"Look at all these people," Doug murmured.

"They were all trying to find you," Aliyah said.

Doug couldn't believe his eyes. They were there for him. Doug couldn't help but wonder what people could accomplish if a community banded together instead of preying on one another, as he frequently witnessed in the neighborhood. He recalled how the slaves of Bentonville banded together. They nursed the injured and sick among them and buried and honored those who perished. When one person fell, another helped him or her stand again. The sight of the people in the park gave Doug hope everyone could care like the slaves of Bentonville.

"Let's get you home and look at your head," Wanda said.

"I'll help you, Mrs. Timmons," Aliyah offered.

"Thank you, Aliyah. That's very nice of you," Wanda responded. "Isn't it, Doug?"

"Yeah, thank you," Doug said through gritted teeth as he endured the pain in his head.

There was something different about the neighborhood. Doug tried to put his finger on it. Despite his aching head and hazy vision, Doug saw the same cracks in the sidewalk, the same bars on shop windows, and the same cars parked along the street. A siren blared in the distance, and dogs barked and howled. A car rolled by, playing loud music. Nothing had changed, but everything was different. It occurred to Doug that sometimes it isn't the world, but you, that's changed.

Doug didn't know if his adventure in Bentonville resulted from a miracle that took him back in time or was simply a vivid dream. No experience in his life had felt more real. Whatever the explanation was, it altered Doug forever.

27

The Path

A cozy ranch-style brick house stood on a carpet of lush green grass at the intersection of two quiet streets. Nearby trees swayed in the crisp fall breeze and displayed vibrant shades of red, orange, and yellow. A cloudless sky allowed an unbridled sun to immerse the neighborhood in radiant light. Despite the cool weather of the day, a man washed a car in the driveway of the house next door. Wanda stepped out of the front door of the house and carefully walked on stepping stones until she reached her paved driveway. A bright yellow leaf drifted in the air and crossed Wanda's path as it gently descended to the ground.

"Hey, Virgil," Wanda said as she waved to the man washing the car. Virgil lifted his free hand, the other submerged in a bucket of suds, and waved back.

Wanda opened the mailbox and removed a few envelopes. She shuffled through the letters, glancing at them before she closed the mailbox and walked back to the house.

Doug sat on the side of his bed and stared out the window, the three buttons on his polo shirt unfastened. A dresser with a mirror hugged the wall. Doug's bedroom window perfectly framed the scene of children playing in a park across the street. Black and white children climbed up the steps of a slide one after another and took turns gliding back to earth. A narrow dirt path cut through a stately, verdant field, bypassing the sidewalks leading to the park entrance. Countless people strolled over the field throughout the years, gradually scouring a trail through the short, dense grass.

Doug watched the children play and laugh. They were just across the street, but the journey to get there took centuries. Doug knew the names of those who helped lead the way. But Lincoln, King, Douglass, Stowe, Truth, Tubman, Brown, and Parks didn't forge a route across the rugged landscape of history alone. Many whose names are unknown made the grueling pilgrimage that abraded a pathway leading to a better future. Doug knew some of those names as well: Maurice, Florence, Vernon, Cecelia, Robert, Lucille, Luke, Homer, Stephen, and Charles. Doug owed it to them and the children across the street to keep striving to make today better than yesterday. The tears and screams of suffering slaves and dying soldiers echoed across generations and demanded it of him.

They demand we all be better.

Every one of us.

A knock on the bedroom door jolted Doug out of his reverie.

"Come on, Doug. We're supposed to meet Aliyah and her mom at the restaurant in half an hour," Wanda alerted her son.

"Yes, ma'am," Doug replied. "I'm almost ready."

"OK, don't take too long."

"I won't."

Doug got up from the bed and walked to the dresser, where he examined himself in the mirror. A prominently placed framed picture of young Doug with his late grandfather sat on the furniture. Doug knew the importance of choosing your heroes wisely, so he kept a reminder of one of his foremost in plain view. The young man grabbed a brush that served as a paperweight for a returned homework assignment and ran it across his head. A large letter *A* adorned the front page in bright red ink. Doug placed the brush back on the dresser, then fastened the buttons on his shirt. He inspected his appearance one last time, peering intently at the mirror.

Isn't that where so many things begin? Doesn't change begin with oneself? The first person you should hold accountable is you. Sometimes we have to change before asking the world to transform. Light radiates outward from the source.

Doug grabbed a bottle of cologne and gave himself a couple of sprays.

"Doug, you ready?" Wanda asked through the door.

"Yes, ma'am. I'm ready," Doug said.

Doug placed the bottle back on the dresser and walked to the door. He exited the room and pulled the door closed behind him. Doug ventured into a world filled with happiness and sorrow, love and hate, possibility and roadblocks. But he left contempt and bias behind. Maybe we can too.

It's important to remember the past. The footprints in the sand behind us reveal where we were, but also how far we've come. The path ahead is up to us.

All of us.

About the Author

Shayne Whitaker was born in California and lived throughout the United States as a child. Abandoned by his mother when he was four years old, Shayne lived in a foster home before returning to the custody of his father. After spending nearly ten years in poverty and neglect, he was placed in an orphanage in Oxford, North Carolina, a place he considers his hometown. He attended Gardner-Webb University and served in the Army National Guard. His first book, *The Homeless Man's Journal*, chronicles many of the experiences of his life. He makes his home in North Carolina with his five beloved rescue cats.

You can connect with me on:
- 𝕏 https://twitter.com/ShayneWhitake10
- f https://www.facebook.com/AuthorShayneWhitaker

Also by Shayne Whitaker

The Homeless Man's Journal

Based on a true story. While waiting at his usual bus stop, Ben discovers a notebook that tells the life-changing story of a homeless man who once slept there. The Homeless Man's Journal chronicles the experiences of author Shayne Whitaker. Abandoned by his mother when he was only four years old, Shayne embarked on an odyssey full of hardship, poverty, and abuse that crisscrossed the country. The Homeless Man's Journal will stir your emotions and remind you that the power to persevere is within us all. Join the author on an amazing journey where he sees the worst in people but also discovers the innate goodness that exists in the world. Homeless when he began writing the book, Shayne found hope in the idea that success consists of getting up just one more time than you fall.